Denise N. Wheatley loves happy endings and the art of storytelling. Her novels run the romance gamut, and she strives to pen entertaining books that embody matters of the heart. She's an RWA member and holds a BA in English from the University of Illinois. When Denise isn't writing, she enjoys watching true-crime TV and chatting with readers. Follow her on Instagram @Denise_Wheatley_Writer, X @DeniseWheatley, BookBub @DeniseNWheatley, and Goodreads Denise N. Wheatley.

Rachel Astor is equal parts country girl and city dweller who spends an alarming amount of time correcting the word *the*. Rachel has had a lot of jobs (bookseller, real estate agent, 834 assorted admin roles), but none as, *ahem*, interesting as when she waitressed at a bar named after a dog. She is now a *USA Today* bestselling author who splits her time between the city, the lake and as many made-up worlds as possible.

HOMETOWN HOMICIDE

DENISE N. WHEATLEY

A SPY'S SECRET

RACHEL ASTOR

MILLS & BOON

First Published in Great Britain 2024
by Mills & Boon, an imprint of HarperCollins*Publishers* Ltd
1 London Bridge Street, London, SE1 9GF

www.harpercollins.co.uk

HarperCollins*Publishers*
Macken House, 39/40 Mayor Street Upper,
Dublin 1, D01 C9W8, Ireland

Hometown Homicide © 2024 by Denise N. Wheatley
A Spy's Secret © 2024 by Rachel Astor

ISBN: 978-0-263-32247-7

0924

This book contains FSC™ certified paper and other controlled sources to ensure responsible forest management.

For more information visit: www.harpercollins.co.uk/green

Printed and Bound in the UK using 100% Renewable Electricity at CPI Group (UK) Ltd, Croydon, CR0 4YY

HOMETOWN HOMICIDE

DENISE N. WHEATLEY

To my aunts, Sharon and Glenda. I love you!

Prologue

"9-1-1. What is your emergency?"

"Someone's trying to break into my house!" a woman screeched into the phone.

Operator Nia Brooks shot straight up in her chair. The buzz within Juniper, Colorado's communications center was louder than normal as the phone lines had been dead for hours. Increasing the volume on her headset, she scanned the computer screen for the caller's location.

"What is your address, ma'am?"

"Three eighty-two Barksdale Road."

"And you said that someone is trying to break into your house?"

"*Yes*. A man has been banging on the back door and fighting with the knob for several minutes now. I'm here alone, and…"

The woman fell silent. A loud thud penetrated Nia's eardrums, followed by a deep, muffled howl.

"Do you *hear* him?" the woman hissed.

"I do," Nia replied, forcing a calm tone as her fingers flew across the keyboard. "I'm already in contact with the police dispatcher alerting them to the situation. Law enforcement should be heading your way. Just stay on the line with me—"

"Listen," the woman interrupted, her voice breaking into a jagged whisper. "I told you I'm here by myself. I don't have any weapons. If this maniac makes his way inside my house, I have no way of protecting myself. So *please* tell the authorities to hurry up!"

She paused at what sounded like a bat pounding the door.

"Leave me alone!" the woman screamed. "I'm on the phone with 9-1-1 and police are on their way!"

"Yes, they are," Nia assured her. "I can see that law enforcement is en route to your house. And they're aware that this is a high-priority emergency situation."

Quivering sobs rattled Nia's headset as the woman whimpered, "They need to hurry up and get here. This man is about to break down the door. When he does, he might try to kill me!"

"Are all of your windows and doors locked?"

"I think so—yes. I turned off all the lights, too, hoping that would somehow run him off. Obviously it didn't work."

"Well, the secured windows and doors should keep him at bay until police arrive. In the meantime, I'll be right here on the line with you. What is your name, ma'am?"

"Linda. Linda Echols."

"Okay, Linda. When the knocking first began, did you happen to take a look outside and get a glimpse of the man?"

The woman paused, only the sound of her unsteady breaths swooshing through Nia's headset. "I—I did. Just once. When the banging started. I looked out to see what all the commotion was about and tried to tell him that he had the wrong house, not realizing he was trying to break in. He insisted that he was exactly where he was supposed to be. But he's dressed in all black and looks to be wearing a mask and—*wait!* I think he might be…"

She went silent again.

"Linda, talk to me. Tell me what's going on. I don't hear anything."

"Yeah, neither do I. Maybe he finally decided to stop—"

Boom, boom, boom!

Nia cringed at the rapid succession of thumping.

"Linda?"

Silence.

"Linda! Are you okay? What is he doing now?"

"He just picked up one of my patio chairs and is slamming it against the window! He's gonna break it and get inside. I need for the police to get here. *Now!*"

Just as Nia enlarged the map on her screen and checked the responding officer's location, a message from dispatch flashed below it.

Inform the caller that police are on the way, but due to construction they've been rerouted, causing a delay.

Clenching her teeth, a frustrated grunt gurgled in Nia's throat. This was the hard part of the job—the part that she couldn't control. It pained her, being on the front line with the victims from behind a desk as opposed to in person.

"Where are the cops?" Linda rasped. "Are they almost here?"

"They're still on the way. But there's roadwork near your home that's blocking the direct route. So as soon as they get around that they'll arrive at your house. And like I said, I'll be right here with you until they—"

Crack!

Nia jerked in her chair as the sound of shattering glass pierced her ears, followed by Linda's guttural scream.

"He's getting in!"

Inhaling sharply, Nia asked, "He's getting inside the house?"

"Yes! He just smashed the sliding glass door!"

Nia pounded the keyboard with an update to dispatch while clambering footsteps stuttered through her headset.

"I'm still here with you, Linda. What's happening now?"

"I'm running upstairs to hide inside my bedroom closet. *Please* tell the cops to hurry up and get here!"

A faint shuffling echoed in the background.

"He's inside the house!" Linda whisper-screamed as the sound of shoe soles squeaked across the floor.

"Hey!" a gravelly voice roared. "Get your ass back down here!"

"Linda," Nia began, struggling to maintain her composure, "are you inside the bedroom yet?"

"I am now."

"Good. Make sure you lock the door. Can you push a dresser or a chair or some sort of heavy object in front of it?"

"I can try, but I don't think I can move this chest of drawers across the carpet!"

Eyeing the map on her screen, Nia checked the responding officer's location. Her chest tightened at the sight of the vehicle's marker. It was at a standstill.

The intruder's demands boomed in the distance, followed by Linda's hysterical cries.

Bam!

"He's forcing his way inside the bedroom!"

A throbbing pain pulsated over Nia's left eye. She pounded her fist against the desk, watching helplessly as the responding officer's vehicle finally began to move.

"Linda, the police are making their way to your house.

Is there anywhere inside the bedroom you can hide? The closet? Or bathroom?"

The other end of the call went silent.

"Hello?" Nia called out. "Hello! Are you still there?"

"I'm gonna kill you," she heard a man grunt.

"Linda!"

A jarring thump preceded heaving gasps.

"I'm gonna kill you," the man muttered again over the sound of gut-wrenching gurgling.

Nia's body weakened at the thought of Linda being killed.

Come on! she wanted to scream after seeing that police were still several blocks away from the victim's house.

Just as she typed another message to dispatch alerting them to the severity of the situation, the call dropped.

Chapter One

Officer Drew Taylor kicked in the cracked wooden panels hanging from the door of Shelby's Candy Factory before stepping inside. The place had been closed for years and sat abandoned on the land bordering Juniper and Finchport. Since it was in Juniper's jurisdiction, the town had made plans to demolish the property last year and build affordable housing in its place. But then protestors had stepped in, insisting that the historic landmark merited preservation.

The powers that be agreed to halt demolition after activists promised to renovate the building. Their plan to turn it into a multipurpose community center, however, had yet to happen after fundraising efforts failed. In the meantime, the factory remained vacant—and dangerous.

Teens had been using the space to throw wild parties while squatters saw it as a place to hang out, drink and sleep for days on end. Law enforcement did their best to keep out the riffraff. But the moment they drove away, loiterers and partygoers sneaked right back onto the scene.

Shelby's had become a point of contention for most Juniper residents. The quaint town of just over 10,000, located right outside Denver, prided itself on a welcoming spirit, solid family values, neighborly kindness and tight-knit bonds. Many of the cafés, boutiques and service businesses had been passed down from generation to generation. The hardworking community strove to maintain a glowing reputation, which was vital considering many of Denver's tourism dollars trickled over into Juniper's agricultural museum, vintage car shows and antique mall.

Most residents felt as though Shelby's had become a stain on the town. Nothing good had come of allowing it to remain standing—especially now, as Drew had been called there to investigate a dead body.

He and his partner, Timothy Braxton, walked across the dilapidated main level in search of the crime scene. Layers of dust covered the 3,000 square feet of cracked cement flooring. Shards of glass were scattered everywhere as large holes marred the cloudy picture windows. Pulleys once used to lift heavy candy-filled cauldrons were still in place, as were a few of the cooling tables and taffy-spinning machines.

"Officers, over here!"

Drew and Timothy made their way past a row of drop roller machines toward the back of the factory. The stench of decomposing flesh hit before Drew even laid eyes on the victim.

"Oh my God…" Timothy uttered, holding his hand to his nose.

A deceased woman's body sat propped up in a metal folding chair. She'd been bound and gagged. Dried blood had pooled around her neck and chest.

Drew's stomach lurched at the sight. Juniper rarely saw crimes this brutal. Thefts, drug deals and bar fights were the norm—not vicious murders committed by demented killers, who, the officer feared, would kill again.

The victim looked to be in her mid to late twenties. Five foot six if he had to guess, and about 135 pounds minus the postmortem bloating. Her long, dark brown hair was a tangled mess. If he hadn't seen the back of her white T-shirt, he would've thought it was a reddish brown as the front had been completely soaked in blood. Layers of duct tape were wrapped around her wrists and ankles. While her dark blue jeans appeared to be intact, she wasn't wearing any shoes.

"Any word on who the victim is?" Drew asked Officer Davis.

"Yep. Her name is Katie Douglas."

"So she had ID on her?"

"No. When the call came in over the radio that a body had been found, whoever tipped off law enforcement knew the victim but asked to remain anonymous."

Drew bent down and studied the woman's skin. Judging by the green discoloration, along with the mixture of blood and foam leaking from her mouth, she'd been dead for a few days.

He pulled a handkerchief from the pocket of his black cargo pants and waved off several blowflies before holding it to his nose. "Have you found any evidence that might contain DNA?"

Officer Davis held a brown paper bag in the air with a gloved hand. "So far, just a piece of duct tape with a bloody fingerprint that I spotted near the victim's feet."

"Good. Let's make sure we get that sent off to the crime lab as soon as possible."

"Will do. Oh, and there was one more thing…"

The officer handed over a brochure. Drew slipped on a pair of latex gloves before taking it. "What is this?"

"An event calendar for Latimer Park's recreational center. We found it stuffed inside the victim's hand."

"Hmm, interesting…"

In between the blood stains, Drew studied the activity details. There was a wide variety of them, from pumpkin-carving contests to crafting classes. "I wonder if she's somehow affiliated with the park. But I don't see her name listed as an instructor or host on any of the events."

Peering over his shoulder, Timothy asked, "Are there any handwritten notes on it? Or phone numbers?"

"Nope. Nothing. We'll send this to the lab as well. See what DNA might be detected. We should also stop by Latimer Park and pick up a calendar on the way back to the station. I wanna have that on hand just in case we can somehow trace the victim to the park."

Drew made his way toward the back wall. A door that was normally boarded up had been yanked from the hinges. "Hey, Davis, where's the forensic team?"

"They're on the way."

"And the medical examiner?"

"She's at the hospital wrapping up an autopsy. She should be here soon."

"Can you let me know when she arrives? I'd like to speak with her."

Officer Davis's eyelids lowered, as if he wanted to question Drew. Instead he replied, "Uh…yeah. Sure."

Ignoring his confusion, Drew pulled out his cell phone and took several photos of the scene. After nearly ten years on the force, his colleagues still didn't seem to understand his behavior once he slipped into investigative mode. Drew had a habit of taking over, oftentimes making a list of duties

for his fellow officers while collecting forensic evidence on
his own. Today would be no different.

As he began filming a video, Drew contemplated what
the victim had gone through before being murdered. Had
she been drugged and kidnapped? Did she know her killer?
Was it someone she'd trusted?

He squeezed his eyes shut, thinking of how this could
have been someone he knew. The thought sent a streak of
anger through his chest that pushed past his lungs and out
his mouth in the form of a loud grunt.

"You all right?" Timothy asked, following him into the
alleyway behind the building.

"No. I'm not. I've gotta do something here. As a matter
of fact, I don't wanna wait on the forensic team. I've got
my kit in the trunk of the car. I'll let the medical examiner
handle the processing of the body while I collect whatever
evidence I can find. Fingerprints, shoe prints, blood trails—
anything I can get my hands on. I've got a bad feeling about
this one, Tim. If we don't catch the suspect soon, trust me,
he *will* kill again."

DREW STOOD OUTSIDE Chief Mitchell's door gnawing at his
bottom lip. The chief never called him to his office. At least
not for a one-on-one meeting. Usually when he wanted to
talk he'd call Timothy in with him. This time, he specifically asked to speak to Drew alone.

Just as he raised his fist to knock, the door flew open.
Officer Davis came charging out.

"Hey, man!" he said, giving Drew a hearty slap on the
back. "Listen, great job at the crime scene today. Way to
step up and take the lead. Oh, and congrats!"

"Thanks. But wait, congrats on what?"

"The chief will tell you. I'm late for an appointment. Let's catch up tomorrow!"

Remaining planted in the doorway, Drew's brows furrowed as the officer darted down the hallway.

"Hey, Taylor!" Chief Mitchell called out. "Come on in. That damn Davis has such a big mouth. He never could hold water, could he?"

"Not since I've met him, sir, which was during our days at the academy. But what is he supposed to be keeping from me?"

"Close the door and have a seat. That's what I need to talk to you about."

Drew made his way inside the cluttered office. While pulling out a worn burgundy tweed chair, he eyed the cardboard boxes stacked against the empty filing cabinets. Framed pictures and certificates that had yet to be hung were propped against the wall. Containers of unopened supplies hugged the side of his desk. No one would know the chief had taken over the space almost thirty years ago considering it looked as if he'd just moved in.

"So," Chief Mitchell began, his chubby jowls quivering, "Officer Davis just updated me on the crime scene at Shelby's. Such a shame, finding Katie like that. Poor girl…"

"Sir, are you okay?" Drew asked after the chief's voice broke.

"Yeah, yeah. I'm good. I went to high school with the victim's father. So I feel somewhat connected to this case. Her dad called me this afternoon and the man was inconsolable. I promised him we'd do everything in our power to catch the sick son of a bitch who did this to his daughter. Which is where you come in, Officer Taylor."

Drew nodded, his eyes drifting toward the stack of boxes

sitting directly behind the chief. The one on top caught his attention. "Linda Echols" was scribbled across the side in bold black letters.

It had been almost a year since her murder occurred, leading to one of the toughest investigations Drew had ever worked. No viable evidence was found at the scene of her home invasion. With the house being in an isolated area, no witnesses came forward and no security footage surfaced. Every lead hit a dead end. Eventually, the case went cold.

Since Linda's death, not a day had gone by that Drew didn't think about it. He'd grown extremely close to her family while working the investigation. After speaking to Linda's mother on an almost daily basis, he made a promise to catch her killer. When that didn't happen, he'd considered quitting the force. But it was Chief Mitchell who had encouraged him to remain onboard.

"You'll never make an arrest if you're no longer a member of Juniper PD," the chief told him. When Drew expressed feeling like a failure after making a promise he couldn't keep, his boss stopped him. "Listen, son. This was your first lesson in understanding that sometimes, working in the field of criminal justice means playing the long game. Hell, some cold cases don't get solved until twenty or thirty years down the road. But the key is, if you work hard enough, they eventually will. So keep your head up and hang in there."

Those were the words that kept Drew on the force, prompting him to pin a photo of Linda inside his cubicle as a reminder to never give up on trying to solve her case. And now, after hanging a picture of Katie next to hers, Drew hoped the investigation would somehow come full circle and lead him to Linda's killer. He had to consider the possibility of the cases being connected, considering both women's throats had been slashed and Linda's attacker was still on the loose.

"Well," Chief Mitchell said, pulling Drew from his thoughts, "let's talk about why I asked to meet with you. When Officer Davis and I were discussing the crime scene, he mentioned how you really stepped up and took on a leadership role with getting the reports completed, holding critical conversations with the medical examiner and forensic team, and gathering evidence. Then of course there were the photos and videos you captured… Keep this up and you'll be stepping into my shoes once I finally decide to retire."

"*Wow.* That's, uh…that's quite the compliment coming from you, Chief. Thank you."

"Of course. It's a compliment well-earned. And the reason I'm saying all that is because I'd like for you to head up the Katie Douglas murder investigation."

Drew sat straight up, turning his ear in the chief's direction. "I'm sorry. I think I misheard you. What did you just say?"

"I said I'd like for you to be the lead investigator on the Douglas case."

The weight of the request sent him slumping in his chair. Hundreds of thoughts flew through Drew's mind. There were at least three other officers who were more qualified than him. Officers who'd been with the Juniper PD way longer and weren't still carrying the burden of Linda Echols's cold case.

"I—I don't know what to say," he stammered. "This is such a huge investigation, and—"

"Wait, are you saying that you don't want to take this on?"

"No, no. It's not that. I'm just thinking about all the other officers who have more seniority than I do. Like Nelson or Harper or Adams—"

"Officer Taylor. I'm asking *you*. Davis wasn't the only one who came to me with great feedback on the way you handled that crime scene today. I received calls from the medical examiner and head of forensics. They both sang your praises. Not Nelson's, Harper's, or Adam's. Nor anybody else's on the homicide team. *Yours*."

Pulling in a puff of air, Drew leaned back, his eyes glazing over as he stared into the speckled drop ceiling. Moments like this were the reason he'd joined the force. This was his time—his opportunity to prove he was capable of getting a murder solved.

"So what do you say, Officer Taylor. Are you in?"

Gripping the arms on his chair, Drew slid to the edge and looked Chief Mitchell directly in the eyes.

"Absolutely, sir. I'm in."

Chapter Two

Nia pulled a mirror from her drawer and checked her reflection. The beach waves she'd carefully flat-ironed through her long chocolate brown bob that morning were still intact. But her T-zone was shiny and lip gloss had faded.

Glancing at the time on her laptop screen, she saw that the special officers' meeting called by Chief Mitchell was set to begin in ten minutes.

"Just enough time to freshen up," she muttered, grabbing her makeup bag and swiping powder across her nose and gloss over her lips.

A knock against her cubicle's frame sent her jumping in her chair.

"Good morning, Officer Brooks."

Nia spun around, rolling her eyes at her smirking work bestie and former 9-1-1 colleague, Cynthia Lee. The pair had grown close while working together in the emergency services department. After Linda Echols's devastating murder last year, Nia was hit with the desire to serve a bigger purpose. Within days she submitted a transfer, and with Chief Mitchell's blessing, joined the police academy.

"Good morning, Cyn. What are you doing away from the call center this early?"

"Well, I've been here since five this morning. So I'm on my break. But here's a better question. What's with the flowing curls and face full of makeup? You got a hot date or something?"

"*Please.* Don't start with me. I'm just making sure I look presentable for the officers' meeting."

"Yeah, right. Presentable would've been a neat ponytail and dab of lip balm, like *I* normally wear," Cynthia quipped, propping her hands underneath her cherubic freckled face. "But you look like you're getting ready for a photo shoot. It's not like you even need all that with your gorgeous skin, those modelesque cheekbones and incessant gym visits. I mean, you keep the men's heads turning around here." She paused, glancing over her shoulder before whispering, "Could all the primping have anything to do with *Drew*?"

Nia grabbed her arm and pulled her farther inside the cubicle. "Will you lower your voice? Better yet, cut that talk out altogether. You know I'm not into Drew like that."

"Oh, do I really? Because last time I checked, you've been pining after that man ever since you started working for Juniper PD."

"Lies," Nia rebutted, checking her reflection one last time before slapping her compact shut. "Now I may have mentioned that Drew is a handsome guy—"

"Juniper's very own Boris Kodjoe to be exact."

"But you know my rule. I don't date coworkers. Plus Drew seems like such a grump. Like he's always in a bad mood. Not to mention he's never paid an ounce of attention to me."

"First of all, most people meet their partners at work, so you need to toss that rule out the window. Secondly, how would Drew even know you're interested in him? It's not like you've ever gone out of your way to talk to him. Or say hello even."

"Isn't your break over yet?" Nia asked, pushing away from the desk.

"Nope. I've still got five minutes left."

"Well, I need to get to the conference room. So we'll have to table this conversation for later. Or better yet, just forget about it."

"Look," Cynthia said, stopping Nia before she brushed past her. "Do me a favor. At least try and sit next to Drew during this meeting. Maybe start up a conversation. Say good morning. *Something.*"

"Enjoy the rest of your morning, Cynthia," Nia retorted before rushing down the hallway.

"Hey! Are we still on for lunch?"

"Yes, see you at noon!"

The conversation was out of Nia's head before she reached the conference room. All eyes were on her when she walked through the door. Gripping her notebook tighter, she ducked her head while searching for an empty chair.

The majority of the other officers were already there— including Drew. Cynthia hadn't been totally wrong in her assessment of Nia's feelings for him. She had been crushing on the officer ever since her first day of work. Aside from his ruggedly handsome good looks, there was a kindness behind his brooding, intense gaze. Drew was popular among their peers, oftentimes managing to drum up a few laughs despite his no-nonsense attitude. That, along with his impressive career accomplishments, made him one of the most well-respected officers within the department.

But Nia never allowed her crush to go too far. And while she had no intention of breaking her "no dating colleagues" policy, it wasn't as if he was available anyway. Rumor had it he'd been seeing someone for years.

Tables for two were set up alongside the conference room walls. The only empty space left was directly behind Drew. Just as he glanced in her direction, Nia dropped her gaze to the floor. Her calf muscles burned as she rushed past him and plopped down into the chair. Hoping he hadn't seen her ogling him, she flipped to an empty page in her notebook, then nervously bounced her pen against the table.

Drew turned slightly. He didn't look directly at her, but judging by the curl in his downturned lips, something was annoying him.

The pen, she thought. *Stop banging the pen!*

The second Nia's hand froze midtap, Drew turned back around and faced the front of the room.

Her jaws clenched with embarrassment while he proceeded to talk to his partner, Timothy. When he spoke, the indentations in his biceps flexed as he waved an arm in the air. Tim's jokes sent him twisting in his chair, those gleaming white teeth lighting up the entire area. Nia's lips parted after he ran his strong, nimble hands over his freshly cut hair. She couldn't help but wonder what they'd feel like pressed against her body.

Just as her thoughts trickled from her head down to her tingling chest, a commotion erupted near the doorway. The room grew silent when Chief Mitchell approached the podium.

"Good morning, everyone. I'm sure you're wondering why I called this meeting on such short notice. But don't worry. I'll get right to it, then let you go as we've got a lot of work to do. I recently received a call from Finchport

PD's chief of police, and he was telling me about a mentoring program that he's implemented within the department."

"Ugh," Drew grunted, slumping against the wall. "Here we go. Something else to add to my plate that I don't have time for..."

When a series of groans rippled through the room, the chief held up his hand. "Hold on. Before you all go shooting down my idea, just hear me out. I know we're all busy, but none of us are too busy to help out a fellow officer. Now, Finchport's chief has partnered his veteran officers with rookie cops in order to help them adjust to working on the force. As many of you know, being out on the street feels a lot different than training in the academy."

Drew leaned toward Timothy, whispering, "If anybody on this force can't navigate the streets of Juniper, then they need to rethink their career choice. It isn't like this is LA or Chicago."

"Maybe," Timothy replied. "But what about the Katie Douglas murder? Or Linda Echols for that matter? Both of those incidents reek of big-city crimes."

"True. However, cases like those are such a rare occurrence around here. Or so I hope..."

"Listen," the chief continued. "The more Chief Garcia and I discussed his mentoring initiative, the more I thought about our department and how vital a program like that could be for us. We've talked a lot about mental health here and the benefits of checking in with one another to make sure we're all in a good headspace. While the higher-ups have provided a variety of resources, I think a mentorship program would be a great addition to the work we're already doing to improve the team's overall well-being."

Chief Mitchell signaled Officer Davis, who began placing white envelopes in front of each officer.

"I've already taken the liberty of assigning mentees to each of the veteran officers. The name of the person you've been teamed with is inside the envelopes that Davis is passing around."

Nia's legs bounced underneath the table as she anticipated who she'd be paired with.

"Ouch," she hissed when her knee hit the metal edge.

Once again, Drew's head turned slightly toward her. That look of irritation had reappeared. This time, Nia wanted to say, *Stop taking your frustrations out on me!* But instead she pressed her hand against her knee, attempting to rub the pain away without making another sound.

As Officer Davis neared their section, Drew's head adamantly shook from side to side. "I highly doubt that the chief would ask me to mentor someone. Not when I've just been chosen to head up the biggest investigation of my career."

"That's *exactly* why he would've assigned you to a mentee," Timothy argued. "What better way to learn the ropes than to watch a pro catch a killer firsthand?"

"Thanks for the reassurance," Drew deadpanned. "But *no* thanks to a rookie getting in the way of my work—"

He paused when Officer Davis approached his table.

"Hey, Officer Taylor, congratulations again on landing that Douglas case."

"Thanks, man. I appreciate you putting in a good word for me."

"No problem. The accolades were well-earned after the way you took charge of that crime scene."

Nia held her breath when Officer Davis handed him an envelope.

"Oh, no," Drew huffed, refusing to take it. "That can't be for me. I was just telling Tim that Chief Mitchell wouldn't have assigned a mentee to me. I've already got my hands full."

Officer Davis flipped the envelope over and eyed the name on the front. "I don't know what to tell you, other than the fact that this clearly says 'Officer Drew Taylor.'"

Emitting a low grunt, Drew snatched it from his hand. "Fine. I'll talk to the chief once this meeting is over."

"Suit yourself. But I think you'd be an excellent mentor to one of our rookies."

"I couldn't agree more," Timothy added.

After Officer Davis moved on to another table, Nia noticed Timothy push Drew's envelope toward him.

"Aren't you gonna open it?" he asked. "See who you've been assigned to?"

"Nope. Because it doesn't matter. I can't be a part of the program. And it's not that I don't think this is a great idea. It's fantastic. I just don't have time for it."

Nia wished she were bold enough to interject. To tell Drew how having a rookie by his side to assist in his investigation would be an asset rather than a disruption. An extra set of eyes on case files, surveillance footage and crime scenes would only bring him closer to solving Katie's murder. But rather than intervene, she remained silent for fear of him biting her head off.

"So what are you gonna do if Chief Mitchell insists you take on a mentee?" Timothy asked.

"Quit."

"Yeah, right."

As the officers broke into laughter, Nia muttered, "That is so messed up."

Both men slowly swiveled in their chairs.

"I'm sorry," Drew said. "What did you just say?"

Nia's mouth fell open. She hadn't intended for those words to slip out of her head and through her lips.

"You weren't listening in on our conversation," Drew probed, "were you?"

"No! Of course not. I was... I was just—"

He reached back and tapped his hand against her table. "Calm down, Officer Brooks. I'm only kidding."

When he pulled away, his fingers brushed against hers. The rush of electricity that shot up her arm sent Nia falling against the back of her chair.

Just as Drew threw her a strange look, Chief Mitchell banged his knuckles against the podium.

"All right, everybody, let's quiet down for a second so I can wrap this up. Now that you've all had a chance to find out who you've been assigned, I'd like for you to get to know your mentorship partners better. Go out for coffee or lunch. Take time during your breaks to go on ride-alongs together. Share investigative stories. Mentors, be generous in offering up guidance to your mentees. Find ways to help them get acclimated to the department, the community and the rules of the Juniper PD. Most importantly, work on creating real, lasting bonds. Remember, you are your brothers' and sisters' keeper. Now, before we go, does anybody have any questions?"

Drew raised his hand. "Yes, sir. I do."

"Go ahead, Officer Taylor."

"What about those of us whose workloads are too heavy to take on a mentee at this time? Can we withdraw our names, then jump back in the next time around?"

"There is no such thing as a workload being too heavy.

We're all swamped. It's called sacrifice. And you'd be the perfect mentor, Officer Taylor. Especially with this case you're currently working. Three sets of eyes are better than two. Consider yourself lucky to be adding another person to your team of investigators. Now," Chief Mitchell proceeded, looking around the room without giving Drew a chance to respond. "Any other questions?"

"When does the program start?" Timothy asked.

"Immediately. And I expect for the mentors to take the lead. Reach out to your mentees first. You all are the more experienced of the two. So lead by example. Set something up, then get moving on the mentoring." He paused, glancing around once again. "Anything else?"

A quiet murmur swept through the room as officers spoke quietly among themselves.

"Okay, then," Chief Mitchell said, "this meeting is adjourned. As always, my door is open if anyone would like to stop by and talk in private."

Drew pushed away from the table and jumped to his feet. "Yeah, I'll be the first one doing just that."

"Let it go, Taylor," Timothy said. "The chief has spoken, and I don't think he's going to change his mind. Not to mention I think he's right."

"Yeah, well, we'll see about that. He may be singing a different tune once we talk one-on-one about all the pressure I'm under." Drew snatched up his unopened envelope and shoved it inside his back pocket. "I'll let you know how it goes."

Nia watched as he trudged out of the room. She'd been so wrapped up in his and Timothy's conversation that she hadn't noticed Officer Davis slide her envelope onto the table.

She stared at it, praying that she'd been assigned someone who, unlike Drew, would be enthusiastic about the program and happy to mentor her.

Timothy stood as she tore it open. "Who'd you get, Officer Brooks?"

"I don't know. Let's see…"

Her stomach dropped at the sight of the bold black letters typed across the page.

"So?" Timothy said. "Who's the lucky mentor?"

She turned the paper around. He leaned forward. "'Officer Drew Taylor'? Oh, no. And of course you'd be sitting right behind us. I'm sure you overheard our entire conversation."

"I did." Nia shoved the sheet back inside the envelope. "No worries. I'm sure after Officer Taylor has his conversation with the chief, I'll be assigned to someone else."

"Judging by the tone Chief Mitchell took when Drew gave him pushback, that's highly unlikely. But either way, good luck."

"Thanks. I'm definitely gonna need it."

Chapter Three

It'd been almost two weeks since Drew had been assigned as Nia's mentor. And he'd yet to reach out to her. Timothy had been on his case about it, insisting that he set something up before Chief Mitchell stepped in. But Drew wasn't worried. He'd scheduled a reminder to contact her one day this week. For the time being, his mind was focused solely on the Katie Douglas investigation.

The chief had put in a call to the head of the crime lab down in New Vernon to prioritize the evidence collected at the scene and the results were in—neither the blood nor fingerprints matched any offender profiles in CODIS.

Drew was beyond disappointed as he was certain they'd find a pairing. In his mind, Katie's death was too violent an act for the killer not to have any priors. The officer still believed his suspect had murdered before. He just hadn't been caught yet.

The only clue Drew had to go on was the Latimer Park event calendar. He was convinced there was some sort of message behind it. After he and Timothy stopped by the park and picked up a new brochure, they'd pored over every past and upcoming event. They had even spoken with Katie's friends and relatives to find out if she was somehow connected to the park or any of the activities. As far as they knew, she wasn't.

Drew questioned whether there was a husband or boyfriend in the picture. There wasn't. Katie was single, never married and hadn't fallen out with any exes or friends as far as they knew.

The current state of the investigation had left Drew frustrated and stuck back at square one. The case was all he could think about. He didn't want to drop the ball and watch the case go cold, which meant keeping himself completely immersed in it.

But then there was that damn mentoring program, looming in the back of his mind. Drew imagined getting on Chief Mitchell's bad side and losing the case altogether after stalling on contacting Nia.

Just do it, he thought, spewing a string of curses before rolling over to the other side of his king oakwood bed and grabbing his cell phone.

He checked the time. It was almost 6:00 a.m. Nia usually didn't arrive at the station until a little after eight. Drew had no idea why he knew that. Nevertheless, he sent her a text in hopes of finally getting their first meeting over with.

Good morning, Officer Brooks. Officer Taylor here. Are you free for coffee this morning before work? If so, we can meet up at the Cooper's Cake and Coffee on Motley Boulevard near the station at 7:00 a.m. Does that work for you? Let me know.

Drew sent the message, then made his way through the spacious primary bedroom, the soles of his feet cushioned by the warm cork flooring. He lived in the ranch-style home he'd grown up in, which he'd moved into after his parents left for North Carolina a few years back. Once he was convinced that they were in Charlotte to stay, Drew sold the loft that he'd owned across town.

He thought letting go of the place would be tough. He'd owned it since senior year of college and it held a lot of memories—the most recent being one that he'd rather forget.

Stepping inside the white marble bathroom, Drew turned on the shower and grabbed his toothbrush. His mind drifted to the day that his ex-fiancée moved into the loft. Ellody was the one who'd assured him that his bachelor days were over. His home quickly became theirs as she added her own personal touches, leaving an indelible mark on both the decor and the energy.

After their breakup, he knew he couldn't stay there, which was why he'd jumped at the chance to rent out the loft and set up shop in his childhood home. The eventual sale of his place felt cathartic, confirming that he had finally gotten over his ex.

Drew's pinging cell phone pulled his eyes toward the screen. It was a response from Nia.

Good morning, Officer Taylor. Nice to hear from you. Yes, I'm available to meet. I'll see you at Cooper's at 7. Looking forward to it.

Despite the irritation rumbling through his chest, he replied, Great, see you then.

"You're getting thirty minutes, tops," Drew said to himself before composing a message to Timothy.

Hey, meeting up with Brooks for coffee at 7. Let's connect at Latimer Park afterwards. I wanna take a look around the place. See if we can figure something out on the Douglas case. Does 7:45 work for you?

He hit Send, then jumped in the shower. Anxious to get to the park, he decided to give Nia twenty minutes instead.

DREW ENTERED COOPER'S a few minutes late and glanced around for Nia. The 1950s-style café was packed. He moaned at the sight of the line that was practically out the door. Every shiny red table and booth was occupied. Drew had passed on brewing a pot of coffee at home since he'd expected to grab a cup here. But from the looks of the crowd waiting to place their orders, he'd have to get through the meetup without it.

"Officer Taylor!" someone called out from the back of the shop.

Through the throng of patrons, he spotted Nia waving her hand in the air. He acknowledged her with a nod, then made his way across the black-and-white tiled floor toward her table.

As he got closer, Drew noticed how nice she looked. Nia normally wore her hair pulled back into a bun. Today it was down, with soft curls cascading around her slender face. Red lipstick set off her bright, sexy smile. And she wasn't in uniform. Instead, she was wearing a fitted cream cashmere sweater and tight gray jeans.

"Good morning, Officer Taylor," she said, extending her hand. "Thank you again for meeting with me. I've been looking forward to this since…well, since Chief Mitchell assigned you as my mentor."

"Yeah, sorry for the delay in reaching out," he uttered, taking her hand in his. "As you know, I've been working the Katie Douglas case. Things have been tough, considering it's not going as I'd hoped."

"Hmm, I'm sorry to hear that…"

Several seconds passed before Drew realized he was still holding on to Nia. For some strange reason, he couldn't get past the soft sensation of her palm pressed against his.

Gesturing for Drew to have a seat, Nia asked, "What's going on with the investigation?"

As they settled into the booth, something about her warm tone and concerned expression lowered his guard. "Well, we got the results back from the crime lab, and nothing matched up with a criminal profile in the database…" Drew's voice trailed off when a server placed two drinks and a tray filled with food onto the table. "Wait, what's all this?"

Nia's lips spread into that alluring smile she'd greeted him with. "I got here about fifteen minutes early and noticed it was getting pretty crowded. So I decided I'd better hurry up and order something for us. That way we wouldn't have to wait." She slid a cup and two items wrapped in plastic in front of him. "I didn't know if you'd be hungry. So I ordered a spinach omelet wrap for you. And of course I had to get us both slices of Cooper's famous cinnamon swirl crunch cake."

"Wow. And here I was thinking I'd have to pass on my morning dose of caffeine. Thank you. For all of this." Pulling the lid off the cup, Drew took a sip. "Hold on. How did you know my coffee order? You must've texted Tim and asked him."

"Nope. I've heard you around the station mentioning how

you can't get your day started without a cup of dark roast with a splash of soy milk and one packet of raw sugar."

"Hmph, I didn't realize you were paying that much attention to me."

"I—well, I guess I just have good ears, or..." Nia hesitated, wringing her perfectly manicured hands.

"I'm kidding," Drew said, chuckling at how easy it was to throw off the rookie. "Don't worry. I know you're not stalking me or eavesdropping. Even though you *did* jump into my conversation with Tim during that mentorship meeting."

Her tense expression broke into a slight smirk.

"So is this how it's gonna be?" Nia asked. "Are you going to haze me throughout our entire mentorship?"

"I might..." Drew quipped, relaxing against the padded seat cushion. "No, but seriously. I appreciate this. I'm gonna have to take it to go though. I'm meeting Tim at Latimer Park and need to leave soon."

"Oh...okay."

The disappointment in Nia's soft tone was apparent. But her wide eyes appeared hopeful, as if she was waiting for an invitation to ride along with them. Drew wasn't totally against the idea but decided to hold off on extending an invitation.

"What time are you and Officer Braxton meeting up?" she asked.

"About seven forty-five." Drew pulled his cell from his black leather jacket. "Speaking of Tim, he never did confirm. That's not like him."

"Maybe he's sleeping in late?"

"I doubt it. He usually hits the gym every morning at five, and it's almost seven-fifteen. I'm sure he'll get back to me soon. Anyway, why don't we talk a little bit about your past experience and what made you want to become a police officer?"

Nia's brows lifted as she slid to the edge of her seat. The glimmer in her eyes reminded Drew of the excitement he'd felt during his time as a rookie.

"Well," she began, "as you know, I worked as a 9-1-1 operator for eight years before joining the force."

"Right. I did know that."

"There was something about those calls I'd receive and the rush of adrenaline pumping through my body whenever I'd send emergency services out to assist the victims. It made me feel vulnerable and helpless in a strange way. Like there was more I could be doing. Eventually the desire to serve a bigger purpose hit, and I began contemplating making a move to the force."

"Really? Why is that? Our 9-1-1 operators are vital. They're the first point of contact between the victims and law enforcement. Without them, we'd be completely uninformed and disorganized."

"I agree. But for me, I felt the need to be more present. Out there on the front lines, assisting firsthand rather than sitting inside the call center."

"Okay. I feel you on that…"

Drew's voice trailed off when a deep frown overtook Nia's cheery expression.

"There's, um," she began, her tone almost a whisper. "There was one call in particular that really turned things around for me."

"Oh? Which call was that?"

"Linda Echols."

Nia's response disarmed Drew's cool disposition. Recoiling at the pull in his chest, he nodded stiffly. "Yeah… That was a tough one. Were you the operator who handled it?"

"I was. I'll never forget how powerless I felt on the other end of that call, struggling to keep Linda calm while trying to send help. But the responding officers had trouble getting to her house. The attacker got to her before they could. I can still remember the shrill intonations in her screams, and how she kept saying that if he makes his way inside, he's going to kill her." Nia paused, clawing at the napkin underneath her coffee cup. "I was devastated when I heard she'd been found inside her bedroom closet with her throat slashed."

"I hope you're not blaming yourself for any of that."

"I try not to. But I did. For a long time. That guilt is what prompted me to join the force."

"Well I know for a fact that Chief Mitchell was thrilled to welcome you to the department. I mean, he *really* sang your praises in particular. Every chance he'd get, he would talk about how you're an excellent addition to the squad."

"Yeah, that was really nice of him," Nia murmured, her lush lips curling into a half grin.

The sight of her spirits lifting motivated Drew to continue. "I don't know if you're aware of this, but we'd hear little tidbits about which recruits were doing well and standing out. Your name was always at the top of everyone's list. Your sharp instincts, high level of intelligence, dedication to the Juniper community…nothing but good things were spoken about you. So remember that whenever those feelings of guilt start to hit. Let those traits be a reminder that what happened to Linda was in no way your fault. You did all that you could to try and save her. And hey, you never know. Now that you're on the force, maybe you'll get an opportunity to help solve her cold case."

Sitting up a little straighter, Nia's eyes connected with his gaze. "You know what? You're absolutely right."

A loud rumble floated through the air. Drew grabbed his stomach and glanced around the café, hoping no one else heard it. When a soft giggle slipped through Nia's lips, he realized she had.

"Why don't you take at least one bite of that wrap?" she suggested. "Because clearly you're hungry."

He peered down at his phone again. Still no word from Timothy. "Might as well." After noticing she hadn't unwrapped hers, Drew asked, "Aren't you going to eat?"

"I will. Once I get to the station."

"Why don't you eat now? Tim hasn't gotten back to me yet, so I've got time."

Wrinkling her nose, Nia tapped her fingers against the table.

"What's wrong?"

"Nothing. It's just…a little embarrassing."

"What's embarrassing?"

"I'm too nervous to eat," Nia murmured through tight lips.

"Nervous? Why?"

"Is that a real question? I don't think you realize how intimidating you can be, Officer Taylor."

He dropped his wrap and searched her face for a sign of humor. There wasn't one. "I had no idea anyone thought of me as intimidating. Would it help if you start calling me Drew instead of Officer Taylor?"

"It might…" she replied while slowly peeling the plastic off her wrap.

"Good. So tell me, Officer Brooks. When it comes to this mentorship program, what are you expecting from me?"

"Now hold on. It wouldn't be fair for me to call you Drew if you don't call me Nia, would it?"

"I guess it wouldn't be, *Nia*. So go on. I'm listening."

"Well, aside from all the things Chief Mitchell mentioned during the meeting, I'd love to just shadow you. If that wouldn't be too much trouble…"

"It wouldn't be. And before you continue, can I just apologize for whatever you overheard me saying to Tim at that meeting? I'd just been assigned the Douglas investigation, and—"

"You don't have to explain anything. I get it. I figured I'd find a way to win you over eventually. Hopefully the coffee and breakfast was a good start."

"Oh, this was an excellent start. By the way, how much do I owe you?" he asked, reaching for his wallet.

"You don't owe me a thing. Consider this a thank-you for taking the time to meet with me."

A streak of guilt stabbed Drew in the gut. He'd been so resistant to meeting with Nia, and she had turned out to be more gracious than he ever could've imagined. "You're welcome. Next time is on me. Now, back to you wanting to shadow me."

"Yes. I'd love to help out with the Katie Douglas case however I can. Of course I wouldn't get in the way of things or overstep my bounds. But it would be great if I could experience the ins and outs of a murder investigation firsthand."

"I don't think that would be a problem. But let me talk to Tim first. He's my partner, and out of respect for him, I should figure out what role he's going to play beforehand. Is that cool?"

"Of course. And just know that I'm willing to take on whatever role I can, no matter how big or small."

"I'll keep that in mind..." After checking the time on his cell again, Drew scrolled through his notifications. Nothing from Timothy. "We should probably head out. I still wanna take a look around Latimer Park before I check in at the station."

Nia was slow to gather her things. Judging by her fallen expression, Drew sensed she didn't want to leave.

"Thanks again for inviting me to coffee," she said. "This was good. I think it may have been the most we've ever spoken since I started working for the Juniper PD."

"Oh, now you're trying to make me out to be some standoffish introvert," he joked, following her toward the exit.

"That could not be further from what I'm saying!"

As he held open the door, Drew couldn't help but notice the sway in Nia's curvy hips. She brushed up against him, her touch sending an electric shot straight to his groin.

Don't even go there...

When they reached Nia's silver Acura, she clicked the alarm. "I'll see you back at the station. Good luck at Latimer Park. I hope you and Officer Braxton find something useful."

"Yeah, about that. I still haven't heard from Tim. And as Chief Mitchell likes to say, two sets of eyes are better than one. So, if you want, you can follow me to the park."

Pressing her hands together, Nia replied, "I'd like that," before the words were hardly out of his mouth. "I've got my evidence collection kit in the trunk, too. So if I stumble upon anything viable, I'll be prepared to collect it."

Drew couldn't help but chuckle at her enthusiasm. It was actually endearing.

You're doing it again, he thought before backing away.

"Sounds good," he told her. "I'll lead the way."

"Hey!" Nia called out just as he reached his car. "I forgot to mention that I know Latimer Park's recreation manager. If she's there, I'll see if we can get in and talk to her about that event calendar you found on the victim. Maybe she knows something."

"That would be awesome. Thanks."

Drew climbed inside his car and glanced in the rearview mirror, making sure Nia was behind him before pulling out. When she waved, he gave her a thumbs-up, then left the lot. As he drove down Sandpiper Road, wise words from his father popped into his head.

The universe works in mysterious ways...

Considering Nia's unexpected involvement in the investigation, Drew thought of how interesting it would be if she became the catalyst to solving the case.

Chapter Four

Nia eased up on the accelerator, realizing she'd been tailing Drew's car way too closely. But she couldn't help herself. The thrill of working the Douglas case had her emotions coursing full speed. Determination surged the strongest as she was eager to prove her capabilities, and hopefully, solidify her spot in the investigation.

Drew's cool, laid-back attitude had come as a pleasant surprise. Nia assumed it would take weeks, if not longer, to crack his hardened demeanor. But their meetup, albeit brief, gave her hope that his mentorship wouldn't be nearly as dreadful as she'd expected.

The get-together did nothing, however, to quell Nia's feelings for him. If anything, they'd intensified. Oddly enough, she didn't feel as though the sparks were one-sided. There were several moments when Drew appeared a bit flirty. The way he'd wink at her after saying something funny or flash a suggestive half smile while agreeing with a point she'd made. Those small gestures hadn't sent warm sensations stirring through her center for nothing.

Hold on, Nia told herself mid-thought. *Don't go getting ahead of yourself...*

Drew's bright taillights pulled her back into the moment

as they drove across the Sparrow Lane Bridge. Nia's heart-beat quickened when Latimer Park appeared in the distance.

Cottonwood and Early Richmond cherry trees were scattered along the outskirts of the lush, sloped landscape. Stay-at-home parents bordered the playground as children rode the merry-go-round and climbed monkey bars. Tennis lessons were in session, and several young men were practicing their free throws on the basketball court.

It was hard to believe that such a beautiful, active space was now tainted by a possible connection to Katie Douglas's murder.

Just when Drew made a slight turn onto Candlewood Avenue, he reached out the window and signaled to Nia, then quickly pulled over. She parked behind him, craning her neck to see what was going on.

After waiting for him to get out of the car, Nia peered through his rear windshield and saw Drew's cell phone glued to his ear. A few minutes later her phone rang. It was him.

"Hey, what's going on?" she asked.

"Chief Mitchell just called. We need to get back to the station. Something's happened to Tim."

"*What?* Is he okay?"

"I don't know. But judging by the chief's tone, it sounds serious. He just got a call from Tim's mother saying that he's been rushed to the emergency room. Hopefully Chief will know more by the time we get there."

"Got it. I'm right behind you."

NIA AND DREW pulled into the station's parking lot and charged into the building. While he headed straight for Chief Mitchell's office, she stopped at her desk.

"Keep me posted!" she told him.

He spun around, his brows wrinkled with confusion. "Wait, you're not coming with me?"

"I—I didn't know if you wanted me there."

"I definitely want you there. Whatever's going on, I could use all the support I can get."

The officer's worried expression almost prompted Nia to wrap him in a warm embrace. Instead she nodded, following him to the chief's office.

They barely reached the doorway before Drew asked, "What's going on with Tim? Any updates since we last spoke?"

Chief Mitchell ran his hands through his thinning gray hair. "Have a seat, you two."

While Nia sat directly across from the chief, Drew paced the creaking wood floor.

"Chief, you're scaring me," he said. "What happened to Tim?"

"He, uh…he was in a really bad car accident on the way home from the gym this morning. It was a hit-and-run. According to a witness, another vehicle that was driving behind him accelerated, then rammed into the back of Tim's car. He spun out of control and slammed into a tree."

"Oh my God," Drew moaned, slumping into the chair next to Nia's.

"He was thrown from the vehicle and suffered several injuries," Chief Mitchell continued. "A concussion, broken bones, a punctured lung…"

"Is he showing any signs of brain damage?" Nia asked.

"They're not sure yet. The doctors are still running tests. But the good news is Tim's breathing on his own. He's been put in a medically induced coma just in case he experienced any brain swelling and to give his body a chance to heal."

"Was the witness able to get a license plate number?" Drew croaked.

"No, unfortunately. But he did say that the collision seemed intentional. Instead of going after the driver, he went to help Tim and call an ambulance."

"I should probably go to the hospital," Drew said. "Check on his family and make sure they're doing okay."

The chief nodded in agreement. "Good idea. I'm sure his mother would appreciate that. And I hate to bring this up, but now that Tim is out of commission, what are we going to do about the Katie Douglas investigation?"

"Yeah," Drew uttered, running his hand along the back of his neck. "I can't head that up alone. I'm gonna need a partner."

"Do you have anyone in mind?"

The question straightened Nia's back. Her head swiveled from Chief Mitchell to Drew, then back to the chief.

"I do, actually," Drew responded. "Officer Davis was the first person I thought of since he and I worked so well together at the crime scene."

The chief's gaze drifted toward Nia. She bit down on her jaw, desperate to throw her hat in the ring. But she held back. She'd been on the force less than a year. Officer Davis had way more experience. Nia knew she didn't stand a chance against him.

"What about Officer Brooks?" Chief Mitchell asked.

Huh?

She perked up, her face growing hot with anticipation while awaiting Drew's response.

"I'm sorry," he muttered. "Come again?"

"I said, what about Officer Brooks?"

As Drew remained silent, Nia held a hand in the air. "Should, um...should I leave, or—"

"No, no," the chief said. "You should stay. Maybe help plead your case on why you'd make a good partner on this investigation."

She turned to Drew, cringing at the slight scowl on his face.

"That won't be necessary," Drew huffed. "Because it's not gonna happen. Now I agreed to the whole mentoring thing. But this is where I draw the line. I need a veteran officer by my side who's familiar with crime scenes and evidence analysis. Someone who can put leads and tips and pieces of the investigative puzzle together to get this case solved."

Chief Mitchell kept silent while sipping from his World's Best Granddad mug. His lack of a response seemed to set Drew off as the officer sprang from his chair, continuing his rant while pacing the floor once more.

Holding her hand to her chest, Nia pulled in a sharp breath of air and peered over at Drew. The intensity in his wild eyes and erratic hand gestures were jarring. He was speaking about her as if she weren't even in the room. His behavior was far from that of the cool guy he'd appeared to be at Cooper's—the one who seemingly welcomed her into the investigation. Now that things had gotten real, the chief's suggestion sent him spiraling.

"Please, Officer Taylor," Chief Mitchell said. "Calm down. Have a seat. Let's talk this out. Do you need some water, or coffee—"

"No," Drew interrupted, throwing himself into the chair. "I'm fine. I'm just worried about Tim. And the investigation, of course."

"Which is all perfectly understandable. Do you still think

you're capable of handling the case considering the news about Tim? Because if you're not, I can always pass it on to another officer."

"Of course I am, Chief. Regardless of what's going on around me, I'm completely up for it."

Tension sucked the air from the room. Nia clenched her toes inside her combat boots while awaiting Chief Mitchell's response. But he just sat there, patting his fist against the desk. Judging by the look on Drew's poker face, he was done pleading his case.

Finally, after several moments of pained silence, the chief said, "Officer Taylor, keep in mind that Officer Brooks isn't new to the Juniper PD. She's worked within the department for years."

"Yeah, as a 9-1-1 op—"

"Hold on. I'm well aware of her former position. My point is, Officer Brooks is familiar with this town, the rules of the department and the inner workings of crime and apprehension. She won Telecommunicator of the Year five years in a row. That award isn't easy to come by."

Chief Mitchell paused, as if waiting for Drew to reply. But the officer remained silent.

"What I'm saying is, Officer Brooks is special. She's sharp. Her attention to detail is uncanny. Her communication and leadership skills are exceptional. The level of care and respect she's shown to victims is unmatched. She has helped solved crimes by simply asking the right questions during 9-1-1 calls. You don't come by those traits easily or often. When you do, you have to utilize them. What better way to do that than to partner with Officer Brooks on this case?"

"With all those accolades," Drew grumbled, "maybe you should just assign the case to her."

"Keep it up and I just might."

That's it, Nia thought, no longer able to withstand the awkward conversation. Just as she grasped the arms of her chair to stand, Drew emitted an exasperated sigh.

"Fine. I'll partner with Ni—I mean Officer Brooks. Not that I have a choice in the matter," he added under his breath.

"Good decision," Chief Mitchell said, ignoring the second half of Drew's response. "Officer Brooks, are you good with this?"

"I am, thank you. I really appreciate your kind words as well as this opportunity."

"Of course you do," Drew whispered toward his feet.

Nia glared in his direction, that crush she'd had on him fading by the minute.

"It's all well-earned," the chief told her. "Now, I'll be expecting a report from you two on the Douglas case in the next few days. Officer Taylor, maybe you can take Brooks down to Shelby's Candy Factory so she can assess the crime scene in person. Who knows—maybe she'll come across something that you and the other officers missed."

It was obvious that the chief was baiting Drew. Nia braced herself, waiting to see if he'd bite.

"I'd love for that to happen," he responded, holding his arms out at his sides. "If she does, that just means we'll be one step closer to solving the case."

"Now *that's* what I like to hear," Chief Mitchell boomed. "Teamwork. It makes the dream work, right?"

"Oh, please…" Drew hissed through clenched teeth.

"All right, you two," the chief continued. "Unless you've got something else for me, I think we're done."

Charging to the door, Drew said, "I'm going to the hospital to check on Tim. I'll have my phone if anyone needs me."

"Hey!" Chief Mitchell called out. "Be sure to check in with me as soon as you can. Let me know how he's doing."

"Will do."

Drew left the office without giving Nia so much as a glance. Ignoring the uncertainty banging against her temples, she slowly stood.

"Thank you again, Chief. I promise I won't let you down."

"I know you won't. That's why I assigned this case to you. Now get out there and prove Officer Taylor and anybody else who may be doubting you wrong."

"Yes, sir."

Those words were all it took to send Nia back to her cubicle with her head held high. Just as she sat down, someone approached from behind. It was Drew.

"Here you go," he said, slamming a file down on the desk. "This is everything I've got on the Douglas case. I would advise you to read through every single word of it and examine those crime scene photos from top to bottom. We'll make plans to go to the candy factory in the next day or so. For now, I just need to make sure Tim is okay."

"Understood. Please send Tim my well wishes. And hey, Drew? Just so you know, I'm really looking forward to working on this investigation with you. I may not be the most experienced officer on the force, but I promise I'll do everything I can to help solve this case."

He responded with a grunt before walking away.

"Nice chat," Nia mumbled.

Shrugging it off, she reminded herself that getting justice for Katie was all that mattered, whether Drew wanted her help or not.

Chapter Five

Drew felt like crap as he pulled back into the station. Seeing Tim connected to all those tubes while surrounded by machines, concerned doctors and worried loved ones had been devastating. It was a reminder that anything could happen at any given moment. And there were bigger concerns in life than him being partnered with a rookie cop.

The hospital visit was a wake-up call that left him feeling ashamed of his meltdown. The disrespect he'd shown toward Chief Mitchell and Nia was unacceptable, making his first order of business a talk with his boss, then his newly appointed partner.

Drew entered the department and made a beeline for the chief's office. The door was open. He approached it cautiously, knocking lightly on the frame.

"Hey, Chief, you got a sec?"

"I do," he replied, without looking up from his cell phone. "But hang on. Chief Garcia from Finchport is gonna be calling me any minute now. He wants an update on how our mentorship program is working out. Speaking of which..." He paused, finally peering up at Drew. "How's the mentoring going between you and Officer Brooks? Last I heard you two hadn't connected yet."

"Actually we did connect. Over coffee this morning."

The chief set his phone to the side. "Well, that wasn't what I expected to hear. But it certainly makes me happy. Is it safe to assume you two got along okay?"

"Yes. We got along just fine."

"Good. Because after the way things went during that meeting earlier…" Chief Mitchell hesitated, then pointed at Drew. "You're one of our main leaders around here, Officer Taylor. And I expect for you to act like it. At all times. The behavior you displayed in my office earlier today in front of Officer Brooks was disgraceful. You're better than that. So I'm hoping to never see that side of you again."

"That's actually why I stopped by, sir. I wanted to apologize. You're right. And you have my word that it'll never happen again."

"Apology accepted. Was I your first stop since returning to the office?"

"Yes, you were."

"I'm guessing you know what the second stop needs to be?"

Drew shoved his hands inside his pockets and walked back toward the doorway. "Yes, sir, I do."

"Good. Trust me, Officer Brooks is gonna be a great asset to your investigation. Now get to work. Oh, and thanks for the update on Tim. I'm glad to hear the doctors are planning to reduce the meds that are keeping him in the coma. Did they say what they're expecting to happen once the dosage is lowered?"

"They're hoping he'll open his eyes. Respond to sights and sounds. Grip his mother's hand. Things like that."

The conversation was interrupted when Chief Mitchell's

phone rang. "That's Chief Garcia. We'll catch up later. In the meantime, you know what you've gotta do."

"I do. And I'm on my way to do it now."

Drew sauntered toward the rookie cubicle area. Heads turned as he appeared to be talking to himself. But he was practicing which version of an apology he would give to Nia.

When he approached the desk, her chair was empty.

Good, he thought, realizing he wasn't quite ready for a face-to-face just yet. The day had already been heavy enough. Plus he couldn't seem to mentally compose a decent enough apology.

"Hey, Officer Taylor," a soft voice murmured behind him. "Were you looking for me?"

Dammit...

"Yuh—yeah," he stammered. Noticing she'd gone back to the formalities, he contemplated reminding her that she could call him Drew. But he resisted. After the way he'd behaved earlier, he didn't blame her for shutting down their friendly rapport. "Do you have a minute?"

Nia set a freshly poured cup of coffee on her desk and sat down, pointing to a chair in the corner. "I do. Please, have a seat. How is Officer Braxton doing?"

"He's already showing some slight signs of improvement. I was just telling Chief Mitchell that the doctors are hoping to start pulling him out of the coma tomorrow."

"Oh, good. I've been putting in my fair share of prayers all morning." She went quiet, her dazzling deep brown eyes searching Drew's face. "How are you holding up?"

I don't deserve your kindness, he almost blurted. The amount of concern this woman was showing toward him was inexplicable.

"I'm holding up okay. Knowing that Tim is getting better has me feeling cautiously hopeful. Thanks for asking."

Drew rocked back in his chair, suddenly lost for words. The fragmented apologies he'd just mentally rehearsed completely slipped from his mind now that he was in Nia's presence.

Freestyle something, he told himself, glancing over at her. She stared back expectantly, making no attempt to fill in the awkward gap of silence. He didn't blame her. This situation was on him to fix.

"Nia, if it's okay that I still call you that, I need to address the way I behaved this morning during our meeting with Chief Mitchell. I don't wanna use Tim's accident as an excuse, but hearing that he'd been hurt sent my mind reeling. Then after finding out how bad off he was, I honestly didn't think he was going to make—"

His voice broke underneath the weight of his words. When Nia reached out and clutched his hand, warmth radiated from her smooth skin, easing his pain like a soothing balm. "Look, I'm getting off track here. I want to apologize for the way I treated you. You didn't deserve that. And just to be clear, I have no doubt that you'll be an asset to this investigation."

"Thank you, Drew. I appreciate you saying that. Apology accepted." She held his gaze, flashing that same bright smile that had caught his attention when he'd entered Cooper's. "Listen, why don't we forget about what happened earlier and start over with a clean slate?"

"I'd like that."

"Good." She opened the case file and flipped through the police report. "Now that we've gotten all that out of the way, come closer. I'll go over what I've been working on since you've been gone."

"Oh? So you've been working my case without me?" he teased in an attempt to lighten the mood.

"I've been working *our* case without you. But anyway, I was looking through these notes and saw that Katie Douglas's family found her cell phone inside her apartment, which they turned over to law enforcement."

"Right. Officer Mills is downloading and researching all the data now. Once he's done, he's gonna provide me, well, now *us*, with all the pertinent info. So we'll find out who she'd been calling, texting, messaging on social media... those sorts of things."

"Yes, I spoke with Officer Mills about that. He confirmed that he'll be tracking her digital footprint as well, which is good. I'm curious to know where she'd been prior to her murder. In the meantime, I asked if I could take a look at the apps on her phone. One that stood out was the Someone for Everyone dating app. Did you know she was a member?"

"No, I didn't. But after speaking with her family, I did find out that she wasn't seeing anybody."

"As far as they knew."

Hunching his broad shoulders, Drew leaned in and studied the notes. "That's true. I just assumed they would know. Especially her sister. They seemed pretty close."

"Trust me, that doesn't mean a thing. Take my younger sister Ivy, for example. I used to think we were as tight as could be. Then one day I found out she'd been dating some guy for an entire year who I knew nothing about. People oftentimes hide things from those they're closest to. Especially when it comes to relationships."

"You make a good point. With that being said, we should reach out to the app's administrator as soon as possible."

"I'm already on it," Nia responded before flipping open her notebook. "I reached out to their customer service department requesting access to Katie's account. We need to know who she'd been in contact with and whether she made plans to meet up with anyone before her murder. Since so many people communicate solely through the app, there may be information we won't find in her emails, text messages and call log."

"Wow. You really are on it. I love the way you're taking such strong initiative." Drew hesitated, fiddling with the crown on his stainless steel watch. "Wait, you seem to know an awful lot about this whole dating app thing."

Nia ignored the remark. But her subtle smirk let him know she'd heard him loud and clear. "So anyway, I'm still waiting to hear back from the company. I had to contact them through the app since I couldn't find a phone number. I'll let you know as soon as they reach out."

"Sounds good. Nice work on all this—"

"Oh, wait!" she interrupted. "Before I forget, I got ahold of Latimer Park's recreation manager. Her name is Dawn Frazier by the way. She said that Katie's name doesn't ring a bell. After searching through the activity database, she found that Katie had never registered for any classes or programs. So as far as Dawn knows, she was in no way connected to the park. But Dawn did say we could come by anytime to speak with her and search the premises."

Drew eyed Nia while fidgeting with his goatee. He would've expected the average rookie to passively wait for him to return from the hospital, set up a meeting, then sit down together to discuss the next moves. But not Nia.

Clearly she was well above average, proving every word that Chief Mitchell had spoken about her to be true.

Two traits he'd failed to mention, however, were her tenacity and assertiveness—characteristics Drew found to be most attractive in a woman.

"Again," he said, "good work. Thank you."

"No problem. I was thinking—maybe you should send a patrol car out to Latimer Park to keep an eye on things. You know, just in case the killer left that event calendar at the crime scene to hint at what might be coming next."

"That's not a bad idea. Even if Katie isn't directly linked, there could still be some sort of connection. We'll run it by Chief Mitchell and see what he thinks. If he gives us the okay, I'll get someone assigned to the job as soon as possible."

"Excellent."

Drew reached for one of the crime scene photos just as Nia closed the file. Their hands met. His fingers slid between hers, rousing a heat so intense that he lurched in his chair.

"Sorry," he uttered, slow to pull away.

Nia's narrowing eyes drifted from his hand to his lips. "So…what's next?"

"Why don't we head to the candy factory so you can check out the crime scene. Then we'll stop by Latimer Park if there's still enough daylight."

Rolling away from the desk, she grabbed her tote. "Sounds like a plan."

"Cool. I'll get my stuff and meet you out front."

While Nia headed toward the lobby, Drew watched her walk away, his pupils shifting to the swing of her graceful stride.

Turn around, he thought, tearing himself away from the hypnotic sight.

The officer couldn't decide which was more impressive—Nia's beauty or her savvy. Either way, he was glad to have her on his team.

Chapter Six

Nia stretched out on her cream leather sofa, kneading her fist into her quads after an intense spin class. The day had been long. She'd stayed at the station way past six, then stopped by the grocery store before heading to the gym.

Cozying up against a green suede pillow, Nia was hit with a bout of loneliness. The chilly autumn night left her wishing she had someone to come home to. It'd been almost two years since she had been in a serious relationship. In the past week, she and Drew had spent countless hours together, which only magnified her single status. It almost felt like punishment, working so closely with the man she'd been pining after for years.

Landing a case of this magnitude early in her rookie career was a dream. Nia had hoped that fact alone would hold her attention so that she wouldn't be laser-focused on Drew. Yet the complete opposite had occurred. Seeing him in uniform, taking charge and handling the investigation with such skill and ease, only made him more appealing.

Once the pair had teamed up, Nia realized she'd only scratched the surface of who really Drew was. Underneath the tough exterior was a thoughtful man who always took her thoughts and theories into consideration. That had been pretty surprising after the meltdown he'd had in Chief Mitchell's office. But aside from his investigative acumen and meticulous critical thinking skills, it was Drew's appreciation of her contributions that impressed Nia the most.

The drawback, however, was that her feelings for Drew were growing beyond her control. Her slight crush had been manageable. But these new emotions were beginning to get the best of her. And it was frustrating that she couldn't do anything about it.

Nia closed her eyes. Mulled over the moments alone she and Drew had been spending together. Just that afternoon when they were inside the cluttered evidence room he'd slipped past her, his hard chest pressing against her back. She'd gasped and spun around, her breasts brushing against his taut bicep as he reached out to steady her.

Self-control left her body when she quivered within his grip. Drew just stood there, his parted lips indicating he'd felt her reaction. Those massive hands lingered on her hips. Their mouths were so close that as he exhaled, she inhaled the sweet scent of cinnamon espresso on his breath.

Nia's desire for Drew no longer appeared one-sided. But dating a colleague was still off-limits. Being a Juniper police officer meant everything to her. If she and Drew got together, then broke up, her dream job would become a nightmare as Nia knew she didn't have the stomach to face an ex every day.

"Oh, well," she sighed, turning up the volume on the Tennis Channel. As Chanda Rubin reviewed the day's top matches, she grabbed her phone and swiped open the Someone for Everyone app. There were several messages, but none from the administrator in response to her Katie Douglas request.

Drew had been right about one thing—Nia did know her way around the dating app. What he didn't know was that she'd been a member for almost a year.

After Linda Echols's murder, Nia had grown depressed. She became obsessed with work and began isolating herself socially. Friends insisted that she needed to get out more and start dating, if for nothing else than to help take her mind off the tragic death. It had taken quite a bit of convincing on their part. But after they assured Nia she could easily connect with the perfect match through a dating app as opposed to a bar or club, she gave in and joined Someone for Everyone.

Nia had only been out with a few of the members. Two of them lived in nearby towns and one resided in Denver. None had worked out. But she hadn't given up hope just yet.

After swiping through several lackluster profiles, Nia clicked on her inbox and scrolled through the messages. She stopped at the sight of a man's profile picture. He appeared tall, his slim-fitting navy suit tailored to a tee. His flawless deep brown skin glowed as he flashed a sexy, mischievous half smile. His dark, piercing eyes looked as though they were staring right at her. The gaze was somewhat haunting, but at the same time intoxicating.

"Hmm…" Nia murmured before opening his message.

Hello, beautiful. My name is Shane Anderson, and I am new to the Juniper area. I just stumbled across your profile, and I must say, you are quite lovely. I would love to get to know you better. If the feeling is mutual, please feel free to respond to this message. I hope to hear from you soon…xx, Shane

Nia reread the message at least three times. It may have been short, but it was one of the more gentlemanly introductions that she'd received. Most men asked what her plans were for the evening and whether she was available to hook up. And by *hook up*, it was clear they weren't referring to dinner or drinks.

Curiosity coursed through Nia's fingers as she clicked on his profile. The headline read, Shane, 38. Always up for meeting great people and experiencing new adventures. About Me: Works hard as a wealth management advisor Monday through Friday so that I can venture out and explore the world on weekends. Loves to laugh. Hates Brussels sprouts. Might challenge you to a dance-off in the middle of the club.

A soft smile teased Nia's lips as she took a sip of Merlot. "So you're handsome, smart and seem to have a good sense of humor. Nice start."

She scrolled down and continued reading.

What I'm Looking For: A woman who isn't afraid to laugh at herself, loves to travel, doesn't mind dog cuddles, is confident and secure, and knows what she wants. If we're a match, she would totally be down to explore this thing called life with me.

"I think this one might have potential," she said before opening his photo album. There was a picture of him sitting out on a massive backyard deck, a golden retriever nearby. Then one of him rock climbing inside the Pier 48 Fitness entertainment complex. From the look of his cut physique, he spent a fair amount of time in the gym.

The rest of the album contained an array of travel photos—from deep-sea fishing in Cabo San Lucas to skydiving along the Amalfi Coast. As his profile headline stated, Shane did indeed seem to live an adventurous life. Nia wondered if she could keep up. Aside from becoming a police officer, the most daring thing she'd ever done was take a midnight ghost tour through downtown Colorado Springs one Halloween weekend.

Deciding that Shane had potential, Nia replied to his message.

Hello, Shane. Thank you for your message. It's nice to "e-meet" you. My name is Nia, and as a lifelong resident of Juniper, I do hope you're enjoying my hometown thus far. To answer your question, yes, I would like to get to know you better. I'll start things off. After viewing your profile, I saw that you are quite daring. Have you found any fun activities here in town that have satisfied your adventure-seeking spirit? If not, I've got a few ideas. Looking forward to hearing from you...xx, Nia

"Now I just need to google thrilling things to do in Juniper."

Soon after she hit Send, Nia's phone pinged.

"That was quick."

A mix of hope and excitement simmered in her chest as Nia reopened the text thread between her and Shane. There were no new messages.

"What, what's happening here?"

She refreshed the page. Still nothing new.

Then an email notification appeared at the top of the screen. The message was from Drew, and the subject read "Case Report for Chief Mitchell—Final."

Nia's mind immediately shifted to thoughts of the investigation. The pair had spent the majority of the day composing the report. It had gotten late, and Drew knew she didn't want to miss her spin class. So he was kind enough to let her go while he stayed back and added the final touches.

Hey Nia, the message read. I hope your class went well. I've attached the final case report for the chief. Take a look and let me know what you think. If you don't have any changes, we'll send it first thing in the morning. Looking forward to hearing from you. Have a good night. Drew

Nia clicked on the attachment and scanned the report. They'd started off by bringing Chief Mitchell up to speed on their visit to Shelby's Candy Factory. For over two hours, the officers combed the area where Katie's body had been discovered. Just when they were about to give up, Nia found a piece of cardboard underneath the cold pressing unit. It contained a dirty shoeprint impression that looked to be the sole of a size eleven in men's. Luckily for them, the distinct treads with beveled edges and slanting lugs were clearly visible. Drew took photos and sent the fiberboard off to the crime lab for testing.

Through a shoe-sole pattern classification system database, Nia discovered that the print belonged to a Lacrosse AeroHead Sport hunting boot. Despite knowing the print could belong to anyone as there had been plenty of people in and out of the factory, she and Drew were hoping that the print would prove viable in helping to track down their killer.

Next was a summary of their visit to Latimer Park. After inspecting the area, nothing appeared suspicious. Dawn, the recreation manager, wasn't able to share much more than she already had during her phone conversation with Nia. Their brief meeting ended with her promising to keep an eye out and let law enforcement know if anything strange occurred.

After getting the okay from Chief Mitchell, Drew had assigned Officer Davis to patrol the park. Days went by with no abnormal activity. Davis questioned whether the crumpled event calendar found at the crime scene was relevant to their case.

"Don't give up," Drew had told him. "You never know what we may find."

But nothing could convince Officer Davis that the Latimer Park stakeout wasn't a waste of time. He didn't think the killer would make a move with a patrol car present. Nia and Drew felt his presence would deter the killer from making a move at all. In the midst of the debate, Davis requested that the stakeout be called off. So Drew wrapped up the report asking that Chief Mitchell make the final decision.

Nia replied to the email confirming the report was good to go, then took another sip of wine. She needed a break. Ever since the chief partnered her with Drew, the case was all she thought about. It was difficult enough knowing there was a killer on the streets of Juniper terrorizing the community. But the pressure to prove herself while struggling to not overstep her bounds had become an even heavier burden to bear. The search for balance was beginning to wear on Nia and a reprieve was in order—which was why the message from Shane had come at the perfect time.

Just as she grabbed the remote and turned to the Oxygen channel, her phone pinged again. This time, it was a text from Drew.

Hey, it's me again. Thanks for the green light on the report. On another note, Officer Davis talked to Chief Mitchell this evening, and Chief decided to stop the surveillance on Latimer Park. I'm really disappointed as I'm sure you are too since we both believe that the event calendar is no coincidence. I'll talk to the boss in the morning and try to change his mind. Fingers crossed. Have a good night.

Dread poured over Nia as she slammed her phone against the couch. Of course the calendar was no coincidence. But trying to defend their hunch without further proof, signs of suspicious activity or a viable connection between Katie and the park seemed impossible.

Nia stared at Drew's message, rereading it a couple more times before composing a response that wouldn't reflect the anger ringing inside her head.

Thanks for the update. I'm really disappointed to hear that as well. Let's just hope that Chief Mitchell is right and nothing comes of the calendar being left at the scene. Hope you have a good night as well.

After sending the message, Nia opened the Quick Eats app and ordered a buffalo chicken sandwich with a side of loaded fries instead of the salad. News of the canceled stakeout left her craving comfort food.

Just as she refilled her wine glass, her cell pinged again. Nia assumed it was Drew and swiped open her phone without checking the notification. The Someone for Everyone heart-shaped icon flashed on the screen, indicating she had a new message.

She sat straight up and opened it. A text from Shane appeared.

Hello Nia. It's nice to "e-meet" you as well. Beautiful name, btw. Thank you for your quick response. Did I mention that I love a woman who's prompt? But anyway, as I'd stated in my previous message, I'm new to town. I recently began working for a brokerage firm, and let's just say I've been earning every single penny! Once my schedule frees up a bit, I would love to meet you in person, maybe for a nice dinner or some live jazz music. Until then, I hope we can keep the conversation going here. That way, once we finally do meet, it'll feel as if we already know one another. That said, it's lights-out for me as the alarm is set for a 4:00 a.m. training session at the gym. Have a wonderful night, gorgeous. Looking forward to hearing from you again soon...xx, Shane

Nia's pulse began to throb as she reread the message. She debated whether to respond now or wait until the morning. After a mental back-and-forth, she decided to hold off so as not to appear too eager.

The minute she set her cell down, thoughts of the investigation crept back into her head.

Enough, Nia told herself. She'd dedicated enough of her day to the case. It was time to focus on something a little more pleasant—like the message exchange with Shane.

Thanks to him, her evening was ending on a high note. "So let's keep it there," she murmured, grabbing her phone and scrolling through his photos once again.

Chapter Seven

Drew floored the accelerator, flying across Sparrow Lane Bridge, then tearing down Candlewood Avenue. He tried Nia's cell again. The call went straight to voicemail.

"Nia," he huffed. "I've been trying to reach you for the past hour. I hope you're getting my calls and texts. I need you out at Latimer Park. *Now.* A couple of joggers found a dead body on a bench over by the duck pond. Chief Mitchell and the forensic team should already be there. I'm pulling up now. Call me when you get this message."

After parking along a side street near the tennis courts, he sprinted across the freshly cut grass. Panic swirled through his lungs as he choked on shallow breaths of air.

It was a little past six-thirty in the morning—too early for the recreational areas to be occupied. *Thank God.* The last thing Juniper PD needed was for people to catch sight of the gruesome scene.

Yellowish-orange light broke through dark clouds as the sun began to rise. A few of the officers who'd worked the overnight shift were already there, wrapping yellow Police Line tape around lodgepole pine tree trunks. In the center of it all was a shallow duck pond. Birds were splashing about, their fluttering wings flipping over banana water lilies in response to all the commotion.

On a black wrought-iron bench right across from the water sat a woman's body. Her head was slumped over, and just like Katie Douglas, her throat had been slashed. Blood drenched her off-white bomber jacket. Her hands and feet were bound with duct tape. And a piece of paper was stuffed inside her right hand.

"Hey, Taylor!" Officer Davis called out. "I just got a text from the chief. He should be here any minute. Any word from Officer Brooks?"

"No, not yet. I've sent several messages and left voice-mails. Her phone must be out of juice because she never turns it off."

The thought of something happening to Nia flashed through Drew's mind. *Don't do that*, he told himself, gritting his teeth in frustration.

As he approached the victim, Drew's grip on the evidence collection kit tightened, his stomach turning at the grisly sight. The woman looked to be no older than twenty-five. A long dark braid hung down her back. From what he could tell, her height and weight appeared to be almost identical to Katie's. The similarities between the two crime scenes were uncanny. Either they were dealing with a copycat killer, or their suspect had struck again.

"So what do you think?" Officer Davis asked. "Is it possible we might have a serial killer on our hands?"

"Not only is it possible, but in my opinion, it's highly likely. And apparently he's got a type. Notice the parallels between this victim and the last?"

"Yeah, I do. You know who else comes to mind when I compare the two?"

"Let me guess. Linda Echols."

"You got it."

Staring down at the ground, Officer Davis dug his heel into a clump of grass before emitting a forced cough. "Hey, uh… Officer Taylor? There's something I need to say to you. I feel terrible after insisting that Chief Mitchell take me off the park surveillance job. You're the lead investigator on this case, and I should've listened to you and believed that hunch you were feeling about the clue left at the last crime scene. You knew it might lead to something like this. But I got impatient. Blew it off, thinking the killer was playing some sick game rather than tipping us off."

"Actually, it was Officer Brooks who was adamant that we keep watch on the park. I just wish I'd been more aggressive in trying to convince Chief Mitchell to change his mind. But the reality is neither of us can do anything about what's happened here. What we *can* do is put every effort into catching this maniac before he kills again."

"Agreed." Shoving his hands in his pockets, Officer Davis slowly backed away. "But I just can't shake the guilt of knowing this victim's blood is on my hands. I could've prevented this. From here on out, trust that I've got your back and will follow your lead until we get this case solved."

"Thanks, Davis. I appreciate you saying that."

"Officer Taylor!"

The sight of Nia running toward Drew eased his tense shoulders.

"Hey, where have you been? I was starting to worry about you."

"I'm so sorry I didn't call you back," she panted. "My phone battery died right after your first text came through.

So what's the latest? Are the joggers still here? Have they been questioned yet?"

"They were questioned briefly by responding officers but weren't able to offer up much info. I'd like for us to interview them more thoroughly down at the station."

Drew followed Nia's gaze as she pointed toward the street. "The medical examiner just pulled up. I'd better slip into some protective gear before we get started. I'll be right back."

As he watched Nia hurry off, Officer Davis nudged Drew's shoulder.

"What's up?" Drew asked him.

"Yeah, that's my question to you. What's up?"

"What do you mean?"

Nodding in Nia's direction, Officer Davis replied, "What's going on between you and Brooks? I noticed how quickly your mood lifted the second she ran over here."

Drew's eyes narrowed at the officer's sly smirk. "I'm just glad to know she's all right after not hearing back from her earlier."

"You sure that's all it is?"

"Yeah. I'm positive." Drew broke the officer's inquisitive stare and pulled on a mask and gloves. "Look, we need to get started on the crime scene analysis while the medical examiner processes the body. I wanna move on that ASAP so I can take a look at whatever's inside the victim's hand."

With a slow nod, Officer Davis caught the hint and dropped the subject. "You got it, boss."

DREW EASED INTO a seat inside Earl's Steakhouse and waited for Nia to arrive at the table. She'd been stopped near the entrance by a group of old friends from college. After being introduced, he had stood around waiting as the girl talk commenced. But once they began discussing bridal showers and TikTok makeup tutorials, he excused himself and followed the hostess to their booth.

After he and Nia had spent the day processing the crime scene, Drew offered to treat her to dinner. Sending her home alone straight from the station just didn't feel right. As her mentor, he wanted to make sure she was okay and offer up a little moral support over a nice steak and glass of cabernet.

Drew peered over the top of the menu, watching as Nia's friends fawned all over her. Whatever she was saying had them completely captivated. Nia had that effect on people wherever they went. When she walked into a room, everyone took notice. Whenever she spoke, those around her stopped and listened. Nia was a natural-born leader who had that *it* factor. Her beauty only added to her appeal. The more she and Drew worked together, the deeper his admiration grew. And if he were being honest, his attraction as well.

The moment she pivoted and headed toward the table, Drew dropped his head, diverting his attention back to the wine list. Before doing so, he caught a glimpse of her fading smile. There was a look of agony behind her tired eyes. He wasn't surprised, considering they'd spent hours at Latimer Park, scouring the crime scene for evidence. This being Nia's first encounter with a murder victim, her discomfort showed—the slight gagging, watering eyes and excessive fidgeting. He'd recommended she work on completing the police report while he processed the scene. But she refused, insisting she was fine.

Drew appreciated Nia's endurance as she ended up being an essential part of the analysis. She was the one who had initiated the fingerprint search, dusting the bench with a dark powder and using clear adhesive tape to lift the prints. She'd spotted a muddy shoeprint near the victim's feet that the other officers missed. To record that pattern, she and Drew used a sheet of rubber layered in gelatin to lift it off the soil's surface. And then there was the cigarette butt Nia had found floating near the edge of the duck pond that she'd retrieved before the birds got to it.

It was quite a rousing sight, watching the awe on their colleagues' faces as they observed Nia's work. They'd never seen her in action since this was her first time processing an active crime scene. Drew on the other hand was accustomed to her procedural acumen. But even he was impressed when she immediately recognized the pattern on the shoeprint. It contained the same beveled edge treading as the Lacrosse hunting boot impression found at Katie Douglas's crime scene—convincing both officers that the women had been killed by the same perpetrator.

"Hey," Nia breathed, pulling Drew from his thoughts as she slid into the seat across from him. "Sorry about that. I haven't seen some of those women in years. We had a lot to catch up on. But anyway, thanks again for suggesting this. I cannot tell you how much I needed it."

"Of course. It's the least I could do considering all the great work you put in today. Plus I still owed you after our coffee outing."

"Oh, please. With the amount of wine I'm about to drink? You'll wish you would've covered the coffee date instead—" She froze, a deep shade of crimson coloring her cheeks. "I'm sorry. But did I just refer to our mentoring meeting as a *date*?"

"Yes," he replied, chuckling at her horrified reaction. "I believe you did."

Her mouth fell open, but no words were spoken as she began fanning her face with the specials menu.

"Hey," Drew murmured, flashing a relaxed smile. "It was just a little slipup. Actually it was more like a welcome faux pas. We needed something to take the heaviness off of the day."

Nia's tense expression softened. Reaching across the table, she gave his hand a squeeze, her fingertips teasing his palm. "You're right. Because today was definitely a lot to deal with."

He barely heard her as a tingling sensation shot up his arm. When it snaked below his belt Drew straightened up, turning his attention back to the menu. "So…anything look good?"

"Everything looks good. And I didn't eat a thing today. I'm actually surprised I have an appetite after seeing…"

"Are you okay?" Drew asked after her voice trailed off.

"Yep," she quickly replied, forcing a tight grin before burying her face in the menu. But he could still see the creases of worry lining her forehead. "I'm thinking of getting the barbecue-glazed salmon with a side of garlic mashed potatoes and roasted asparagus. What about you?"

"I'm going with the bone-in rib eye, loaded baked potato and spring sweet peas."

"*Aaand* I've got that," someone chimed in.

Drew's head swiveled, not realizing the server had approached. After taking the rest of their orders, she rushed off just as the officers' cell phones pinged. Drew grabbed his first.

"Oh, good. We've got an ID on the victim. Her name is Violet Shields. Twenty-six years old. Her parents identified the body at the medical examiner's office."

Biting down on her bottom lip, Nia's eyes remained stuck to her screen.

"Did you receive this text as well?" he asked her.

"No, mine is from Dawn at Latimer Park. And it's not good news. She reviewed last night's surveillance footage. The cameras captured the basketball and tennis courts and the playground. But nothing near the duck pond."

"*Dammit.* I wonder if there's footage of anyone walking past those areas. Unless the suspect entered the park through the back area near the trees, Dawn should've seen him making his way toward the pond."

"You're right. I've already asked that she forward the footage to us so we can review it ourselves, but I'll remind her to do that now."

Drew paused when a server approached with their wood-grilled octopus and drinks. Once she was out of earshot, he said, "Hey, there's something else I want to talk to you about."

"*Okay...*" Nia uttered. "I'm listening."

"I was talking with Officer Davis this morning before you arrived at the crime scene. He mentioned how much he regretted removing himself from the Latimer Park surveillance assignment. So on behalf of him, myself *and* Chief Mitchell, I wanna apologize."

"Drew, you don't have to—"

"No, no, I do. We really dropped the ball on that. You were the one who initially made that suggestion, and you were one hundred percent right. Had the department taken heed, maybe Violet's murder could've been avoided. So, moving forward, just know that I'll push harder for what you want. Because obviously your instincts are a hell of a lot stronger than some of these veteran cops."

"Thank you for that, Drew. But like I was going to say, there's no need for you to apologize. It wasn't your decision. It started with Officer Davis and ended with Chief Mitchell."

"True." He took a sip of his whiskey sour while Nia filled their plates with octopus. The gesture warmed him, sparking memories of what it felt like being out on a date. The fire it incited within his gut. The excitement, the anticipation of what would come later.

Everything you shouldn't be feeling for Nia...

"Drew?"

"Yep?" he uttered, so buried in his thoughts that he hadn't noticed her handing him a plate.

"Where did you go just now? It seemed like you faded out or something."

"Oh, sorry. I, uh… I was just thinking about Officer Davis," he lied. "And how he swore to never make a rash decision that could cost someone their life again."

"Good. Hey, switching topics for a quick sec. How's Tim doing?"

"He's doing well. Better than the doctors expected, actually. He's out of the ICU, and so far, there are no signs of any brain damage. They're not sure how much longer he'll be in the hospital, but afterwards I'm pretty sure he's going to have a lengthy stint in rehab. They keep saying he's lucky to be alive."

"Any new leads on the driver of the car that hit him?"

"No, unfortunately. Tim didn't get a look at it. And since the accident occurred on a rural road where there were no houses, we weren't able to obtain any surveillance footage." Drew rammed his fork into a tentacle. "I don't know why, but something is telling me that accident was intentional."

"Meaning?"

"I'm wondering if Tim was targeted. And whether the crash is connected to this murder investigation. Because it happened right after Katie Douglas's body was found. Could it have been the killer's way of trying to throw us off, and leave the department with one less officer on the case?"

"Could be. At this point, I wouldn't count any theory out." Nia swiped open her cell and pulled up a photo. "We haven't had a chance to discuss the clue left inside the victim's hand at Latimer Park. What do you make of it?"

Drew studied the image of the wedding invitation Nia had snapped at the crime scene. The thick cream pearlescent stock and gold print was smeared with blood. But he was still able to make out the wording. At the top were two initials, *T* and *I*. The names of the couple set to exchange vows, Terrance Gauff and Ingrid Porter, were printed underneath. The wedding location was at the bottom—the Charlie Sifford Country Club.

"Well, I definitely think it's alluding to what our killer has planned next. And I bet we're on the same page regarding next steps."

"What—that we should set up surveillance at the club?"

"Exactly. Which is why I already spoke to Chief Mitchell and he assigned Officer Ryan to the job. He's patrolling the place as we speak."

Nia held her glass in the air. "Now *that* is some good news I needed to hear. Cheers."

Tapping his glass against hers, Drew's gaze lingered on Nia until the server approached with their food.

"You know what I suggest we do?" Drew asked. "Pause all talk of the investigation and enjoy our dinner."

"Yes, good idea."

Drew eyed her plate, adding, "You know what else would be a good idea? Sliding a piece of that salmon onto my plate."

"Oh, really now," Nia retorted, pointing her fork toward his entrée. "How about we make a trade? A slice of my salmon for a piece of your steak?"

"Deal."

As Drew cut into his rib eye, the tension in his shoulders slackened, which he credited to the change of subject. But underneath that theory lay the fact that Nia's presence had put him at ease.

Yet while the case discussion had ended, thoughts of the investigation persisted. The wedding invitation left at the scene was a stark reminder that the clock was ticking. And it was only a matter of time before the killer would strike again.

Chapter Eight

Nia pulled into the driveway of her tri-level townhome and willed her fatigued legs to carry her to the door. The day had been exhausting—both physically and emotionally. Dinner with Drew did lighten the load of the investigation. But by the end of the meal, she was fighting to keep her eyes open. He'd insisted on ordering key lime pie for dessert, which only exacerbated her exhaustion. Now that Nia was finally home, climbing into bed was the only thing on her mind.

Nia stopped at the mailbox on the way in. Just as she opened the lid, a light flickered inside the house.

She hesitated, peering through the canted bay window's sheer curtains. Every light in the living room was off. Yet the kitchen light was on.

But...how?

She could've sworn she'd turned it off that morning.

You're just tired. You rushed out to the crime scene before 6:00 a.m. Probably left the light on by accident...

Grabbing the stack of envelopes from the mailbox, Nia made her way inside. She kicked off her boots, switched on a lamp and shuffled through the mail.

"Bill, bill, junk, another bill—"

She froze when the last envelope came into view. It didn't

have her full name on it, nor her address. The letters *NIA* were handwritten across the middle in bold black letters.

"What the hell is this?"

She tore open the envelope and snatched a thick cream pearlescent card from it. Scanned the beautiful gold print, then dropped it to the floor. Her hands shook as she bent down to pick it up.

It can't be. You're just seeing things...

But upon further inspection, Nia realized her eyes weren't deceiving her. In her hand was an invitation to Ingrid Porter and Terrance Gauff's wedding—the same invitation they'd found at the crime scene. And in the lower left-hand corner was a bloody fingerprint.

"No, no, no..." she muttered.

Nia grabbed her purse, almost ripping the zipper trying to get to her cell phone. With trembling fingers she fumbled through the call log and dialed Drew's number. The call went straight to voicemail.

"Drew! Call me as soon as you get this. I got a wedding invitation in the mail today that matches the one we found at Latimer Park—"

The kitchen light went out again.

Her phone fell by her side. She glanced at the alarm control panel hanging by the door. It had been disabled.

What the...

Terror grabbed hold of Nia's joints as she stumbled against the wall. Without taking her eyes off the kitchen entrance, she reached down and pulled her gun from her purse.

Stay calm. This is what you were trained to do.

Standing straight up, Nia pointed her weapon toward the doorway. "Hey! Whoever's in here, just so you know, I am a police officer. I am armed. And I *will* shoot you. So come out into the living room with your hands up!"

Silence.

She ducked down while inching along the back of the couch. "This is your final warning. Trust me, this is not a game." Curling her finger around the trigger, Nia yelled, "Either come out, or I will—"

"Don't shoot!"

The kitchen suddenly lit up.

"Who the hell is that?" Nia called out right before her sister, Ivy, came bouncing into the living room.

"Niaaa! Hey, girl! Oh, how I've missed you, *seesto!*"

"Ivy! What are you doing here? And why would you scare me half to death like that? I almost shot you!"

"Come on, now. You weren't gonna shoot me."

"The hell I wasn't!"

Ivy jumped into her arms, ending the rant as her wild curls smothered Nia's entire face. Typical Ivy—showering her sister with love to deflect from the issue at hand.

"Anyway, I've missed you, too," Nia said, relenting, before she embraced her sister. But as she grabbed hold of Ivy's bony back, she quickly pulled away. "Wait, what's going on with you? Why do you feel so tiny?"

"Because I *am* tiny." Holding her scrawny arms out at her sides, Ivy spun a three-sixty, showing off the skintight black pleather dress clinging to her rail-thin figure. "I've lost fifteen pounds since the last time you saw me."

"Yeah, well, the problem is you didn't need to lose any weight. Whatever look you've got going on isn't healthy."

"Have you forgotten that I'm in the entertainment industry? You know how it is. The thinner you are, the bigger your chances of becoming a star."

Nia watched through worried eyes as her sister flitted back into the kitchen. Ivy, also known as the black sheep of the Brooks family, had a checkered past that plagued her for years. She'd hung out with a rough crowd during high school and had gotten herself into trouble on numerous occasions.

Those incidents of stealing from local stores for fun, vandalizing the property of people who'd allegedly wronged her and being caught drinking after hours at Latimer Park had left a stain on her reputation. After barely graduating, she'd run off to Los Angeles to pursue a singing career. She and Nia had managed to remain close over the years. But Ivy's erratic behavior remained a point of contention in their relationship.

"So," Ivy said, bouncing back inside the living room with two glasses of wine, "what have I missed since I've been gone?"

"First of all, I don't need another glass of wine. I had plenty during dinner."

"Oh? Dinner with who? Someone special you haven't told me about?"

Plopping down on the couch, Nia replied, "Nope. Just a coworker."

"Hmm," Ivy purred, sliding into the spot next to her. "That's what your mouth says, but that glimmer in your eyes is telling a completely different story. Spill the tea, sis! Tell me all about him."

"There's nothing to tell. Like I said, he's a coworker." When Ivy handed her a glass, Nia turned away. "No, please. Trust me, I've had enough. All I need at this point is a glass of ice water and my bed. I am exhausted. Speaking of which, I wish you would've told me you were coming to town. I wouldn't have stayed out so late."

"Don't worry. There will be plenty of time for us to spend together since you'll be seeing a whole lot more of me."

"What do you mean?"

"Well…" Ivy avoided Nia's eyes as she picked at a rogue thread hanging from her hemline. "I don't know exactly when I'm going back to LA. So I'll be here for a while."

Judging by the look of Ivy's pouty lower lip, Nia knew what that meant. Ivy was running from something.

"Where are you staying? With mom and dad?"

Suddenly, Ivy's scowl curled into a sugary sweet grin. "That's what I wanted to talk to you about. I was hoping that maybe I could, you know…"

"Oh, no," Nia interrupted, shaking her head so adamantly that her gold hoops slapped her cheeks. "Absolutely not. I was just assigned to a *huge* case that could make or break my career. I do not have time to keep an eye on you."

"Why would you have to keep an eye on me?"

"*Please*. Is that even a real question? Or should I pull up your police report and remind you of all the mess you've gotten yourself into over the years?"

"Can you please stop throwing that up in my face? All that happened forever ago. I'm not the girl I used to be. I've grown up."

Crossing her arms over her stomach, Nia watched as Ivy guzzled her wine, then picked up the second glass she'd poured. "So, tell me, what brought you back to Juniper?"

"I just needed a break. You know how LA can be. Hectic. Grueling. *Expensive*. Plus I got tired of the whole auditioning grind. Singing my heart out day after day, week after week, while working my ass off to make ends meet was getting old. Even though I'd land a few small gigs here and there, they weren't getting me anywhere."

As Ivy slouched down farther into the couch, Nia suspected she wasn't telling the whole truth. Her sister was known to be secretive. She'd always been a wild card, making spontaneous decisions without thinking of the repercussions. So the abrupt move back home didn't come as much of a surprise.

"Well, you should know that now isn't the best time to be in Juniper," Nia warned.

"Why not?"

"Haven't you seen the news? We've got a serial killer on the loose."

"Wait, you've got a *what*?"

Nia tossed her hand in the air for extra emphasis. "There is a serial killer hunting down women in Juniper. He's binding their wrists and ankles, slashing their throats and leaving their bodies on display in public places."

"Oh my God," Ivy moaned, covering her mouth in disgust. "That is…that is *sick*."

"Yes, it is. And I'm assisting the lead investigator on the case—"

"Wait, *you*? But how? You're still a rookie. You just made it onto the force."

"It's a long story. Look, my point is, this partner of mine is a hard-nosed veteran who's working the biggest case of his career, too, and he's depending on me. So I don't have time to be looking after you and making sure you're staying out of trouble."

"And you won't have to," Ivy insisted. "I've already reconnected with several old friends, so if I need anything, I can go to them. Plus I landed a job bartending at the Bullseye Bar and Grill. So I'll be fine."

"Oh, so you told everybody you'd be in town except for me? Even though *I'm* the one you want to stay with?"

Giving Nia's thigh a playful pinch, Ivy squealed, "Yes! Thanks again for letting me crash here."

"Yeah, yeah. Just make sure you stay out of trouble."

Ivy suddenly grew quiet while staring down into her glass. Watching as her sister's eyes filled with tears, Nia didn't interpret the mood switch as a sentimental sign of missing home. It was something deeper. Something troubling.

Knowing Ivy, the more Nia probed, the more she'd withdraw. So Nia decided to leave it be, at least for the time being. She was completely drained. The talk could wait until tomorrow.

"Listen," Nia said, brushing Ivy's bangs out of her eyes. "I'm gonna need for you to be careful. I haven't forgotten about those old friends of yours and how they operate. They weren't the best people. And from what I hear, they've only gotten worse. More importantly, with this killer on the loose, I don't like the idea of you running around town and bartending until the early hours of the morning. Things have changed since you left."

"As hard as it is for you to grasp this fact, I can take care of myself. Stop worrying so much. I'll be fine."

Before Nia could respond, Ivy drained the second glass of wine, then hopped up from the couch.

"Wait, where are you going?"

"To change clothes. I'm getting together with the girls tonight. They're throwing me a little impromptu welcome home party at Army and Lou's Jazz Club. You wanna come?"

"Absolutely not. It's already late and I have to be back at the station early in the morning. How are you getting there?"

Pressing her hands together, Ivy pleaded, "I was hoping you'd let me borrow your car. *Pleeease?*"

"No, ma'am. I highly doubt that you'd bring it back in time for me to make it to work. Can't one of your friends pick you up?"

"I guess one of them will have to, won't they?"

"I guess so."

"Fine," Ivy huffed, charging up the staircase. "I'll call Madison. Oh, and nice way to welcome your baby sister home."

"Maybe the welcome would've been much nicer had my baby sister told me she'd be here instead of breaking into my house and scaring the hell out of me."

"It's not breaking in when I used the key you gave me!"

"It is when I don't even know you're in town!"

The sound of Ivy's silver cowboy boots pounding the stairs grew louder in response. Nia ignored it and turned on the television, now wide awake thanks to her sister's unexpected arrival.

A flash of sparkly cream cardstock caught Nia's eye. She shot to her feet and ran to the console table by the door. After being startled by Ivy, she'd forgotten all about the wedding invitation left inside her mailbox. Nia had also forgotten about Drew, who'd yet to call her back.

She checked the cell. No text notification from him either. She tried calling again. The call went straight to voicemail. *Dammit.*

Nia left another message, snapped a photo of the invitation and texted it to Drew. Once the message was sent, she dead-bolted the door and grabbed her gun off the table. Just as she set the alarm, her phone rang. It was him.

"Are you okay?" he asked the second she picked up. "I got your voicemail and saw that text. What is going on?"

"*A lot*. I'm fine though. A little shaken up, but I'm okay."

"Good. Sorry it took so long to call you back. I stopped by the gym on the way home because after the day we had, I needed to get in a workout. I didn't realize my phone was on silent. But about that invitation. First of all, do you need for me to come over there? Because I can—"

"No, Drew. You don't have to do that. It's late. And I know you're tired. Plus I've got my Glock right here next to me."

"Okay. Well, if that changes, just let me know. I'm sure getting that invitation was disturbing to say the least. Assuming it was left by the killer, that means he knows where you live. And with that being said, are you *sure* you don't want me to come—"

"I'm positive," Nia interrupted once again, hating the idea of being a burden.

"Look, do me a favor. Put the invitation inside a plastic bag and bring it to the station tomorrow. We'll send it to the crime lab first thing and have it tested for DNA."

"I will." Nia paused at the sound of a glass crashing to the floor right above her head. "Oh God..."

"Wait, what was that I just heard?"

"My sister is upstairs destroying my house."

"Ivy's in town? I didn't know she was coming to visit."

"Yeah, neither did I. When I got home she was already here and scared the crap out of me."

"Nia!" Ivy screamed from the top of the landing. "Do you have any hair mousse?"

"No, I do not!"

Drew's throaty chuckle floated through her ear.

"What's so funny?"

"You and your sister, sounding like two teenagers."

"Interesting you should say that. Because she's acting like a teenager, asking to borrow my car and whatnot. I'm still trying to figure out what she's doing back in Juniper. I have a feeling she's keeping something from me. I'll get it out of her eventually."

"Does she know about this homicidal predator out here roaming the streets?"

"She does now. But Ivy's the type who thinks nothing will happen to her. She's already got me worrying. Especially after hearing that she'll be bartending at Bullseye."

"Look, you've got enough on your plate. I don't want your blood pressure to go up because you're stressing over your sister. I'll talk to the guys and ask them to keep an eye on the bar during her shifts."

"Drew, that is a lot to ask. Are you sure it wouldn't be too much trouble?"

"I'm positive."

"Thank you," she murmured, her quiet tone buzzing with warmth. "I really appreciate it."

"Of course. Oh, and before I forget, I heard back from the joggers who found the victim's body at Latimer Park. They're going to come in tomorrow morning and talk with us. I don't know how useful it'll be since they didn't see much. But sometimes when these witnesses are questioned at the station, they suddenly remember things they'd initially forgotten."

"Good to know. Let's hope that's the case." Nia hesitated when Ivy came clomping down the stairs. "Listen, I'd better go. My sister is getting ready to leave, and I need to give her one more lecture before she heads out."

"Yes, please do. If anything comes up, call me. And don't forget to keep your gun close. Unless you decide otherwise, I'll see you in the morning."

Nia sat there, contemplating whether or not she *should* decide otherwise.

You'd better not. Between all that wine you drank and your vulnerable state, there's no telling what you might do if he comes over...

"Thanks, Drew. I'll see you in the morning."

"Yeah, um...see you then."

There was a tinge of disappointment in his low tone. Nia wondered if it stemmed from his desire to be there with her or the fact that he was just tired. He disconnected the call before she could inquire.

"Okay," Ivy said, strutting into the living room as if she were on a catwalk. "What do you think?"

Nia looked up from her phone and almost fell off the couch. "What in the world are you wearing?" she asked, glaring at the sheer black negligee and glittery platform heels.

"*What?* I think I look good! And according to my nine thousand-plus followers on TikTok, they think so too."

A flash of anger shot through Nia as her sister snapped several selfies. "You aren't taking any of the warnings I gave seriously, are you?"

"Of course I am! I already told my girls about the investigation. Madison is planning on covering the case on her YouTube channel. Oh! And she wanted me to ask if you'd be willing to do an interview with her. You know, on behalf of the Juniper PD. Maybe that partner you mentioned could go live with her, too. Ooh, and what about your boss? Chief Marshall, or whatever his name is."

"It's Chief Mitchell. And, no. None of us are going on some YouTube channel to discuss the case. Besides, I thought Madison's channel was all about makeup and fitness."

"It is. But true crime is really hot right now. A lot of vloggers are doing this thing where they apply their makeup while covering cases. You've gotta keep up, big sis."

A loud engine roared out front.

"Maddy's here!" Ivy exclaimed, teetering toward the door to the beat of a blaring horn. Right before Ivy stepped outside, Nia grabbed her arm.

"Hey, listen. You need to be careful. Keep your eyes open and call me if anything comes up. Don't go wandering off by yourself or get too friendly with every person you see. Most importantly, please don't do anything illegal."

"Yes, *mother*. Now wish me luck. It's open mic night and the winner gets five hundred dollars."

"Good luck. Oh, and try not to stay out all night!"

"Bye!"

As Ivy went bouncing toward a red Toyota Supra, Nia stepped onto the porch and waved. She could barely hear Madison scream her name over the loud house music.

Worry pricked her skin watching the pair speed off into the night.

She's grown, Nia reminded herself. *She'll be fine...*

The night air was cool. And eerily peaceful. Nia eyed the broadleaf evergreen shrubs lining her rock garden, imagining some stranger audaciously invading her space.

The killer had dropped an ominous hint. He wanted her to know that he was aware of her connection to the case. Leaving the invitation was his attempt to extinguish her efforts. But it wasn't going to work. If anything, it would serve as fuel to further ignite her drive.

When she stepped back inside the house, a thought dropped in Nia's head like a hammer to a nail—security cameras were mounted over her front and back doors.

How could you forget that?

She threw her head back in relief and glanced at the top of the door.

"What the…"

The security camera was gone.

Nia rushed inside the house and bolted the door, then grabbed her phone. This time when she dialed Drew's number, he picked up on the first ring.

"Hey, what's up?" he asked. "Is everything okay?"

"No, everything is not okay. I need for you to come to my place. *Now.*"

Chapter Nine

Drew flicked a packet of raw sugar inside his coffee and stared across the conference room table. Nia's distraught expression pained him. The investigation was not going as he'd hoped. And now that she had become a target, it felt as though he was failing her.

The DNA evidence found at Latimer Park matched the evidence from Shelby's Candy Factory. Yet law enforcement still couldn't figure out the suspect's identity since no match had turned up in the national database.

The interview with joggers who'd discovered Violet Shields's body was a complete bust. Not only did they have nothing to report from the crime scene, but they'd brought their children into the station hoping they could tour the facility.

Surveillance footage saved to Nia's computer from the day the wedding invitation had been delivered didn't reveal much. The suspect had not come fully into view after crossing the neighbor's lawn and creeping up onto the porch from the side railing.

From what the officers could tell, he appeared slender and was dressed in all black. A mask covered his face and his head and shoulders were hunched over, making him unrecognizable. The steel rod swinging from his hand, however, was visible. Once he'd reached the landing, the camera shook violently before it went crashing to the ground. Nia's neighbors had allowed her to view their security footage. But none of their cameras were positioned to capture images of her house.

Despite his coffee being steaming hot, Drew took a long sip. The bitter burn on his tongue somehow cancelled the frustration brewing in his chest. The conference room table was covered with every piece of evidence they had collected. He'd suggested they start back at square one and work their way through each crime scene in hopes of stumbling upon something they'd missed. So far, both he and Nia had come up empty.

"This is so aggravating," she said, fiddling with the cap on her water bottle. "All these reports, all the photos, the DNA evidence... But still no suspects. The biggest disappointment was that bloody fingerprint found on the wedding invitation inside my mailbox. I just knew it would link us to our suspect."

"Yeah, same. The fact that it belonged to Violet Shields was just another sinister way for the killer to taunt us. What about that Someone for Everyone app? Have you heard back from the administrator?"

"No, not yet." Nia grabbed her phone and swiped it open. "But I'll check again, just to see if something came through since the last time I looked. I'll also do some online digging to find out who the owners are and get in touch with them directly."

"Good idea. While you do that, I'll have Officer Ryan work on getting a subpoena. That way they'll be forced to hand over the information whether they want to or not.

We've waited long enough for a response, which is ridiculous considering our request pertains to a criminal investigation…"

Drew's voice trailed off as Nia smiled at her phone screen.

"What's got you grinning over there like a giddy schoolgirl?"

"Nothing!" She fumbled her cell before sliding it to the side. "I was just—just checking on that response from the administrator."

"Any word from them?"

"Nope. No word yet."

Nia's bottle almost slipped from her hand. She caught it just in time, but not before a stream of water trickled onto the table. Quickly wiping it up with her sleeve, she snatched a report and pointed at the notes. "I've been meaning to ask about Violet's cell phone. Any luck tracking it down?"

"Not as of yet."

Drew watched as Nia's attention remained on the document. He hadn't known her for long. But he knew her well enough to realize when something was off. And she'd been acting strange all morning.

"Hey, is everything all right?"

"Yeah," she uttered a beat too soon. "Everything's fine. Why?"

"You just seem a bit…distracted. Is it that wedding invitation or your security camera going missing? Or what about your sister? I know you were caught off guard after the way she dropped in unexpectedly."

Finally looking up at him, Nia replied, "*Yes*. That's it. I think the fact that Ivy came storming back into town like a tornado has thrown me for a loop. But again, I'm fine.

Thanks for asking. Anyway, back to Violet's cell phone. Does her family think they may be able to find it?"

Drew could smell her lie from across the table. Clearly Ivy's visit had nothing to do with the joy on Nia's face after she'd checked the dating app. He was dying to ask what she was hiding. But it was none of his business. Not to mention he shouldn't even be concerned.

So why do you care?

Ignoring the annoying voice in his head, Drew said, "Violet's family is on top of the search for her cell. They're gonna try and track it down inside her house which, according to them, is a bit of a mess since she had some hoarding tendencies. I've also contacted her phone provider. So even if we can't get our hands on the actual device I'll have a record of her activity."

"Good. Because there is the chance that the killer took it. I'm guessing Violet didn't share her phone's location with anyone?"

"Nope. Nor did she utilize the Find My Device feature. And that's part of the problem. The more I've spoken with her family, the more I realize just how private of a person she was. According to her father, she was also dealing with issues of paranoia. Violet was convinced that if she used any sort of tracking technology, people outside of her family and friend circle would be able to trace her whereabouts."

Nia clicked her tongue while flipping through the photos of Violet's crime scene. "And what ends up happening? Someone still managed to hunt her down and kill her." Stopping on a close-up of the victim's slashed throat, she glared at it, then shoved the whole stack inside the folder. "Where do we go from here, Drew?"

"Great question..."

He rocked back in his black ergonomic chair and scanned the piles strewn in front of him. The documents became a blur of chaos as his mind sought out an answer.

When he leaned his elbows onto the table, Drew's laptop awoke from sleep mode. Katie Douglas's Facebook page popped up. He reached over and enlarged her profile picture. She stared back at him, her head tilted toward the sun while throwing up a peace sign.

"That picture is so haunting," Nia said. "Katie looks so happy and vibrant. And *alive*. To look at her there, knowing she's dead now, is just—just so disturbing."

"Yes, it is…"

Nia's words sparked a fire in Drew that pushed him away from the table.

"I got it," he said, pounding his fist into his palm.

"I'm sorry. You what?"

"I got it! I've got the answer. You and I are going to print out photos of Katie and take them down to Shelby's Candy Factory."

"And do what? Hang them up in hopes that someone will recognize her? I don't know how effective that'll be considering the place is abandoned. And the people who hang out there aren't the type to wanna assist law enforcement."

"Here's what I'm thinking. First we'll use social media to get some intel on when the next underground rave is happening. Once we find out, we'll show up with Katie's photo in hand and ask the attendees about her. Maybe she used to hang out there. Who knows, the killer may even hang out there. Either way, the answers we're looking for might be with the people who party at that factory."

Grabbing her notebook and flipping it open, Nia said, "I like that idea. I like it a lot. On another note, you mentioning a rave brought the whole use of illegal substances to mind, which made me think of the victims' toxicology reports. Have the results come back?"

"No, not yet. But I'm curious to know whether any of them were drugged. I'll put in a call to the medical examiner's office once we're done here and find out when we can expect them. As for now," he continued, pulling up his email, "I'm gonna send Officer Ryan a message asking if he's got intel on the next rave since he's usually up on those types of events."

"You know who else might know something? Ivy. I wouldn't be surprised if some of her old friends were the ones throwing them. I'll shoot her a text now."

As Nia typed away on her phone, Drew peered across the table, taking in her natural beauty. While it was on full display, there was something different. Her eyes, usually sparkling with enthusiasm, appeared dull, almost lifeless. Her lips were never without some shade of gloss. Today, they were bare. While she was still giving her all to the investigation, that fire and drive were missing, as if her spirit had been broken.

"Hey, Brooks," he said, trying his best to sound casual, "how are you holding up?"

Her fingers froze over the phone screen. "What do you mean?"

Those fluttering eyelids indicated that she knew exactly what he'd meant. Drew was slow to respond, empathizing with Nia as he thought back on his days as a rookie cop. They hadn't been easy. The need to appear tough overrode moments of vulnerability. He'd seen Nia the night that invitation showed up in her mailbox and the security camera went missing. She had been damn near inconsolable, falling into his arms the moment he stepped through the door.

But now, as she sat in front of him at the station, Nia was struggling to appear resilient, as if she wasn't being affected by the case. He needed her to know that she didn't have to put up a front for him. Their relationship was a safe space— a soft place to land when everything around her hardened.

"You know," he began, his husky tone laced with sincerity, "you don't have to put on an act for me. You've been through a lot. It's okay to be open and show emotion. You may be a police officer, but you're also human. I just need to know that you're all right. If you're not, I wanna do everything in my power to get you there. I can put a patrol car on duty to keep an eye on your house twenty-four seven. Hell, I'll even stay with you for the time being if that's what it'll take to make you feel secure."

Slowly setting her phone aside, Nia blew a heavy sigh. Her body shifted as she finally looked him in the eyes. "Thank you, Drew. Honestly? I am still shaken up. I don't even go into the kitchen to get a glass of water without taking my gun with me. But I'm working through it. At this point I'm more concerned about Ivy. She's the one who's constantly running around town, coming in at all hours of the night. I've talked her into carrying a can of pepper spray everywhere she goes, so that's made me feel a little better. And the camera your friend installed has helped ease my anxiety, too, so…"

"So, you're hanging in there?"

"Yes. I'm hanging in there." Her pursed lips spread into a faint smile. "I appreciate you looking out for me."

Drew's chest pulled at her gratitude. It was confirmation that his words of encouragement were well received.

Nia's response deepened his need to protect her, triggering a surge of emotions that fueled his burgeoning attraction.

Pull back...

He downed a swallow of coffee before grabbing his phone. "I should call the medical examiner's office. Get an update on those toxicology reports."

As he dialed the number, Nia's cell pinged. Her face lit up after checking the notification. A twinge of jealousy stirred in Drew's gut as he wondered what sparked the wave of happiness this time.

Cool out, his inner voice warned once again.

He left the medical examiner a voicemail, then turned his attention back to his laptop, acting as if he hadn't noticed Nia ogling her phone.

"You are not gonna believe this," she said, handing him her cell. "Read that text from Ivy."

"Text from Ivy?" Drew repeated, his neck burning with shame.

And here you were, assuming she was chatting with a man...

He took the phone and scanned the message.

Hey big sis. Funny you asked about the next event at Shelby's. There's a rave happening at midnight tonight. But you DID NOT hear that from me and you'd better not tell your cohorts. If it gets shut down, everyone's gonna assume I snitched thanks to you being a cop. So keep it on the hush!

"Wow," Drew said. "You know what this means? The universe is working in our favor. Tonight is gonna generate some solid new leads. Thanks for contacting Ivy and getting that intel."

"Of course. Thanks for coming up with the idea to pass out Katie's photo at the rave. We make a good team," Nia added with a wink.

The small yet sensual gesture sent a rush of heat straight through Drew's gut that roused below his belt. Forcing his eyes toward the clock hanging above her head, he said, "It's already after twelve. Why don't we figure out tonight's game plan over lunch? Then maybe cut out early. If the rave doesn't start until midnight, we should probably try and get some rest."

"Good idea. These days, I'm never even out until midnight, let alone arriving somewhere at such an ungodly hour."

"Same here. I never had late nights like this unless it was…"

Drew's voice faded as memories of the last New Year's Eve he and his ex-fiancée spent together crashed his mind.

"Unless it was what?" Nia asked.

"Never mind." He slammed his laptop shut and shot to his feet.

"Are you okay?"

"Yep. I'm fine," he told her, despite being far from fine.

Drew wished he had it in him to justify his reaction. To explain why the conversation had turned so triggering. But now was not the time or place to discuss the tragedy surrounding his personal life.

Chapter Ten

Nia and Drew stood outside Shelby's with Katie's flyers in hand, waiting for the partygoers to arrive. They were both dressed in dark, casual clothing and baseball caps in an attempt to blend in with the crowd.

So far, only a few people had trickled inside through a kicked-in side door, carrying lighting and DJ equipment. They'd been less than helpful when the officers flashed Katie's photo, insisting they needed to get inside and set up.

"I'm just imagining all the illegal drugs that are gonna be flowing in and out of here tonight," Nia said.

"Yeah, and unfortunately, we'll have to tackle that problem another night. We're here on a different mission. I don't want anything blocking our road to the killer."

Nia took notice when a group of young men hopped out of a pickup truck. "Here we go," she said, leading with Katie's photo as she approached. "Excuse me, have any of you seen this woman here at the factory? Or anywhere in the vicinity?"

Barely looking at the picture, they muttered an almost inaudible "Nope" before pushing past her.

Spinning around in frustration, she shouted, "Hey!" and followed the men. "You didn't even look at the—"

"Hold on," Drew said, grabbing hold of her mid-confrontation. "Let them go. The night is young. There'll be plenty more people to talk to. This investigation is a marathon, not a sprint. Tonight will be no different. All it's gonna take is one solid tip to lead us in the right direction."

Her arms relaxed within his grip. *Regroup*, Nia thought, feeling less like a lead investigator and more like a newbie fresh out of the academy. She stood taller, straightening the flyers in her hand. "You're right. I'll tamp down the aggression and play it a little cooler."

"Good. But don't lose that fighting spirit of yours. It's one of the traits I admire most about you."

Reassurance permeated within her as Drew's hand slid toward the small of her back.

"I won't…" she murmured.

The candy factory stood far back from the street, with little light surrounding the area. The building's dilapidated wood exterior looked as if it might come crashing down at any given moment. Nia couldn't understand why anyone would want to step foot inside the place. But once it was no longer considered an active crime scene and the police tape was removed, the ravers, drug addicts and squatters began using it again.

"Are you warm enough?" Drew asked when a chilly breeze blew by.

Nia zipped her tan leather jacket up to her chin and hovered closer to him. "I am now."

She took a breath, staring up at the streaks of dark gray clouds scattered across the sky. Her squinting eyes couldn't make out one single star hidden within them. The grim atmosphere was as bleak as the reason they were there. Nia just hoped their efforts wouldn't be in vain.

Boom!

The pair jolted when heavy bass rumbled from inside the factory.

"Sounds like the party is getting started," Drew said.

"Judging by all the headlights rolling up to the curb, we've got some new arrivals, too."

Anticipation swelled in Nia's chest as a crowd began to gather. She held the flyers tighter, slipping one in between her fingers to quickly pass along.

Within seconds, people came rushing toward them like a tsunami, storming past so briskly that the officers hardly had a chance to say hello. They shoved Katie's photo into the partygoers' hands anyway, shouting, "Do you know her?" while praying for a response. Almost everyone blew them off, barely glancing at the picture before tossing the flyer to the ground.

At one point Nia attempted to march inside the factory. But Drew held her back, insisting she remain calm.

"Hey, keep your head," he told her. "I don't want you getting caught up inside of there. It's too many of them and not enough of us. We've just gotta stay patient. And persistent. There's still a ton of people out here. Trust me, we'll find somebody who knows something."

Shuffling her feet to shake the excess energy, Nia nodded. "Once again, you're right."

Techno music blared through the factory's shattered windows as ravers continued to pour inside. Nia's throat burned as she yelled over the blaring drum machines. No one appeared to be listening as throngs of people brushed past her as if she weren't there. Some of them even shoved the flyers back at her. Just when she considered tossing the rest of the pictures in the air and giving up, Drew called out her name.

"Over here!" he shouted after they'd briefly gotten separated. He was surrounded by three men and two women. All of them were dressed in torn black T-shirts, leggings and platform boots, with spiked hair dyed every color of the rainbow.

As Nia scanned the group, Drew said, "Three of these guys said they've seen Katie."

"Here at the candy factory?"

One of the men pointed toward the end of the street. "No. A couple of blocks over at the Green Lizard lounge."

"When was the last time you saw her there?" Drew asked.

Shrugging his scrawny shoulders, he looked to one of the women. "I don't know. Do you remember, Adina?"

"I think it was like a couple of weeks before her body was found."

"So you know about her murder?" Nia probed.

"Um, *yeah*. I think it's safe to say everybody in this town knows. And the word is spreading. This is the first rave they've thrown at Shelby's since her death." She paused, gesturing at the huge crowd. "All these people aren't from Juniper, obviously. But after DJ Onslaught dedicated tonight to Katie, everybody from all over Colorado decided to come out and pay their respects."

Leaning toward Drew, Nia whispered, "Interesting. Most of the people we've talked to claimed to have never heard of her."

A member of the group who was sporting a purple mohawk nudged Adina. "We'd better get inside before they close the doors on us."

As they backed away, Drew called out, "Hey, thanks for that info!"

"So what do you think?" Nia asked. "Should we stay out

here and see who else might know something? Or head over to the Green Lizard?"

He checked his watch, then looked out at the crowd. Partygoers were getting rowdier by the minute, practically climbing over one another trying to get into the factory. "Why don't we head over to the Green Lizard before they close? Maybe someone on the staff or even some of the patrons have seen Katie there."

"It would be even sweeter if they captured her on surveillance video at some point. Then maybe we could see who she was hanging out with, talking to, leaving with…"

"Yeah, that would be nice. Let's go see what we can find out."

Drew offered Nia his arm before pushing his way through the crowd. Her body pressed against his as he led the way, protecting her from the throng of ravers.

She'd gotten so used to looking out for herself that Nia forgot what it was like having a caring, capable man by her side. Despite Drew being a colleague, he was beginning to feel like something else. Something more. And as delusional as that may have been, it felt damn good.

When they reached the car, Drew pulled out his cell phone.

"Who are you calling this late?" Nia asked.

The moment the question escaped her lips she gasped, slapping her hand over her mouth.

"Drew, I—I am so sorry. I shouldn't have asked you that. I mean…obviously you can call whomever you want whenever you want. I don't know what possessed me to be so nosy."

"It's all good," he quipped, his sexy half smile riddled with amusement. "I was actually going to check my voicemail."

"Gotcha," Nia mumbled, biting down on her loose tongue before climbing inside the car.

Please let that be the last time you make a fool of your-self...

BY THE TIME Drew pulled into Nia's driveway, it was almost 3:00 a.m.

After leaving Shelby's, they'd headed straight to the Green Lizard. The lounge was located in a part of town that Nia seldom frequented, so she wasn't familiar with the establishment. When Drew parked in front, she realized why.

The bar looked more like a rundown shack than a place of business with its wrinkled metal roof, weathered wooden planks and foggy glass-block windows.

"Last call was fifteen minutes ago!" the bartender had yelled when they walked through the dented steel door.

"We're not here to order drinks," Drew told the puny, bald-headed man. "We're here on official police business."

The second he flashed his badge, the bartender dried his crooked fingers on his filthy apron and called for the manager. She came out from the kitchen with a towel wrapped around her head, as if she'd just washed her hair.

"May I help you?" the burly woman barked, her sparse eyebrows furrowing into her deeply creased forehead.

Nia couldn't take her eyes off the colorful tattoos running up and down both her arms. Snakes slithering around bushels of flowers spread from her wrists to her shoulders. As Drew explained why they were there, the manager began eyeing Nia so suspiciously that she stepped away, pulling out her phone and snapping photos of the lounge.

The seedy establishment appeared more like a long hallway than an actual tavern. Nia walked the length of it, the soles of her boots sticking to the warped hardwood floor. While the red fluorescent lighting was dim, it wasn't dark enough to hide the cracked vinyl barstools, dingy white walls and grimy poplar tables. Even though drinks were no longer being served, there were still several people with beer bottles in hand hovering around an old laminate jukebox.

It didn't take long for the manager to warm up to Drew. He had that effect on people—especially women. Nia attributed it to his deep, calming voice, disarming charm and uncanny ability to come up with the best one-liners at just the right time. Two minutes into a conversation and strangers felt as though they'd known him for years. The fact that he was devastatingly handsome in a rugged, approachable type of way didn't hurt matters, either.

The highlight of the night occurred when the manager admitted that Katie had been a regular at the bar, then handed over surveillance footage from the last time she'd seen her there. Nia had sung Drew's praises the whole way home for prying that evidence from the prickly woman's hands.

And now, as he walked Nia to the door, she couldn't bring herself to say good-night.

"You know I can't wait until tomorrow to watch that video, right?" she said. "I am *far* too riled up for that."

"You know what's funny? Neither can I."

"Well, then, since neither of us are ready to call it a night, why don't you come inside? I've got a refrigerator full of bar food that Ivy brought home from Bullseye and an unopened bottle of Merlot."

"That sounds amazing, actually. Because I'm starving, my fridge is currently empty and I'm all out of wine."

"Oh, wow. Yeah, you needed this invitation for more reasons than one," Nia joked before leading Drew inside.

All the lights were out, which meant Ivy wasn't home. Nia switched on a couple of lamps before tossing her things onto the console table.

As she sauntered through the living room, Drew followed closely behind. Nia could feel his eyes roaming her body. The sensation sent a shiver straight to her core.

"Should I pour the wine while you prep the food?" he asked, stopping near the couch while unzipping his camo jacket.

"No, I've got it covered. Why don't you relax. Have a seat. Watch some television while I get everything together."

The suggestion hadn't come from a place of hospitality. Nia didn't trust herself to move about the kitchen with Drew in such close proximity. It was late. She tended to make rash decisions during the wee hours of the morning—especially when it came to her libido.

"Thanks for the kind offer," he told her, "but I'd rather help you instead. That way we can get to the surveillance footage faster, and if you're up for it, maybe watch a movie afterwards."

The suggestion hung in the air like a delectable offering, waiting to be devoured.

"I'd like that," Nia replied with no hesitation.

She hovered near the fireplace as Drew pulled off his coat. She wished he hadn't worn a fitted black T-shirt as it set off his broad chest and bulging biceps.

"I—I, uh…" she stammered, pointing toward the kitchen. "I'm gonna go heat up the food."

"I'm right behind you."

Drew was slow to follow as he eyed the colorful abstract paintings hanging from the walls and black-and-white photos lining the mantel. "I love your place. And this kitchen... Is it newly renovated?"

"It is. I needed a fresh new look. So I switched out the white appliances for stainless steel and replaced the dark wood cabinets for these cream ones. They really brighten up the room, and it all works together to give off the contemporary feel I was going for."

"I agree. Everything looks great." He ran his hand along the granite countertop, brushing up against Nia as she pulled takeout containers from the refrigerator. When her hips grazed his groin, she jumped back.

"Ooh, sorry," he said, palming her back as if to steady her. "I was trying to get to the wine glasses."

Yeah, right...

Ignoring Drew's struggle to suppress a smirk, Nia pointed above his head. "They're in the cabinet to your left."

"And the wine?"

"In the corner next to the coffeemaker."

Nia filled a platter with buffalo wings, truffle mushroom flatbread and onion rings, then placed it in the microwave.

This isn't fair, she thought, watching the food rotate. Having Drew there, inside her home, felt too good. Too right. Their conversation flowed too easily. And the attraction was too strong. This was the first time she'd met a man who seemed perfect in every way. Yet he was off-limits.

"Hey," Drew said, tapping the laptop sitting on the counter. "Can we use this to review the surveillance footage?"

"Yep. Go ahead and start it up."

Once the microwave buzzed, Nia grabbed everything and set up shop on the island.

"Are you sure you've got time for all this?" he asked.

"I do. Why?"

"Well, I've already taken up the majority of your day. *And* night. There isn't anyone special who'd expect to be here with you right now?"

He's fishing...

A long sip of wine fueled her response. "Officer Taylor, are you trying to figure out whether or not I'm seeing someone?"

Nia expected a swift denial. Instead she got a head nod followed by a crooning, "Maybe..."

A tug of silence swirled between them. She turned away and began preparing their plates, taking her time before responding. Taking her lead, Drew busied himself by inserting the USB drive into the computer. His expression was neutral, as if he wasn't pressing for a response. His bouncing knees, however, told her that he was eager for a reply.

"To answer your question, no. I'm single."

Drew's brows shot up toward the ceiling. "Really?"

"Yes. Why is that so shocking?"

"Well, I mean you're beautiful, intelligent, you crack great jokes and are passionate about the things you love. You're family-oriented, and the list goes on. Bottom line, you're everything a man would want in a woman."

His words sent Nia's heart pounding against her ribcage as she slid onto the stool next to his. While she'd sensed their attraction was mutual, she had no clue his admiration ran that deep.

"Wow," she uttered. "That, uh…that was pretty unexpected. But so nice. Thank you."

"You're welcome. I'm just stating the obvious. I can't imagine you haven't heard that from a man before."

"I have. In bits and pieces from different men. It's just surprising coming from you. I didn't think you paid attention to those types of things since all we seem to talk about is the investigation or departmental policies or—"

"Anything that isn't personal?" Drew interjected.

"Yes, exactly."

"You're right. In case you hadn't noticed, it takes me a minute to warm up to people. It isn't easy letting my guard down. Especially when it comes to situations like ours. We were partnered up during a pretty tough time. But now that I've gotten to know you, I've come to realize that you're pretty damn amazing, Nia."

Those words sent her swooning so hard that she almost fell from the stool. Propping her hand underneath her chin, she replied, "Well, I could easily say the same for you. Getting to know you has been a pleasant surprise. Not what I'd expected after the way things went down at that mentorship meeting. Let's just say I'm glad I was wrong about you."

"Thank God I was able to redeem myself," Drew joked before quickly turning serious. "So why aren't you seeing anyone?"

Nia bit into a slice of flatbread, chewing slowly while contemplating her response. "I guess the short answer is I refuse to settle."

"And what would settling look like for you?"

"Getting involved with a man who doesn't want to commit. Who isn't kind and respectful and doesn't work hard. I actually keep a mental checklist of must-haves. And if I can't tick them all off, then I pass. My friends think I'm asking for too much and should reassess my criteria. But I refuse to."

"As you should. Nothing you're asking for is unreasonable." Drew picked up his glass and leaned into her, his touch igniting sparks between them both. "Here's to you finding everything you want and deserve in a partner."

You're everything I want in a partner, Nia almost blurted. Her gaze drifted from his inviting eyes to his soft lips. They parted slightly, leaving her questioning how they'd feel pressed against hers. How he'd feel inside of her...

Shifting in her seat, she asked, "What about you? Are you seeing anyone?"

"Nope. I'm single."

"Hmm, that's not what I expected to hear."

"Yeah, well, my dating life isn't something I normally talk about."

When Drew's lips twisted into a tight expression, Nia hesitated, waiting for him to elaborate. But he didn't, instead draining his glass, then refilling it.

"You don't have to talk about it if you don't want to," she told him.

"I know. But I probably should. Holding it in hasn't been the healthiest way to cope." He picked at the cheese oozing from a mozzarella stick before proceeding. "I was engaged once. To a police detective from Aurora named Ellody. She'd moved to Juniper to be with me and was commuting back and forth while figuring out what she wanted to do with her career. But we soon realized that the distance was what made us work. Once she came here permanently, problems arose that left me questioning whether or not we were even compatible."

"What type of problems were you having?" Nia probed, unable to contain her curiosity.

"Well, when it came to finances, for instance, she was more of a spender while I'm more of a saver. I'm a neat freak, and she didn't mind a lot of clutter. She enjoyed nights out while I'm more of a homebody. Things like that. It got to the point where our differences began to outweigh the good between us. After admitting to that, we decided it would be best to end the relationship."

"Hmm, that couldn't have been easy. Especially when you two were planning on getting married."

"No, it wasn't, but..." Staring down at his steepled hands, Drew uttered, "That's not where the story ends. A few months after Ellody moved back to Aurora, we reconnected. I think we both realized we'd be better off as friends. Just as we began building a platonic relationship, she was killed in the line of duty."

"My God, Drew. I am so sorry. I had no idea..."

"Thanks. Like I said, it's something I rarely talk about. Since then, I haven't really dated. That experience was so devastating that I've pretty much closed myself off to the whole relationship thing." After a long pause, he tapped his hand against the island, then pulled the laptop closer. "But anyway, enough about me. Let's get back to business."

As Drew clicked on the portable drive, Nia pushed her plate to the side, her appetite transforming into a slight bout of nausea. Hearing the news of his ex was tragic. And while she was sympathetic toward his loss, the consequence was duly noted—Drew was not ready to love again.

"Okay, here we go," he said when an image of the Green Lizard's interior appeared on the screen.

The bar was packed. Every stool was occupied. There were rows of people standing behind them, vying for the bartender's attention. The tables were full. Groups of people with drinks in their hands were bouncing to the music.

Peering at the screen, Drew nibbled on a buffalo wing. "Any sign of Katie yet?"

"Not yet. But I'm looking."

Ten minutes into the video, Nia tapped the screen. "I think that's her. The woman in the red sweater and skinny jeans. Isn't that Katie?"

The pair watched as she approached the bar, then turned and faced the crowd.

"Oh, yeah," Drew said. "That's definitely her. Let's see who she's there with."

A group of women approached Katie, embracing her before starting up an animated conversation. As they spoke, two men walked over. One of them was wearing a baseball cap. Nia couldn't make out his face, but he appeared tall and athletic, with wide shoulders and a narrow waist. He hugged Katie tightly, then held her in his arms while whispering in her ear. The twosome began swaying back and forth. Another couple of minutes passed before his friend and the group of women drifted off, leaving Katie and the man alone.

"It's interesting how this guy has his cap pulled down so low," Nia said. "Like he doesn't want anyone to recognize him."

"Yeah, it is. Notice how he's keeping his head down, too. As if he's aware of the surveillance cameras and is trying to avoid them."

"Right. And he's staying glued to Katie's side."

The officers leaned in closer as the man began pulling her by the waist.

"Wait, what is he doing?" Drew asked.

"It looks like he's trying to drag her out of the bar."

The sight of Katie reaching for her friends was unsettling, even though she didn't appear to be under duress.

"This is so eerie," Nia said. "Here Katie's laughing and

joking and having a great time. Little did she know she'd be murdered in a matter of days."

Just when it appeared as though Katie and the man were moving toward the exit, the screen flickered, then blacked out.

"Wait," Nia muttered, "What just happened?"

"I don't know."

Drew pounded the Enter and Escape keys. Both officers jolted when a new video popped up. The bar's parking lot came into view. Within minutes, Katie and her companion came back into frame.

"All right," Drew said, "we've got action again. Now let's just hope we can get a look at the guy's face this time."

The officers watched as Katie approached a large black SUV. The man opened the passenger door for her, then stared down at the ground while walking around to the driver's side.

"Come on," Nia said, both officers leaning in so close that their noses almost touched the screen. "Please look up. Show us your face…"

Suddenly, rain began to pour. The man in the video hesitated, looking up at the sky.

Air caught in Nia's throat as she struggled to process the image on the screen. But as a flash of lightning illuminated the video, there was no mistaking the man's identity.

It was Officer Davis.

Chapter Eleven

Drew pulled into his garage and headed inside the house. Tossing his messenger bag onto the kitchen table, he headed straight for the refrigerator. The half-empty bottle of wine he'd uncorked a few days ago was still sitting in the door. He resisted the urge to grab it and down the remaining malbec.

Just as he reached for a can of sparkling water his cell phone buzzed. A throbbing pain hit his left temple at the sight of Chief Mitchell's name.

"Please, no bad news," Drew mumbled before picking up. "Chief Mitchell. What's going on, sir?"

"Officer Taylor, listen. I just got back into town from my brother-in-law's funeral and wanted to follow up on the Officer Davis situation. Did you and Brooks get a chance to question him about that Katie Douglas surveillance footage?"

"We did, after he finally showed back up to work today. I'm curious about that sudden leave of absence he took."

"I think someone tipped him off about the video, so he knew you were coming for him. What did he have to say for himself?"

"First I asked why he hadn't told us that he knew Katie. He claimed he didn't think it was important enough to mention."

"Oh, come on," the chief grunted. "I don't believe that for one minute. Davis is a veteran officer, for God's sake. He knows information like that is important."

"That's exactly what I told him. After questioning him for almost thirty minutes, he finally admitted to why he hadn't come clean. He thought being connected to a murder victim would be a bad look for the force. Plus he's in a long-term relationship. So he had no business being out with Katie in the first place and didn't want his girlfriend to find out."

"What an idiot," Chief Mitchell bemoaned. "Okay, then. So are we ruling him out as a person of interest?"

"Yes, we are. No one in the department knows this except for Officer Brooks, but I had one of the crime lab technicians compare Davis's fingerprints to the evidence found at the crime scenes. They weren't a match."

"Good to know. And of course that'll stay between us. So what do you and Brooks have planned next? Do the three of us need to sit down and discuss a new course of action?"

Drew set the can of sparkling water back inside the refrigerator and pulled out a bottle of beer. The conversation was going to require something stronger than LaCroix.

"She and I have put together a game plan. We've been spending a lot of time studying the case file trying to figure out what type of person our suspect is. His character traits. What drives his behaviors. Things like that."

"And how exactly are you two doing that?"

"We're following the FBI's method. Evaluating each crime that's been committed, analyzing the scenes, studying each victim and reviewing the police reports with a fine-tooth comb. It's obvious the homicides are linked since the DNA evidence matched up. Plus those ominous clues that are being left with the victims."

"Speaking of which, I'm surprised nothing came of the wedding invitation left at Latimer Park. The nuptial already took place at the country club without incident."

"Yeah, I was shocked by that, too." Drew reached inside his bag and pulled out Violet Shields's autopsy reports. "There's gotta be something we're overlooking. Officer Brooks and I have been over the evidence hundreds of times, yet we haven't come up with any new leads."

"Keep digging, Taylor. I have faith that you two will get this case solved. In the meantime, if you need me, you know where to find me."

"Thanks, Chief." Drew's cell phone pinged against his ear. "This is Officer Brooks calling on the other line now. We'll check with you tomorrow."

He tapped the Swap button. "Hey, what's up, Nia. Chief Mitchell and I were just talking about—"

"Drew," she panted. "I need you to come to my house. Something is wrong here."

Vaulting from the chair and grabbing his keys, he headed straight for the door. "What's going on?"

"I just got home, and while I was walking up the driveway, I heard some weird, creepy ringing coming from the back of the house. So I walked around to the backyard and saw that all of my deck furniture had been rearranged. And there were two sets of wind chimes hanging from the lamp posts."

"Have you talked to Ivy? Maybe she hung them—"

"No," Nia interrupted. "It wasn't Ivy. I already talked to her and she hasn't touched a thing. And she knows I hate wind chimes, so she never would've put them up. But that's not all. Someone wrote the words *back off, bitch* in red paint across my patio table."

"I'm on my way there now. Are you still outside on the deck?"

"I am. I'm looking around trying to see if any more damage has been done."

"Do you have your gun?"

"Of course. It's right in my hand, locked and loaded."

"Listen to me, Nia. We're dealing with a deranged killer here. I don't want you roaming around out there alone without any backup. Go inside the house, lock up and wait for me to get there. I won't be long."

DREW PULLED INTO Nia's driveway and parked at the bottom near the gate. He climbed out and drew his gun, scaling the fence before entering the backyard.

The lush green lawn didn't appear to be touched. Neither did the pink butterfly bushes and green holly shrubs. But the cream-cushioned wicker loveseat, chairs and ottoman were all sitting in a straight line along the aluminum railing. Drew remembered Nia having each piece surrounding the stone firepit.

An eerie clanging rang out. His head swiveled toward the bronze tiki torch poles. Two sets of shiny blue wind chimes swung from the canisters, creating a deep, sonorous tone that sent a chill straight through him.

After pulling on latex gloves, Drew removed the bells and placed them inside a paper bag, then sent Nia a text letting her know he was there. Within seconds, the back door swung open and she came charging out.

"Thank God you're here," she moaned, running straight into his arms.

Drew's embrace tightened as she trembled against his chest. "Are you all right?"

"Not really." Nia pointed toward the house. "Somebody tore down the security camera I had mounted over the door."

With an arm securely wrapped around her waist, he led her to the doorway and studied the steel base hanging off the brick exterior. "Have you had a chance to look at the surveillance footage yet?"

"No. I wanted to wait until you got here so we could watch it together." Her head fell against his shoulder. "And that isn't all…"

"What else is going on?"

Without responding, Nia grabbed Drew's hand and led him inside the house. There, sitting on the kitchen counter, was a gift.

"What is that?" he asked.

"A present, I guess. Someone left it on my back doorstep."

Drew stepped cautiously toward the small box, eyeing its elegant silver wrapping and cream satin bow.

"I was afraid to open it," she continued. "It could be a bomb or some sort of poison, like abrin or anthrax."

"Something's telling me this isn't that type of thing. My guess is that it's another clue."

Nia backed away from the counter while shaking her head. "I don't know, Drew. I think we should contact the Postal Inspectors. They've got the specialized screening equipment needed to handle this sort of thing."

"I don't think I can wait that long. I wanna know what's in the box now." He pulled an N95 respirator mask from his bag and covered his face. "Stand back."

She hovered in the doorway while he unwrapped the box and peeled open shimmery tissue paper, revealing some sort of lacy white material.

"I can't just stand here and watch this," Nia declared, re-entering the kitchen. "Hand me a pair of gloves and mask."

Drew waited for her to slip on the protective gear before removing the lacy object and holding it in the air.

"Is that…a garter?" she asked.

"Looks like it. Why in the hell would someone leave this on your doorstep?"

"I have no idea."

Several moments passed before Nia finally spoke up, her thin tone tinged with trepidation. "I hope this doesn't have anything to do with one of my exes. I've got a couple who were bitter as hell when I broke things off. When I followed my dream of becoming a police officer, that really set the last one off."

"Would either of these exes happen to know that you hate wind chimes?"

"Oh, absolutely. At some point, one in particular tossed around the idea of us getting married, too, which I immediately shot down."

"Hence him leaving a garter belt at your doorstep, alluding to you missing out on being his bride? If he's keeping up with the news, then he'd know you're one of the lead investigators on the case. He could've done this as a way to throw you off your game."

"Yep. And he was petty as hell, too. So I would not put something like this past him."

Nia cringed at the thought as she reached inside a drawer and pulled out a plastic baggie. After snapping several photos of the garter, Drew slipped it inside the bag along with the gift box and wrapping paper.

"I'll get this to the crime lab first thing in the morning. See if it matches up with anyone in CODIS."

"And in the meantime, I should go through my last ex's garbage to try and find a disposable cup, a straw…anything that would contain his DNA."

"Um, let's wait on the results from the lab before you go doing all that. You never know. This time we just might get a hit. For now, why don't we check out the surveillance footage from the backyard?"

"I'll pull it up."

As Nia launched the video, Drew thought about Ivy. "Hey, you mentioned that your sister has been staying with a friend from work, right?"

"I did. It's just easier that way since she doesn't have a car. She and her friend Madison set their schedules so that they'd cover the same shifts. It's such a relief, because knowing Ivy, she'd be on public transportation or hitching rides with strangers at all hours of the night."

Drew glanced at the back door, reminded of the security camera that had been stolen. "Yeah, that is a relief. For her at least. But what about you? I could put a cop car on the block to keep an eye on your house. I'd feel much better if you weren't here alone though. Is there anywhere else you could stay for the time being? Your parents' house? Or Madison's? At least until we get a suspect in custody."

"Uh, *no*. Madison has at least two other women who work at Bullseye living with her, and that isn't counting Ivy. As for my parents, they've got my uncle Jeffrey staying with them, plus they've somehow managed to hoard every piece of furniture they have ever purchased in life inside that house. So there's no room for me. But don't worry. I'll be fine right here in my own home, with my doors locked, security system on and Glock fully loaded."

When Drew studied Nia's strained expression, he could sense the tension behind her narrowing eyes as they peered at the computer screen. Rather than stress her out further, he took the hint and dropped the subject.

"The surveillance footage is up and running," she said, turning the laptop in his direction. "It was recorded this morning. I left for work at about seven forty-five, so the suspect got here sometime after that. I'll speed up the video until we see some movement."

Several minutes passed before Drew nudged her hand. "Hold on. Go back a few seconds. I think I just saw something."

"Okay. I'll slow it down, too. I think I may have seen a shadow come into view, but I'm not sure…"

The thirty-seven minute mark flashed on the screen when Nia began replaying the tape. Just as she set the view percentage to 150, someone jumped the fence near the driveway, then hid behind the side of the house.

"Did you see that?" Drew asked.

"I did. Let me rewind it again."

After playing the footage back once more, he realized the perp was moving too fast to get a good look at him. He appeared to be wearing a red flannel shirt, black cargo pants and Timberland boots. His head was covered with a red baseball cap, and his face was hidden behind a black mask.

"I'm trying to see what this man looks like," Nia said, rewinding and replaying the footage again, "but he's covered from head to toe. From what I can tell, he looks tall. And slim. Unlike my ex."

"His silhouette is actually similar to the suspect who knocked the camera off the front of your house."

"It sure is. So we're probably dealing with the same person here."

A few seconds later, the film showed the security camera beginning to shake.

"Will you look at this," Nia lamented. "This guy is using the same tactic he did when he stole the other camera."

"And he made sure to knock it down before rearranging the furniture, hanging the wind chimes and leaving the garter. I'll give it to him. The man is going to great lengths to remain unrecognizable."

When Nia dropped her head in her hands, Drew placed an arm around her.

"I'm so sorry," he murmured. "We're gonna catch this guy. That much I can promise you."

"Yeah, but how? And why the sudden attack on me? Is it because I'm connected to the investigation, or is this something more? Something deeper?"

Drew bit his jaw as he stared at the black-and-white static flickering across the screen. "Unfortunately, I don't have the answers to those questions. *Yet.* But I will. Because one thing I don't do is make promises I can't keep."

She nodded, muttering into her hands, "This is such a mess. Did you see the article on the front page of *The Juniper Herald* this morning?"

"I did. And I noticed a few of the guys around the station reading it, then slamming their laptops shut when they saw me. That headline was scathing, too. 'Juniper PD Doesn't Have What It Takes to Catch a Killer.'"

"Yeah, that really pissed me off. More support and less criticism would go a long way here." Nia hesitated, staring at Drew through damp eyes. "But...*do* we have what it takes?"

"Of course we do. You know our motto. This is a marathon. Not a sprint. Like Chief Mitchell once told me, working in the field of criminal justice means playing the long game. And if we work hard enough, we'll get this case solved."

Straightening her back against the stool, Nia replied, "You're right. So where do we go from here? Back to the criminal profile we've been building?"

"I think that would be our best bet. I was just telling the chief that once we have a good understanding of who we're dealing with, we'll have a better chance of apprehending him."

"I'll pull that document up now," she said right before her cell phone pinged.

Drew watched as her tense expression softened, the light suddenly returning to her deep brown eyes. Resisting the urge to peer down at her phone, he said, "Good news?"

"Yeah, that was Ivy. Since we've got this maniac roaming the streets, I've asked her to check in with me a couple times a day, just to let me know she's okay. Surprisingly it's working. She just got to Bullseye and is covering somebody else's shift, so she'll be there until late tonight. She's gonna let me know once she's off and back at Madison's."

"I like that you're keeping up with her."

Or are you relieved to hear that she wasn't communicating with a man?

Ignoring the irritating thought, Drew asked, "Does Ivy know what's been going on here at the house?"

"She does. Which is why she rarely comes back here now. But I told her that whenever she needs to drop in to make sure I'm home first."

Drew's gut urged him to reiterate that it would be good if Nia found somewhere else to stay. At least for the near future. But he refrained. After she'd made it clear that she wanted to remain in her house, he knew he couldn't force her.

"So let's talk about this criminal profile we're building," Nia said. "So far, we've deduced that our suspect is between the ages of thirty-eight and forty-five. He's about six feet tall, maybe a little taller, and no more than a hundred-and-eighty pounds. He is intelligent and well educated, with at least a bachelor's degree. We think he's extroverted and charismatic, and meeting these women in social or public settings, like bars, clubs and gyms. He's familiar with Juniper but probably doesn't live here, and he's definitely killed before."

"Right." Drew swiped open the Notes app on his phone and tapped the bulleted list of profile traits. "He's methodical. Very careful in his planning. Which has a lot to do with why he has yet to be caught. Our suspect is mission-oriented in that he's going after young women and killing them in the same manner. He also enjoys the control he has over the victims once he gets them alone."

"And since the women's toxicology reports came back negative, we know they were fully aware of what was happening to them during their attacks. It's as if the suspect doesn't want them to be sedated because he gets off on their fear."

The clicking of Nia's laptop keys suddenly stopped. She moaned loudly, leaning to one side while clutching her hip.

"Are you okay?" Drew asked.

"I am. I think it's these stools. The sleek Italian lacquer look seemed like a good idea when I was remodeling the kitchen. But they're not the most comfortable pieces of furniture I own." She glanced over at the clock on the microwave. "I'll tell you what. It's dinnertime, and I haven't eaten yet. Have you?"

"No. You called right after I got home from the station. I ran over here so fast that I didn't get a chance to even think about food. But now that you mention it, I'm starving."

Grasping the metal sides of her seat, Nia slowly stood. "Why don't we take this into the living room where we can stretch out on the couch, and I'll order takeout?"

Drew's lips parted. But he failed to respond while watching her dip to one side and knead her gluteal muscles. The move accentuated every curve in her fitted navy slacks, leading to thoughts of those long, lithe legs wrapped around his waist.

"So what do you think?" she asked, looking up at him.

Quickly turning away, he said, "That sounds good," while hoping she hadn't noticed him gawking. "We could do Thai or Mexican…"

"Ooh, yes. Mexican would be perfect." She grabbed her phone and began typing away. "I'll order from Zapata Cove since we both love that place. Can you grab a bottle of cabernet sauvignon from the fridge? Then we'll head to the living room and get back to work."

"You got it."

Drew collected the wine and glasses, then followed Nia out of the kitchen. On the way past the island, he caught a glimpse of the evidence bags. They were a stark reminder of the imminent danger surrounding her home.

His grip on the bottle tightened. Somehow, he had to convince her that she could no longer stay there alone.

Chapter Twelve

Nia tapped her fingernails against her glass and glanced around The Sphinx Hotel's bar once again. There was still no sign of Shane Anderson.

She pulled her cell phone from her snakeskin clutch and opened the Someone for Everyone app. After scrolling through the messages, she tapped on the last one he'd sent her.

Hello beautiful. I'm so glad you're available this weekend. Can't wait to meet you. I'll see you Saturday night at 7:00 p.m. inside the Sphinx's Solar Lounge bar. Looking forward to it. xx, S

Nia closed out of the app, then immediately reopened it, deciding to send Shane a message in case he'd forgotten about their date.

Hi there. I'm at The Sphinx, sitting at the bar inside the lounge. Hope everything is okay and you're still able to make it. xx, N

She checked the time. It was 7:41 p.m. She'd give him ten more minutes. If he hadn't arrived by then, she would leave.

"Another pinot grigio, ma'am?" the bartender asked.

"No, I'm fine for now. Thank you."

Nia gripped the stem between her fingertips and twirled the glass along the mahogany bar's shiny surface. The uncertainty bubbling inside her chest had exploded into pangs of anxiety. She'd been looking forward to this evening all week. Thanks to the investigation, she couldn't remember the last time she'd been out socially. As for an actual date, it had been months.

Nia needed this night. Her entire life had begun to center around work. There was no reprieve. The majority of her days were filled with frustration considering the case had hit a wall. No amount of evidence analysis, criminal profiling, interrogating or surveilling had delivered any answers. The clues she and Drew had gathered revealed no new leads. And the DNA left at the crime scenes, which they continuously ran through CODIS, had yet to identify a suspect.

But the investigation wasn't Nia's only concern. There was also Drew. The more time the pair spent together, the deeper her attraction grew. It was getting to the point where she couldn't be around him without blushing underneath his piercing gaze or tingling at the slightest touch of his hand. His presence was beginning to drive her crazy. Yet there was no getting away from him. They had a killer to apprehend. So in the meantime she needed a distraction, and Nia was hoping it would be Shane.

After pulling the neckline of her cream sweater dress over her plunging cleavage, Nia took another look around the bar. This was the first time she'd been there since the hotel had been renovated. The lounge was sleek, with its midnight blue walls, warm crystal pendant lighting and contemporary pewter furniture. The seductive ambience set the perfect mood for a date. But from the look of things, it appeared as if Nia would be going solo.

Other than a few couples scattered about and a rowdy bridal party, the place was fairly empty. She checked the entrance. Still no tall, dapper man dressed in a suit walking through the door to meet her.

Just as she drained her glass, Nia's phone pinged. She almost choked on the last swallow of wine trying to check the notification. Hoping to see Shane's name, she swiped open the screen. Disappointment pushed her back against the chair at the sight of Ivy's message.

Hey! Just letting you know I'm working another double shift tonight then going out afterwards. If you don't hear from me again, it's because I'll be passed out on Madison's couch. Luv you!

For a brief moment, Nia considered stopping by the Bullseye and hanging out with Ivy for a bit. She hated the idea of having gone through over two hours of preparation just to head back home. Somebody needed to see her new dress, wavy curls and perfectly applied makeup.

But by the time she paid for her drink and headed toward the parking lot, all Nia wanted to do was curl up on the couch with a deep-dish pizza and a gruesome horror movie to match her mood.

"I cannot *believe* this man just wasted my time," she grumbled, slamming the car door and revving the engine.

She pulled out of the lot and jetted down the street. The bottoms of her feet went numb inside her tan stiletto boots as she pressed down on the accelerator. Light reflecting off the streetlamps blurred. Lost in her thoughts, Nia was reminded of why she seldom put herself out there. The inevitable disappointment was unbearable.

But she'd grown tired of sitting around the house waiting for someone to come along. As her mother always said, the man of her dreams wasn't going to just come knocking at her door. "Don't waste the pretty," she would tell her. "Get out there and let him find you."

And I did. Just to get stood up.

Nia made a left turn on Dobel Lane, her stomach rumbling with emotion as hot tears stung her eyes. The truth of the matter was right in front of her, but she'd blocked it from her mind. This had nothing to do with Shane or being stood up or putting herself out there in hopes of finding the right man. The right man was already in her life. It was Drew. Yet there was nothing she could do about it. Because Nia still didn't feel comfortable dating a colleague, and Drew was still healing from his tragic past.

"So basically," she whispered, "stop worrying about a relationship and focus on the investigation."

The words burned as they left her lips. All practicalities aside, there was no denying that she wanted love in her life.

As she made a left turn down Mountain View Drive, Nia turned on her high beams. Streetlights on the long stretch of road were few and far between. The lack of sufficient lighting almost caused her to hit a deer last time she'd driven here.

So concentrate, she thought, willing herself to keep her eyes on the street and off the phone as she checked for a message from Shane.

The farther she drove, the more Nia felt as if she were heading down a bleak, never-ending passageway. Loneliness simmered inside her head. Despite having no one to go home to, she focused on curling up on the couch with that pizza and movie.

Just as she turned on the radio, a pair of blinding headlights lit up her car's interior. Nia peered into the rearview mirror. It looked as if someone was trying to get her attention. But then the lights flickered erratically, appearing defective.

Thinking nothing of it, she turned up the volume on a '90's R & B satellite station, bobbing her head as Mary J. Blige's "Real Love" piped through the speakers.

"I'm searching for a real looove," Nia sang. "Someone to set my heart free…"

She stopped abruptly, realizing the lyrics were doing nothing to lighten her mood. Neither did another glance at her phone as there were still no new notifications.

Nia contemplated calling Drew under the guise of discussing the investigation. But she really just wanted to hear his voice. A witty Drew-ism or inside joke would undoubtedly lift her spirits.

The screech of spinning tires squealed behind her. Whipping her head toward the side-view mirror, Nia noticed the car with the flickering lights tailing her.

"What in the hell are you doing?"

She shifted her focus back to the dark road in front of her. Craning her neck, she hoped the intersection would come into view. It didn't. She still had a ways to go.

Nia pressed down on the accelerator. Maybe if she sped up the tailgater would back off. He didn't.

An unnerving sense of panic took hold of Nia's joints. Her head jerked from right to left. There was nothing but massive ponderosa pines standing guard on either side of her. She faced forward, gripping the steering wheel tighter while eyeing the pitch-black stretch of road.

Vroom!

The revving engine blared loud enough to drown out Nia's music. As the car loomed closer, she reached inside her clutch and felt around for her gun. Just having it in her lap would make her feel more secure. And if she needed it, she'd be ready to use it.

Her eyes darted from the rear-to side-view mirrors as she struggled to keep an eye on the road. "*Dammit*," she hissed, her fingers scrambling over her keys, wallet and compact. But no gun. It wasn't there.

"Where the hell did I..."

Her voice trailed off as she remembered rushing out of the house so quickly that she'd left it inside the hall closet.

A string of curses spewed from her lips as the car rode her bumper. Pounding the voice control button on the steering wheel, she yelled, "Call Drew!"

Please pick up.

On the third ring, he answered.

"Hey, Nia. I was just thinking about you. What's going on?"

Stay calm. Maybe it's nothing and you're just being paranoid.

She blew an unsteady exhale as the sound of his voice soothed her unraveling nerves. "Hey, Drew." Before she got started, Nia took another look in the rearview mirror. The car seemed to be farther away. The sight slowed her racing heartbeat to a semi-normal pace.

"Are you okay?" he asked. "You sound strange."

"I'm—I hope so. I was out at the Solar Lounge, and I'm on my way home now—"

"Wait, you were hanging out at The Sphinx Hotel?" Drew emitted a light chuckle. "Which one of your bougie girlfriends recommended that place? I heard that since the renovation, the drinks start at about thirty dollars a pop and the attire is designer only."

Normally his teasing would've summoned a laugh. But not tonight.

"Nia? You still there?"

"Yes, I'm here. Sorry. I'm on Mountain View Drive and this dark stretch of road has completely thrown me off—"

Her voice broke. Emotions swelled in her throat. Hearing Drew on the other end of the phone sent words dangling from her tongue that she had no intention of sharing.

"I've had a really rough night," she divulged.

"Why? What happened?"

His tone, thick with alarm, disarmed Nia. Tears welled as she pulled in a rush of air. "I wasn't out with my girlfriends. I was on a date. Or at least I was supposed to be. But I got stood up."

She held her breath, waiting for him to respond. The other end of the line went silent. Nia checked the phone to see if the call had dropped. Reception in the area was known to be spotty.

"Drew? Can you hear me?"

"Yes. I can hear you. So, you were out on a date?"

"I was *supposed* to be on a date. But the guy didn't show up."

"Who's the guy?"

His voice was laced with irritation, leaving Nia wishing she'd never brought it up.

Too late for that now...

"His name is Shane. Shane Anderson. He's new to Juniper."

After a long, awkward pause, Drew asked, "Where did you two meet?"

What's up with the interrogation? she almost blurted. But instead she replied, "We connected through a dating app."

Nia winced at the sound of his repulsed sigh.

"A *dating* app? Really, Nia? So I guess you've forgotten there's a deranged killer running around town. Despite you being a police officer and all, it isn't very wise of you to be hooking up with random strangers—"

"Okay, hold on," she interjected, instantly regretting her decision to call him. "First of all, I'm not *hooking up* with anyone. This man and I have been corresponding for quite some time now, and all we were planning was to meet up for drinks. Secondly, I like to think that I'm a pretty good judge of character. He seemed nice, he's successful... Nothing about him screamed crazed murderer."

"Come on, Nia. You're smarter than that. Do you know how many murderers *seem* nice? Have families? And lead normal lives outside of killing people on the side?"

Curiosity eclipsed her annoyance as Drew rambled on. His genuine concern for her safety was obvious. But his snarky commentary seemed rooted in jealousy. Nia knew she could take care of herself. After living in Juniper her entire life, she didn't need a lecture on how to move around town—nor did she want the investigation to hinder her love life.

But Drew wasn't completely wrong in his sentiments. And she didn't want the night to put a damper on their partnership. So she relented, saying, "Look, I hear you. You're right. You can't judge a killer by his outward appearance."

"*Thank* you. And look, I'm not trying to tell you how to

live your life. I'm just looking out for your safety. Because I would hate for something to happen to you—"

Bam!

Nia's forehead banged against the steering wheel. She bounced against the back of the seat, her wide eyes unable to make out the road ahead.

Disoriented, she gripped her pounding head and blinked rapidly, struggling to clear her blurred vision.

"Nia?" Drew said.

Boom!

Her car careened toward the side of the road, skidding along the gravel before spinning out of control.

"Nia!" he yelled. "What the hell is going on?"

The vehicle that had been tailing her came flying toward the driver's door. She pounded the accelerator and jerked the steering wheel. The car missed hers by a few inches. Swiveling toward the back windshield, Nia watched as the car swerved along the shoulder.

"Drew!" Nia screamed. "Somebody hit my car. I—I'm being attacked!"

"Where are you?"

"I'm still on Mountain View Drive."

"Hold on. I'm coming to you now."

As the assailant's vehicle backed away from the shoulder, Nia slammed the accelerator into the floorboard. "Don't bother. By the time you get here, I'll be long gone."

"Listen to me, Nia. Do not go home. Go straight to the police station. Better yet, just come here. My house is closer to Mountain View. My gun and I will be waiting right out front. I'll text Officer Ryan and the other officers on duty and send them your way."

"Thank you," she choked, her fingers cramping around the steering wheel.

Nia's eyes darted toward the side-view mirror. The assailant's car was gaining speed. "I'm trying to get a look at the make and model of this vehicle. But it's so damn dark out here. I think it's some sort of black sedan."

"I'm guessing you can't see the license plate either?"

"No. Not at all."

"Don't worry about it," Drew assured her. "I'll get it when he comes my way. I'm already outside waiting. You've got your weapon in hand, right?"

She gritted her teeth, pissed at herself for leaving it behind.

"*Nia?* Are you still there?"

"I'm here. I, um... No, I don't have my gun. I was so busy rushing out of the house that I forgot to grab it."

Several moments passed before Drew spoke up.

"Don't let that happen again," he warned. "*Especially* when you're going to meet up with a stranger."

"I won't," she told him, her voice small against his commanding tone.

Nia's angst subsided briefly when the intersection appeared up ahead. But just as she reached the corner of the road, those flashing headlights glared behind her.

Trepidation hit as she contemplated what would happen if she stopped—the attacker would ram her into the four-way crossing. But driving straight through could cause an accident.

Pivoting from right to left, Nia saw no cars in the vicinity. The vehicle behind her loomed closer and didn't appear to be slowing down.

Just go!

She floored it, flying through the red light, then making a sharp left turn.

"Where are you now?" Drew asked.

"On Kennedy Boulevard." She glanced in the mirror. The assailant's car was right behind her. "And I've still got company."

"Well, just keep coming this way. Officer Ryan and the rest of the crew are en route."

Nia sat so rigidly that her back began to spasm. She leaned forward, shuddering when the other driver's engine roared. The increased speed sent clouds of smoke billowing through the air. He laid on the horn, causing her to swerve uncontrollably.

"Dammit!" she shrieked, jerking the steering wheel from side to side while struggling to regain control.

Gambel Oak Street was up ahead. She was only a couple of blocks away from Drew's house.

You're almost there...

"Talk to me," he said. "Can you still see the vehicle—"

Boom!

"He hit me again!" Nia screamed. "Where the hell is my backup?"

The sound of pounding footsteps beat through her car's speakers.

"That's it," Drew panted. "I'm coming to you. Now!"

"No, just stay where you are! I'm almost there."

The attacker's ultrabright high beams were blinding. Nia angled her rearview mirror until the lights reflected off his windshield. Within seconds, his car went spinning before coming to an abrupt halt.

"*Yes!* I think I may have..."

Nia's voice faded at the piercing screech of tires as the assailant's car skidded along the pavement.

A glance in the mirror sent her chest pounding. Her assailant was back on the road and gaining speed.

Hooking a sharp left onto Belle Lane, Nia huffed, "I'm right around the corner from your house. And I finally hear sirens. Tell the other officers to block off each end of your street so that this maniac will be surrounded."

"I'm on it."

She drove toward another intersection. The light was red. As vehicles heading north drove through their green light, she ran hers, bobbing and weaving through traffic until reaching the other side.

"I'm on your block, Drew!" Nia said after making a right turn down Burr Ridge Avenue.

"I see you. Keep coming this way!"

Relief cooled her burning skin at the sight of him standing in the middle of the road. Cop cars hovered on either end of the street. Nia pulled in front of Drew's house and waited for the car that had been terrorizing her to appear. It didn't.

"Where is this guy?" Drew asked, his head swiveling from one end of the block to the other.

"I don't know. He was—he was just…"

Swallowing the whimper creeping up her throat, Nia climbed out, desperate to apprehend her attacker. Wobbling legs sent her stumbling against the doorframe. Drew caught her, holding on tight as Nia's body collapsed against his.

"It's okay," he assured her. "You're fine. I've got you."

She wrapped her arms around his waist and stared down the street. Officers jumped out of their cars and drew their weapons, covering every inch of the vicinity. The assailant was nowhere in sight.

"He knows," she said, her head falling against Drew's chest. "He knows I was coming to your house. So he kept going."

Drew held her close while calling Officer Ryan. "Hey, the suspect didn't follow Nia all the way here. I need for you all to get back out there and find him."

As he continued giving the officer instructions, Nia closed her eyes. An incoming migraine throbbed over her right eye. The roar of an engine sent her shaking in Drew's embrace. But it was Juniper PD, speeding off in search of the assailant.

"Wow," Drew uttered. "That bastard really did a number on your car."

Nia's eyes shot open. The left side of her bumper was completely hanging off while the trunk had been rammed into the backseat.

The terror that had been pulsating through her joints ignited a fiery anger.

"Drew, it's time to come up with a new game plan."

"It most certainly is. And we will. For now, I'll have forensics analyze your car while we do everything in our power to hunt down your attacker."

Too exhausted to respond, Nia reached inside the car and grabbed her cell phone.

"What are you doing?" Drew asked.

"Calling an Uber. I've been enough of an imposition. I just wanna go home, crawl into bed and—"

"Nia," he interrupted, "are you being serious right now? First of all, you're far from an imposition. You are my partner. It's my duty to be here for you. Secondly, I don't think you need to go home. You shouldn't be alone right now. Why don't you stay here with me?"

The suggestion eased Nia's bruised emotions. The offer to stay was touching. And tempting. Despite her desire to show strength in the moment, she softened underneath the weight of Drew's concern.

"I'd like that," she whispered. "Thank you."

"Of course. And just so you know, that invitation is open-ended. You can stay here for as long as you want."

With his arm securely wrapped around her, Drew led Nia up the walkway. Her head, no longer throbbing, fell against his shoulder as her mind churned in a hundred different directions.

She thought about Shane standing her up and the violent car chase that followed. Were the two incidents related? And did they somehow link back to the investigation?

"Come on in," Drew said, opening the door and leading her inside. "Make yourself at home. Anything you want or need, just say the word."

The sight of his softly lit living room came into view. The crackling fireplace cast a warm glow over the space. Cream throw pillows lined a chocolate brown leather sofa. Linen drapes hung from the windows. A game of chess sat in the middle of a plush coffee table ottoman. The faint scent of espresso lingered in the air.

Nia exhaled, the tension in her body slowly dissipating.

"You all right?" he murmured, his lips so close to her ear that his breath teased her lobe.

"Not yet. But I will be."

Chapter Thirteen

Drew trudged out of Chief Mitchell's office and returned to his desk, collapsing into his chair. His boss had requested an impromptu update on the case, and it killed him that he had nothing new to report.

It had been almost two weeks since Nia's attack. Police were unsuccessful in tracking down her assailant. With no new leads on the serial killer investigation, the chief was getting frustrated. The amount of pressure that the media and community were putting on the department was becoming unbearable. Chief Mitchell had even asked Drew whether he thought it would be a good idea to let one of the more seasoned homicide detectives take over the case.

"Absolutely not," Drew told him. "Officer Brooks and I are keeping the homicide team up-to-date and welcoming their input. However, we've put a lot of work into this investigation and the momentum is building. Trust me, we're getting closer."

His vow seemed to work as the chief ended the meeting without bumping his lead officer status. But even Drew was getting tired of hearing himself make promises that he had yet to keep.

It's time for some action…

The unsolved case wasn't the only thing bothering him. It had been almost a week since Nia returned home. After days of keeping watch on her house, Officer Ryan saw no signs of suspicious activity. So she felt comfortable enough to go back. Drew, on the other hand, did not—especially now that Ivy was seldom there anymore. He'd expressed that to Nia, even adding that she was more than welcome to keep staying with him. But she'd refused, while promising to remain on high alert at all times.

Drew sensed that Nia felt she'd become a burden staying at his place. What she didn't realize was that her presence filled his home with a comfort he'd missed. Since losing his ex, that void was something he hadn't even acknowledged until Nia came along.

Working and living together had created a deeper bond between them. They'd spend time at the station piecing together evidence while continuing to build their criminal profile. At night they'd hang out at his place, avoiding talk of the investigation while preparing dinner or playing Scrabble. Their organic connection was intoxicating, to the point where Drew found himself imagining Nia being more than just a colleague.

It'd felt like a punch to the gut when she told him she needed to go back home. The news almost caused him to profess his feelings for her. But Drew held back, knowing how resistant Nia was to workplace romances. He did, however, wonder how long he could keep this up. Because at some point he'd have to face a hard truth—he had completely fallen for her.

Drew took a sip of his lukewarm coffee and focused on the computer screen. Katie Douglas's Instagram feed was still on display. He'd been scrolling through it before being

called into the chief's office, hoping to get a better understanding of her lifestyle. He studied each post, scrutiniz-
ing the captions along with the locations and people she'd
tagged.

One thing was for sure—if anybody was looking for
Katie, all they'd have to do was turn to her social media
to find her. By the time he'd gotten to the third post, Drew
knew that she'd worked as a marketing coordinator at Next
Level Productions. Her Friday nights were spent at The
Golden Standard for happy hour. Every other Saturday,
Katie and her sister had gone for manicures and pedicures
at Betty's Day Spa. A little further in and he learned she'd
been a regular at the candy factory's raves.

As Drew searched for photos taken at the Green Lizard
lounge, he realized there were none. There also wasn't any
evidence that she'd hung out with Officer Davis. Drew assumed the pair had some sort of understanding since he
was in a relationship.

Things had been icy between him and Officer Davis since
news of the fling surfaced. Drew couldn't get past the fact
that Davis hadn't come clean in the beginning. He could've
seen something that may have assisted in the case. In Drew's
eyes, any officer willing to put his own personal interest
over a murder investigation didn't deserve to be on the force.

A loud clamor and string of "Good mornings" pulled
Drew from his thought. He peeked over the top of his cubicle wall, watching as Nia sauntered toward the break room.
His eyes weren't the only ones following the officer as several heads turned in her direction.

"Ugh," he grumbled at the sight of their ogling expressions.

The buzz of an incoming text message from Tim served
as a welcome distraction.

Taylor! Hope all is well, man. Just checking in with a quick update. I'm doing at-home physical therapy sessions three days a week now. So improvements are happening. Hoping to be back on the force soon. How are things going with the investigation? Any updates on the jerk that hit me?

Drew swallowed down the sizzle of defeat burning his throat. Not only was the investigation at a standstill, but they had yet to find the driver who'd hit Tim.

Just as he began composing a response, footsteps sounded near his desk.

"Drew!"

He spun around and saw Nia standing over him, a thin sheet of perspiration covering her face.

She shoved her cell phone into his hand. "Look at this!"

Peering at the screen, he homed in on a photo of her sitting at a bar. She was all done up, wearing a beautiful cream dress and sipping a glass of wine.

"Hmph," Drew grunted before handing her the phone back. "You ran over here in a panic just so I could tell you how good you look in that picture?"

"*No*," she hissed, jamming her fingertip against the screen. "Read the text underneath it."

"The what?" He leaned in and eyed the message.

How gorgeous were you on this night?? Too bad you got stood up. Better luck next time. And another thing. Keep hunting for the Juniper serial killer and watch the bodies pile up...

"Wait—someone just sent this to you?"

"Yes," Nia confirmed, pulling up a chair. "From an anonymous number. This photo was taken the night I went to The Sphinx Hotel to meet up with that guy from the dating app. I'm convinced he's behind this. Behind *all* of this."

"All of this, meaning…"

"The security cameras being knocked off my house. The wedding invitation, garter and wind chimes. The rearranged deck furniture. The car chase. And maybe even the murders. Keep in mind we connected through the same dating app that was found on Katie's phone. If we get ahold of Violet's cell and find out she was using the app, too, then I think that'll pretty much confirm my suspicions."

"Speaking of that dating app, I need to follow up with Officer Ryan on the subpoena situation. Did you ever hear back from the administrator?"

"No, I didn't." Nia opened Someone for Everyone on her phone. "But you know what's interesting? The day after Shane stood me up, he completely disappeared off the app. His profile is gone and so are all of his photos and the messages we exchanged."

"Yeah, that's very interesting. And telling." Drew paused when he heard Officer Ryan's voice nearby. "Hey, Ryan! What's the latest on the subpoena we sent to that dating app?"

"The administrator objected to it. So I filed a motion to compel. Now I'm just waiting to hear back from the court."

"All right. Keep me posted."

Drew emitted a frustrated groan before draining his cup. "I need more coffee. And some answers regarding this damn investigation."

As Nia stared at his computer screen, he turned it toward her.

"I've been going through Katie's social media trying to

figure out her patterns. See where she'd been going. Who she'd hung out with."

"I've been doing the same thing with Violet. And I'm noticing that their Instagram feeds are practically identical. Same aesthetic, same amount of oversharing. Both of their lives were like an open book."

"And that's a dangerous way to live these days. Which is why I mostly avoid social media. The couple of accounts that I do have are set to private."

A knock against Drew's cubicle sent both officers spinning in their chairs.

"Hey, Officer Mills," Drew said. "What's up?"

"I heard you two over here discussing the investigation. Did you get my email?"

"No, I didn't. When did you send it?"

"Early this morning. You know how you'd been waiting on Violet Shields's family to locate her cell phone?"

"I do."

"Well, I reached out to them and got the name of her carrier, then put in a request for the data. The company's working on gathering it now."

"What about a warrant?" Nia asked. "Won't they need that before releasing the information?"

"They will, which is why I put in an urgent request for one this morning. I should receive it later today. Once I turn that over, the carrier said they'd send the data ASAP."

"Mills." Drew gave the officer an enthusiastic high five. "My man. Thank you for doing that."

"Of course. Teamwork makes the dream work. Isn't that what Chief Mitchell always says?"

"Indeed it is. Oh, and speaking of teamwork, could you be sure to include Officer Brooks on any correspondence you send to me? Since we're partners on this case, whatever I need to see, she'll need to see as well."

Officer Mills glanced down at Nia, his grin fading into a sheepish expression. "Sure thing, Taylor. Sorry about that, Officer Brooks. I'll head back to my desk and forward everything to you now."

"Thanks. I'd appreciate it."

Nia gave Drew a look as the officer shuffled off. "I guess some of these guys still see me as the rookie cop, standing on the sidelines while you do all the work."

"Just give them some time to get used to things. I'm sure once Tim was unable to work the investigation with me, several of these guys thought they'd get his spot. So there might be a little envy happening here, too. But don't sweat it. They'll get over it. Especially after you and I solve this case."

"And even if they don't, I'm grateful that you have my back. On a positive note, I see why you pushed so hard for Chief Mitchell to hire a tech expert earlier this year. Between Katie's and Violet's phone data, we should definitely get some—"

"Officer Taylor!"

Drew and Nia both jumped to their feet at the alarm in Chief Mitchell's voice.

"Where the hell is Officer Taylor?" he asked, scrambling around the middle of the floor.

"I'm right here at my desk, sir. What's going on?"

The officer recoiled when Chief Mitchell turned to him, his pale expression distorted with agony. "I just got a call. There's been another murder."

"There's been a *what*?" Nia snapped. "Where? Please don't say the Charlie Sifford Country Club."

"No. It was at a residence—eight-four twenty-one Birch-wood Lane. I need you two to get over there immediately. Officer Davis got the initial call over the radio and he's already en route. I'm right behind you."

"We—we're on it," Drew choked, turning to Nia.

The touch of her hand gave him a shot of reassurance.

"We got this," she said, somehow knowing that was exactly what he needed to hear.

"Thank you," he whispered before they jetted toward the exit.

Chapter Fourteen

Drew could hear the panic in Nia's voice as they sped down Stoney Drive, then turned onto Birchwood Lane.

"If we're dealing with the same killer here," she breathed, "then he's switching things up on us. Why would he suddenly go from public to private property? Especially after the last clue was all about the country club?"

"Good question. He's probably trying to catch us up. Confuse us so that his next moves won't be too obvious. Either that, or this murder has nothing to do with our investigation."

"I would hate to think that we've got *two* killers on our hands."

The instant Drew pulled in front of the victim's home, Nia hopped out of the car and lifted the trunk. Both officers slipped on their protective gear, grabbed their evidence collection kits and rushed up the walkway.

Officer Adams had already begun cordoning off the exterior of the red brick split-level house. He nodded, telling them, "Officer Davis and a couple of the homicide detectives are already here. The victim's body is on the third floor inside the primary bedroom."

Drew gave him a thumbs-up and approached the entrance. He paused, checking for signs of forced entry. Both the door and frame appeared to be completely intact as there were no dents or scrapes. The doorknob and locks looked to be untouched.

Upon entering the living room, Drew noticed that nothing appeared out of place. The eighty-inch television was still mounted on the wall. The pristine pale blue sofa and loveseat hadn't been damaged. All of the crystal vases and copper statues were still standing.

The scent of fresh paint mixed with wood and adhesives filled the air. That new construction smell alerted him that the house may have recently been renovated.

To the right of the living room was the kitchen. The home's open floor plan allowed Drew and Nia to see straight into it. Neither of them could make out a speck of dirt on the white marble countertops, and the stainless steel appliances shone from a distance.

"Why don't we head upstairs and—"

Drew stopped when a man came charging through the front door.

"Where's my wife?" he yelled. "Where is my *wife*?"

Officer Adams grabbed him before he made it to the staircase.

"Sir, I'm gonna need for you to step back outside with me. We'll talk on the front lawn."

The man pushed the officer away, insisting, "Get the hell off of me! I want to see my wife."

Drew and Nia waited until Officer Adams convinced him to leave the house before proceeding up the stairs.

"Poor guy," Nia said. "I wish we could've stopped and talked to him."

"I know. But Adams will handle it. We need to get to the crime scene and find out what we're dealing with here."

Drew's breathing quickened as he heard voices coming from inside the bedroom at the end of the hallway. He ran his hand along the back of his neck, a stinging heat kindling around his collar.

They approached the doorway. Sunlight streamed through the half-open venetian blinds, brightening the large, airy space. The coppery scent of blood drifted through the air. As officers milled about, Drew noticed that this room, like the others, appeared to be in perfect condition. The grey velvet king-size bed had already been made, with its silver duvet pulled tightly into each corner and the decorative pillows in a precise line along the crystal-tufted headboard.

Not a piece of clothing or pair of shoes was strewn about the floor. A designer handbag was propped along the edge of a mirrored vanity. It looked to be full and the zipper was securely fastened. Next to it was a porcelain Tiffany jewelry tray, which held a pair of diamond earrings, a platinum wedding ring set, a gold Omega watch and a framed photograph.

Drew bent down, staring at the couple in the picture. They were lying on colorful towels at what looked to be a beach resort. The woman's long, curly hair draped down her back. Her head was nestled against the man's chest—the same man who'd just burst through the front door. At the bottom of the photograph was the caption "Living, laughing and loving on our Bahamian honeymoon…"

"Here's a photo of our victim and her husband," Drew said to Nia.

"Sad. Look at them. They appear to be so in love."

"Yes, they do."

He gave the room another once-over. "One thing's for sure. This doesn't look to be a robbery."

"I agree. Nothing looks to be out of place."

Several officers were gathered in the far right corner. "Let's go take a look at the victim," Drew said.

"Right behind you."

As he walked past the bathroom, Drew noticed that the toilet seat was up. He found that odd considering the victim's husband was allegedly away from the home at the time of her murder. In that case, the seat should have been down. He made a mental note to dust it for prints, then approached the crime scene area.

Blood spatter covered the pale gray nightstand and eggshell-colored walls behind the victim. Her hands and feet were bound with duct tape. A deep, jagged gash had been slashed across her throat. An enormous amount of blood had poured from the wound, seeping into the cream Berber carpeting and turning her satin lavender nightgown a deep shade of brown.

"This feels like déjà vu all over again," Nia said. "Our victim looks to have been killed the exact same way as Katie and Violet. She's also petite with dark hair. But again, the big difference is this crime was committed inside her home."

Leaning forward, Drew studied the victim's head. "Hey, take a look at her hair. Notice how long it was in that photo we just saw? According to the date on the picture, it was taken recently. And look at it now. It appears to have been chopped off. Literally."

Nia moved in closer. "Oh my God. It does. You can tell by how uneven the ends are. It doesn't even look to have been cut with scissors. If the assailant did this, he must've used a knife."

"Yeah, the same knife he used to slit her throat, because I can see clumps of dried blood in her hair from here. And look. There are long strands of hair scattered across her body."

"This is so…so *sick*. Is he killing, then collecting souvenirs now, too?"

"Could be. If that's the case, the crimes are escalating. I think our suspect is getting a thrill out of committing these murders—taunting us by leaving clues at the crime scenes and now taking it up a notch. It's like he's daring us to apprehend him before he kills again."

Noticing Officer Davis hovering near the detectives, Drew called out, "Hey, Davis, were you the first one on the scene?"

"I was."

"Who called this in?"

"The neighbor who lives right here on the corner." He motioned to the white-framed casement window, pointing at the house on the left. "The guy told the 9-1-1 operator that he was afraid the victim may be in distress after hearing screams coming through his bathroom window. He let us inside the house, too."

"How'd he let you in?"

"He used a spare key the husband gave him in case of an emergency."

"Did he say why the husband felt it was necessary to give him that key?" Nia asked.

"Yeah, the husband travels a lot for work and his wife is a type 1 diabetic. Since the neighbor is a retired physician, the husband thought it would be a good idea for him to have access to the house in case his wife experienced some sort of health crisis."

"Did you get the impression he had anything to do with this?"

"No, not at all. He appears to be at least seventy-five to eighty years old. The man was dressed in plaid pajamas, a terry-cloth bathrobe and house slippers when he walked over. It looked as if he'd just rolled out of bed."

"All right," Drew sighed, running his hands along his goatee. "Has anyone called the medical examiner's office yet or do I need to take care of that now?"

"I put in a call as soon as I established that the victim was deceased. She'll be here shortly."

Drew gave him a nod of appreciation. It was the first decent exchange the men had shared since the Katie debacle. "Were you able to walk through the house and see if you could figure out the suspect's point of entry?"

"Not yet. I've been up here helping these guys process the scene."

"Officer Brooks and I will take a look around downstairs, then come back up and see what evidence we can collect."

Giving him a slight nod, Officer Davis inhaled sharply, as if he had something to add. Drew waited for him to continue. But he just stood there awkwardly, his mouth opening and closing several times before he backed away and rejoined the detective.

Drew sensed that he wanted to discuss the Katie situation. Now, however, wasn't the time. He had a case to solve.

"You ready?" he asked Nia before leading her out of the bedroom.

On the way downstairs, the victim's husband could be heard wailing out on the front lawn.

"We need to talk to him before we leave," Drew said. "I wonder how he found out about his wife."

"My guess is that the neighbor called and told him. I've been debating whether he may have had something to do with this. But the way he came tearing through the door with that look of fright on his face? I don't know. Plus he and his wife appeared so happy in that honeymoon photo."

"Not to mention he gave the neighbor a spare key in case his wife experiences a diabetic episode. My gut is telling me that he's not involved."

"Yeah, same."

The pair walked through the living room and back to the family room.

"Another area that appears to be untouched," Drew said, eyeing the row of neatly placed navy pillows lining a tan suede sectional and flat-screen television hanging from the wall.

A wedding photo sat prominently on top of the fireplace mantel. He walked over and stared at the black-and-white picture. The couple was holding hands while running through a grassy meadow. Their smiles radiated through the glass casing. Drew could feel their joy, which vibrated throughout the entire house. Yet today, because of some sick bastard, the lives of the groom, their families and friends would be forever shattered.

"Drew!" Nia called out. "Come and take a look at this."

He approached the sliding glass doors that led out onto the backyard deck.

"This door was unlocked and slightly open. I wonder if the victim forgot to secure it, because nothing appears to have been tampered with or broken. The lock is still intact. This may be how our suspect made his way inside the house."

"Or how he exited. Since there were no signs of forced

entry at the front door, there's a possibility that our victim knew the suspect and willingly let him in." Drew knelt down and studied the doorframe. "I wish we could figure out the motive behind these attacks. Why these women? I know they've each got their similarities. Katie and Violet were both single, outgoing and pretty heavy fixtures on the Juniper social scene. But this victim is different. She was married. The murder took place inside her home. What's the connection there?"

"Good question, assuming it's the same killer."

"Exactly. We need to know more about this victim. Starting with her identity. Did you happen to get her name while you were talking with the detectives?"

Nia flipped through the pages in her notebook. "You know, I didn't. We'll find out as soon as we head back up—"

"Hold on," Drew interjected, pointing to the doorframe. "Check this out."

Nia moved in closer as he shone his flashlight toward a partial bloody fingerprint. "Hmm, good catch. I'll see if I can lift an impression of it."

Both officers snapped photos before Nia pulled a bottle from her evidence collection kit.

"What is that you're using?" Drew asked.

"Amido black reagent."

"Nice. That's my preferred chemical of choice for developing blood evidence. I once had a partner who'd use luminol solution, which usually ended up ruining the proteins and genetic markers needed to detect DNA."

"And since luminol is water-based, I bet it diluted the blood impressions, too."

"That's exactly what would happen."

Drew looked on as Nia began applying the reagent to the print. "Where did you learn how to do all this?"

"I minored in forensic science in college and periodically take classes to keep my skills sharp."

"So you always knew you wanted to do this kind of work, even though you started off in the emergency services department?"

"I did. And working as a 9-1-1 operator gave me a nice head start. Before becoming a police officer, I already had a good understanding of how the radio works, proper protocols, the computer system. Plus I went in knowing how to handle victims and what's expected of law enforcement. Being at that call center really did help prepare me for the streets."

"That's awesome, Brooks. I love hearing about your journey to joining the force." Just as Drew pulled a roll of fingerprint tape from his bag, his cell phone pinged. "Chief Mitchell got held up at the station but he'll be here shortly."

"Good. I'm glad we can report that we've found some evidence. I have never seen him as shaken up as he was today."

"Yeah, neither have I."

Drew looked on as the amido black reagent slowly turned the proteins in the blood a shade of dark blue. Once it had dried, he carefully applied the tape, lifted the print, covered the tape with plastic and placed it inside a brown paper bag.

"That should do it," he told Nia. "Let's head back up and check in with the detectives."

As they walked through the living room, Drew glanced out the window. Officer Adams was still standing on the lawn talking to the victim's husband when the medical examiner's van pulled up. The sight sent the man to his knees.

Officer Adams quickly helped him up and sat him inside the squad car.

Drew wished he could do more to ease the husband's sorrow. But there was nothing more important than the task at hand—processing the scene so they could hunt down the killer.

"Hey, Officer Taylor!" Officer Davis called out from the landing. "Can you and Officer Brooks come up here? I need to show you something."

Charging up the stairs, Nia stopped Davis on the way inside the bedroom. "Hey, have you identified the victim yet?"

"I have. Her name is Porter. Ingrid Porter."

"Got it. Thanks."

As Nia began writing the victim's name down in her notepad, Drew noticed her hand freeze on the page.

"What's wrong?" he asked her.

"That name. Ingrid Porter. It sounds so familiar."

"According to one of the detectives," Officer Davis said, "she was born and raised here in Juniper. Maybe you went to school with her or something?"

"That could be it. But I'm not sure…"

"Well, while you try and figure that out, this is what I wanted to show you two."

Officer Davis held up a glossy trifold brochure. Before Drew could make out the wording, his eyes drifted toward the top right side. A single bloody fingerprint was smeared along the edge.

"Hey," he said, pointing toward it. "Did you see that—"

"Wait!" Nia exclaimed, pulling out her cell phone and scrolling through the camera roll. "I remember where I heard that name, Ingrid Porter."

"Where?" Drew and Officer Davis asked in unison.

"She's the woman who got married at the Charlie Sifford Country Club. Look, there's her name on the wedding invitation the killer left at Latimer Park."

Drew stared at the phone screen, tension swirling inside his head. It was all coming together. The invite. The garter. Those clues leading up to Ingrid's murder had nothing to do with the country club itself. They were about the woman getting married there.

"*Damn*," Officer Davis muttered. "Well, now we need to use the clue that was left at this crime scene to figure out the killer's next move."

"Wait, what are you talking about?" Nia asked. "What clue?"

The officer held the brochure in the air again.

"This menu to the Bullseye Bar and Grill."

Chapter Fifteen

Nia awakened to the sound of her pinging cell phone. After yesterday, she had turned the volume all the way up while awaiting Ivy's call. So far, she'd heard nothing and had barely slept.

Opening one eye, Nia grabbed the phone from the nightstand and swiped it open. A text notification appeared on the screen. Finally, a message from her sister.

Hey, sis! Sorry I didn't reach out sooner. The girls and I heard about the latest murder. So tragic! Sounds like she was targeted. No one at Bullseye thinks we're in danger though. STOP worrying about me. I'm good!

Nia sat straight up in bed and replied in all caps.

IVY, THIS IS NOT A JOKE! THE KILLER HAS ALREADY TARGETED ME AND CLEARLY HE KNOWS YOU'RE MY SISTER. SO WHY WOULDN'T HE TARGET YOU?? YOU ARE IN FACT IN DANGER! CALL ME ASAP!!

Nia tossed the phone back onto the nightstand and rolled over. Once her eyes adjusted to the dark room, she gasped, throwing off the comforter. Faint shadows of chairs and floor lamps loomed around her. Nothing looked familiar. She sucked in a panicked breath, confused by the faint smell of coffee.

A knock at the door sent her shuddering against the headboard. And then, it all came rushing back. Yesterday, after finding out Ingrid Porter was their latest victim, then discovering the Bullseye menu at the crime scene, Nia told Drew she couldn't bear going home alone.

"And you don't have to," he'd told her before gently taking her hand in his. "Not tonight or any other night for that matter. You can stay with me for as long as you want."

Nia remembered the plethora of emotions coursing through her mind. Gratitude spun the fiercest. At this point, the feelings she'd been harboring for Drew had blossomed into something more than just a crush. The sentiments ran deep, fusing a mix of admiration, appreciation and deep attraction.

After processing the crime scene, he'd driven her home and waited patiently while she packed a bag.

"This goes without saying," he had told her while setting up the guest bedroom, "but please, let me reiterate that there is no end date to how long you can stay here. You have an open-ended invitation."

A knock at the door pulled Nia from her thoughts.

"Good morning," Drew called out. "Are you up yet?"

"I am!" she lied. "Just one second..."

Hopping out of bed, Nia slipped on her satin lilac robe, ran her fingers through her tousled curls, then threw open the door.

"Sorry about that. Good morning."

"Hey, I hope you're hungry." He glanced down at the cup

of coffee and platter filled with fruit and breakfast breads in his hands. "I didn't know what you'd want to eat, so I went to Cooper's and picked up a little bit of everything."

"I see. That was so thoughtful of you. Thanks."

She took the mug and stepped to the side as he entered the room, placing the platter on the desk. Glancing in the mirror, Nia cringed at her disheveled appearance. The plan was to wake up early, shower and pull herself together before Drew laid eyes on her. Yet here she was, fresh out of bed and looking a rumpled mess. It didn't help that he was fully dressed and perfectly groomed.

"Hey," she began, "do you mind if I freshen up a bit, then we can enjoy breakfast together in the kitchen?"

"Of course!" He grabbed the platter and hurried toward the door. "I'm sorry. I didn't mean to bombard you. I, uh—I guess I got a little overzealous now that you're back in the house. Plus we had such a rough day yesterday, so I figured an early breakfast would be nice. And…well, now I'm just rambling. But you get the gist of what I'm trying to say."

"I do. I appreciate it. *And* you."

As Drew hovered in the doorway, Nia couldn't help but smile. His thoughtfulness, albeit a bit awkward, was quite endearing. "I won't be long getting ready."

"That's fine," he said, glancing down at his watch. "We've got plenty of time before we're due at the station." He turned to walk out, then took a step back. "Hey, were you ever able to get ahold of Ivy?"

Rolling her eyes, Nia went over to the nightstand and grabbed her phone. "Yes, *finally*. But not until a few minutes ago. She and her coworkers are safe. Of course she blew off my warning. Ivy still isn't taking any of this seriously. I'm telling you, the girl thinks she's invincible, just like she always has. She's the type who believes the universe will keep her covered."

"Yeah, well, this time she really needs to take heed. I hope you can get through to her."

The pair fell silent, Drew's gaze remaining on Nia as he stepped into the hallway.

"I'll leave you to it."

The moment he closed the door, Nia hurried to the bath-room and put a rush on her morning routine. While she made it into the kitchen in less than forty-five minutes, it looked as though she'd taken much longer to pull herself together after putting a little extra care into applying her makeup and flat-ironing soft waves into her hair.

"I just received an email from the crime lab," Drew said once she took a seat at the table. "There was no DNA evi-dence found on those wind chimes in your backyard or the garter. I'm guessing the suspect must've worn gloves."

"That makes sense. But if he wore gloves then, why wouldn't he have used them while committing the mur-ders?"

"Maybe he did. Think about the method he used to mur-der the victims. This guy is extremely violent. So violent that he could've worn gloves and torn them while perform-ing the acts."

Nia nodded, spreading her plain bagel with strawberry cream cheese. "You make a good point."

"We'll see what comes of the fingerprint evidence taken from this latest crime scene. Until then, let's keep working with what we've got. Violet Shields's phone records should be coming in any minute now that Officer Mills has sub-mitted the warrant to the carrier. As for Ingrid's cell phone, we got lucky after finding it inside her purse. Mills is going to start downloading the data today."

"You know, I had a theory that all these murders were linked to the Someone for Everyone app. But Ingrid was married. So I doubt she's connected to the killer in that way."

"Yeah, well, you never know..."

Flipping her notepad open to the most recent bulleted list, Nia asked, "What do you mean?"

"I mean, stranger things have happened. People do have affairs, flings, no-strings-attached types of situationships. Hell, a lot of people use those dating apps for quickie one-night stands."

"Something's telling me that's not the case here. But like you said, you never know. I can't help but think about Ingrid's husband though. He was so distraught over her murder. News that she was being unfaithful would tear him apart."

Nia lurched in her chair when Drew jumped up and began pacing the floor.

"What's going on?" she asked. "What are you doing?"

"I just thought of something." He picked up his cell phone and began typing away.

"Um, are you gonna tell me what you thought of?"

"I will," he said, placing the cell back down, then refilling their coffee mugs. "Just let me see what comes of this first."

Within seconds, his phone buzzed. Drew almost knocked it off the table trying to grab it.

"I'm dying to know what you're up to," Nia said, craning her neck to get a look at the cell.

As his eyes darted across the screen, he yelled, "Bingo! See, that's exactly what I thought."

"*What's* exactly what you thought?"

"I just sent a message to Ingrid's husband asking how he and his wife met. I'll give you one guess as to what he responded."

Pressing her palm against her forehead, she rasped, "If I were to say through the Someone for Everyone app..."

"Then you would be absolutely right."

"*Drew*," Nia shrieked, hopping up and throwing her arms around him. "You are a genius! So Ingrid was on the app, too. See, now we *really* need for Someone for Everyone to turn over the victims' membership information."

"Agreed. It's just a matter of time now that Officer Ryan has filed a motion to compel their objection to the court. At this point, I'm almost certain the administrators have something to hide."

"Not only that, but I'm sure they don't wanna deal with the controversy of having a member who's a serial killer. Whatever the case may be, this is good. We've now got a common thread linking two of our three victims. We'll see what comes of Violet's cell phone data once it comes in."

Drew quickly sobered up as he slumped back down in his chair. "You mean three out of four. Because unfortunately, you're now included on that list."

It was a little after 1:00 p.m. when Nia and Drew settled in at a table in the back of the Bullseye Bar and Grill. The place was packed with lunchtime patrons as almost every rustic table and booth was filled. Industrial fans whirled from the high exposed ceiling. Jumbo flat-screen televisions hung from each wall, showing practically every sporting event from basketball to soccer to tennis. Nooks hidden within the wood-paneled walls housed dartboards, pinball machines, foosball tables and cornhole boards.

Nia wished she were there for the honey-glazed wings, frothy mugs of beer and a round of pool. But she and Drew were on a stakeout of sorts, looking to see who'd drift in and out during Ivy's shift.

While she tried not to appear as worried as she felt, Nia was actually terrified for her sister. She hoped that by showing up to the bar in person, Ivy would take heed of the danger she was in—especially after refusing to call Nia back that morning.

Sis, you're really killing my vibe, Ivy had texted shortly before Nia arrived at the station. If I wanted to live my life in fear while constantly looking over my shoulder, I would've just stayed in LA!

Nia asked what in the world that last statement meant as Ivy never told her she was fearful of anything back in LA. Of course the question went unanswered. Typical Ivy—full of secrets and short on admissions.

"Will you look at this girl?" Nia said to Drew while pointing toward the bar. "Ivy is back there just laughing and joking as if she doesn't have a care in the world."

"Well, in Ivy's mind, she doesn't. But that's part of the reason why we're here. Hopefully our presence will prove to her that this is a serious matter, and she needs to move with caution."

"I highly doubt that's gonna happen. She seems to think we're here on a social call. The way she was introducing us to everybody when we walked in, as if we're her guests of honor as opposed to two police officers investigating a serial killer..." Nia paused, grazing her nails against her palms while watching Ivy wiggle her hips as she shook a Boston Shaker high in the air. "She needs to grow up and understand that it's gonna take more than just good vibes and a positive aura to help keep her safe."

"Hey, you never know. Maybe that'll work for her."

"Please tell me you don't believe in all those woo-woo theories, too."

Drew reached inside his beige utility jacket, playfully digging around. "I might. Let me grab my tarot deck and pull a few cards. See what they have to say about all this."

When Nia's expression twisted in frustration, he said, "Look, I get it. You're worried about your sister. But I'm just trying to lighten the mood because there isn't much you can do about her behavior. Just as you've stated time and time again, you cannot control Ivy. All you can do is advise her, which is exactly what you're doing."

"I know, I know." She picked up her fork and stabbed at her Caesar salad, no longer in the mood to eat. Thoughts of her sister becoming the next victim had ruined her appetite.

Glancing around the restaurant, Drew said, "Have you noticed anybody looking suspicious?"

"Yeah, how about everybody in here!" Nia quipped, only half joking.

Her gaze fell on a young man sitting at the bar who was there when she and Drew arrived. He was tall and lean, appearing well-groomed with his freshly trimmed Caesar haircut and goatee. When Nia walked past him, she'd noticed his half-eaten bowl of pasta, indicating he had been there for a while.

"What about that guy?" she asked Drew, pointing at the man as he stood on his stool's footrest and leaned over the bar.

"Which guy?"

"The one in the navy blazer and khaki chinos. He's giving me narcissistic, former frat boy vibes with the constant high-fiving and shoulder bouncing whenever a new song comes on."

"Oh, yeah. I noticed him when we first walked in. He definitely likes attention. I picked up more of a former collegiate athlete, still-living-in-his-glory-days type of vibe off him."

"Either way, something seems off. He's doing entirely too much. And of course my sister, who is a douchebag magnet, has been entertaining him the whole time we've been here."

Nia watched as Ivy rocked her hips back and forth, then poured the shaker's contents into a martini glass. When she slid it toward the man, he blew her a kiss, causing Nia to almost choke on a slice of grilled chicken.

"You know," she said, "when Ivy first got back to town, I told her to be careful and watch who she buddies up with. And look at her. Entertaining every man sitting at the bar. Especially the one who looks like the Preppy Killer."

Tapping his finger against Ingrid's police report, Drew replied, "Well, on a positive note, maybe she can give us some much needed intel since we're not getting anywhere with the evidence that's been left at these crime scenes."

"That would be nice. Notice I didn't even get my hopes up when it came to that bloody fingerprint on the Bullseye menu recovered from Ingrid's crime scene. And just as we'd suspected, it belonged to Ingrid."

"Yep. Another taunt aimed at us. As for Ingrid's husband, Terrance, Officer Adams's notes confirmed that he has a solid alibi. He was at work at the time of her murder."

"And I know the neighbor's officially been ruled out, too. What about the Ring camera footage? I noticed the cameras over the front and back doors. Any word from Terrance on that?"

"Another dead end," Drew grumbled. "Terrance told Officer Adams that the Wi-Fi got really spotty around the time of their home renovation. Plus he and Ingrid were in the process of upgrading the security system. So for the time being, the service was down."

"We need to talk to the neighbors then. See if their cameras captured any footage."

"Officer Adams was on top of that. While we were processing the scene, he interviewed the neighbors to find out if they saw or heard anything. We'll follow up with him once we get back to the station—"

Drew was interrupted when Ivy came strolling over to the table. She plopped down in the seat next to Nia's and planted a kiss on her cheek.

"Hey, big sis!" she squealed, her words a bit slurred. "Hey, big sis's partner."

Nia held her hand to her nose. "*Ivy.* I know that isn't alcohol I smell on your breath. It's barely lunchtime!"

Ivy giggled, tilting her head to one side. "Oopsies… You've got Gene to blame for that. He and I have been taking shots of whiskey ever since he got here. You know how it is. Hashtag that bartender life!"

"Yeah, how about hashtag you need to slow down," Nia rebutted. "I'm guessing Gene is the guy sitting at the bar who's been vying for your attention ever since we got here?"

"Yep, that's him. Isn't he cute?" She turned and wiggled her fingers at him. He immediately hopped up and began making his way toward them. "No!" Ivy called out, gesturing for him to sit back down. "I'm taking care of some business here. I'll be back soon. Just give me a few minutes!"

He tossed her an exaggerated scowl before returning to his stool.

"Ivy," Nia began, "listen to me. This serial killer investigation is not a joke. Things are really heating up and I'm gonna need for you to start taking your safety more seriously. Now, I'm glad you're staying away from my house. But as for all these wild late nights, the drinking, the taking up with strangers—it's got to stop."

"I agree," Drew chimed in, his eyes softening with concern as he stared across the table at Ivy. "I don't know if your sister has shared this with you, but if not, I trust that you'll keep it to yourself as we can't risk compromising the investigation. But at this latest crime scene, the killer left a Bullseye menu near the victim's body."

"What?" Ivy shrieked so loudly that several patrons turned and stared. "Nia, why didn't you tell me that?"

"When did I have a chance to? I've been trying to reach you since last night, but you refused to call me back!"

Nia looked to Drew, silently urging him to interject before her exchange with Ivy turned into a full-blown argument. He gave her a discreet wink before jumping in.

"Ivy, Nia and I aren't trying to scare you. We just wanna warn you that the streets aren't safe. Your sister is one of the lead investigators on this case, and thanks to all the news media coverage, I'm sure everyone in the community knows that. She's become a target. That Bullseye menu left at the crime scene indicates you may be one as well."

"Oh my God," Ivy moaned, her head falling onto Nia's shoulder.

"Remember when you first got back to town?" Nia asked. "And I told you that Juniper is a different place than it was when you left? Well, this is why. So just watch yourself.

Cut out the late nights. Don't go out alone. Be more private on social media. And if you're doing any online dating, cancel your memberships. At least until we get this maniac locked up."

"Yeah!" someone yelled loudly.

Nia watched as the guy at the bar Ivy had been talking to jumped up from his stool and pumped his fist in the air. "Let's go, Buffaloes!"

"What is his deal?" Drew asked.

"He played college football and he's a huge sports fan."

"So he's a friend of yours?"

"We're getting to know one another. He's actually a talent scout in the music industry, and he promised to help me book a few gigs around town. Maybe even something big at one of the venues in Denver. Starting with, drumroll please, the Rose Theater."

"The Rose Theater?" Nia echoed skeptically.

"Yes. The famed Rose Theater, better known as the venue that can make or break a performer's career."

"Um, Ivy?" Drew chimed in. "You do know that place has been under renovation for months, and it may not reopen for another year or so."

"Oh, really?"

"Yes, really," Nia replied, tossing her sister a tight side-eye. "I can't believe you actually fell for the game this man is running on you."

"I didn't fall for anything, little Miss Paranoia. What, you think I just took him at his word? I did do some research. And after looking Gene up, I saw that he has some pretty notable credits to his name. But anyway," Ivy continued quickly before Nia could inquire about said credits, "I'd better get back to work. Oh! And before I forget, Gene is trying to get me on the schedule to perform at Army and Lou's new artists' night next weekend. If he does, you two have to promise me that you'll come."

Drew looked toward Nia, who was slow to respond.

"Pleeease?" Ivy begged, pressing her hands together. "It would mean the world to me. If I get this, it'll be the first real singing gig I've booked in…in *months*. I could really use the support."

"Well, after all that," Nia told her, "how can I say no? Now I can't speak for Drew, but of course I'll be there."

"Nope," he said. "You can speak for me on this one. Because I'll be there, too. As a matter of fact, I wouldn't miss it."

Despite talking directly to Ivy, Drew's eyes were on Nia. She could tell by the glint in his gaze that he knew this was important to her. She mouthed the words *thank you* before turning back to her sister.

"So then it's settled. We'll see you next weekend at Army and Lou's."

"If I book the gig."

"When you book the gig," Nia assured her before glancing at the time. "Listen, it was good seeing you, and I'm really glad we had a chance to talk. But Drew and I should probably get back to the station. We've got a lot of work to do."

"So soon?" Ivy whined.

"Yes, ma'am. As much as we'd love to spend the day here watching sports and playing foosball, we've got a number of murders to solve."

"Ivy," Drew said, handing her his credit card, "it was nice to finally meet you, and thank you for everything."

"It was nice meeting you, too, you're welcome, and please, put that credit card away. Your money is no good here."

"No, Ivy," Nia said. "You don't have to do that."

"Nope. Everything is on the house. Family eats and drinks for free. Now get out of here and go solve your case."

After saying their goodbyes, Nia noticed Drew slip a fifty-dollar bill inside Ivy's hand. She tossed him a wink of thanks, then headed toward the door.

On the way out she gave Ivy's friend Gene one last glance, searching his eyes for that cold, blank look she'd seen in so many killers' mug shots. He didn't have it. When Ivy walked back behind the bar and leaned toward him, he gently covered her hands with his, giving her a bright smile that appeared sweet and genuine.

"So what are you thinking about your sister's acquaintance?" Drew asked.

"I don't think he's our guy."

"Neither do I."

As the pair climbed inside the car, their phones pinged simultaneously.

"Uh-oh," Drew uttered. "Can you check your cell and see what's happening?"

"Yep. It's an email from Officer Mills." Nia swiped open the message. "Oh, *wooow…*"

"What's going on?"

"Violet Shields's cell phone data just came in."

"And?"

"She was an active member on the Someone for Everyone app."

Chapter Sixteen

"Drew!" Nia called out from the guest room.

"What's up?"

"Did I tell you that Ivy texted me about ten times today, reminding me about her show tonight?"

"You did. And you know what I say? Let the woman have her moment. This evening means a lot to her."

Drew fastened his slim-cut gray slacks, leaving unsaid that he was just as excited for the night as Ivy, if not more so.

Toward the end of the week, Ivy had shared the news that she'd booked the gig at Army and Lou's. Tonight would mark the first occasion that he and Nia were getting dressed up and enjoying some time together away from the station in an official social capacity.

The past several days had been nothing short of chaotic. After Ingrid Porter's murder hit the news, Chief Mitchell was forced into defense mode, appearing on every local news channel to discuss the case. The department had been accused of being inadequate and inefficient. The towns-people were insisting they bring in the FBI. A couple of outlets and podcasters even portrayed Drew and Nia as being a pair of bumbling idiots who were being outwitted by their suspect.

The pressure to solve the case was getting to everyone. But no two officers were more affected by the insults and scrutiny than Drew and Nia. At first, she'd told Ivy that they couldn't make it to her show, feeling as though the evening would be better spent working the case. But Drew quickly reminded her that she was still a human being. Focusing on the investigation 24/7 wasn't healthy. Together, he and Nia had put in enough hours that week alone to fill up a month's worth of work for some officers. So when Ivy messaged Nia asking if she'd changed her mind, Drew insisted that Nia RSVP for them both.

After throwing on his blazer, Drew spritzed a few pumps of cologne on his neck, then headed to the living room. Of course he'd beaten Nia there. She had been groaning for the past hour and a half about how she couldn't figure out what to wear and that it was a bad hair day.

Drew blew her off, knowing she was exaggerating. Since Nia had been staying at his place, he'd seen firsthand just how many items of clothing she owned. And when it came to her hair, it didn't matter whether she had it wrapped in a bun or flowing freely over her shoulders. Either way she always managed to look beautiful.

"Nia!" he called out, glancing at his watch. "We're gonna be late. It's already past seven o'clock. Isn't your sister going on at eight?"

"Yes, she is!"

"Well, we'd better get a move on. I'd like to get a good table and order a bottle of champagne before the show starts."

"Ivy already reserved a table for us up front. We'll be sitting in the VIP section, where there's bottle service."

"Ooh," Drew uttered, strolling over to the gold-framed

mirror in the hallway and giving himself another once-over. "All right then. Fancy…"

The moment he heard high heels clicking across the floor, Drew spun around, stretching his neck as Nia rushed into the living room. When she came into view, he almost fell against the wall.

While he'd expected her to look nice, he had *not* expected all of this. She was wearing a black strapless leather dress that stopped somewhere in the middle of her thighs. The outfit showcased every ample curve on her slender body. Her hair had been pulled back into a sleek ponytail, and sparkly dangling earrings shimmered along her delicate neck. Her matte red lipstick set the look off, as did the silver stilettos with straps that snaked around her ankles.

"You… I—I think you look…" Drew stammered, completely lost for words.

"I know, I know," Nia said, hurrying over to the coatrack and pulling down a sheer floor-length duster. "I'm late. But I ended up having to throw my hair into this ponytail because it kept frizzing. And the dress I'd originally wanted to wear is at my house, so I had to settle on this one. I hope it doesn't look too snug. And these *shoes*… This is the first time I've ever worn them, so I'm gonna try my best not to waddle around like a walrus when I walk—"

"Nia," he interrupted, taking the duster out of her hands and helping her into it. "You look stunning. Absolutely stunning."

She turned to him, her frazzled look spreading into a slight grin. "I do?"

"Yes. You do. Trust me, you're going to be the most beautiful woman there."

Drew stopped himself. Had he gone too far? Said too much?

Just as he thought to apologize, Nia kissed him softly on the cheek and whispered, "Thank you," confirming that the last thing he needed to be was sorry.

"Just stating the facts," he mumbled, relishing the scent of rose perfume radiating from her neck.

On the way to the car, he couldn't control his ogling as his eyes traveled every inch of her body. His teeth clenched when the stir in his groin responded to the sight. While her hips swayed to the rhythm of her sexy walk, he wondered how much longer he could suppress his growing desire for her.

DREW PULLED OPEN Army and Lou's frosted glass door and followed Nia inside. The moment she gave the hostess her name, they were led down the long wood-paneled hallway lined with black-and-white photos of all the jazz greats who'd performed there over the years.

They stepped down into the dimly lit, intimate main room of the club where the featured performers appeared. The place was already packed as every table and seat at the bar was occupied.

"Follow me to the stage!" the hostess shouted over the house band that was playing a rendition of John Coltrane's "Naima." "Ivy made sure we got you all set up in the VIP area. Once you're seated, the server will be over to take your food and drink orders."

Drew's breath caught in his throat when Nia reached back and grabbed his hand. Practically every man's head turned in her direction as they made their way through the crowded club. Admittedly, it felt good being by her side. And just as he'd told her, Nia was by far the most beautiful woman in the club.

A server approached the table the moment they were seated. Drew ordered champagne and a couple of appetizers to start. If she was up for it, he planned on taking Nia somewhere else for a nice, quiet dinner afterwards.

"I am so excited!" she said, pressing her hands against her voluptuous chest. "I haven't seen Ivy perform in years. Whenever she'd land a gig here or in LA, I was always too busy with work to attend. So tonight is really special." She slid her arm across the black bistro table and clasped Drew's hand. "Especially with you being here. Thanks again for coming with me. It means a lot. I wouldn't have wanted to be here alone because...you know."

"I do know. You don't have to thank me. Being here with you is my pleasure. And I'm happy to support your sister's dream. Plus, like I said before, we both needed a night out. This case is getting to us both, and—"

Nia held her finger to his lips. "*Shh*. You can't do that. You're going against the rules. We're not supposed to discuss the investigation tonight. Remember?"

As her skin pressed against his mouth, Drew resisted the urge to grab her hand and kiss it. "You're right. I'll drop it."

The moment was interrupted when Cynthia and a couple of other 9-1-1 operators approached the table. After chatting for several minutes, Drew tapped open his phone's home screen. It was six minutes to eight o'clock.

He tapped Nia's thigh, then pointed toward the stage. "It's almost showtime..."

"I know!" she gushed, bursting into rapid applause.

When the server came over with their champagne and appetizers, Cynthia and the others said their goodbyes, then hurried back to their table. Nia picked up a glass and held it in the air.

"To Ivy's performance tonight. May it be amazing and lead to all her dreams coming true. And…to us. May we continue to fight the good fight until we catch the killer."

Drew smirked, clinking his glass against Nia's. "I would do to you what you did to me and press my finger against your lips considering you just brought up the investigation. But I won't. I don't wanna ruin your lipstick."

"How thoughtful of you," she teased, blowing a kiss in his direction before taking a sip of her drink.

You'd better cut it out, he almost warned, realizing the evening was bringing out another side of Nia. Thoughts of how it would end ruminated as he readjusted his pants leg.

When the music slowed, Nia reached underneath the table and gave his thigh a squeeze. "This is it. It's time for Ivy's performance!"

While she peered at the stage his eyes remained on her. Drew waited for Nia's hand to slip from his leg. It didn't.

"Okay," she said. "It's after eight now. Where is Ivy?"

"Maybe she's still getting ready, or—"

He paused when a woman came running out from behind a curtain. He'd expected for it to be Ivy. It wasn't.

The woman rushed to the stage and whispered something in the bandleader's ear. He nodded, then pulled the microphone off the stand.

"Good evening, ladies and gentlemen! Welcome to Army and Lou's sizzling Saturday night showcase!"

The crowd broke into applause. Nia wiggled in her seat, then raised her hands in the air, clapping louder than anyone around them.

"If Ivy is peeking out into the audience from backstage," she said, "I want her to see me cheering. You know, just in case she's got the jitters."

"You're such a good big sister," Drew said with a wink before turning his attention back to the man on the mic.

"Thank you for coming out tonight. We've got a roster full of extremely talented artists ready to perform for you. So prepare for some intoxicating rhythm, boisterous blues, vivacious vocals and hypnotic harmonies. First up on to-night's schedule *was* the lovely, talented Ivy Brooks."

"Was?" Nia uttered. "What does he mean, *was*?"

"But I've just been informed that Ivy has yet to arrive. So we're gonna move on to our next rising star, Mario King, then bring Ivy up later tonight. Mario, come on out here and show the people what you've got, my man!"

"Drew, did I just hear him correctly? Ivy isn't here?"

"That's what he said. Maybe she got caught up at work and is running late."

"Nooo..." Snatching open her clutch, Nia pulled out her cell phone. "Ivy wouldn't have missed this for the world. It's all she's been talking about this week. Plus she took the day off. She wanted to make sure she was at the sound check on time this afternoon. She'd even mentioned staying here until tonight so that she wouldn't be late for the show."

"Has she called or texted you?"

"No, not since early this afternoon." Nia turned in her chair, frantically searching the club. "I wonder if any of her friends from Bullseye are here. And that guy who booked this gig for her. What was his name? Gene? He's supposed to be here, too. Have you seen him?"

Drew peered out at all the unfamiliar faces. "No, I haven't."

When Nia jumped up and rushed through the crowd, Drew tossed some cash onto the table and followed her. She stopped at the hostess stand.

"Excuse me," she said to the woman who'd seated them. "Are you involved in scheduling the artists' performances or arranging the sound checks?"

"I am. I keep track of the calendar for the manager. You two were guests of Ivy Brooks, right?"

"Right. She's my sister. Her sound check was scheduled for this afternoon, and she was supposed to perform at eight o'clock. But the bandleader just said that she's not here."

The hostess opened a brown vinyl planner and flipped through the pages. "Hold on. Let me take a look at today's sign-in sheet."

Sensing that Nia was on the brink of breaking down, Drew wrapped an arm around her. "Try and stay calm. I'm sure Ivy is fine. It's been a long time since she's performed. Maybe her nerves got the best of her and she had a change of heart."

"I doubt that. Ivy doesn't get nervous to the point where she wouldn't show up. My sister is the most confident woman I know. Believe me, she wouldn't have let anything get in the way of being here tonight. Unless…"

As her voice trailed off, dread pounded Drew's frontal lobe. In his ten-plus years of being a police officer, that all-too-familiar sensation meant one thing—something was wrong.

"Here she is," the hostess said, pointing at one of the appointments scribbled inside the calendar. "Ivy Brooks. Her sound check was scheduled for two o'clock. But she didn't show up."

Drew felt Nia lean further into him. He held her tighter before asking the hostess, "Did she call and try to reschedule?"

"No. Which I thought was strange after she'd called several times throughout the week just to confirm she was still on tonight's roster. But no one here at the club has heard from her at all today."

Pulling Drew toward the exit, Nia shouted, "We need to find my sister!"

Chapter Seventeen

It had been nine days since Ivy went missing.

After Nia and Drew left Army and Lou's, they'd rushed to Bullseye, praying that Ivy had had a change of heart and gone to work. But they were told that she never showed up. On the way out the pair ran into Madison. She hadn't seen Ivy since she'd left the apartment earlier that day.

Despite Madison having just left home, Nia begged Madison to take them back to her place. She needed to see for herself that Ivy wasn't there. When they arrived, Nia and Drew spoke to the landlord and learned that the building had no security cameras. None of the buildings in the area looked to have any, either.

Once inside Madison's unit, the officers searched every corner of the cramped one bedroom. There was no sign of Ivy.

Before leaving, Nia went through her sister's things. She'd found a duffel bag filled with what looked to be the things Ivy had planned on taking to the club the day of her performance—a slinky red floor-length gown, makeup bag, curling iron and rollers. Packs of peppermint and chamomile tea to soothe her throat. Her journal.

What was most alarming was the sight of her keys, wallet and cell phone. Ivy never would've left the apartment without those essential items.

That's when Nia and Drew rang the alarm. They issued an alert with Juniper PD as well as the surrounding areas, informing the agencies that it was likely her sister had been kidnapped.

"Hey," Drew said, "how are you holding up?"

Nia jumped at the sound of his voice.

"Sorry," he continued, slowly entering her cubicle and placing a brown paper bag on the desk. "I didn't mean to scare you."

"You're fine. It's me. I've been so jumpy that any little noise sends me leaping ten feet in the air."

"I know. Which is why I've been stuck to your side twenty-four seven ever since Ivy…"

"Went missing," Nia finished for him, struggling to sound stronger than she felt.

He took a seat, propping his chin in his hands while studying her expression. "You're doing it again."

"Doing what?"

"Getting in your feelings. Shuffling through everything you think you've done wrong or could've done differently. Stay out of the weeds, Nia. Fly above it all and keep your head in the now." He pointed toward the bag. "Since you refuse to step away from your desk for food these days, I picked up a turkey club and cup of tomato soup for you from Cooper's. You won't be any good in the search for your sister if you don't start taking better care of yourself."

"I know. But food is the last thing on my mind right now. I'm already sick to my stomach at the thought of what happened to her. Or the idea that she might be—"

"Held captive somewhere," Drew interjected firmly. "And

I get that. But still. At least try and take a couple of sips of soup while we go over the recent developments. Chief Mitchell wants an update on the case this afternoon."

Nia reached inside the bag and pulled out the sandwich. The scent of freshly cooked bacon drifted from the foil wrapping. Normally that would've sent hunger pains rumbling through her gut. Today it triggered a bout of nausea.

"So," Drew said, opening his well-worn composition notebook. "Here's what we've got for the chief so far. The rest of the DNA evidence found at Ingrid Porter's house came back from the lab. The fingerprints lifted from the sliding glass door and toilet seat matched that of the suspect's we found at the other victims' crime scenes. After running it through the database once again, we still didn't get a hit."

"Got it," Nia said, typing the notes into her computer as Drew spoke.

"We looked into that guy, Gene, who booked the singing gig for Ivy. His fingerprints didn't match the suspect's, plus he has a solid alibi."

"Right. He'd spent the day with his wife and newborn baby, and wasn't able to leave the house the night of Ivy's performance. Should I add the part where he's a sleazy bastard who was hitting on my sister even though he's married, and—"

"Hold on," Drew cut in. "You're not wrong. But we should probably leave those particulars out of the report."

"If you insist."

Nia continued typing, acting as if she was actually adding the details to the document. When Drew broke into a deep, throaty chuckle, she couldn't help but laugh.

"Wait, is that a smile I see on your face?" he asked. "And did I just hear an actual giggle escape those lips?"

"Yes, you did. You've somehow managed to make even the hardest moments more bearable. That's one of the things I love most about you."

"Ooh, there are things you love about me? Wow, Officer Brooks. You just made my day."

A palpable energy swirled between the pair as they both fell silent. Just when Drew reached for Nia's hand, she cleared her throat and turned back to the computer. "All right, what else have we got?"

Slouching against the back of his chair, he responded, "The court granted our motion to compel Someone for Everyone's objection to the subpoena. So the administrators have no choice but to comply by the deadline."

"Okay, I've got that recorded. Anything else?"

Drew blew a pensive sigh. "Lastly, we need to tell Chief Mitchell everything that you found inside Ivy's journal." He slammed his notebook shut. "But first, you should probably start by telling me."

After saving the document, Nia grabbed the diary and shifted in her seat. She hated having gone through something of her sister's that was so personal. Reading her innermost thoughts and private actions, let alone sharing them with Drew and Chief Mitchell, felt like a betrayal of their sisterhood. But Nia had no choice now that Ivy had gone missing. This was a matter of life and death. And she was willing to do whatever it took to get her sister back.

Nia turned to one of the pages she'd bookmarked with a pink sticky note. "Okay, so, I'll just give you a brief overview of what Ivy had going on back in LA, because

I think some of this had a lot to do with why she left the city so abruptly."

"All right," Drew said, cracking open his notebook again and jotting down notes. "I'm listening."

"Earlier this year, Ivy started working for an elite men's social club called Legacy. Have you heard of it?"

"No, I haven't. What's it about?"

"It's basically an underground secret society of sorts. Membership consists of prestigious business owners, judges, attorneys, investment bankers—you get the idea. It's like a brotherhood. These men meet up and unwind over top-shelf spirits, expensive cigars and high stakes poker games while debating politics and brokering business deals."

"Interesting. What type of work was Ivy doing for the club?"

"She was just bartending as far as I know. But the thing is, Ivy was being paid a lot of money. In cash. That part makes sense, because I never could figure out how she'd managed to pay rent on a two-bedroom apartment in a Beverly Hills high-rise. The question is, was she making all that money just serving drinks? Or was there more to it than that?"

"Good question. Because the average bartender definitely isn't making enough money to live in that area."

"Exactly." Nia flipped to a page that had been bookmarked with a yellow sticky note. "I'm thinking that the members were throwing a lot of money at the women who worked for the club as a way of grooming them. Hoping the professional rapport would grow into something more."

"Was there anything in Ivy's journal that gave you that impression?"

"Well, a few months into the job, she'd mentioned that the

club's dynamics started to change. Some of the patrons' behavior became dodgy and demanding. Their requests went from business to personal. There was one man in particular whose actions had become downright inappropriate with his aggressive flirting and pleas for a date. I looked through the entire journal for his name, but Ivy never mentioned it. She only referred to him as The Donor."

"The Donor," Drew repeated, rapidly taking notes, then biting down on the tip of his pen. "I wonder if he was one of her big tippers."

"That's what I'm thinking. One name that Ivy did mention pretty often is Coco. She's someone who also worked for Legacy. I found her contact information in Ivy's cell phone and left her a voicemail message. Hopefully she'll get back to me soon. But in the meantime, that's what I've got."

"That's a good amount of information to work with. At least we have a substantial report to turn in to the chief and some solid leads to look into." Drew tossed his notebook onto the desk and slid closer to Nia. "Listen, I know things are tough right now, but I want you to stay positive. And trust that we're going to find your sister."

She nodded, unable to verbally respond for fear that a fresh batch of tears would start to fall.

"Ready to go meet with Chief Mitchell?" Drew asked.

After taking a couple of swallows of soup, Nia gathered herself, then stood. "Yes. I'm ready."

NIA INCREASED THE volume on her cell phone and set it in the middle of the coffee table. She and Drew were sitting on his couch with the latest episode of "Black Cake" muted and their bowls of shrimp risotto only half-eaten.

Their evening had been interrupted when Ivy's coworker Coco finally returned Nia's call.

"So this men's group, Legacy," Drew said. "It isn't based in just one state?"

"No, it isn't," Coco replied. "The members live in California, Nevada, Arizona and Colorado. And they meet in major cities throughout those states. That's what makes the group so difficult to trace."

"Got it," Nia said. "Now, let's get back to Ivy. If she was dealing with all this harassment from the members, well, one member in particular, why didn't she just quit the job?"

"Because the money was too good. But then something happened, and the president of the club fired her. Since she and I were so close, I ended up getting fired, too."

Nia threw Drew a look before he asked, "When you say something happened, what exactly do you mean?"

"I, um… What I mean is, she knew too much."

"What exactly did she know?"

The other end of the phone went silent.

"Coco?" Nia said. "Are you still there?"

"Yeah, I'm here. I just… I really don't feel comfortable talking about this over the phone."

"Well, is there any way we could meet up in person?"

Another long pause.

"Did she hang up?" Drew whispered just as Coco's low grunt rumbled through the speaker.

"Look," she said, "that's not possible. I'm leaving for New Mexico tomorrow night. I've gotta get out of here. After what's happened to Ivy, I just don't feel safe anymore."

Clenching her teeth together, Nia willed herself to keep pressing. "Where are you now?"

"At my parents' cabin in Lake Astor."

"What if we meet you there, before you leave town?" Drew suggested. "I promise that we won't take up too much of your time."

Nia slid to the edge of the couch, balling her hands into tight fists while awaiting the response.

After what seemed like forever, Coco finally uttered, "Fine. Be here tomorrow at two o'clock sharp. I won't have much time to spare. I'll give you thirty minutes, tops."

"Thank you, Coco," Nia told her, grabbing the phone and swiping open the Notes app. "You have no idea how much this means to us. Where is the cabin locate—"

"I'll text you the address."

Before they could say another word, Coco disconnected the call.

"All righty, then," Drew said, staring at the phone screen. "I certainly hope she's more helpful than that tomorrow."

Collapsing against the back of the couch, Nia rubbed her tired eyes. "It's fine. I get it. She's frustrated and obviously scared. I'm just glad that she agreed to meet with us and pray that whatever she knows will lead us to Ivy."

Drew glanced at the clock, then picked up their bowls. "It's getting late. I'm sure you're probably exhausted. Why don't we head to bed? We've got a big day tomorrow."

"I'm right behind you."

Nia turned off the television and grabbed their glasses. On the way to the kitchen, she noticed a slight spring in her step, driven by a boost of optimism. The call with Coco felt like more than just another empty possibility. It seemed like a tangible tip.

After straightening up, she and Drew headed down the hallway, stopping in front of the guest bedroom.

"You were great today," he said. "We're making good progress."

"Thanks. Just ten minutes ago I was feeling so confident. But now all of a sudden I'm starting to worry about tomorrow. What if Coco gets cold feet and decides she doesn't want to tell us anything? Or what if she skips town before we can even get to Lake Astor—"

"Nia," Drew interrupted, taking her hands in his. "None of those things are going to happen. Coco gave us her word and I believe she'll come through. She and Ivy are close friends. She wants her to be found just as badly as we do. So just relax. Don't put all that unnecessary stress on yourself by running a bunch of fake scenarios through your head."

"You know I have a bad habit of doing that. And I know I need to stop."

Drew leaned in and gently kissed her forehead. Closing her eyes, Nia's hands skimmed his broad shoulders, then rested against the back of his neck. The feel of his lips against her skin was comforting, rousing a stir of emotions deep within her.

The moment intensified when Drew slipped his arms around her waist. As his body pressed against hers, she felt a bulge against her thigh.

Abruptly pulling away, he muttered, "We, uh…we'd better get some rest."

Nia didn't respond, while eyeing Drew intently. Nothing in his lingering stare indicated he wanted to leave.

He brushed several strands of hair away from her face. "I hope you sleep well."

"You, too." She took a step inside the room, hovering in the doorway. "Hey, Drew?"

"Yes?"

"I don't want to be alone tonight."

"You won't be," he murmured, straightening the teardrop pendant on her necklace. "I'll be right next door. If you need anything, just call out my name."

Her body shivered as his fingertips delicately grazed her neck. "Let me put it this way. I don't want to *sleep* alone tonight."

The pair didn't break their gaze as she backed into the bedroom. A deep sense of longing spun through Nia's core when Drew followed, closing the door behind them.

Chapter Eighteen

The rows of dark green Douglas fir trees lining Ensley Lane were all a blur as Drew navigated the winding road. He glanced over at Nia, whose pulsating temples had to be aching by now as they'd been going nonstop since the officers left the station.

"How much longer until we get to Lake Astor?" she asked for a third time.

"About fifteen minutes. Maybe a little sooner since traffic is pretty light."

Drew reached across the console and slid his hand over hers. While she didn't glance in his direction, her fingers intertwined within his. He knew she wasn't in the mood to talk. So he continued to let the smooth jazz flowing through the speakers fill the gaps of silence.

Waking up with Nia lying in his arms felt surreal after their explosive night of lovemaking. They'd poured every pent-up emotion into the moment. Drew could still feel the sensation of her supple skin lingering on his lips. He'd wanted more of her this morning. But the moment she had opened her eyes Nia was all business, anxiously anticipating their meeting with Coco.

Once they arrived at the station, she immediately began

digging into the investigation. She'd followed up with Someone for Everyone as the company had yet to submit the subpoenaed documentation. The court-imposed deadline was fast approaching, prompting Officer Ryan to look into having the app shut down until they complied.

At twelve-thirty sharp Nia charged Drew's desk, insisting that they head to Lake Astor just in case Coco decided to leave for New Mexico early. According to the navigation system, they were set to arrive almost thirty minutes earlier than the two o'clock meeting time. Drew just hoped the afternoon wouldn't lead to disappointment.

"In five hundred feet," the navigation system announced, "turn left onto Sandcastle Road. The destination will be on your right."

Nia's grasp on his hand tightened as she leaned forward, staring out the window. "We're almost there."

Within minutes, a two-story cabin deckhouse appeared in the distance. The bright afternoon sun gleamed against the floor-to-ceiling windows. Silverleaf maple trees surrounded the property's vast acreage, with a sizable lake flowing along the side of the home.

As Drew tapped the navigation screen and ended the route, Nia rapped on the window.

"What is going on out here?"

He pulled up to the house's vast front yard, then slammed on the brakes. Yellow caution tape had been wrapped around the lower deck and several nearby trees. Law enforcement officers dressed in hazmat suits were scattered across the front yard. Farther in the distance, a white sheet lay near the edge of the river.

The sight turned Drew's stomach. He peered over at Nia, whose hand covered her mouth.

"I think I'm gonna be sick," she gagged.

"Let's just stay calm," he told her, his steady tone masking the trepidation coursing through his body. "We don't know what's going on here yet."

"I think I have a pretty good idea."

Drew threw open the door and jumped out. "Let me go talk to the officers, then I'll come back and let you—"

"Absolutely not," Nia interrupted, climbing out and following him up the driveway. "I'm coming with you."

Together the pair rushed over to a group of officers. One in particular approached them with his arms in the air.

"Hey!" he shouted. "I'm gonna need for you to get back. This area is closed off."

Drew flashed his badge then extended a hand. "Sir, my name is Officer Taylor, and this is Officer Brooks. We're with the Juniper PD and were scheduled to meet with Coco Campbell here. She told us that her parents own this place."

Despite the detective's face being covered with a mask, Drew noticed his fiery glare soften. "Oh, my apologies. I'm Detective Reynolds with the Lake Astor PD. And um…yeah. I'm sorry to have to tell you this, but Ms. Campbell is dead."

"Oh my God," Nia moaned, doubling over in shock. Drew grabbed her right before she went tumbling to the ground.

"Did you two know her personally?" the detective asked.

"Not exactly," Drew told him. "I'm sure you've heard about the serial killer case we're working up in Juniper. Officer Brooks and I are the lead investigators, and Coco had some information that we were hoping might lead us to the suspect."

Detective Reynolds ran his thumbnail across his brows. "Oh boy. Welp, I wonder if the information she was planning to share has anything to do with her murder."

Nia stood straight up and pulled in a long breath of air. "Coco was a friend of my sister's, Ivy Brooks. She's gone missing." Gesturing toward the sheet covering her body, she choked, "Who found her? And was her throat slashed?"

"A couple of deer hunters were out here early this morning and spotted the body. Judging by the looks of her swollen lips and bruising around the neck, we're thinking she died by asphyxiation. But of course the medical examiner will need to perform an autopsy to confirm that."

"So she wasn't bound at all?" Drew asked.

"No, she wasn't."

Pivoting away from the officers, Nia uttered, "That means we really could be dealing with two killers here."

A couple of men dressed in dark gray suits appeared from behind the house. Alongside them was an extremely petite woman dressed in pink pajama pants and a brown leather aviator jacket. Her shoulders shook as she sobbed uncontrollably, using her long red hair to wipe away the tears.

Detective Reynolds pointed toward the group. "You two may wanna speak with Elena. She was a friend of Coco's. They were supposed to drive down to New Mexico together today. Once she's done with the homicide detectives, I'll send her over."

The officers exchanged business cards, with Reynolds promising to reach out once the crime scene evidence came back from the lab.

As soon as the detective walked away, Nia leaned into Drew. "I have got the worst feeling that Ivy is dead."

"Don't say that. You have got to keep your head in a good space, Nia. If for nothing else, for the sake of your sister. That's the only way you're gonna get through this. We'll be hoping for the best until we can't anymore. Now let's see what this friend of Coco's has to say, all right?"

When she failed to respond, Drew reached down and lifted her chin. His chest pulled at the pain in her eyes. "You heard what Detective Reynolds said. Coco's cause of death is nothing like the other victims. Her murder may not have anything to do with this case we're working." He knew the statement was wishful thinking on his part. But Drew was desperate to say something, *anything*, to prevent Nia from falling apart.

"Hey!" Coco's friend Elena shrieked as she ran toward Drew and Nia. "You're Ivy's sister?"

"I am. You're Elena, right?"

"Yes," she whimpered before collapsing into Nia's arms.

Drew grabbed both women as they teetered back and forth. "Why don't we go sit inside the car and talk?"

"Good idea," Nia told him while they both helped a stumbling Elena across the lawn.

Once inside the vehicle, the officers pulled out their notebooks and turned to the back seat where Elena was sitting.

"I know your sister," she croaked. "Very well. We worked together for Legacy. It's like this high-society men's club. Did you, um…did you know anything about that?"

"I didn't. At least not until Ivy went missing and I read about it in her journal. What type of work do you do for the club?"

"I bartended at the meetings. Just like Ivy. But I quit and was about to move to New Mexico with Coco, until…" Her voice broke as a low groan gurgled inside her throat.

"We're so sorry for your loss," Drew said. "Can I ask why you quit the job?"

"Yeah," she sniffled, wiping her nose on the sleeve of her

coat. "Because just like Ivy, I was sick of all the harassment and gross behavior. The members treated us like we were their property or something. And they were never reprimanded. We were just expected to take it. Which most of us did because the money was so good. I'm actually surprised Ivy didn't fight harder to keep her job when she was fired. She was getting paid more than most of us. But I get it. Ivy was sick of the guys asking for more than just friendly conversations and dinner dates. When she was let go, her plan was to return to Juniper and focus on her singing career."

"Is one of the guys you're referring to known as The Donor?" Nia asked.

"Yep, he's one of them. He's the main one, actually."

"Do you know his name?"

"Yeah. It's Ethan Rogers."

"What do you know about him?" Drew probed.

Biting down on her cuticles, Elena mumbled, "If I get into this, you all have got to promise me you'll keep my name out of it. Because those Legacy members are a trip. And I do not wanna end up like Coco and Iv—" She paused, her head jerking in Nia's direction. "I'm sorry. But, I mean…"

Instead of appearing solemn, there was a determination in Nia's taut expression.

"You have our word," she told Elena. "Now tell us everything you know about Ethan."

Pride erupted inside Drew's chest at her strength. In that moment, he couldn't have been prouder to have her as his partner.

"Ethan," Elena spewed. "Where should I even start. He and Ivy got really cool when she first started working for Legacy. After a while, he started buying her all these ex-

pensive gifts and paying her rent. He was there for her as a friend, too. And eventually, as a protector."

"Wait," Nia interjected. "What do you mean as a protector?"

Rolling her eyes toward the roof of the car, Elena emitted a loud snort. "Yeah, so Ivy had a fan club of sorts back in LA that included a stalkerish ex-boyfriend and an overly friendly neighbor. When she and the boyfriend broke up, he wouldn't leave her alone. He kept popping up at her apartment, begging her to take him back. He'd call and text nonstop. Leave flowers and love letters at her front door. She'd made it clear that there wasn't a chance in hell they'd rekindle the relationship. But the man just wouldn't give up."

Drew paused his note-taking and turned to Nia. "Did you know about any of this?"

"No, I didn't. I hadn't read about any of it in Ivy's journal, either." She nodded in Elena's direction. "Sorry, go on."

"Yeah, so as for Ivy's incel of a neighbor…*whew*. That weirdo would magically appear everywhere she went. The grocery store, the gym, her singing gigs. Eventually it got to be too much, and she told Ethan what was going on with both guys. I don't know what that man did. But soon after she talked to him, the harassment just stopped. The next time Ivy saw Ethan, he told her that she wouldn't have to worry about either of the guys ever again."

Both Drew and Nia sat there, neither wanting to ask the inevitable. Several moments passed before Drew finally spoke up.

"What, uh…what exactly do you think Ethan did to the men?"

"Either he beat their asses or threatened to. Because after that, whenever Ivy ran into the neighbor, he'd barely speak, duck his head and keep it moving. As for the ex-boyfriend, he ended up moving to Florida to live with his brother."

"Hmph," Nia sighed. "Well, I'm glad to hear he didn't kill them. But wait, if Ethan was looking out for Ivy and doing all these nice things for her, why did they fall out?"

"Because the more he did, the more he expected. Ivy was content with just being friends. Ethan wasn't. Over time, his feelings for her grew into some sort of twisted infatuation. It became dark. And menacing. I'm telling you, the man was obsessed."

"Do you think he has anything to do with Ivy going missing?"

Elena paused, twisting her hands together as tears welled in her eyes. "I do."

Piercing silence filled the car. Drew's pen stopped in the middle of the page before he expanded the probe, asking, "What about Coco's murder? Do you think he's involved in that as well?"

"I do. Because just like Ivy, she knew too much."

"What did she know?"

"I'm not exactly sure. But it had something to do with him and another club member named Vaughn Clayton. Vaughn is a big-time attorney who's running for senator here in Colorado, and Ethan is the head of his fundraising committee. If you ask me, everything about their partnership is shady. And I think Ivy and Coco discovered a few things that the men didn't want to be known. Exactly what I don't know. But that's just my two cents."

"Are you still in touch with anyone who works for Legacy?" Nia questioned.

"*Hell* no. None of those bitches deserve my friendship. I was so good to all of them. But when I needed backup after complaining to our manager about the way I was being hassled, nobody had my back. They all turned on me. They're all about the money. I'm not surprised though. Those girls have yet to learn that all money isn't good money."

Slamming her notebook shut, Nia thanked Elena for the information, then nudged Drew's arm. "We need to find this Ethan guy and have a talk with him."

"I agree. Why don't we head back to the station and figure out where to—"

"I know where you can find him," Elena interrupted.

"Where?"

"At the next Legacy meeting."

"Do you know when and where it'll be?" Drew replied skeptically. "You know, since you no longer work for the club or speak to your ex-colleagues."

"I still have a couple of connections within the club. I heard that the guys are getting together this Friday night at Richard's Cigar Lounge in downtown Denver. The meeting starts at eight o'clock sharp."

Nia tore her notebook open and wrote down the information. "Good to know. Thank you."

"Oh, and there's one more thing you should know," Elena said.

"What's that?"

"Ethan Rogers sometimes goes by another name. He claims it's for business purposes. But I think there's more to it than that."

Pausing his pen, Drew's eyes drifted from his notebook to Elena. "Oh, really? What's the other name?"

"Shane Anderson."

Chapter Nineteen

"9-1-1. What is your emergency?"

Nia turned up the volume on her phone and held her breath, shivering as the night breeze blew past her. Crouching down behind a row of perfectly manicured boxwood shrubs, she took another look around the vast backyard.

"Hello, 9-1-1," the operator repeated. "Do you need police, fire or medical?"

"I need the police," Nia hissed, barely able to force the words from her constricting throat.

She craned her neck. Stared out toward the massive white pines lining the back of the yard. That shadowy figure she'd just seen darting through the pruned tree trunks was nowhere in sight. Neither was Drew, who should've been there by now.

Juniper PD's plan to raid the Legacy club meeting at the cigar lounge had gone completely awry. And Nia had no one to blame but herself. She was the one who'd insisted that Ethan, also known as Shane, was the only person who could lead them to Ivy. If they confronted him at Richard's, she feared they'd never find her sister. So she insisted they hold off and follow him after the meeting.

Once Ethan and Vaughn left the lounge together, law enforcement trailed the men to the house on Webb Hill Road. Unbeknownst to Nia, who had driven her own car from Juniper to Denver, she'd been the first officer to arrive on the scene. A flickering bulb hanging over the coach house's porch had caught her attention. She'd sent Drew a text letting him know she would meet him there.

Desperately hoping to get to her sister, Nia exited her vehicle and began casing the house's exterior. At one point she could've sworn she'd seen Drew hovering near the coach house doorway, signaling her over. But as she got closer, Nia realized the short, stocky figure dressed in all black was not him.

As she approached, the man lunged at her. She panicked, freezing underneath the grip of his strong, massive hands. Everything happened so fast that Nia didn't have time to draw her weapon. A brief tussle ensued. She'd managed to land a right hook, then slip from his grasp, only to roll her ankle while running to safety.

"I'm sorry, ma'am," the operator said, jolting Nia from her thoughts. "Could you please repeat that? And speak up a bit, if possible?"

"I. Need. *Help!*"

She fell to her knees, her feet aching and head pounding simultaneously.

"What is your location?"

"Forty-two Webb Hill Road."

"Can you tell me what's going on there?"

Covering her mouth, Nia whispered, "I've been attacked. I was able to get away, and now I'm hiding in the backyard. The assailant is still out there somewhere. I'm a Juniper police officer and my team was supposed to meet me here, but we got separated. So now I'm alone, it's pitch-black and I can hardly see a thing."

Frustration stiffened Nia's limbs. She stared up at the gloomy, cloudless sky. Only a few dim streams of light beamed from the scattered stars. They did nothing to break through the relentless darkness blanketing the yard.

"I've got law enforcement heading your way. What is your name, ma'am?"

"Officer Brooks. Officer Nia Brooks—"

Bang! Bang!

"Hello? Officer Brooks? Were those gunshots I just heard?"

"Yes!" Nia screeched into the phone.

"Were you struck?"

"I…no, but I—"

Bang!

Nia hit the ground, narrowly dodging the bullet that flew over her head. A scream threatened to escape her lips. But she bit down on her jaw, knowing one wrong move could end her life.

"Listen to me, Officer Brooks. I'm going to need for you to take cover and stay on the line with me. Denver PD is already en route, okay?"

"Okay. *Please* tell them to hurry."

Blades of grass cut into Nia's cheek as she inhaled the damp, earthy dirt. She thought back on her days of working as a 9-1-1 operator. Being on the other side of danger felt surreal. This moment was eerily similar to the night she'd received the call from Linda Echols. With one exception— Nia was armed.

She unholstered her Glock 22 and squeezed the grip, bracing herself for another round of gunfire.

"Officer Brooks, my name is Sydney. I'll be right here on the line with you until police arrive, all right?"

"Yes, thank you, Sydney." Nia clutched her throbbing ankle, peeking through the bushes as her attacker sprinted across the back of the yard. "How much longer until they'll be here?"

"Just a few more minutes. Hang in there."

A sobering thought crossed Nia's mind—Drew still wasn't there. She wondered if they'd crossed paths with Denver's police department. "Has anyone in your department heard from the Juniper PD?"

"Not as far as I know. But I'll send out a message to dispatch and find out. In the meantime, have you spotted the shooter again?"

"I think I see him lurking in the wooded area behind the backyard. But I'm not sure. I've got my weapon drawn and I'm ready to shoot if necess—"

Boom!

"Officer Brooks! Are shots being fired again?"

The phone went silent.

"Officer Brooks, talk to me. Are you okay?"

"Yes," Nia finally uttered through shallow breaths.

Just as another round of shots rang out, someone yelled in the distance, "Officer Brooks! Where are you?"

"Drew!" Nia screamed.

The sound of his voice eased the tension coursing through her body. She hopped to her knees, peering through the bushes while waving an arm in the air. "I'm over—"

Bang!

A bullet ricocheted right past her shoulder.

"Stay down, Brooks!" Drew yelled. "The other officers are surrounding the premises—"

Boom!

Drew's voice faded as a loud thud echoed through the air.

"Officer Taylor?" Nia shouted. "Officer Taylor!"

Another bullet flew past her ear. She burrowed deep within the grass, gripping her chest after what sounded like a body dropping to the ground.

Sirens blared right before footsteps pounded the winding driveway's pavement.

"Police! Drop your weapon and come out with your hands up!"

Nia recognized the voice. It was Chief Mitchell.

"Officer Brooks," Sydney said into the phone, "I'm still here with you. It sounds like the police are on the scene."

"Yes, they're here," she moaned, her tone flattened by the thought of Drew being shot.

I've got to get to him...

Nia slid to her knees. Curled her finger around the trigger while glaring through the brush. The officers' darting flashlights spilled across the lawn. She scanned the yard for the shooter as an urge to call out Drew's name singed her tongue.

Don't do it...

"We need paramedics at forty-two Webb Hill Road!" Sydney yelled through the phone. *"Stat!"*

Dread pricked Nia's skin. An ambulance was probably being called to the scene for Drew.

You cannot let this man die...

Her eyes burned with determination just as she caught sight of the black-clad husky figure she'd seen earlier, creeping toward a sloped rock garden. He hid behind a boulder, then shot at the officers.

"Take cover!" Chief Mitchell commanded.

Nia took aim. Fired one bullet. The shooter fell onto his back.

"We got him!" someone yelled before law enforcement charged the attacker.

Jumping up and running in the opposite direction, Nia's legs went numb right before she crumpled to the ground.

Get on your feet! a voice screamed inside her head.

She dug her palms into the ground, steadied herself and stood, then pressed on in search of Drew.

"Officer Brooks?" Sydney asked. "Are you still there?"

"I am," she panted into the phone. "But I need to hang up and check on my partner."

"Understood. Good luck, Officer."

Disconnecting the call, Nia stayed low while charging across the backyard.

"Drew!" she screamed, spinning in circles while frantically searching the grounds.

Her vision blurred with fear as she peered through the darkness. Chaos reeled all around her. Law enforcement darted in between the trees and bushes. Flashlights beamed in every direction. Gunshots intent on taking down each officer in the vicinity were firing at every moving target.

"Take cover!" Chief Mitchell yelled. "And don't shoot unless you've got a clear shot!"

Ignoring the directive, Nia kept moving, stumbling through the thick patches of grass. Another round of bullets whizzed through the air. She wanted to stop but couldn't. Not until she found Drew.

"Nia! Over here!"

"Drew!"

She sped toward him, almost falling to the ground before collapsing into his arms. "I thought you were—"

"Don't even say it. I'm fine. Now we've got to stay focused. I just saw Ethan and Vaughn run inside the house. I'm gonna have Officer Davis bang on the front door while we force our way in through the back." He paused, staring out at the lawn. "After the way those guys came at us with their guns blazing, I have no doubt they're hiding something in there."

Trembling at the thought of her sister being found dead, Nia stared at Drew, searching his tense expression for a glint of hope. Their eyes met. He pulled her close, the energy flowing within his embrace filling her with reassurance—as if he knew what she needed without having to be told.

For a brief moment, Nia thought about their night together. They'd been so wrapped up in finding Ivy that they had yet to discuss it. But what was understood didn't need to be explained. She knew the opportunity to express their feelings would soon come. In this moment, however, their only goal was to get her sister back.

"It's time to move in!" Chief Mitchell yelled.

As he directed several officers toward the front of the house, Drew shot the lock off the back door. He kicked his way inside with Nia following closely behind, staying low while spreading out inside the dark dining room.

"Police!" he yelled. "Whoever's in here needs to make themselves known. Come out with your hands above your head!"

Nia flinched at the sound of Officer Davis's fist pounding the front door, then fell to the floor when bullets came rushing past them.

Drew grabbed her arm and pulled her behind a stately oak hutch.

"Take cover!" he warned law enforcement as they bum-rushed the living room.

Tightening the straps on her bulletproof vest, Nia rose to her feet.

"There's no one in my line of vision," she whispered, pressing her head against the back of the unit while glancing around the corner.

"Same here. I'm trying to figure out where the shots are coming from."

Officer Davis threw a hand in the air, signaling toward the staircase. Drew gave him a thumbs-up, then placed his hand over his head, indicating he'd cover him.

Just as the officer made a move, a blast of bullets flashed once more.

"The assailant is to the right of the stairs!" Nia shouted.

Together, she and Drew fired back while Officers Davis and Ryan slid underneath the dining table. Glass shattered over their heads as slivers of champagne flutes crashed to the floor. For a brief moment, both sides ceased fire. But the echo of bullets still rang through the air.

"There's another shooter upstairs!" Drew warned.

Nia stooped down, checking to make sure the other officers hadn't been hit. They each nodded before raising their weapons.

"Ethan and Vaughn must have split up," she told Drew. "One is covering the front door while the other is covering the back—" She stopped at the sound of Officer Mills's voice.

"Get down on the floor! Hands over your head. Now!"

An audible gasp came from the room to the right of the staircase, followed by the loud thump of metal hitting the floor. Nia's arms trembled as adrenaline ripped through her body. Repositioning her gun, she pointed it toward the doorway, hoping the shooter would appear.

Drew stepped around Nia and threw the other officers a signal. "That was the shooter's magazine. He's out of bullets. Let's move in!"

He led the squad toward the room just as a man appeared in the doorway.

"Drop your weapon!" Drew yelled. "Get those hands in the air!"

As the officers swooped in, Nia froze. Faint screams filled the gaps of chaos circling around her. She turned her ear in the direction of the pleas. Through the darkness, she was able to make out a door near the back of the dining room.

She darted toward it. Reached for the knob. When the door failed to open, Nia ran her hands along the frame. A metal bolt scraped at her palm. She rammed it to the side and yanked at the door once more. The second it cracked open, a dark figure appeared from behind a curtain hanging from the dining room's windows.

"Dre—" Nia called out right before a gloved hand covered her mouth. The bitter taste of leather grazed her tongue. In one fell swoop she was pulled behind the curtain and knocked to the floor.

Nia's gun fell from her hand and slid across the hardwood planks. She threw an elbow, jabbing her attacker in his side. A chilling grunt rumbled from his mouth.

"You *bitch*," was all she heard before his hand slid from her mouth to her throat.

"Drew..." Nia wheezed, his name dissolving in the air as pressure crushed her neck.

Kicking out at her attacker, she struggled to make contact. But he slid from side to side, making it impossible to land a blow.

Nia's eyes rolled into the back of her head. Shallow streams of breath seeped through her quivering lips. She reached out, her hand shaking as she tried to hit the floor. Grab Drew's attention. Tell him she was in danger.

"Die, bitch," the man rasped. *"Die!"*

Drew... Nia screamed in her mind as the word couldn't escape through her constricting lungs. She struggled to see through the darkness. To catch a glimpse of her attacker. A sheet of sweat covered her face as her body went limp. Everything around her grew hazy, then blackened. A dizzying spell filled her head as she felt herself fading.

"Nia!"

Footsteps pounded the floor as the sound of Drew's voice brought her to. The grip on her neck loosened, then released.

Boom!

A kick to the gut from Drew's boot sent her attacker rolling across the floor. Officer Ryan swooped in and pounced, subduing then handcuffing who she now realized was Ethan.

Blinking rapidly, Nia slowly sat up and clutched her throat. Willed herself to regroup. And find Ivy.

"Nia!" Drew panted, pulling the officer to her feet. "Are you all right? Ethan... He just—he came out of nowhere. And I thought you were right behind me. I should've kept a better eye on you. I am so sorry!"

"It's okay," she gasped. "I'm fine. I just need to get my bearings—"

Faint screams came from the lower level.

"Ivy," Nia said. "I think I hear Ivy!"

Drew held her up as she stumbled toward the door. Throwing it open, Nia screamed out her sister's name.

"I'm down here! In the basement!"

Taking the stairs two at a time, Nia practically skied through the darkness. "Ivy! I don't see you. Keep talking!"

"Hold on, Nia!" Drew called out, pulling her back. "Where's your gun?"

She pressed her hands against her body before pointing toward the ceiling. "*Dammit.* I dropped it when I was being attacked."

He drew his weapon and covered her. "Stay close and let me lead the way. We don't know who may be lurking around down here."

Hovering near Drew's side, Nia called out Ivy's name once again. "Make some noise, Ivy! Where are you?"

"In here!" she yelled as the sound of banging rang out.

Nia ran her hands along the wall in a frantic search for a light switch. "I can hardly see a thing. Drew, *help*!"

Within seconds, the room lit up. Nia looked over and saw him standing across the way, gripping a metal pull string hanging from a lightbulb.

"*Thank* you," she uttered while eyeing their strange surroundings.

Sheets of plastic dangled from the ceiling, their edges crumpled against the dusty floor. Exposed wood and insulation lined the unfinished walls. The few pieces of furniture scattered around the spacious area were covered in paint-splattered drop cloths.

"*Nia!*"

The sound of Ivy's voice sent the officers rushing toward a back corner. A thick, dirty canvas tarp hung across the wall. Nia yanked it to the floor, revealing a narrow wooden door. It was secured shut with an alloy steel padlock.

"Ivy, stand back!" Nia yelled. "Step away from the door!"

Drew took aim and blew off the lock, then kicked down the door.

"*Ivy!*" Nia screamed, rushing inside. Relief rattled her

chest when her sister appeared inside the dimly lit make-shift bedroom.

Stumbling around a gray chest of drawers, Ivy fell into her arms.

"Thank God you found me," she sobbed.

Holding her as tight as she could, Nia said, "Of course we found you. But…how did this happen? How did you get here?"

A guttural moan vibrated against Nia's shoulder as Ivy's body wracked in agony. "I was getting ready to go to the sound check at Army and Lou's, and there was a knock at the door. I thought it was Madison, there to give me a ride during her break at Bullseye. I didn't even look through the peephole before opening the door. When I did, Ethan was standing on the other side. I just knew he was gonna kill me right there on the spot and freaked out. The second I screamed, he attacked, covering my mouth and pushing me back inside the apartment. All I remember is the sting of a needle being jabbed into my arm. When I woke up, I was inside this tiny hellhole."

Nia was overcome by a flood of emotions as she held her sister tighter. "Well, we're here now. I'm just so glad we got to you in time, before…" Her voice broke. She couldn't bring herself to say the words *before he killed you.*

The thought of Coco sprang to mind. Nia couldn't tell Ivy what had happened to her, either. At least not yet.

Tramping overhead alerted the officers that there was still work to be done. Holding on to Nia's shoulder, Drew said, "Keep your sister safe," before turning to Ivy. "We're so glad you're okay. Once we secure this place, we'll get you to the hospital. In the meantime, we need to arrest these bastards."

Chapter Twenty

Drew and Nia entered Chief Mitchell's office, neither of them able to wipe the smiles off their faces.

"Welcome back, Chief. How are you feeling?" Drew asked, pointing at the sling cradling his boss's left arm. During the shootout Chief Mitchell had been hit in the shoulder, landing him in the hospital for a couple of days, then at home for over a week.

"I'm feeling pretty good thanks to a little time off and eight hundred milligrams of ibuprofen every six hours. What've you two got for me?"

"A lot," Drew replied, sliding a copy of the case file across the desk. "Have you been keeping up with the reports we've emailed to you?"

The chief sat straight up and flipped open the file. "I have. But I wanna hear everything I've missed direct from you two. So have a seat and fill me in."

Raising her hand in the air, Nia said, "Wait, before we get started, can I just share with you that my phone, along with Officer Taylor's, has been ringing off the hook ever since Ethan and Vaughn were arrested?"

"And you're not alone in that," Chief Mitchell replied, chuckling into his coffee mug before taking a long sip. "I think every member of this community has called singing the department's praises. It's safe to say they're all breathing easier these days, thanks to you two. But anyway, let's get to it. Give me a rundown of the interrogations."

"So," Drew began, "as you can probably guess, both men turned on one another the second they started talking. Ethan claimed that Vaughn had been misappropriating the funds he'd donated to his senatorial campaign to bankroll his lavish lifestyle, then accused him of being Juniper's serial killer after he'd had multiple affairs with the murdered women."

"Did he mention what his motive would've been?"

"He did. According to Ethan, Vaughn was worried that the women would leak details of their liaisons and ruin his political career."

"*And* his marriage," Nia added. "But as for Ivy's friend Coco, Ethan alleged Vaughn killed her because she knew about the misused funds. He was afraid she'd blow the whistle."

"What about Ivy?" Chief Mitchell asked. "Vaughn wasn't worried about how much she knew?"

"He was. According to Ethan, Vaughn wanted her dead, too. But Ethan wouldn't allow it, and claims he was keeping her safe at his house so that Vaughn couldn't get to her."

The chief reached across the desk and switched on the fan. "So what did Vaughn have to say for himself?"

"Brace yourself," Drew responded, flipping through his copy of the report. "Because Vaughn presented a completely different side to this sadistic story. Officer Brooks and I started off light. We questioned him about the whole misappropriated campaign funds situation first. He claimed that Ethan was the one who'd misused the money by making illegal donations in hopes of influencing policies that would benefit his businesses."

"Then," Nia interjected, "without being prompted, Vaughn went straight to the murders. He called Ethan a possessive, controlling sociopath who met each of the victims through Someone for Everyone and killed them after they broke things off with him. And according to him, Ethan actually *owns* the dating app."

"A fact that he kept hidden after registering the company as an anonymous limited liability," Drew said.

"Hmph," Chief Mitchell huffed. "Sounds to me like both of these men could've had a hand in all this."

Shifting in her chair, Nia said, "Well, just to add another odd layer to an already twisted story, I actually connected with Ethan through Someone for Everyone. During Vaughn's interrogation, he claimed that since Ethan had been rejected by Ivy, he went after the next best thing."

"Meaning...you?"

"Yes. Exactly. But the night we were supposed to meet up, he was a no-show. Ethan felt as though he'd be betraying Ivy by going out with me. Then when he found out I was one of the lead investigators working the serial killer case, Vaughn claimed that it was Ethan who began stalking and harassing me in hopes of disrupting the investigation."

"Wow," Chief Mitchel grunted. "And the plot thickens..."

Drew threw Nia a look, then slid another report across the table. "Let's get to the good stuff, shall we?"

"What is this?" the chief asked.

"A present from the forensic lab. They processed the evidence in record time and we've already got the results back."

"And?" Chief Mitchell boomed through a widening grin.

"Ethan's DNA matched the evidence collected at the

crime scenes of Katie Douglas, Violet Shields and Ingrid Porter. Those footprint impressions Officer Brooks discovered at Katie's and Violet's crime scenes matched a pair of size eleven Lacrosse AeroHead Sport hunting boots that we took from Ethan's house. Blood evidence found on the soles matched both victims' DNA."

"Good work, Brooks."

"Thank you, sir."

"What about Vaughn? Anything come back on him?"

"Oh, yeah," Nia said. "His DNA matched perspiratory evidence found on the body of Coco Campbell. That gave credence to Ethan's claim that she was aware of the illegalities involving Vaughn's campaign, prompting him to kill her before she could expose his illicit campaign activity. *And…*" Nia pivoted in her seat, giving Drew's shoulder a nudge. "I'll let Drew share the rest."

Chief Mitchell looked up from the report. "Go on. I'm listening."

"So, once Ethan's DNA was entered in the criminal database, one of our department's cold cases was cracked. Remember Linda Echols?"

"Of course. How could I forget?"

"Well, the nightgown Linda was wearing the evening she was murdered contained Ethan's DNA. After speaking with her sister, I found out Linda was a member of Someone for Everyone at the time of her death. We didn't figure that out earlier because she used a fake name on the app."

Pounding his fist onto the desk, the chief rocked against the back of his chair and stared up at the ceiling. "This is the best news I've gotten all year! See, I knew it. I knew you two would somehow get that case solved, too." He shot back up and pointed at Drew. "Aren't you glad that I—"

"Yes," Drew interrupted before Chief Mitchell could finish his statement. "I am *ecstatic* that you insisted I team up with Officer Brooks. Now let's get back to the case before things start getting mushy around here. I still believe that either Ethan or Vaughn caused Tim's car accident due to his involvement in this investigation. But before you even say it, I already know that charge can't be filed since I have no supporting evidence. Nevertheless, I'd be remiss if I didn't at least bring it up."

"Well, we'll continue to keep an eye out. If some sort of evidence does emerge, then we'll file charges. What's the status of the third suspect involved in the shootout?"

"Turns out he was a private security guard hired by Ethan to patrol his home. He's the one who attacked Nia when she first arrived on the scene."

"What's his status?"

"Still in the hospital in critical but stable condition."

Running a hand over his injured shoulder, Chief Mitchell replied, "And once he's discharged he'll go straight to prison. On another note, how did your call go with the district attorney?"

"Great," Drew told him. "She's planning on charging Ethan with four counts of first-degree murder, aggravated kidnapping, attempted murder and conspiracy. Vaughn's being charged first-degree murder, conspiracy, and aiding and abetting. In the meantime, both men are being held without bond."

"Oh, that is *awe*—" The chief groaned, wincing while gripping his shoulder.

"Are you okay?" Nia asked just as his cell phone rang.

"Ugh, I will be. I guess I should've listened to my wife when she told me to stay home a few more days to recuperate. But how could I when all this excitement was happening around here?" He glanced down at the phone. "Speaking of my wife, I'd better grab her call. I'll circle back with you both this afternoon. Thanks again for the great work on this investigation."

"You're welcome, sir."

As Drew followed Nia out of the office, his eyes drifted down to her hips. He shoved his hands inside his pockets, reminding himself that it wouldn't be appropriate to wrap her up in his arms in front of the entire department. Yet in that moment, he felt so full. Emotion was churning inside his chest. With Nia by his side, the pair had managed to solve one of the biggest cases in Juniper's history.

In the midst of it all, memories of their steamy evening together occupied his mind more often than he'd like to admit. As the case continued to heat up, however, there hadn't been time to address that night and talk about whether either of them wanted more.

But now that Ethan and Vaughn were finally behind bars, Drew planned on sitting down with Nia and putting it all on the table, sooner rather than later.

Epilogue

One month later...

Nia pressed her hand against her chest as she approached the door to Army and Lou's. Peering through the frosted glass, she could already tell that she was overdressed. Most patrons were wearing jeans and button-down shirts, or leggings and oversized sweaters. Nia must have missed the memo. She'd chosen a mini tuxedo dress, which she thought would be appropriate since the Juniper PD was gathering to celebrate Drew's promotion to detective.

The moment she stepped inside the club, all eyes were on her. Nia greeted everyone through a stiff smile, squeezing past the crowd of people lining the hallway. She focused on the photos hanging from the wall rather than the ogling expressions on clubgoers' faces.

A loud, familiar roar of laughter echoed from the back of the main room, signaling that her colleagues were gathered near the stage. As she headed that way, a waving hand caught her attention over by the bar.

"Hey, Officer Brooks!"

Nia waved back while Officer Ryan made his way toward her.

"Wow," he uttered, eyeing her from head to toe. "You look...*fantastic*. I don't think I've ever seen you all dressed up like this. Wait, are those real diamonds on your shoes?"

"I wish," she said, laughing as the officer offered her his arm.

"This place is packed tonight," he said. "I'll escort you to the spot where the manager roped off a section for us."

"Thanks, Officer Ryan."

Nia teetered on her heels, struggling not to bump into anyone on the way to their section. The atmosphere was electric as strobe lights shone down on a quartet playing a rendition of Dizzy Gillespie's "Get Happy." The dance floor was packed with couples swinging to the rhythm of the music. And almost everyone there looked to have a drink in their hand and a smile on their face.

Several officers greeted Nia as she approached. While responding with enthusiastic hellos, there was only one thing on her mind—finding Drew.

Her heart stuttered the moment she laid eyes on him. He looked up, as if he could feel her presence. Nia's lips curled into a soft smile. Unlike the other officers, Drew had dressed up, appearing so handsome in his slim-fitting beige suit and crisp white shirt. He tossed her a sexy head nod while his eyes roamed her body. They paused on her arm, which was still nestled within Officer Ryan's. The grin on Drew's face quickly shriveled in a confused scowl.

"We've got a ton of food set up here," the officer told Nia, motioning toward platters filled with buffalo wings, pepperoni flatbread and Philly cheesesteak sliders. "And there's wine, champagne, and of course, beer. If you want a craft cocktail, you'll have to order that at the bar. Or I'd be happy to go over and grab something for you. Anything you want. Just say the word."

Nia's skin prickled as he leaned in closer. She slipped her arm out of his grip and said, "Thanks, but I'm fine for now."

When she walked over to the table and poured herself a glass of ice water, he followed.

"You know," he began, swinging his mug of beer toward the dance floor, "I love this song. Would you like to—"

"Hey, Ryan!" someone called out behind them. "Why don't you at least let Officer Brooks settle in before you try and make a move on her?"

Nia didn't have to turn around to know that it was Drew.

Raising his hands in surrender, Officer Ryan replied, "It isn't even like that. I was just being friendly. No need to get testy, *Detective Taylor.*"

"Ooh, I like the sound of that," Drew retorted. "Thanks, *Officer Ryan.*"

Drew wrapped his arm around Nia's waist and led her to a quiet corner. "Damn, that man wasn't even trying to hide the fact that he's got a crush on you."

"Give him a break. He's a nice guy."

Nia's limbs tingled with nerves as several of their colleagues eyed them curiously. But that wasn't the only reason she was feeling anxious. She had yet to talk to Drew about their intimate night together. There hadn't been much time for personal matters. Soon after the killers were arrested, Drew was hit with the news of his promotion. Adjusting to the position and heftier workload practically took over his life. Nia, however, could no longer suppress the things she needed to get off her chest.

Suddenly, the room felt excruciatingly warm. She almost choked on the thick, steamy air circulating around them.

Taking a long sip of water, Nia fanned her face before setting the glass down.

"What's going on?" Drew asked. "Are you okay?"

"I, um…" she said right before her cell phone buzzed.

"Let me guess. That's your sister texting you."

Nia smiled and showed him the message. "Of course that's Ivy texting me."

Hey big sis! Just checking in, as you've insisted I do every minute of the day. My audition for I Made It to Broadway is tomorrow morning so I'm heading to bed. Wish me luck!

"Nice," Drew responded. "Tell her I said good luck, too. How's her move back to LA going?"

"Good. Really good. She's happy to be back out there working on her craft."

"Glad to hear it." Drew moved in closer, taking Nia's hand in his. "Can I just say that you look absolutely stunning tonight?"

"Thank you. Listen…" She hesitated, distracted by everything going on around them. After glancing over her shoulder to make sure no one was within earshot, she continued. "There's something I need to tell you—"

"Wait," he interrupted. "You must have forgotten that tonight is my big night. Shouldn't you be holding a glass of champagne in celebration of my promotion?"

"Yes, I should be. But…"

"But what?"

"I can't."

"Why not?"

Nia stared into his inquisitive eyes as perspiration dotted her forehead. "That's what I wanted to talk to you about."

"Uh-oh. You're starting to scare me. What's going on?"

She reached out, straightening his lapel before resting her hand against his chest. "I'm pregnant."

Drew's pecs stiffened against her palm as his eyelids fluttered in confusion. "I'm sorry. It's so loud in here. I actually thought you said that you're *pregnant*."

"I did. I am pregnant."

"Wait," he uttered, taking a step back. "Are you…are you serious?"

"I am."

Between his long pause and twitching eyelids, she didn't know what to make of his reaction.

"Nia, please don't play with my emotions like this."

"I wouldn't do that. I'm being totally serious. But your response is starting to scare me. Could you say something? *Anything?* Are you happy? Is this good news? Or…"

A wide grin covered his face.

"Of course this is good news!" he yelled, sweeping Nia off her feet and twirling her around. "Baby," Drew continued, lowering his voice. "We're gonna have a *baby*?"

"Yes. *Yes!*"

She held his face in her hands as their lips met, sealing the sweet moment with a tender kiss.

"Thank you, everyone!" the bandleader boomed into the microphone. "The Jazzets and I are gonna take a brief break while I turn the mic over to one of Juniper's finest, Chief Bruce Mitchell. Take it away, Chief."

Nia slowly pulled away from Drew. "Maybe we should go back over. I have a feeling our boss might be looking for you considering you're the man of the hour and all."

"Maybe we should. And if he calls me up, I'll try my best not to share the most thrilling news I've ever received before in my life with everyone here."

"Oh, *please* try your best not to do that!"

"I promise I won't." Drew held her chin in his hands, gently kissing her one last time before they returned to the group.

Chief Mitchell grabbed the mic and waved at the crowd. "Thank you, Evan. Hey, Detective Taylor, would you mind joining me up here?"

Nia looked on proudly while Drew headed to the stage, clapping the loudest among their cheering colleagues.

"Hey," Cynthia muttered in her ear. "What was that all about?"

"What was what all about?"

"Don't play coy with me. You know what I'm talking about! I saw you and Drew standing over in the corner all hugged up, making googly eyes at each other and whatnot."

"We'll talk about it later," Nia told her without taking her eyes off the stage.

"Yeah, okay. Just know that you *will* be spilling the tea as soon as Chief Mitchell is done with his speech."

The chief held his hands in the air to quiet the crowd. "Detective Taylor, on behalf of myself and the rest of Juniper PD, I would like to congratulate you on your promotion to detective. This well-deserved position is a testament to the outstanding work you've done for the department. Not only are you an excellent investigator, but you are a leader and the prototype of what anyone working in law enforcement should strive to be. We're all lucky to have you on the force, and for many of us, even luckier to call you a friend. Thank you for all that you've done, and most importantly, for spearheading Juniper's serial killer investigation."

Applause rippled through the room as Drew stepped to the mic, nodding humbly. "Thank you so much for those kind words, Chief Mitchell. I don't know if I've earned all that praise just yet, but hey, you're the boss, right? So far be it from me to disagree."

As the crowd broke into laughter, Drew's gaze drifted to Nia.

Oh no, she thought, that intense look in his eyes screaming *Join me onstage*.

"But seriously," Drew continued, "I certainly didn't solve the biggest case of my career alone. I had the help of this entire department. We were like a fine-tuned machine—everyone played their part. There was, however, one person who stood out from the rest."

Everyone turned to Nia. She crossed her arms over her chest, squeezing tightly while wishing the floor would open up and swallow her. Being the center of attention had never been her thing.

Cynthia reached over and uncrossed her arms. "Hey, relax. This is your moment, too. And you deserve it just as much as Detective Taylor. So enjoy it."

Sucking in a swift breath of air, Nia stood taller and shook out her arms. "You're right," she whispered, bracing herself as Drew proceeded.

"Some time ago, Chief Mitchell decided to implement a mentorship program within the department. I had just been assigned to this case and didn't think I'd have the time nor the patience to serve as a mentor. But the chief insisted, and as you know, what he says goes. So here I was, stuck with mentoring Officer Brooks."

The crowd burst into laughter while Drew's shining eyes homed in on Nia, as if she were the only person in the room.

"Then my partner and good friend, Officer Timothy Braxton, got into a terrible car accident. Thank God he made it out alive and is doing well. But back then, while I was concerned with his injuries and overwhelmed with the investigation, Officer Brooks and I were forced together on a deeper level as we worked to solve the case." Drew paused, then held out his hand. "Officer Brooks, would you please join me onstage?"

Loud clapping rattled her eardrums. She remained frozen in her stance, holding her breath while her colleagues chanted her name.

"Nia," Cynthia hissed, giving her a nudge, "get up on that stage and celebrate your accolades, girl!"

Wringing her hands together, she prayed her stilettos would hold her up as she wobbled toward Drew. He took a step down and extended his arm, then led her to the mic.

"Officer Brooks, it goes without saying that this case would not have been solved without you."

"Well, I don't know about all that, but—"

"No, it's true. I'm just glad that I didn't push back *too* hard. Because I wouldn't have realized that I'd been handed the perfect partner." He paused, slipping his hand along the small of her back. "Or gotten the chance to fall in love with you."

Rippling cheers rolled through the entire club. But Nia barely heard them. And when Drew leaned in and kissed her in front of everyone, she didn't care that all eyes were on them.

The moment their lips separated, she murmured, "I'm in love with you, too."

Nia wasn't sure whether he'd heard it. But judging by the beat of his pounding heart, she was certain that he'd felt it.

* * * * *

A SPY'S SECRET

RACHEL ASTOR

Prologue

Something had been off with Justin for weeks.

The change was subtle—most people would never no-tice—but the Sparrow's training taught her to spot incon-sistencies. She couldn't pinpoint what it was, exactly, but he was acting strange. And when he kissed her goodbye that fateful Tuesday morning, a thought hit her like a truck, filled to the brim with trepidation.

Oh God, he's going to ask me to marry him.

Was that even something she wanted?

Judging from the way her stomach flopped when the thought crashed through her brain, it wasn't. Except, Justin was the best guy she knew. She only trusted two people in the world, and he was one of them.

In their business—a business literally built on lies—trust was in short supply, only coming after years of earning it. And Justin had earned it. He'd been her partner for four years before they ever got romantically involved. It was inevitable the relationship would eventually turn into something more.

But they'd only been a couple for eight months.

Of course, time acted differently when you were in the spy business. Forced to depend on someone to keep you safe when they held your life in their hands made everything more intense, heightened. And as her communications tech for years, he'd kept her safe through inconceivable danger.

Lately though, things were less...exciting. Which of course had been inevitable too.

Maybe she was reading too much into things. They'd only been living together a few months, after all. And even that had been more out of convenience when the lease came up on his apartment. She owned this huge, beautiful place with plenty of space, and it seemed like the logical thing to do. But now that the thought had entered her brain, she needed to know.

Justin wouldn't be back for hours.

So she began to search.

Thoughts jolted through her. Thoughts like *too soon*, *bad timing* and... *I have to get out.*

Sparrow's training taught her how to conduct a thorough search while making sure to keep everything intact. Neat. No suspicion aroused.

She came up empty in the house. Deep down she suspected she would. If a ring existed, she knew where it would be.

The shed.

Justin had the small building delivered when he moved in.

"I could never do this stuff in my old apartment, but I've wanted this for years," he'd said.

And it didn't matter to Sparrow. Her property had plenty of space, tucked out of the way from prying eyes, far away from the city. She loved being lost in the desert. And so, the shed was installed. A dark room for his photography. No matter how advanced technology got, Justin swore something about film was truer, more real. There was an art to it.

Sparrow thought his passion was endearing.

What would she do if she found a ring? Make hints that it was too soon? But how could she possibly do that without rousing his suspicions that she'd discovered it? Justin was trained to spot lies too.

Sparrow flung the shed door open and flicked on the light. Everything appeared in order. *Exacting* order. One more thing that differed between the two of them. Sparrow wasn't messy, but she wasn't anal either. Working under-cover meant blending in, and she always thought Justin's obsessive neatness was too over-the-top to blend. But no one would ever discover his perfectionism way out here, so she let it go. Although, when she routinely found her toiletry bottles lined up with the labels all facing front and in order from shortest to tallest, she always wanted to mix them all up into a disorganized group. One time, she did exactly that. He'd come up behind her, grasping her in a tight hug, as if he was physically trying to stop her. "I love that you love a little chaos," he'd said.

"It's hardly chaos," Sparrow replied, pulling gently out of his grasp.

The bottles were once again lined in military precision the next time she came into the room.

The urge now to mix up the shelves of chemicals, film and tools was immense, but she was far too professional. Start at one end and be methodical. Leave no stone—or bottle—unturned.

I have to get out.

Stop, she told herself. *Things are fine. Why do you always search for trouble whenever things are going well?*

Unfortunately, she knew the answer. Because she always found trouble. And when she tipped over a black plastic chemical jug in the middle of ten other black plastic chemical jugs, hearing a telltale click of a door unlatching, she realized she'd found it once again.

For a second, she actually wished she'd discovered what she'd gone looking for. She'd realized in the past few minutes, with absolute clarity, she did not want to marry this man, but still, a ring would have been so much better than this.

Sparrow shot off a quick text before she pulled the trapdoor, which had unlatched from the floor when she tilted the bottle. Annoyance rolled through her. The bastard did this on her own property right under her nose, probably during the Marseille job when he claimed he was sick. She should have caught it. She'd been trained to catch things like this. Trained not to trust anyone. But she did. She trusted Justin. Sure, he had his idiosyncrasies, but this was Justin.

I have to get out.

Sparrow grabbed for her gun, but it wasn't there. Of course it wasn't. All her weapons were in the house. But she couldn't turn back. Irritation and curiosity fueled her forward.

Until a moment ago she believed she had control. Of her life, her career, of everything. But suddenly nothing was true anymore. And with the passion of a thousand sports fans whose team had just lost, she hated that she'd been played.

The bunker was pitch-black. She lit the screen on her phone to search for a switch, but there was only a simple light bulb with a string. She pulled it, sucking in a breath, bracing herself for anything.

Still, she was not prepared for what she saw.

Surveillance.

A typical spread. Photos of the target. Maps of where they'd been. Movements tracked down to the minute. Schedules.

But it was the face of the target, staring back from all those photos, that almost broke her.

Her face.

Some of the pictures were from before she'd even met Justin. Years before. Of her shopping, eating…sleeping. Newspaper articles from when her parents were killed ten years ago. Family history. Not that there was anyone left anymore.

The pictures and articles grew older as she moved down the wall.

She reached up to pull the string on the second light above her.

Click.

No light came on. In an instant she understood her fatal mistake. A barely audible squeal pierced her ears. And then the blast.

Blinding, deafening, jolting her forward. Backward? She didn't know.

Pain.

And as the world began to go black, Sparrow had only one thought left.

I have to get out.

Chapter One

Five years later...

Zach was annoyed. This time of year was always so...much. Everyone in town seemed to think the annual Apple Cider Festival was the best thing ever, and sure, most of the people in town made half their year's salary during the week as several thousand people from all over the state and beyond flocked to town, so he could kind of understand, but man, all these tourists were just so...touristy.

The bell above the coffee shop door chimed, his shoulders rising further toward his ears. It was the third time in the last five minutes he'd heard its tinkling ring, messing with his focus.

"Oh my gawd, this place is so stinking cuuuuute," the woman who'd entered said.

Zach closed his eyes and pulled a long breath in through his nose. *Breathe*, he tried to encourage himself, *just breathe.*

"Welcome to The Other Apple Store," Ava said from behind the counter.

Somehow, she actually seemed to enjoy when these people barged into her life and her store. Of course she did—that was Ava Katz. Good with everybody. Always kind. Always patient. Although she'd only been in town for five years, and he'd been here his whole life, so maybe the novelty hadn't worn off for her yet.

The woman whose jangle interrupted Zach turned to her friend, gasping with excitement fit for a teen pop concert. "Did you hear that? The Other Apple Store! Like the computer one except, like, this one actually sells real apple stuff."

"I know!" her counterpart squealed.

They erupted into a shriek slash giggle slash "oh my gawd" fest. And Zach just knew they'd gone shopping for their Apple Cider Festival uniforms of cable knit sweaters, boots with wool socks peeking out and winter hats with giant pom-poms at some overpriced hipster store too. A small growling groan escaped him before he could catch it.

Ava beamed while Zach tried not to say anything more under his breath. She caught his eye and pumped her eyebrows at him like she was having the time of her life.

Which, knowing Ava, she probably was.

It was one of the things he loved most about her—she seemed to find genuine enjoyment in almost anything.

He shook the thought from his head, reminding himself he wasn't supposed to love anything about Ava. She was off limits—too important a friend—a friendship he couldn't risk with silly, romantic notions.

Maybe if he'd made a move in those first months after she'd arrived in town…but that time was long gone. He remembered the first time he saw Ava, laughing and joking with the movers like she'd known them all her life.

She'd stopped him in his tracks.

She was beautiful, but it wasn't just the way she looked. There was something about the way she treated the movers. Like kindness was her religion.

But Chloe had been his focus, only five back then, and time for romance didn't exist. Now, all these years later, Ava and Zach had both put each other so wholly in the friend zone it was far too late for anything else. Besides, he'd learned that lesson with Kimberly. Never date a friend. There was too much to lose.

And he honestly didn't know who he'd be anymore without Ava's friendship.

It was too important.

She was too important.

Another flurry of giggles shocked him out of his thoughts, the ladies trying—and failing—to pick something out at the bakery counter.

"Everything looks so goooooood," one of them said.

Zach couldn't stop his eyes from rolling. They weren't wrong, but why did they have to be so loud and all "Look at me! Look at me!" about everything? But Ava never lost her hundred-watt smile, her patience rivaling that of a saint. She shot him a quick wink, which reminded him he didn't have to be such an old curmudgeon about the festival, but honestly, these people were a nightmare to deal with. He thanked his lucky stars he didn't have to work part-time in the gift shop anymore like he did in high school. Talk about a horror show.

"Apple Fritter, Caramel Apple Cake, Apple Spiced Cookies. You sure do have a lot of apple stuff," the second tourist said.

"Well," Ava replied, still genuinely charmed by the women, "it is the Apple Cider Festival after all." Her smile grew even wider, and her eyes sparkled.

"Oh my gawd, you're right!" the first woman squealed. She jump-turned toward her friend and gasped. "I just had the *best* idea. We should buy one of everything!"

Her friend's eyes went wide as if the woman had discovered gold or cured cancer or something. She began to nod vigorously. "We totally should! We are here all weekend, after all!"

Ava packed up their enormous order and sent them on their way with complimentary cups of apple cider you would have thought were filled with diamonds the way they'd reacted.

"This town is so friendly! No wonder Trixie and Alistair recommended this place so highly."

Zach had never been so happy to hear the little bell over the door as he watched them walk out. The sigh he let out might have been a bit more audible than he'd intended.

"You okay there, Zach?" Ava called from behind the counter.

He looked at her, more serious than he'd ever been. "I honestly don't know how you do it."

She shrugged. "I'll never get sick of this. All the people, the energy, the excitement…the apples," she said. He didn't know how she could routinely make her eyes twinkle the way they did, like a kid on Christmas morning. "And speaking of apples," she continued, sneaking into the kitchen and returning with a plate covered in a napkin. "I present to you—" she paused both for effect and to fling off the napkin with a flourish "—the Apple Butter Glazed Spiced Pecan Blondie!"

He stared at her, expressionless. "The name's a bit of a mouthful, isn't it?"

But Ava simply grinned. "Not as much of a mouthful as you're about to have," she said, grabbing the fork off his plate and shoving a bite into his mouth before he could say another word.

And of course, the dessert was perfection. Like everything she baked. As he chewed the buttery, sweet goodness, he couldn't help but wonder how he'd gotten so lucky as to be her resident taste-tester.

"That is good," he said, "really good. But how come you're always trying your new stuff out on me?"

"Ah, there are two reasons," Ava said. "First, you're always here."

He tilted his head in agreement. He basically considered The Other Apple Store his unofficial coworking space.

"And second," she continued, her smile widening, "if even you, Old Mr. Grumpy Pants, like something, I know I've got a winner."

And as Zach's eyes rolled so hard he nearly saw his brain, hers sparkled brighter than ever.

HONESTLY, AVA LOVED how grumpy Zach was. Like her very own little Grumpy Cat in human form. He came off unbearably gruff to new people, but once you got to know him, everybody loved him—even his grumpy ways. Especially his grumpy ways. Because he was the most generous, empathetic, helpful old grump anyone could be lucky enough to know.

"Besides, you were the first person to welcome me to Ambrosia Falls, so I guess I have a soft spot for ya," she said, shoving his shoulder a little.

He smiled.

She remembered the first time she'd seen that smile. Her first day in town had been a long one...after an even longer month. She'd been holed up in the safe house all alone—not supposed to even glance outside, though she obviously took a peek once in a while. A person isn't meant to not see the outdoors, to not get a glimpse of sunshine.

She didn't get much of a say in what her house would be like—she couldn't exactly leave protection to go house shopping, but she did get to pick out her furniture—thank you online shopping! She could only hope everything would go with whatever house she landed in. Ava purposely picked things different from her old place, which had been minimalist, stark and modern, and thank goodness she did. The giant old Eaton farmhouse would have looked ridiculous decked out like that. But she'd chosen comfortable and cozy things, and after a bustling day of movers and unpacking, things felt more settled.

But it had been so...quiet.

Alone again, Ava thought. Hadn't she always known she was destined to live like this? To always be on the outside looking in? Why would a new town be any different? Except she was out now. She wasn't a spy anymore. She wasn't Sparrow. Relief and a little sadness washed over her. For a while she had loved that life. The excitement, the danger... but it got old faster than she had thought.

In theory Ava didn't have to worry about letting people get close anymore. That version of her disappeared off the face of the earth, replaced by this new "normal" person.

But what did that even mean?

And then Zach showed up at her door with a welcome to the neighborhood gift, a six-pack of beer. The night had been so hot the flyaway tendrils that had escaped Ava's ponytail stuck to the back of her neck as she opened the door and got her first glimpse of the man who would become so important to her.

"Hey," he'd said and introduced himself. "This, uh...this was all I had." He lifted the six-pack, looking a little sheepish. "I wanted to bring a bottle of wine or something, but the store was closed and I figured it was better than nothing…"

"It's perfect," Ava said, charmed by the way his words trailed off and he rubbed the back of his neck, clearly uncomfortable. But with the impeccable manners of someone raised in a small town where community meant everything, he couldn't leave a new neighbor waiting without something to welcome them home.

Little did he know how perfect the gift really was, at the perfect time in the perfect little town.

They didn't chat much that night, but his smile, along with the beer, did make her feel welcome. She'd been so terrified normal wasn't possible, yet here she was, normal flourishing all around her.

The bells chimed above the door again, and Zach's face grimaced automatically, but when he saw who entered, his expression quickly changed.

Only one person could put a smile on his face like that. Sadly, it wasn't her, Ava thought.

"Hey, Chloe," she said, not having to turn to know who'd come in.

"Hey, Ava," came the adorable chirp of a voice. "How is your day going?"

Ava turned and smiled. Chloe had to be the most adorable kid ever. Ten going on thirty, she loved to spend time at the coffee shop, preferring grown-up conversations to the ones with her friends. What kind of kid asks the adults in their life how their day is going before the adults get the chance to ask first?

"Even better now that you're here, kid," Ava said, then gave Chloe a sideways, mischievous look. "Got a new one for ya." She held the blondie plate out and grabbed a clean fork off the counter.

Chloe's eyes got wide as she slipped into the booth opposite her dad. "A new one?"

Ava nodded, opening her mouth to speak, but Zach interrupted her.

"Don't ask her what it's called unless you have until next Monday for her to tell you. Just eat it, trust me."

Chloe laughed and nodded, knowing full well how Ava liked to name her recipes after the long list of ingredients. "Don't worry, we'll come up with something amazing."

"I'm counting on it, kid," Ava said, glancing up out the window.

She loved this time of year. The festival helped stoke a tiny longing for something else in her life—something a bit more exciting. She loved this new life, but it was so very opposite of how her world used to be. And sure, a small-town fruit festival wasn't exactly the epitome of intrigue, but the whole town came to life with activity, and that was good enough to quell the yearning.

But as she took in the view of Ambrosia Falls—the glorious colors on the autumn trees, the ever-growing groups of tourists, everybody working hard to erect temporary tents and booths—something seemed…off.

She crossed her arms and tilted her head, trying to figure out what bothered her.

She moved slowly away from Zach and Chloe, toward the door, opening it slowly, the gears of her mind cranking.

The seasonal water tower. Was it…swaying?

Ava glanced at the trees surrounding the town and while a few leaves fluttered gently in the light breeze, it certainly wasn't enough to make the enormous makeshift water tower—filled only once a year to cover the needs of the town as the population quadrupled in size—sway.

And then she heard the groan.

Ava's eyes darted to the tents and cloth-roofed booths near the bottom of the tower.

"Move!" she yelled at the top of her lungs, her feet already in motion.

People turned to see what the commotion was about, but not a single soul appeared the least bit alarmed. "Move!" she screamed again, realizing Annie's booth—the one filled with a year's worth of crocheted sweaters, both for people and pets, as well as hats and baby booties—stood directly under the tower.

The tower began to tilt.

Ava kept screaming, "Move! The tower! Move!" as a few people started to figure out what was going on, their eyes nearly popping out of their heads before they turned to flee.

Annie would never be able to get out of harm's way in time. She didn't have the best hearing, and the fact she needed a walker definitely wouldn't help.

The sound of wood splintering must have finally reached Annie. She began to turn, trying to see what was going on behind her, but there was no time.

Ava dove at her, circling her arm under Annie's the way one might saving a drowning victim and pulling her as far away from the inevitable disaster as she could, hoping she wouldn't do any physical damage to the poor woman.

The sound of the crash brought with it a flashback of the fateful night back at the desert bunker when Ava's whole world imploded, both literally and figuratively. Screams erupted as water exploded from the enormous plastic tank, drowning the street, the booths, and soaking all of the people standing nearby.

An explosive squawking came from Miss Clara's booth as her prize rooster, Captain Applebottom—the fair's unofficial mascot for the past three years running—was hit with the surge. Feathers and water flung from the cage violently before Miss Clara rushed to soothe the poor creature who was somehow, miraculously, still clucking.

When the water finally settled, flowing rapidly over Ava's feet and into the sewer grates on the edges of Main Street, Annie turned to Ava, blinking. "Are you alright, dear?" she asked, calm as could be.

Ava nodded, although she felt more than a little bit away from alright. "Yeah," she said, still panting. "Yeah, I'm alright. Are you?"

Annie looked down at herself as if checking to make sure. "Yes, yes, I think so, dear. Thank you for saving me."

Ava gave the woman a hug—more for her own benefit than Annie's—and said, "Yeah, of course. Anytime."

"Ava!" Zach's terrified scream rose above the rest.

She turned as Zach rushed up to her, putting his hands on her shoulders and surveying her head to toe. "What the hell were you thinking, running in like that?"

"Well." Annie's reply came quicker than Ava could form words. She always had that trouble whenever Zach touched her, no matter how innocent it was. "She was saving my life, of course," Annie said, as if delivering any old sentence.

Ava supposed poor Annie was a bit in shock, looking at her booth. The creations she'd taken all year to make with love and craftsmanship had become flattened mats of soggy yarn, floating pitifully in the muddy water.

"I wonder how on earth something like this could have happened," Annie said, expressing the words everyone was thinking.

Chapter Two

Zach was more than a little relieved everyone appeared okay as he tried to process the situation. Ava had just…taken off. Dove headfirst into danger. He thought he knew her pretty well, had spent nearly every day of the past five years with her, but he honestly would have pegged her as a flight-er, not a fighter.

He was also embarrassed to admit he was more than a little turned on by her bravery and, holy mother-of-pearl, the way she looked with her clothes soaked and clinging to every inch of her. He shoved those thoughts as deep and as far into the corner of his mind as possible.

He still held Ava's shoulders, double-and triple-checking that she was all in one piece. One nonsmashed piece. The water tower had come so close. From his angle he swore it came straight down on them. Right on top of poor Annie and… Ava.

What if something had happened to her? The thought made him instantly sick, and that realization made him even sicker. He'd been working so hard to keep her at arm's length, to center himself solidly in the friend zone.

He lowered his arms and took a sheepish step back, clearing his throat.

"We need to figure out what happened here," Barney from the candle stand said. "Do you think this was an accident?"

For the first time, Zach considered the possibility it might not be.

"Of course it was an accident, you fool," said Miss Clara, the one person in town you could count on to always give Barney a hard time.

"You know, Clara, contrary to your belief, there are things in this world even you don't know every answer to," Barney said. Unfortunately, you could always count on Barney to volley that hard time right back.

The two started bickering like they were in grade school, the volume rising quickly. Others tried to jump in and calm them down, but Zach had watched the scene play out a hundred times before, and it would never work. He raised his hands to his mouth and let out a deafening whistle, quickly regretting it when every eye in town turned toward him.

"Look, none of us knows what happened here. Maybe instead of arguing all day, we could, I don't know, examine the tower and see if we can figure it out?" He glanced from one person to the next to the next, but not a single one backed him up.

Until he locked eyes with Ava. "Sounds reasonable," she said, her breath surprisingly back to normal already, not at all like she'd recently dead-sprinted to save a friend. Suddenly, everyone standing on the street agreed. Zach tried not to take it personally that he'd lived in Ambrosia Falls his entire life, was related to some of these people, yet the moment Ava opened her mouth, they hung on her every word.

Not that he could blame them.

"Well, you guys take care of it then," Barney said, apparently all too happy to spout on about needing to figure everything out, but not too keen on actually doing it.

"Um, who's taking care of it?" Ava asked.

"You two," he said, vaguely waving toward Zach and Ava.

"Makes sense to me," Miss Clara said. "You're the mystery expert, after all."

Zach closed his eyes. "Seriously? The first time in the history of the world you two agree on something, and that something is to send a mystery writer off to solve a real mystery?"

"Sure," Barney said, without a hint of irony.

Zach opened his mouth to argue, but the crowd had already started dispersing, beginning the cleanup before more tourists could arrive.

Ava put her hand on his shoulder. Her touch sent an all-too-familiar jolt through him. "It's fine," she said. "Maybe the whole thing was engineered poorly or something. I mean, a giant tub of water on those spindly wooden legs. This was bound to happen at some point."

"Shouldn't we call the authorities or something?"

Ava shrugged. "I guess if we find something suspicious, but you know as well as I do that unless something catastrophic happens, we're so far out in the middle of nowhere we don't hit anyone's radar."

He let out a long, slow breath. "Yeah," he said, remembering the time Hanson's horse got stolen. The law took six days to come out to investigate, and even then, it was a reserve officer who'd come…one Hanson suspected was sent due to some kind of a hazing situation.

"Honestly, I think we're about as good a choice as any," Ava said. "At least we'll keep it together. Imagine some of the conspiracy theories Jackson or Mae might come up with?" she asked, the spark back in her eyes.

Zach sighed. "Fine, let's get this over with."

They made their way through the rubble, mud and flurry of townsfolk cleaning up with no regard for the fact they might be ruining evidence. They eventually got to the area where the wooden stumps of the base were still sticking out of the ground, the wood splintered and shattered.

"Doesn't look like the legs were cut or anything," Zach said, easily pulling a sharp piece of wood from the jagged stump.

"Termites?" Ava asked.

"I don't know. Might be rot, but either way this doesn't look like anything too nefarious, other than an incredible lack of safety inspection."

Ava nodded. "Well, case closed, I guess. Come on, I'll buy you a beer for the good work. I feel like we both deserve one."

"Yeah." Zach watched as Ava moved back toward the coffee shop, tucking a piece of wet hair behind her ear as she carefully picked her way through the wreckage.

But something still felt off about the whole thing. The water tower was quite literally on its last legs, but still. Why today? The wind wasn't blowing that hard. And what were the chances the tower would fall in the exact direction to put people in harm's way?

He shook his head and threw the splinter to the ground.

Perhaps he wasn't the best person to do any investigating. His writer's imagination definitely got the best of him sometimes.

AVA WATCHED AS the last of the vendors closed up their booths for the night. The rest of the afternoon had gone by in a blur of mud and tourists and baked goods. Zach had been surprisingly focused after the incident, incredibly productive over in his corner frantically typing the afternoon away.

She flipped the sign on the door to Closed, then finally cracked the beer she had promised Zach and set it on his table. She cracked another for herself and slipped into the booth opposite him.

"Well, that was a day," she said.

He slid his laptop aside and pulled the beer toward him. "Definitely something."

Ava took a swig. "Looks like the excitement gave you a shot of inspiration though," she said, motioning to his laptop.

"Yeah, I guess so. Powered through a chapter and a half."

Ava raised her eyebrows. "Nice."

They talked about what happened, then a bit about the festival, and went on to everything else under the sun. Chloe's grandma was with her for the evening, so Zach was in no hurry.

Funny, no matter how much time they spent together, they never ran out of things to say.

But Ava always wondered about one thing, and with three beers behind her, she found the courage to bring up the subject that had been on her mind for years.

"You've never told me what happened with Chloe's mom." She held her breath.

For as long as she'd known Zach, he had been single, and she was more than a little curious why. Then again, she supposed she hadn't been involved with anyone either.

She expected him to wave her off, but to her surprise, he let out a breath and began to speak.

"I thought we wanted the same things. Kimberly was a little hard to please, but I felt like I pulled it off, at least at first. My debut book had been moderately successful, and some real money started to come in, so we were living the dream, I guess," he said, shrugging.

Ava nodded, not wanting to say anything, scared to break the spell.

"We'd been best friends ever since we were kids. She lived down the street, and we'd known each other since before we started grade school. Then when we did go to school, we kept being best friends. We depended on each other for everything."

"Sounds perfect," Ava said, nodding for him to continue.

"It was...mostly. She was adventurous, you know? And I was too for a while. After graduation we went on all these trips...white-water rafting, mountain excursions, zip lining, that sort of stuff. Life was fun, don't get me wrong, but I always felt like I was playing a part. Like it wasn't really *my* life."

Ava could relate so much more than he would ever know.

"She liked the lifestyle more than I did, but we were best friends, and making her happy made me happy." Zach squirmed in his seat a little.

"You know, for someone who makes their living as a storyteller, you don't seem to be all that comfortable when you're telling one out loud."

He grinned. "That's the beauty of the computer. No one to judge until you know you've got it right. I can make as many changes as I want until I'm satisfied."

Ava's neck went hot, trying not to think about what Zach would look like satisfied. She cleared her throat. "I'm not judging you, Zach."

He nodded. "Yeah, I know." He took a long swig of his beer.

"So you were living the dream. What happened?"

Zach tilted his head. "I don't know exactly. I mean, we never discussed having kids, but I assumed, like a fool, I guess, that we both wanted the same things. She got pregnant and, well, it spooked her. She wasn't sure if she wanted a baby, but me," he said, staring off, a grin—elated, but somehow with a sadness to it too—spread across his face, "after knowing a part of me was growing into a tiny human, I couldn't think about anything else. I thought I wanted this life of adventure and travel and freedom, but the second even the *idea* of a kid entered the picture, I became obsessed."

Ava smiled. "Sounds about right."

He nodded. "It's who I am now, but I was a different person back then. I was scared too, but I convinced her to have the baby. And Chloe came along, and we tried for a while, Kimberly tried for a while, but motherhood didn't come naturally. She said she was never meant to be a mom and she left."

"I can't imagine how someone could leave their child."

Zach shrugged. "She was never cut out for it. I suppose I shouldn't have pushed, but I wanted to be a parent so badly. And Kim tries. I mean, she's a parental disaster, but she sends Chloe letters and presents and tries to stop in once in a while, but for the most part, Chloe and I are on our own."

Ava felt a squeeze in her heart. This man she admired so much—tried so hard *not* to admire as much as she did—had done such an amazing job raising a great kid all by himself. "Must have been hard on you all these years."

"The dad part hasn't been hard at all. I feel like you just love your kid and try to make good choices and do your best. The hardest part was losing my best friend, you know?"

Ava didn't know. She couldn't remember ever having a best friend, but she nodded anyway. "I'm sorry. It's hard to lose people." That she did know.

Zach nodded, drifting in his own thoughts. "Maybe Kimberly and I were never meant to be romantically involved. We probably should have stuck with being friends. Everything got screwed up once we became a couple."

Ava nodded. "There's always the chance you're going to lose the friendship if things don't work out."

"Exactly," Zach said. "But I did get the most important thing in my life out of the deal, so I suppose it was meant to be."

Ava smiled. Nodded. *Meant to be.* How nice to live a life where you could believe in "meant to be" and "happily-ever-after and all those fairy-tale notions.

"Well, I guess I better leave you to it," Zach said, probably realizing she still had a lot of cleaning up to do before returning at dawn to start tomorrow's baking.

And the day's baking would be intense. Two assistants were coming in at 5:00 a.m. in order to keep up with the demand.

"Thanks for the beer," he said, packing up his computer.

"And thanks for the story," she said. "I thought I knew almost everything about you, but I guess there's always more to learn."

She hated all the secrets she would never be able to tell him.

As Zach stood to leave, a frantic knock sounded at the door.

Zach sighed. "What now?"

Ava shot him a twinkling smile and went to unlock the door. Miss Clara burst through, nearly knocking her over.

"Miss Clara, what is it? Are you okay?" Zach asked.

"No! No, I'm not okay. You guys…" she said, trying to catch her breath, clearly beside herself. "Captain Applebottom is missing!"

Chapter Three

"This can't be a coincidence," Miss Clara said, looking around as if she might find Captain Applebottom right there in the room.

"A coincidence with what?" Zach asked.

"The water tower, of course," Miss Clara said, though Zach couldn't, for the life of him, figure out what one could possibly have to do with the other. "This has to be the work of those Pieville hooligans."

Zach nearly spit out a laugh trying to imagine the charming older ladies of Pieville creeping around town all dressed up in "hooligan" outfits, which, in his mind, consisted of head-to-toe black, perhaps with those eye masks that tied in the back of their various gray/purple/blue and heavily permed hairstyles. But he couldn't even get a snort out before Miss Clara went on.

"Everybody knows they've been trying for years to take over the festival scene around these parts—I mean, they changed the name of their entire town just to wrangle a few tourists—but if they think they can beat our cozy charm and friendly atmosphere, they have another thing coming."

"Friendly atmosphere. Right," Zach said, risking a glance

at Ava, who looked like she was enjoying every second of Miss Clara's rant.

He couldn't understand how Ava never seemed to tire of the ridiculous, and endless, "emergencies" the people of this town overreacted to on the daily. Or how she seemed to be enchanted by it instead of the correct reaction, which was, of course, exasperation.

"I'm sure Captain Applebottom is fine," he said in his most soothing voice.

Ugh, he hated saying the name of that damned chicken. The bird itself was okay, and he got that it was an homage to the Apple Cider Festival, but why did Miss Clara have to go and name him something so embarrassing to say out loud?

"Fine?" Miss Clara said, her voice screeching a bit. "Fine? That poor creature experienced the shock of his lifetime when the water tower came down this morning, and on top of that, now he's been abducted! How could you possibly say you're sure he's fine?" She broke off, pacing and muttering something under her breath that sounded a bit like, "Don't these people have any idea how important my sweet boy is to this town?"

"But we checked the tower, Miss Clara. You know we didn't find any signs of foul play," Zach said.

Miss Clara stopped her pacing to squint at Zach in a way that revealed how little she thought of his detective skills. "Yes, maybe the wood was rotting a little on the tower, but that does not mean there was no foul play! Anyone could have pushed it over."

Zach tried to picture what that would entail, but came up a bit short. To even think of standing under something, with all that weight teetering above—knowing the structure was so rickety it could simply be pushed over—a person would have to be about as smart as a Popsicle stick…or have gargantuan balls of steel. Or a death wish, he supposed.

"I bet it was that dastardly Mayor Harlinger," Miss Clara continued. "She's been after this town for years."

Dastardly?

Pieville's Mayor Harlinger was a kindhearted seventy-something woman who originally hailed from the Deep South, which she loved to tell everyone about as often as possible.

"Miss Clara," Ava said, grabbing the woman's hands to get her to focus.

And thank goodness for that, Zach thought, since he had no idea what he was supposed to say after the "dastardly" comment.

"I know this is incredibly upsetting," Ava continued. "I'm upset too—and I can't imagine what Captain Applebottom is going through, but if we just think for a moment, we'll all realize that if someone has actually taken him, it's probably because they love him so much and just want a little quality time with him."

Miss Clara blinked at Ava a few times. "You might be right," she said. "Captain Applebottom is a good, good boy, and he loves everyone. But—" tears starting to glint in her eyes "—but what if I never see him again? He's everything I've got in this world."

If asked, Zach would never have admitted it, but he had to swallow a bit of a lump forming in his throat.

Over a chicken.

But damn it, he was a pretty cool chicken. And Zach had no idea how he would ever tell Chloe if something bad happened to Captain Applebottom. The girl had a soft spot for every animal she'd ever met.

"And you're sure the cage wasn't accidentally left open?" he asked, bracing for the full impact of Miss Clara, who let out a tired sigh.

"Of course I'm sure the cage wasn't accidentally left open."

"And there was no ransom note or any other clue?" Zach continued, quite bravely, if he did say so himself.

"I'm pretty sure I would have noticed something like that," Miss Clara answered, and to her credit, she barely even rolled her eyes.

Zach figured he'd better not press his luck by mentioning the unhelpful thought about vagrant coyotes that happened to be flitting around in his mind.

"Come on," he said, holding his elbow out to Miss Clara. "Why don't I walk you home? It's going to be a long day for everyone tomorrow, especially Ava here, and we should all get some sleep. None of us will be any good for—" he cleared his throat "—Captain Applebottom if we don't get some rest."

Miss Clara nodded absently. "Yes, I need to be at my best for the captain," she said. "He's going to need me more than ever tomorrow."

Zach turned back to give Ava a wave good-night, trying his best not to wish it was a very different woman walking out on his arm.

AVA WAVED AND mouthed a quick *thank you* as Zach escorted Miss Clara out of the store. She had a few things left on her list of things to do before she crashed for the night, but if she hurried, she figured she could still get in six solid hours before the alarm went off again. In about equal measure, she was both thankful and bummed that the Apple Cider Festival only came around once a year.

And even with the drama of the day, she still had the baking contest to think about. Sure, the Apple Butter Glazed Spiced Pecan Blondie could be a contender, but she didn't think it had quite the wow factor to win. And being the owner of the town's bakery/coffee shop, she had to make a good showing, or she'd never live it down. And frankly, it wouldn't be great for business, either. Not that it would stop people from coming—she was the only bakery in town, after all—but it would be a year of listening to people be all like, "This is okaaaay, but it's not like she won the contest or anything," and trying to get Ava to lower the prices on her "subpar" baked goods. On top of that, depending on who did win the contest, there could be an entire year of razzing to put up with, and Ava had to admit there were people in Ambrosia Falls she'd gladly take a razzing from, and people she would prefer…um, not to.

But she was way too tired to think up any more appleliciousness tonight, even if she only had a few more days to figure it out. Maybe her subconscious could work on it while she slept.

Ava lowered the blinds, locked the front door and turned off the lights as she made her way through the kitchen to the back door, where her car was parked. She grabbed her purse off the coatrack and came to an abrupt halt.

The back door wasn't locked. Which was completely weird, since the back door was always locked. The kitchen was often empty since she spent so much time out front with customers, so she never risked having it unlocked. And as far as she knew, no one she ever had as extra help on busy days had ever forgotten to lock it either. In fact, none of her fill-in staff even used that door. Unless someone had propped the door open to get some air flow or something, but it kind of seemed strange they wouldn't ask first.

Still, nothing else seemed out of the ordinary and nothing seemed to be missing, so Ava made a mental note to talk with the girls about it, then headed home to catch some much-deserved and much-needed z's.

THE LARGE FLOOR-TO-CEILING windows in the coffee shop made it easy for the Crow to execute his surveillance. These past five years of searching had been the longest of his life, but as he watched from his nesting spot in the bushes across the street, he was finally getting a good look at the Sparrow's every movement.

Sloppy.

Someone like her should know better than to be in the open like that. Of course, it had taken him five years to track her down, so maybe hiding in plain sight wasn't as terrible a strategy as he always assumed.

But none of those thoughts were taking up the most real estate in his mind.

That honor went to the man.

The lackluster nobody of a small-town guy nowhere near exciting enough for the Sparrow. The man who was clearly putting on airs when he made a big show of escorting the old lady home.

Pathetic.

The Crow didn't want him to be of even the slightest consequence—he certainly didn't seem worth it—but after seeing the way the Sparrow interacted with him, the Crow knew something was up. He'd been watching the Sparrow for so long, far before she even knew who he was, far before he'd made her fall in love with him. And if there was anyone on this earth who could read her body language and those sparkling expressions on her face, it was him. He liked to think he knew her better than she knew herself.

Which was how he knew precisely what was going through her mind at that exact moment. She'd be wondering how the darn back door had gotten unlocked. She'd try to explain it away, of course—maybe she'd simply forgotten to lock it herself—but it would niggle at her.

Exactly the way he planned.

He was fine playing the long game. It had been a hell of a long game so far. A few extra hours or days certainly weren't going to bother the Crow. He was a professional who never missed his mark.

Especially now that he'd finally found the only mark that mattered. The mark that had gotten away.

Chapter Four

A couple days later Zach stared out the window, wishing he had a cup of coffee in his hand. It was the same thought he had every morning. He knew he could easily just make it and put himself out of his daily misery, but the payoff when he finally did get that first morning sip was too good to change his routine. Because if he was being honest with himself—something he tried very hard not to do most of the time—he couldn't live without the other payoff of waiting.

Seeing Ava.

Without the excuse of the coffee, he'd have no reason to go to The Other Apple Store until at least lunchtime, and then what would he do with his mornings? Sit at home and try to write? It was plausible, certainly. There was a whole room on the second floor of the house that he'd made into an office. It had an incredible view of the forest behind the backyard, and he'd spent months picking out the right chair that was both comfortable and something he deemed worthy of an author—a high-backed leather number with carved wooden armrests. Any old office chair would not be fit for writing the Great American Novel, after all.

He almost laughed at the thought. He'd never get a word down in that room upstairs. No, he was one of those writers who apparently needed a muse. A damned muse. The notion of it made him feel ridiculous, like a kid who was way too old believing in the tooth fairy, but he didn't know what else to call it. All he knew was after Kimberly left all those years ago, he thought he might never be able to write another word. And he didn't…for a long time. Not until a certain someone moved in next door and all of a sudden Zach felt an itch in his fingertips to write again.

On the days he was being *very* honest with himself—an extremely rare occurrence if he could help it—somewhere deep down he understood it was really that he'd finally found another person who was not so much a muse, but more of a "reason" to do what he did. An inspiration to do something productive with his life. Someone to impress, he supposed. And whenever Zach was around Ava, he simply wanted her to see how hard he was working, which, in turn, made him actually work hard. A convoluted way of getting things done, but effective nonetheless.

Of course, these were all fleeting thoughts Zach routinely pushed way the hell back to the far reaches of his mind, preferring silly notions like muses to explain the phenomenon of his productivity around certain…important people. Not that he'd ever tell another soul about the muse theory either, but it helped him reason away all the time he spent close to Ava.

All those unwelcome thoughts moseyed through his mind as he stared out his front window looking over at Ava's place. Another thought about the fog tried to weasel its way into his brain—something about it being out of place on the warm morning—but it didn't have a chance to settle in before his thoughts turned back to their previous subject. She wouldn't even be there at this hour, but still, he couldn't help but wonder what she was doing at that exact moment.

She'd have gone into the shop to start the day's baking a couple of hours ago already—he always heard her car door slam in the mornings. He knew she tried to be as quiet as possible, and he'd told her the thousand times she'd asked that he never heard a thing, but the truth was, over the years his sleeping pattern had adjusted itself so he would be awake to hear it. Not that it would ever happen in a million years, but it wouldn't hurt to be on similar schedules with Ava for... whatever reason might present itself down the road. Plus, you know, early bird, and worms and everything.

He allowed his mind to wander, an indulgence he only allowed himself once a day during his morning stare out the window, always wishing that bloody cup of coffee he wanted so badly was in his hand.

"Why is it smoky?" Chloe's voice jolted him out of his thoughts...and almost jolted him right out of his skin.

"Jeez, kid, you can't sneak up on an old guy like that."

Chloe rolled her eyes. "Well, if you'd stop daydreaming at the window every morning, maybe you wouldn't be so jumpy. And you're not that old, Dad."

For his own self-preservation, Zach tried to ignore the "that" in her sentence. "I am not daydreaming," he said.

"You were totally daydreaming," she said, and actually patted him on the shoulder. "But it's okay. I get it's part of a writer's job to be all up in your head half the time. Part of the job."

The job. Right. That's definitely what he'd been daydreaming about.

"So what's with the smoke?" she asked again.

"Smoke?" Zach asked, turning back toward the window.

He supposed the fog did look a bit like smoke.

"Yeah. Since you were staring at it so hard, I thought you would have figured out where it was coming from."

It was a bit strange the way it was hovering there, floating ever so slowly like it was just out for a stroll.

He leaned in closer to the window. "I think that actually is smoke," he said.

"Uh, yeah," Chloe said—for a ten-year-old, she really did have the sarcasm of a teenager already. "That's why I was asking."

Worry started to fill Zach's mind. Where the heck *was* it coming from? Suddenly he realized there were few explanations for the smoke that could end well.

"Come on," he said, handing Chloe her lunch as she was grabbing one of Ava's famous apple cinnamon bagels off the counter for breakfast. "We can check it out on the way to school."

Chloe let out a groan. "I don't see why we have to go to school when the only interesting thing that ever happens in this town is happening."

It was the biggest point of contention between the adults of the town and their kids. All the kids figured the Apple Cider Festival should be held before school started up again, not two weeks afterward. Of course, the real point of contention was really that most of the kids simply wanted an extra couple weeks of summer vacation, but that was never going to happen.

"It's not my fault the apples aren't ready in time," Zach said, using the same old line his parents used to give him when he complained.

They hurried out the door, the smell making it even more obvious the haze was definitely smoke and not fog. In fact, Zach couldn't believe he'd thought it was fog at first, or that it took him until Chloe said something to figure it out, but that was kind of what his brain was like when he was letting it run wild. Far too focused on one thing, the rest of the world falling away. It was why he only let his mind go there once a day, then pushed those thoughts aside for the rest of the time. Mostly.

Zach took the long route toward Main Street since much of the direct route was blocked off for the festival. All of Main Street was blocked off as well, but he wanted to get close enough to see what might have been on fire.

"At least it's not getting worse," Chloe said, saying the exact thing Zach was thinking.

"Yeah, couldn't have been too bad," he said, hoping it was true.

Still, it was a fair amount of smoke—it had to be something more than a barbecue or something.

The smoke began to dissipate a bit as they neared the center of town. The fire had clearly been put out, and there seemed to be just a bit of smoldering going on. Still, Zach couldn't help the knot balling up in his stomach the closer they got. There were too many buildings in the way to see for sure where it was coming from, but the smoke seemed to be located somewhere near The Other Apple Store.

Almost immediately his brain started to go off on a tangent about Ava and what would happen if she were in some kind of danger, which of course sent him spiraling to the moment when the water tower had fallen all over again. He swallowed hard, hyperaware Chloe would be able to pick up on any fear, and she'd already seen enough of his panic over the past couple days.

He cleared his throat, hoping to dislodge the lump sneaking up out of nowhere, and pulled his truck over to the curb as close as he could get to Main Street. Which wasn't all that close since he and Chloe were definitely not the only people who wanted to see what the heck was going on.

"Stay put," he said to Chloe, whipping his door open.

"But I want to see!" she said, putting on the "I can't believe you're doing this to me" voice that usually made Zach want to give her everything she'd ever asked for and then some, which was also the surest indication he absolutely should not do anything of the sort.

But he somehow stuffed his panic down long enough to turn back to Chloe. "I'm sorry, sweetheart, but I need to make sure everything is safe before I let you get near where the fire was, okay?"

Chloe did not look at all pleased, but she knew there was no convincing him otherwise when there was even a sliver of a question over her safety at stake. She sighed heavily. "Fine."

"Thank you. Please lock the doors behind me."

The moment Chloe started to nod, Zach took off down the street, headed toward the lingering bits of smoke, desperate thoughts running through his mind.

What seemed like minutes later, though must have been only a few seconds, Zach rounded the last building blocking his view of the coffee shop. Once he hit the sidewalk of Main Street, he skidded to a halt. The Other Apple Store looked…fine. Exactly as he'd left it last night. But there was something else that was definitely not the same as it had been the night before.

The temporary staging area for the annual baking contest had disappeared. Or rather, burned to the ground. The local volunteer firefighters were on scene and had done a good job of containing the blaze to the staging area, which was no small feat considering it was sandwiched into a small lot between the hardware store and the local insurance place.

Several people were milling around the smoldering area, and it only took a moment for Zach to spot the person who mattered the most.

She would have been just as home in jeans and a tank top, and hell if she didn't look damn good in those, but today she was wearing a sundress, white, with a few lacy bits here and there, and cowboy boots making her look every bit the small-town girl she'd become. Her hair was partially tied back, but it was the pieces that escaped, the ones she was always trying to smooth back, that he liked the most. They always blew in the slightest breeze and he wondered if they tickled her sometimes. Of course, even with those stubborn tendrils, Ava was put together as always, and doing what she did best—helping people. Which that day meant handing out coffees while everyone else stood around in shock.

Zach took a furtive look around to make sure no one had witnessed his panic, then turned and walked calmly back to his truck.

He had a worried kid to reassure and get to school on time.

HANDING OUT A bit of coffee was the least Ava could do under the circumstances. She was the one who'd had to wake up half the town since she'd been the first on the scene that morning. The timing was strange, although she supposed she didn't know exactly when the fire started, but she luckily noticed it long before it hit its most violent moments. When she'd dialed the emergency line, there had only been a small flicker in the darkness. In fact, it was only because it had still been so dark out that she saw it so quickly.

It almost seemed like the electrical issues were waiting for someone to be there before they made themselves known. Because it had to be something like electrical issues, right? The problem was, no matter how hard she tried to convince herself it was innocent, just an accident, a heavy sense of unease wouldn't let her go.

She'd run out with her kitchen fire extinguisher, but by the time she hung up and gotten the bloody thing off the wall, the fire was in full swing, and she looked ridiculous holding the small canister.

And now she and the team were way behind on the day's baking, not to mention coffee sales were going to be a bit slower considering she was handing it out for free, but it was the least she could do for the town that had saved her life.

Miss Clara stood alone, staring at the charred remains of the temporary staging area.

"Hey, Miss Clara," Ava said, coming up behind her. "Would you like some coffee?"

But Miss Clara looked like coffee was the last thing on her mind. When she turned, Ava could see her eyes were glistening. "This can't be a coincidence," Miss Clara said.

"I'm sure there's an explanation," Ava replied. "It was a temporary stage. The electrical is older and maybe not exactly up to code."

"Maybe," Miss Clara said, "but when you put it together with the water tower and Captain Applebottom..." Her words fell away as she choked up.

Ava had never had a pet, but she could imagine what it must be like to not know where the creature that mattered the most in the world to you was. A pang of guilt shot through her for not taking Miss Clara's loss more seriously last night. Even if the chicken was safe, the poor woman was still going through a terrible time. "I'll help you find him, Miss Clara. Maybe he just needed a break from all the commotion going on."

Miss Clara sighed. "It's alright dear. You've got a business to run. I've got Carol and Eunice coming to help me search down by the river later this morning. If we need more help, I'll be sure to let you know."

"Okay, Miss Clara. But please let me know if I can do anything. Anything at all, okay?" She practically forced a coffee into Miss Clara's hands, feeling like she had to do something, anything, to help pull her out of her misery. Not that the coffee would do much, but it was all Ava had at the ready to give.

Miss Clara wandered off, hunched over a little more than usual and another pang shot though Ava. She made a mental note to have some baked goods delivered to her house later. If anything, maybe Miss Clara could drown her sorrows in a little home-baked comfort.

"We should see what we can do about getting this cleaned up ASAP," Donna Mae from the antique store said, easing up and gratefully taking a cup of coffee. "Or at least covered up somehow."

Ava nodded. "I suppose it won't look good for the tourists if we have a piece of the festival all charred up at the end of Main Street."

"Exactly," Donna Mae agreed.

Just then, something caught Ava's eye.

It was the same damn thing that caught her eye every day. The same damn thing she tried to make sure did *not* catch her eye every day.

Zach.

He was in her favorite pair of jeans, the ones that were just a little snugger than the rest he usually wore. He didn't wear them often—she suspected they were his laundry day jeans—but when he did, Ava made a point of silently appreciating them.

She sighed.

"Mmm-hmm," Donna Mae said, holding her coffee cup close to her lips but not quite taking a sip. A quick glance confirmed her eye had also caught the man in question, still halfway up the street. "I wholeheartedly agree."

"Sorry?" Ava asked.

Donna Mae gave a knowing smirk. "If I were fifteen years younger, I'd be sighing like a schoolgirl when Zach came around too."

Yikes, apparently the sigh had been a lot more audible than Ava thought. She was going to have to work on her reactions when it came to Zach, or she'd have the whole town talking. Although considering they were two of the very few eligible singles in their age demographic in all of Ambrosia Falls, the whole town had probably been talking nonstop about them for years already.

"Donna Mae," Ava said, rolling her eyes." You know Zach and I are just friends."

"Oh, I am aware, but I can't for the life of me figure out why." Her eyes sparkled at Ava as she finally took her first sip of her coffee.

"Hey," Zach said, finally reaching them. "You guys seem deep in conversation."

"Yup, very deep," Donna Mae said helpfully.

Ava cleared her throat and handed Zach the last coffee from her tray. "We were talking about how we should try to mask this whole scene so the tourists don't get antsy."

"Good idea," Zach said. "I don't think we should disturb

anything yet, but we could build some kind of temporary fence across the front of the lot to hide it as best as we can."

"You are brilliant," Donna Mae said, eyes still sparkling as she gave him a playful swat on the forearm. "I'll leave it up to you all to figure it out." With that she was off like a rocket. A very satisfied rocket whose job there was done.

People in town were always doing that. As soon as Zach joined a conversation, they would make some weird excuse and hightail it out of there. Of course, it happened just as often when Ava joined some conversation Zach was having. If Ava didn't know any better, she'd think the whole town was trying to get the two of them alone as much as possible. Which was absurd considering all the time the two of them spent in the coffee shop when Zach was there working and Ava was holding down the fort.

"Why, whenever there's something to do in this town, does everyone else disappear and we're left in charge?" Zach asked.

Ava made a murmuring sound. "I'm going to take it as a compliment. We're the ones everyone thinks are the most capable."

Zach's retort was less of a murmur and more of a grumpy growl. "I think everyone around here might be a little too lazy for their own good."

"Well, the vast majority of them are retirement age so I suppose they've earned it."

Zach tilted his head in agreement. "At least the hardware store is right there. I'll run in and see if Jackson has any scrap lumber he's willing to donate to the cause. If you can get a couple guys on board to help, we could have it up in less than an hour, I bet."

"See, that's why people leave it up to us. We *are* the capable ones around here," Ava said, shooting him a wink before she headed back to the coffee shop to refill her tray. Maybe she'd be able to bribe a guy or two with some morning caffeine.

She couldn't help but smile as Zach let out another grumpy groan before he headed off to see Jackson, wondering if it was weird that the sound soothed her.

Twenty minutes later Ava was back in the kitchen making a batch of her famous Choco-Jumble cookies, which were pretty much basic chocolate chip cookies except they were her way of using up all the extra bits and chunks of leftover chocolate at the end of a baking day. There was nothing apple about them, so she wouldn't be putting them out in the display case for this week, but they were Zach's favorite, and she decided they could be a special treat to reward the guys building the fence.

Once they were in the oven, she headed to the front of the shop to check the progress of the fence. Amazingly, they were almost done with it. Perfect. The cookies would be ready just in time, and they could have them while they were still warm out of the oven.

Her eyes gravitated, as they so often did, over to where Zach was working. Some of the other guys had shed their shirts as the morning sun's rays got stronger, but sadly, Zach was still fully dressed. She'd only seen him with his shirt off once in all the years she'd known him—the time she happened to be at the pool when Chloe had Lil' Duckies swimming lessons and the parents had to be in the pool with the kids. She didn't know Zach well back then, but that didn't stop the moment from leaving a mark on Ava's memory.

She'd been waiting for an encore presentation ever since. *Stop. Just stop*, she scolded herself. She could not go there.

Yes, of all the people in the world who could be trusted with someone's heart, Zach was at the top of the list. But she'd thought that about someone else once before, and look where that got her. Though from her view out her window, the way Zach had bent down to hold a board in place while someone else wielded the drill, the place it had gotten her wasn't so bad.

She tilted her head a little. Not so bad, indeed.

Not sure how long she'd been staring, she blinked when Zach stood up and looked straight at her, giving her a little wave. Caught staring, she had no choice but to sheepishly wave back, dying a little inside, then force herself to get back to work.

Chapter Five

Once the temporary fence was done, Zach eased into his regular booth, laptop in hand. No one else in town even bothered trying to sit there anymore, which made it feel like the spot sort of belonged to him. He liked the thought of a little piece of Ava's place belonging to him.

Ava set down a plate of four cookies.

"Holy mother of all things majestic. Choco-Jumble. You are a goddess," he said.

And even though it was only a silly little remark, Ava gifted him with a smile that could flash-melt the heart of a snowman.

It seemed like everything had been weird lately—the tourists, the town, the strange occurrences, but one bite of a Choco-Jumble and the world was made right again. He tried not to let out a moan of ecstasy, but it didn't work out.

Ava shot him a little smirk, but then her face morphed into something else. Intrigue? Nah, maybe she just had gas or something.

Once all the other cookie bandits/fence builders had left and her helpers in the kitchen were gone for the day, Ava came to sit with Zach.

"Give me a sec," he said, typing in a sudden flurry until

he finished the section he was working on—things never did turn out the same if you didn't finish the thought in the moment—then flipped his laptop closed. "What's up?" he asked.

"Nothing really," she said. "I just…" She trailed off.

"You just what?" he asked, after her pause became less of a pause and more of a longish silence.

"I don't know. It's just—" She sighed. "Is all of this starting to feel a little fishy to you?"

"Fishy?"

"Yeah. Like with the water tower. And Captain Apple-bottom. And now the contest staging area. All of it put together, it's…starting to feel a little less like a coincidence than I would like."

Zach worked his jaw, staring at her for a minute. He'd been trying all day to push the same thought from his mind, but his brain wasn't having any of it. "The same thought crossed my mind," he said. "I guess I was hoping I was the only one who thought so."

Ava let out a long sigh. "Same here. But at least I feel like I'm not overreacting if someone else thinks so too."

"So what should we do?"

"I don't know. I mean, if anything else happens, I'll feel bad if we don't do anything."

Zach nodded. "You ever get the feeling we hold the fate of this whole damn town in our hands?"

Ava laughed a little, and the sound was like magic being injected straight into his veins. He hadn't meant to use the word "we," like they were in this thing—this moment? this situation? this life?—together, but truthfully, he quite liked the idea of it.

"It is starting to feel like a 'what would they do without us?' scenario," Ava said, still smiling.

"Well, as much as I love this town, how about we do something about that?" he said.

"What are you thinking?"

"I think it might be time to get the authorities involved," Zach said.

After another pause, and some weird expressions weaving their way across Ava's face—he knew every one of those expressions, but he was pathetic at trying to decipher them, even after all these years—she finally conceded. "Yeah, I guess it's time."

Zach pulled out his phone and searched for the authorities in the nearest city. The place was only two hours away, but he suspected a few small incidents in Ambrosia Falls would barely register a blip on their radar. They might even garner a chuckle or two. He'd bet his life what they considered a serious incident was a whole lot different from what the people of his town did.

Still, like Ava said, if something even worse happened and they hadn't at least tried, they'd never be able to forgive themselves.

"Sheriff's Office," came a gruff voice from the other end of the line. The kind of voice that made a person want to immediately hang up for fear they've done something wrong.

But Zach steeled himself and cleared his throat. "Uh, this is Zach Harrison out at Ambrosia Falls."

"Ambrosia what?" the guy on the other end said more impatiently, if that was even possible.

"Ambrosia Falls. Small town about ninety miles north of you. You're our closest law enforcement office."

"Okay?" the man said, making it sound like a question.

"So yeah, anyway, we were hoping you could send someone out to investigate a few incidents that have happened out here over the past couple of days."

There was a hearty sigh on the other end of the line. "And you're sure you're in our jurisdiction?"

"Yes, sir, I'm sure," Zach said, shooting an eye roll Ava's way.

By the look on her face, she was having a grand old time. Honestly, he should have made her call. He'd bet anything that she'd be more successful at convincing these guys to show up. Unfortunately, it was a bit late to decide that now.

"Fine. Let me get something to write on."

He covered the phone with his hand. "He's getting something to write on," he whispered to Ava, whose eyes widened in what seemed to be a surprise/confused combo.

"How could they not have something to write on by the phone at a sheriff's office?" she whisper-yelled with over-the-top drama thick in her voice and a laugh behind those gorgeous deep brown eyes.

"Alright, what is it?" the guy asked.

The guy's voice was something to marvel at, and Zach wondered if he should put the call on speakerphone so Ava could get the full experience of it too, but he decided against it, doubtful whether they'd both be able to keep a straight face.

"Okay, well," Zach began, the guy had a knack for making a person feel nervous, "we have the annual Apple Cider Festival in Ambrosia Falls every year and due to the increase in population, we always have a temporary water tower installed and filled, and the other day the water tower toppled over, nearly taking out a few of our citizens with it."

"How many were injured?" the man asked.

"Well, we got lucky, and no one was injured," Zach said.

"No one was injured," the man said, his waning patience becoming a substantial component to his voice.

"That's correct," Zach said, forging on. "But that isn't the only thing. We also have this makeshift stage where we host our annual Apple Cider Festival baking contest, and this morning it burned to the ground."

"A makeshift stage," the man said.

Zach couldn't help but be annoyed with the way the man kept repeating his words back to him, only in a way that seemed to imply Zach was the biggest chump in the world for bothering him with such petty matters.

"That's right."

The sigh on the other end was even heavier this time. "And did anyone in your—" he cleared his throat "—little town there, bother to take a look at what you think the cause of these…incidents might be?"

"Um, yes."

"And what did y'all come up with?" he asked.

"Well, the water tower seemed to be in a bit of disrepair and so at first we didn't think much of it, but now with the fire, it seems a bit suspicious."

"Uh-huh," the guy said. "So…just so we're all on the same page here, you've had a decrepit water tower, which you only fill once a year, fall down, and then you've had a fire that originated on…what did you call it, oh yes, a make-shift stage. Is that correct?"

Zach was starting to get annoyed with the way this guy was treating the situation. "Right. And there was a third incident as well."

"A third incident, you say. Well, I am utterly on the edge of my seat."

Zach sighed. "Our festival mascot was stolen."

"Your mascot."

"Correct."

"Like, some stuffed apple or something?" the guy said, clearly amusing himself.

"No, our mascot is a live chicken. Um, his name is Captain Applebottom."

This was the point when the laughter started, followed soon after by an alarming amount of wheezing. When it all finally subsided and the guy caught his breath again, he came back on the line.

"Okay, sir, uh," he said as the sound of a page being flipped came over the line, "Zach. I have your number here on the call display. I can't say when we might be able to send someone out to investigate your water tower situation, or your little fire, or," he said, clearing his throat again, "the disappearance of Captain Applebottom—"

Another pause ensued for a bit more laughing, and Zach tried to keep his cool. By the heat in his neck, he had the distinct feeling his annoyance might have been close to reaching the surface.

The man took a few deep breaths to compose himself before continuing. "But I'll be sure to send someone out to your neck of the woods as soon as we can spare the resources."

"Yeah. Thanks," Zach said with little feeling and hung up with even less hope that anyone would ever actually arrive.

"That did not sound promising," Ava said.

Zach shook his head in both frustration and disbelief. "Sounds like it could be days before anyone even thinks about coming…if they decide to come at all."

"Incredible," Ava said. "What if something actually urgent ever happened?"

Zach shrugged. "I guess we're on our own."

She shook her head a little. "Well, I guess I should get back to it. The display case is looking a bit sparse after the lunch rush. Better go see how much stock is left back there and get a start on some fresh batches for the late afternoon crew."

"Sounds good. I'll just be here," he said, motioning to the general area of his booth. "If that's alright with you."

"Wouldn't have it any other way," Ava said, making something swirl a little in Zach's stomach.

And that was when—right after Ava disappeared behind the kitchen door and Zach had barely opened his laptop again—the worst sound he had ever heard reached his ears.

The sound of Ava's blood-curdling scream.

FLASHBACKS OF THE night five years ago flooded Ava's brain. Pain. So much pain. She'd forgotten what that kind of burn felt like. She hoped she'd never feel it again.

Zach burst through the kitchen door, his eyes frantic, searching.

"I'm okay," Ava said, "I'm okay."

But with the amount of pain she was in, she honestly wasn't sure she was okay. The last time she'd felt this kind of pain, she'd been pretty far from okay.

"Show me," Zach said, his voice gruff and demanding.

But there was only fear in his eyes. A fear that hit somewhere deep inside Ava, making her angry that she was the person who caused fear in this man she cared for so much, but also elation that she had the power to make him feel so deeply.

She held her arm out to Zach, who took it gently, peering closely.

"What happened?" he asked.

"I went to check my phone and leaned on the counter with my arm. Except it wasn't the counter, it was the stove I guess, and the burner was on."

"How was the burner on when no one was even in here?" Zach asked, though he was only half listening, clearly far more concerned with inspecting her arm.

"I don't know," Ava said. "It's never been left on before. And I can't even think what the girls might have been using the stovetop for this morning."

In her mind, Ava began to go through the list of baked goods on the menu that day.

"Here, sit," Zach said, pulling up a stool, then turning to the cupboard where he already knew the first-aid kit was kept, having had to grab a bandage every now again, usually for Chloe.

Ava did as she was told, her mind still taking stock of the morning's menu items. "No, there was nothing that needed the stove. The filling for the Candy Apple Glazed Donut Supreme was made ahead of time. I can't figure out why anyone would have turned it on."

"Could someone have bumped it?" Zach asked, coming back to face her, taking her hand gently again.

Ava shook her head. "I don't think so. You have to sort of push in the knob before you turn it. It's a safety feature meant to stop accidents from happening."

"You're lucky there wasn't another fire," Zach said, checking through the contents of the first-aid kit.

"Yeah, I guess so," Ava said, though something about Zach's words sent a sliver of dread down her spine.

"We should clean this," Zach said, gently guiding her off her stool and over to the sink as Ava's mind kept whirling.

The cool water sent a new wave of pain through Ava,

shocking her back to the present. He was so close, using his hands to lather the soap before gently rubbing them on the burn. The gentle pressure momentarily hurt, then subsided as she closed her eyes, concentrating on how his hands felt on her skin. How gentle he was.

This close, she could smell him, a woodsy clean scent she'd come to associate with comfort, though she didn't often get to be so close to it, and she couldn't help but lean in a little more.

"Come," Zach said, and there was so much feeling in the single word as he pulled her gently back toward the stool.

She opened her eyes as they moved, and suddenly the room felt thick with emotion, so thick she could barely breathe.

And so of course she went and ruined it by speaking. "Well, with this and the stage burning down, I guess I won't have to worry about the baking competition." She let out a slight chuckle.

Zach drew his attention away from her hand to her eyes. "Were you seriously worried about it?"

She shrugged. "I always want to make a good showing since I'm the one charging for my baked goods in this town."

Zach grabbed a roll of gauze from the kit and looked directly into her eyes. "Ava, it wouldn't matter what you came up with for the competition. You would have won."

"That's not true," she said, but he cut her off quickly.

"You've won the past five years in a row," he said.

"Only because I stress over it for months in advance," she said. "Except this year, all the stressing didn't even do me any good."

His brow furrowed. "I never knew that about you," he said.

"You always seem so carefree. I didn't think you stressed over anything at all."

If only he knew.

"Sorry to burst your bubble," she said, then put her best carefree face back on.

Well, as carefree as someone who'd just burned the hell out of her arm could be, anyway.

But Zach just made a murmuring sound and got back to work, carefully spreading a thin layer of antibacterial ointment across her forearm. His hands were soft and gentle and felt like they always belonged there...touching her skin. She had a brief thought, wondering how she could have survived this long without that touch to soothe her, and she realized then she never wanted to let the feeling go.

He laid a nonstick sterile pad over the worst of the burn and began to wrap it with gauze, careful not to hurt her. The concentration on his face, so careful, the way he bit his lower lip drawing her attention there, his bottom lip full and looking so soft.

She wondered what his lips might taste like.

Heat began to build deep in her center and she closed her eyes again, inhaling deeply, wanting to savor the moment, knowing she'd want to look back on it for a long time to come.

"Does it hurt?" he asked, and Ava realized he was finished with the bandage.

She blinked her eyes open, and he was there, right in front of her, still holding her arm, taking care of her.

"Hey," he said, his voice so soft. He tilted his head slightly, with a little smile, like he was wondering what was going on in her head.

"Hi," she said, giving him a tiny smile back.

They stayed like that for a moment, volleying silent questions back and forth with their eyes until one of them—Ava didn't know if it was her or Zach, maybe it was both—closed the small gap between them, their lips finally, blessedly meeting.

Ava's mind filled with thoughts. Was this really happening? After all the time spent wondering, resisting, pushing him out of her mind, he was finally here, right in front of her. The moment was surreal and unbelievable, and felt like she had finally found a home in this world.

Zach wrapped his arms around her, deepening the kiss as Ava leaned into him. She let go and fell into the abyss of nothingness that could only be found in the safety of someone who was trusted so deeply the rest of the world suddenly didn't matter at all.

He pulled her closer, onto the very edge of the stool, though it felt like she'd never been so stable in her life. Her arms wrapped around the sturdiness of him, one hand moving down the taut muscles of his back while the other was desperate to find his head, to pull him closer.

And that was the moment the cruel world came crashing back down on her, the pain searing through her arm, shocking her back to reality. A small, gasping wince escaped her lips before she could stop it.

Zach stiffened and pulled back, though he kept his arms around her. Still protecting. Always protecting. "Are you okay?" he asked, the concern heavy in his expression.

"Yeah, sorry. Just forgot about the arm."

And she wanted to keep kissing, to fall back into the oblivion of a first kiss that makes you feel drunk, but the moment was broken. Zach smoothly propped her back onto the stool and pulled away from her.

The moment his touch was gone Ava missed it, and was only slightly consoled when he took her bandaged arm, inspecting it once more.

"It looks okay," he said, finally meeting her eyes again.

"Okay," she said, unsure where everything was supposed to go from there.

Holy shit. She had just kissed Zach. Like really kissed him, and now everything was going to change. And it felt so right, like the change was going to be an incredible thing. But she was scared too. What if he had gotten caught up in the moment and didn't feel the same way about her? What if he regretted it already?

But the thing was, he didn't look like he regretted anything. He looked...happy. Or maybe her happiness was oozing out all over the room and coating him too. Maybe his wasn't even real at all.

Except there had always been...something between them. The kind of thing you knew you couldn't act on until you were ready. Until the time was right. Until all the stars aligned.

And damn if it didn't feel like every star in the universe had lined right up especially for them.

Hadn't she always known they were putting off whatever was going to be between them because they knew as soon as that "whatever" started, it was going to be forever?

She looked down at her arm, which Zach had been holding, then looked at him. He looked like he might have been having the same sort of thoughts running through his mind, but didn't quite know what to do with them either.

What he did do was take a step back, then put his hands into the back pockets of those fantastic jeans and sort of lean back on his heels. "Um, so…" he said, trailing off and looking toward the door to the front of the shop.

Ava tried to smile, but it ended up a little sheepish. "So," she said back, shifting slightly on the stool.

The moment stretched into oblivion.

She opened her mouth to say something, though she had absolutely no idea what that something might be—she just felt like she needed to fill the silence. But Zach apparently had the same thought at the same time, and they both spouted some incomprehensible jumble before each stopped short.

"Sorry, you go," Ava said.

"No, you go," Zach said.

"Um, okay, except I have no idea what I was even going to say." She smiled.

And then he smiled back. "Me neither."

Her shoulders relaxed. He was still Zach. Her best friend.

"So… I guess that happened," she finally said.

He let out a chuckle and pulled his hands from his pockets, taking a tentative step toward her. "Um, yeah. It really did," he said.

Ava thought he was going to come back to her, to give her the one thing in the world she wanted most, which was obviously another long, and hopefully even more passionate kiss—if that was even possible—when his eyes suddenly went wide.

"Is that the right time?" he asked.

Ava's eyes followed his to the clock on the wall. "Shit, Chloe."

"I gotta go," he said, and turned to dash out the door, but just before he reached it, he turned and ran back to her, grabbing her face in both hands and kissing her hard. It was a kiss that said everything Ava needed to know. Because it felt more like a promise than simply a kiss.

She smiled as he dashed through the door.

And smiled as he yelled, "I'll see you later!"

She was still smiling as she heard the tinkle of the bells above the shop door letting her know he had gone.

But then the smile faded as she spotted something on the floor near the other door. The back door. Something had been slipped underneath. But that couldn't be right. It was an outer door, sealed off. And she was sure it hadn't been there when she'd come into the kitchen and burned herself, which meant someone had opened the door while she and Zach had been right there.

Dread oozed up and filled every corner of the room as Ava moved carefully toward the envelope, picking it up from the floor before she could give herself time to talk herself out of it. A quick glance told her the door was sealed tight and locked.

The dread grew thicker as she slipped her finger under the sealed end of the envelope and ripped, pulling the contents out.

And in that moment, she knew, without a shadow of a doubt, she would never kiss Zach again.

Chapter Six

Zach wasn't sure if it had been the best thing that could have ever happened to him, or the worst. Thoughts about how everything started to go south with Kimberly the moment they started being more than friends filled his mind with every doubt imaginable.

But Ava was not Kimberly.

Maybe this time could be different.

And he had to admit. This time felt different. He was feeling things he'd never felt with Kimberly. Maybe it was because he'd known Kimberly his whole life that the relationship didn't carry the same kind of…spark. That was the only word he could think of to describe it. And my God, did the kiss have some spark in it, although it would be better described as lightning, if he was trying to be as accurate as possible.

He'd thought of a kiss like it so many times, pushed away those fantasies just as often and then the moment—the real moment—had completely snuck up on him. Maybe it was the emotional roller coaster he'd been going through when it came to Ava these past few days—the water tower, and then this morning before he knew she was safe from the fire.

The last incident with the burn must have been more than his poor heart could take.

Although he wasn't entirely sure if he'd been the one to initiate the kiss or if she had. He was damned sure thinking about it, that was for certain, but he didn't know who'd actually closed that last, tiny, excruciating gap.

But it wasn't just the kiss that felt different. It was the way he felt inside too. Like the world had a glimmer to it…a lightness. Like he was invincible. No, like he and Ava together were invincible.

Apart, he was just him. But around her, he became someone he liked a whole lot more.

"What's up with you?" Chloe asked, climbing into the truck. "You're never late. I was starting to get worried, you know."

She wasn't necessarily scolding him, but she wasn't *not* scolding him either. Zach decidedly did not like this new side of her. But he *had* been late and couldn't really give her a good excuse.

"I'm sorry, I lost track of time."

Chloe narrowed her eyes. "You never lose track of time."

"I know. I was helping Ava with something, and I forgot to watch the clock."

"So you forgot about me," she said, and Zach couldn't tell if she was legitimately annoyed or if she was just giving him a hard time.

The kid was way too smart, and way too wise for her age.

"I did not forget about you," he said.

Finally, mercifully, she cracked a grin his way. "So…you were hanging out with Ava, hey?" she said, a tone of amused curiosity in her voice.

Zach couldn't help but feel like he was right back in

grade school alongside his daughter. "Chloe," he said, rolling his eyes.

"And you lost track of time," she said, implying something was definitely up.

Zach sighed. "She hurt her arm, and I was helping her."

Chloe's eyes grew wide. "Is she okay?" she asked, a note of concern in her voice now.

"She's going to be fine, don't worry. Has anyone ever mentioned you worry too much for a ten-year-old?"

"Yes. You, pretty much every day," she answered, shooting him a side-eye. "And like you're one to talk," she said.

"But I'm a creaky old adult. It's my job to worry. For the both of us."

Chloe rolled her eyes. "How about we agree it's nobody's job and both stop worrying? Besides, you're only just starting to get a little creaky around the edges."

Zach chuckled a little, amazed, as he so often was, at this kid of his. "Yeah, okay. Deal."

They drove in silence for a couple blocks, then Chloe spoke, spotting the coffee shop up the road. "Can we go get something from Ava's?"

"Not today kid," he said. "I've got stuff to do at home."

He did not, in fact, have stuff to do at home. But he was worried about what seeing Ava again so soon would do to him. That kiss pretty much wrecked him, and he was worried he might lunge for her again the moment he saw her. Which would not be a good look in front of his kid.

And he definitely wasn't going to stare at The Other Apple Store as they passed. Except he found he couldn't stop himself, feeling like a damn teenager desperately hoping to catch a glimpse of his secret crush.

I am in so much trouble, he realized as he craned his neck even further to watch the store for one more second.

IT'S OVER, AVA THOUGHT. *It's all over. He's found me and I have to go on the run again.*

She shuffled through the pictures one more time. The first, a shot of her hugging Annie moments after the water tower had fallen. Then one of Ava—before the firefighters had even arrived on scene at the contest stage—holding her pathetic little fire extinguisher, knowing it was pointless. Next came shots of the back door of The Other Apple Store, as well as her stove, which Ava took to mean that whoever left these photos was taking credit for the strange, seemingly unexplainable incidents in her own place of business.

And then the final shot, which must have been taken with an instant camera, of her and Zach, locked in the kiss they had shared just moments ago.

The bastard had been right there.

It had to be Justin, and he seemed to be having a grand ole time toying with her. Just like he always used to do. It was the one thing about him that bothered her back then—the way he seemed to get pleasure out of making his targets uneasy.

She wondered how long he'd known where she was. Had he been lying in wait all this time? Waiting for proof she'd moved on with her life? That she actually had a life—one she wouldn't want to leave.

She supposed the kiss with Zach would have proved to Justin that she wouldn't be willing to go easily. He wanted her to be comfortable and let her guard down before he made his move.

He wanted her to suffer.

Tears came to her eyes. She should have known better.

She came into this town vowing never to get attached. Sure, she could have friends, ones she would always hold a bit at arm's length, but she would never really let them into her soul. But so much time had passed. Ava didn't know when Zach had wriggled his way straight into the middle of that soul, but she couldn't deny that's exactly where he lived. And somehow, after one person had gotten in, the floodgates opened and now she was pretty much in love with the whole damn town.

She blinked the tears away. This was not the time.

She had work to do.

First things first. Protection.

She went out front to lock the door, putting out a Back in 15 Minutes sign. It wouldn't keep Justin out if he wanted in badly enough, but she couldn't have people wandering in off the street while she did what she had to do. She moved to the closet where they kept the cleaning supplies, conveniently out of sight from any of the front windows, and pulled up a few of the carpet squares she'd laid down to disguise the hatch, quickly pulling it open.

The space wasn't really a basement—more like a glorified crawl space, but it was good enough for what she'd needed it for.

Things she couldn't let others know about.

Ava collected the items she needed, both for protection and for what she knew she'd have to do that evening, then headed back upstairs and took the sign off the door, hoping it would seem to the town that nothing was out of the ordinary.

She had one last important task. A message to send to one of the most important people in her life. The only person who'd remained from her life from before. The one contact in her old life even Justin hadn't known about.

George.

Ava still didn't know how George had managed it. Pulled her from the flaming bunker all those years ago and gotten her to safety and to medical help. She couldn't imagine the strength it must have taken to go down into a smoke-filled hole in the ground to see if there were any signs of life. Then find the will to pull her unconscious body up the steep stairs and back out to the world again. At the age of seventy-five.

He must have been running on pure adrenaline.

Ava opened the browser on her phone, loading up the Buy & Sell page for an obscure medium-sized town somewhere in the heart of Oklahoma. She'd never been to the town, and neither had George as far as she knew, but the online space was where the two of them had communicated for the past five years. They couldn't risk direct contact, of course— George was aging and sometimes needed medical care, so being invisible was no longer an option for him. Thankfully, Justin still didn't know of George's existence, probably still wondered how the hell Ava ever got out of the bunker alive, and so he was relatively safe. Still, Ava couldn't risk Justin even suspecting she'd had help that awful, fiery night, so they kept their communication on the down low.

Ava quickly went into her routine of computer precautions she always took—masking her IP through a VPN and creating a brand-new, encrypted burner email address that would delete itself the moment she hit Send. It wasn't foolproof, but without the tech experts she used to have at her fingertips, it was the best she could do.

She used the email to set up a new account with the site and logged into the Buy & Sell. George knew what to look for. Avocado pits for sale. Ava had noticed a strange trend of people giving away their discarded avocado pits so others could use them to start an avocado plant. Which struck Ava as incredibly strange considering anyone who liked avocados enough to want to grow them would likely have avocado pits of their own to start their plants, but it was, apparently, a thing. Most importantly, a thing easily skimmed past. And in order to make sure she didn't actually get any inquiries about the avocado pits, she put a price tag on them. A small one, about the cost of an actual avocado, which would deter anyone in their right mind from actually being interested in the ad.

But it was what George knew to look for. If Ava ever needed him, she would post about the avocado pits, and vice versa, which would open up a line of communication difficult to trace. Ava spent countless hours skimming that silly Buy & Sell with only the occasional check-in from George. But it was the way it had to be. Anything more direct would be too risky.

She quickly typed up her ad:

Avocado pits, cleaned and dried, healthy? And ready for planting. UnCompromised pits, disease free. Perfect for all you avocado lovers. Call to arrange pickup.

Ava normally wouldn't be so bold as to add the question mark and capitalize the *c* in *uncompromised*, but it was the only way she could figure out how to get her message across to George. If she had a bit more time, she could think of something better, but of all the considerations in a situation like the one she found herself in, time was the most critical. She needed to know if her friend was healthy, and he needed to know she was compromised.

In truth, George had always been much more than a friend

to Ava. He was more like a father figure. He'd been her first handler when she'd become an operative and helped her through those first difficult years. And the years had certainly been difficult. Yes, she'd lost her parents years before and had been a ward of the state for a long time, which meant she didn't have a whole lot in the way of family connections, but still. She had a few friends, and when a person agreed to do the kind of work required—lots of unexplainable travel, frequent changes of appearance, and a sudden influx of money—a person had to let things like friendship go.

Thankfully, George had a huge heart and a soft spot for Ava, and Ava knew no matter what went down in her world, there was a single person she could always count on.

George.

And if anything had happened to him, she wasn't sure she could live with it.

For the next few hours until closing time, Ava waited. The more time passed—each minute seeming like an hour—the more worried she became. The only thing keeping her going was the steady stream of customers thanks to the Apple Cider Festival, a welcome distraction.

She must have checked the Buy & Sell page over a hundred times before she finally got a reply.

All good here, do you need me to come?

Ava felt like she could breathe again, and the weight of about three tons of avocados was lifted from her shoulders. She quickly typed into the Buy & Sell instant messaging window.

Hold tight. I'll keep you posted.

Because before she called in one of the most precious people in the world—especially one who wasn't in the best health—she needed to know exactly what she was up against.

Her first thought was to run. Pack a small bag and get the hell out of Ambrosia Falls as fast as she could. It was exactly what she would have done if she was confident Justin had nothing in the town to hold against her, but Ava realized, with a sick feeling swirling in her guts, there was so much in the town he could hold against her. So many people who mattered.

She shouldn't have let it happen. It was Spy 101—never get attached. Never give your enemy something they can manipulate to get to you.

She'd been sure after being shuffled from house to house as a teenager, and then working diligently not to make personal connections all the years she'd been active, she supposed she didn't think she was capable of those feelings anymore, so they kind of snuck up on her.

It was a monumental mistake, and one she'd regret for the rest of her life if she didn't make this right. And making it right meant one thing…going back to a life she never thought she'd be a part of again.

She needed to bring Sparrow back from the dead.

Chapter Seven

Zach felt like a total creeper staring out the front window. He tried to convince himself it wasn't because he was waiting for Ava to pull up to her house—*just checking to see what the weather's up to!*—but even he wasn't buying it. Thank goodness Chloe was busy doing homework in her room or she'd 100 percent start asking him all kinds of questions.

By now, he knew her schedule almost better than she did, not that he was keeping tabs, or anything, and the strange thing was, she was never this late getting home. He wondered if he should start to worry.

He sighed. Ava was a grown-ass adult, and she didn't need some snooping neighbor wondering what she was up to every waking moment. Even one she'd shared an incredibly passionate kiss with earlier in the day. Heat rose up his torso thinking about the kiss, and he tried to tamp it down by gulping a huge glass of ice water. As fast as he could. Unfortunately, a massive case of brain freeze was all he got for the trouble. Those damn swirly emotions were still lurking in his guts.

But honestly, where could Ava be? Sure, it was possible she had plans with someone else in town, but since Zach was always at the coffee shop, he usually knew about changes in her schedule. He wondered then, if the amount of time he spent around the poor woman might be considered stalking in some circles. And then he wondered if it was a bad thing this was only the first time he'd even thought to consider the notion. Was he being a total pain in Ava's butt all the time? A flurry of panic whirred through his chest until he remembered the kiss. And the way she was completely comfortable around him. And the way she used him as a guinea pig for her recipes.

No, he realized, if she thought he was a big pain in the butt, none of the above would be happening. Still, as if he were back in grade school, he couldn't help but feel like he was doing things all wrong. That's where his mind went when he was all alone and spending way too much time with his thoughts.

When he was around Ava, he felt different. He wasn't nervous. He wasn't worried. He was just him. She had a way of putting him at ease. Maybe that was why he craved being around her so much.

Well, that and the fact he could spend an eternity staring at her and never get tired of the view.

Another hour passed and Zach began to pace. Normally, he would try to pry Chloe away from her phone and get her to do something with him. But he could barely focus long enough to force himself to walk to the back of his house, before rushing back to the front to check the window yet again.

Finally, well after dark, Ava's car pulled into her driveway next door. He breathed out the longest sigh of relief he'd ever expelled in his whole life, then suddenly wondered if he'd left his wallet in the car and headed out to check, careful not to glance her way. The last thing he needed was for Ava to think he'd been waiting for her to come home.

Only after Ava pulled into her garage and her car door slammed, did he allow himself to look up. God, he was being ridiculous, crushing like a thirteen-year-old, desperately wanting to find out if she liked him. He supposed it had been so long since he allowed himself to go there it was expected, but it didn't stop him from feeling incredibly silly and lame as hell.

"Oh hey," he said, as she came out of the overhead garage door, as if he'd only just noticed she was there.

Yup, absolute loser.

Ava looked tired, but eventually gifted him with one of those smiles that reignited the annoying swirly action in his guts, as she hit the button to close the garage. "Hey," she said back.

For the past several hours, Zach had been playing this exact scenario over in his mind, with slight alterations each time it played. Sometimes Ava would come rushing up and fling her arms around him—those were the best ones—and sometimes she would saunter up, all cool-like, with a look in her eye that reminded him they had an exciting little secret. But in none of those fantasy scenarios did she look like she wanted to flee.

Which was exactly how she was looking now. Eyes darting, shifting from foot to foot, and generally seeming as though she was stuck in the most uncomfortable situation she'd ever experienced. It made Zach feel completely awkward and uncomfortable too.

He rubbed the back of his neck. "So, uh, long day, hey?"

"Yeah," she said, nodding a little too vigorously. "Really long day."

Zach had been hoping she'd expand on where she'd been half the damn night, and reminded himself one more time it wasn't any of his business. A concept he hated with the fiery passion of a thousand Red Hot candies and a chaser of Fireball. Should he bring up the kiss? He wanted to bring up the kiss. Except…she wasn't bringing up the kiss, so he probably shouldn't bring up the kiss. If she wanted to talk about the kiss, she would say so.

She shifted her weight one more time.

And then, right after he decided not to say anything, his damned mouth opened itself and started spewing anyway. "So, uh, this afternoon…" he said.

It was barely noticeable, but Zach swore Ava jolted ever so slightly.

She cleared her throat. "Um, yeah…"

"That was, um—"

"Probably a mistake, right?" Ava jumped in, cutting him off and quite soundly crushing his soul into oblivion.

"Right," he said, with an awkward little chuckle. "A mistake…"

"I mean, because we're such good friends and everything," Ava said, her words picking up speed.

Zach nodded in kind of a full-body way, rocking back on his heels. "Yeah, we, uh, wouldn't want to mess anything up."

"Right! Exactly!" Ava agreed, her words full of over-the-top enthusiasm.

And then there was nothing else to say. Just the two of them standing there, staring at nothing, and definitely not looking at each other.

"Um, so… I should be getting in. Kinda tired…you know how it is," she said, along with another weird nodding routine.

"Right, yeah." Zach shook his head a little. "Sorry to keep

you," he said, backing away a step and giving her this strange little wave the likes of which he'd never done in his life.

Zach watched as Ava went up her front steps and into her house. She turned back once, giving him a look filled with regret, making him wonder if she regretted this moment, or the one between them that afternoon.

He went back inside, thoughts racing faster than a bird trapped in a house with the homeowner chasing after him.

"Whatcha doin' outside?" his daughter asked in a small voice, startling him out of the mental hamster wheel.

"Oh..." He looked around.

Why had he gone outside?

"Right, I was looking for my wallet."

Chloe glanced over to the console table by the front door. "That wallet?"

Zach followed her gaze, seeing that his wallet was right in the center of it beside his keys...the keys he was currently holding in his hand and must have picked up from *right* beside the stinking wallet before he'd gone out.

Chloe giggled a little. "A bit absent-minded today?"

Zach forced out a small chuckle. "Yeah, I guess so," he said.

He felt like a damn fool.

But unfortunately, it wasn't because of any wallet.

AVA COULDN'T BRING herself to think about Zach. Walking away from him, telling him the kiss was a mistake...it was, inconceivable. Cruel. Both to her and to Zach.

So she just wasn't going to think about it.

How could she? There was something bigger at stake than his heart.

His life.

The fact that the Apple Cider Festival was going on was in Ava's favor. Every Airbnb and rental property in town had been booked up for Apple Cider months in advance, so Justin would never have found a place like that to stay at. And he would have never held out this long before confronting her if he'd known her whereabouts months ago. Of course, Ava wasn't sure he would have even tried any of the legitimate places to stay anyway. It wasn't his MO.

As the Crow, Justin always thought it was much more badass to hole up in abandoned or unused buildings. Ava had always disagreed with him on the matter, thinking it too risky—it was much easier to spot suspicious activity at a place everyone knew was supposed to be empty, and it had once been a huge point of contention between them. And that day, she decided, it was going to be his downfall, like she always suspected it would be. Especially considering she knew Justin was a bit posh, not likely to use some run-down building as the place he went if there were any other options. And Ambrosia Falls definitely had other options. She could think of at least three gorgeous vacation homes that sat empty this time of year—families who didn't love the crowd of the Apple Cider Festival, but also didn't rent their houses out to tourists.

She had a good idea which houses were empty—she was still the Sparrow after all, trained to remember details—but all evening she'd been confirming with some of the locals. Just "making conversation" in order to substantiate what she already knew.

The rest of the daylight was used to prep for the next day's customers. She knew she'd be out late and would never make it back to the shop early for the morning's baking. So with one last pit stop to give Maureen—her main baking assistant—a key and the code to the alarm system, she headed home to prepare for what was to come.

She'd considered Maureen's safety, of course, wondering if she should be worried about her opening by herself in the morning, but she decided if her evening was successful, there wouldn't be anything to worry about anymore.

Her plan had been coming together for hours. Desperate to find some way—any way—to stay in Ambrosia Falls, she had landed on an idea. One chance she might not have to run. If she were to simply take Justin out, make it so he couldn't hurt anyone she loved, she could go on with her life as it was. She could stay in town, keep everyone safe, and most importantly, figure out what everything meant with Zach.

She didn't take the job lightly. She was a different person than she'd been five years ago, but she still had the training. Still had the ability to do what she needed to do for the greater good. It was just that this time, the greater good was keeping herself and all the people she'd grown to love safe instead of someone else.

Running into Zach outside her house had thrown her off though. Seeing the look on his face when he noticed her there—excited, loving, hopeful…all at the same time—she'd panicked. If her plan for Justin didn't work, she needed to keep her distance from everyone in town. Especially the ones who mattered as much as Zach. Plus there was the little matter of making sure Zach didn't catch a glimpse of the weapons she had concealed around her body. Most people would never notice, but if Zach got close enough to touch her, she'd have a whole lot of explaining to do.

So many feelings had flooded her when she saw Zach— fear something might happen to him, a fierce sense of having to protect him and a heavy dose of straight up lust, something she hadn't allowed herself to wholly feel about him before. But that flipping spectacular kiss had awakened something in her. Something that had been dormant for a very long time.

Had it really been five years since she'd had sex? Good Lord, no wonder her nether regions were churning up a storm of hormones, the likes of which she didn't even remember having as a teenager.

But she had to leave all those feelings behind her.

There was a job to do, and she would only be able to allow those feelings back in if she was successful. It was something she was good at—pushing her own emotions away to do what had to be done.

Ava piled supplies into a large duffel bag. The sooner she could get this over with and didn't have anything to worry about anymore, the better. But her burned arm was not making things any easier. It was amazing how a person could take for granted something as simple as packing without thinking. But with her arm in so much pain, it was no simple feat at all, not to mention the bandage around her arm getting caught in her bag. She thanked her lucky stars that at least it hadn't been her shooting hand.

Once she finally got the damn bag shut, she turned out all the lights in her house, including the outside light. She hoped if Zach or Chloe were watching, they'd assume she'd gone to bed. Not that she thought they'd be paying any attention, but she had to admit, if she didn't have so many other things on her mind, she'd probably be staring out the window toward a certain house, wondering what a certain person inside said house was thinking right at that moment.

Giving it a few more minutes to be sure, she finally slipped out the back door of her house and through the main door to her garage, thinking the whole routine would have been a hell of a lot easier if she'd had an attached garage. After collecting a few more things and stowing them in her trunk, she hit the button for the overhead door, cringing at the loudness. But the noise couldn't be helped.

If she got through this, she thought, she'd get something quieter. Then she realized, if she got through the rest of the night, she would no longer have to worry about it.

As she backed down her drive and out onto the street, Ava let out a long, slow breath, trying to calm her vitals, knowing she would need a steady hand—and a steady mind—for what came next.

She would stake out each of the three properties one by one, starting with the biggest. If Justin was still using the same tactics, chances were he'd pick the fanciest place he could get away with.

She headed to the Williams residence first. It belonged to a kindly older doctor and his wife, who loved to have the place on the river to go boating with their grandkids. There was a cluster of trees on the edge of the large semirural property. That was where Ava headed, parking a half mile down the road where her car would blend in with the others on the street, then made it the rest of the way on foot. Not an easy feat considering the heavy duffle she carried. But the one thing it seemed she had done right was stay in decent shape—not prime form, but decent—which made the trek manageable.

Inside the trees, she set up her surveillance, starting with recording equipment she would leave in case Justin was staying there but not present at that moment, then placing her infrared camera to pick up any heat signatures.

She left her sniper rifle in the bag for now, wanting to get a read on the area and the situation. She sat for twenty minutes, barely moving a muscle. Justin was not there.

She left the recording equipment and made the trek back to her car, scanning the area the whole way. She realized, for all the hunting she'd done before, she'd never known she was the one being hunted. She'd been surveilled back when Justin had been watching her all those years, but she'd been oblivious. It was a very different situation when you knew you were being watched. Every sound, every movement in the shadows had her on edge, and it was starting to play with her mind.

Ava moved to the next house on her list, the Batras place on the other side of Main Street. She didn't know much about the Batras family, only that they came to town about three times a year for a week. She knew them to see them although she hadn't had much chance to chat with the family. But she knew where they stayed. Ambrosia Falls was small enough that most anybody knew where most everybody lived, and she made her way close within a few minutes and surveyed the scene.

There wasn't as obvious a hiding place on this property, since the immediate area was more populated than the Williams place. The park across the street would be risky, but it would have to do.

She made her way to the top fort-like area of the slide, somewhat hidden by the heavy boards all the way around. She'd seen many a kid peeking through the boards, only their curious eyes in view, and now she was about to do the same thing. It was just unfortunate she wouldn't be able to place recording equipment here, since kids would no doubt be back as soon as the sun came up. As it was, she was lucky there were no teenagers hanging in the park that night.

After twenty minutes she was certain Justin was not there. She began to wonder if she had it wrong. Maybe he'd changed his ways, after all, or changed them up since he was dealing with someone who'd once known his routine—but she still had one more place to check.

Lawson's.

This property was the most rural of all, but Ava hadn't gone there first because it had been vacated for the least amount of time. The couple lived in town year-round and loved Ambrosia Falls, but they disliked when the tourists "took over the place." Honestly, they could give old Mr. Grumpy Pants Zach a run for his money when it came to complaining about tourists. They "got the hell outta Dodge," as they liked to say—as often as anyone would listen—the day before the tourists started arriving and were back the day after the festival ended.

Ava assumed Justin had been in town planning and scheming long before the first "strange" occurrence, which didn't seem so strange anymore. But maybe he'd been chomping at the bit and was doing things quickly as ideas presented themselves. It would be the best possible situation really, since it would mean he'd be sloppy, and sloppy was almost always what got a bad guy in trouble.

On foot again, Ava moved in closer to the Lawson residence, her hopes falling the closer she got. Justin would have to be reckless to use this place as his center of operations. It was too secluded, too surrounded by trees—he'd be far too exposed. There were a hundred places Ava could hide and he'd never have a clue she'd been there.

Still, she had to check.

Not worrying too much about where in the trees she settled, she quickly pulled out another set of recording devices and placed them on a tree branch where they wouldn't easily be seen by anyone who happened to be hiking, even though she assumed that didn't happen a whole lot, especially with the Lawsons away. She climbed a separate tree and got her infrared out, her stomach jolting when a very bright, and apparently very warm, figure flashed up on the digital screen.

Someone was most definitely home.

There was always a chance the Lawsons had come home early, but there was only one heat signature—exactly what Ava had been trying to find.

Still, she had to be sure. She was always thorough and didn't make many mistakes. This was not going to be the day that changed.

Her next plan was born when she saw the large rock about ten yards away. The moonlight was strong enough to discern the outline of the large boulder. When she was a kid, she would have loved it. There was something about giant rocks that made her feel like they needed to be climbed and sat on. Being seated on a piece of history, something that had been there for thousands of years felt powerful somehow, especially if it was just high enough not everyone would be able to climb it.

Since she wasn't a kid anymore, Ava didn't have as strong an urge to climb it, but she did wish it was a foot shorter so she could comfortably rest her sniper rifle on it for a stable shot. Then again, nature sometimes had a way of solving problems, and a few minutes later her rifle was planted on that rock, her feet balancing on a large fallen tree. It had taken most of her strength to shimmy over to the rock, but the result was worth it.

She'd have a clear line of sight, and if she could see without a doubt that it was Justin inside those walls, she'd have a clear shot too.

Then, as she gazed through the scope, her heart clenched.

The profile she hadn't seen in years, back to haunt her, as if in a waking dream. And then he turned, facing her fully. She was shocked at how brazen he was, how open and careless he was being. He had essentially announced he was in town. It wasn't like him. Even if he had never been as careful as she was, he'd never been this easy to get to.

Something wasn't right.

But she would never get another chance like this. She couldn't walk away without taking it.

Ava gave herself a few minutes to work through it in her mind, coming at it from every angle, but could not think of a single reason he would purposely be so careless. Maybe he was losing his touch. Sometimes she wondered if he ever had the operative's touch, often wondering if he'd been paired with her back in the day because she would ensure he'd be careful. He was always the brazen one, the one who wanted to charge in without thinking everything through. She'd thought he'd learned a thing or two from her, but maybe he'd gone back to his old ways. His sloppy ways.

Whatever the case, the situation was as it presented itself, and she would not waste this chance at saving the life she'd created these past five years.

She rechecked the wind and stilled her body using the breathing techniques she'd once used on the regular, slowing her heart rate. Justin moved around the kitchen, going from the stove to the fridge to the counter, clearly making a late-night snack.

Still hardly able to believe he was exposing himself the way he was, Ava went into Sparrow mode, clearing her mind of all thoughts, her only focus on the chest of the man inside the house. And then in her mind, the man wasn't a man anymore. And he certainly wasn't the man she'd once shared her life with. Shared every secret with. Almost.

He was only a target. It was the way she was able to get on with what she had to do. Depersonalize the situation. Make it a job. Compartmentalize.

One more slow breath in, and then out through her mouth so slowly, so still…only her finger moving ever so slightly.

The shot was quiet—the silencer doing its job. The only sound was glass shattering as the bullet hit the window and in the same moment, the target went down.

She got him straight to the chest, exactly as she'd intended.

Ava didn't smile. Tried not to think.

It was always that way after a hit. Emotions were tricky things in the moment, and she used all her energy to keep them pushed as far away as possible, focusing on the rest of the job. Putting away her equipment, making any sign of her having been there disappear.

Thankfully, the emotional distress only lasted a short while. Some kind of primal reaction that faded quickly if she didn't let it take hold. By the time she made it into the Lawson house, any residual pangs had wafted away. It was one of the reasons she was good at what she did. Had stayed human enough to stay on the right side—some operatives were apt to switch sides on a whim…or financial incentive—but detached enough to be able to sleep at night. She understood what needed to be done, and not everyone had the capabilities to do it.

Truthfully, she hadn't been sure she was still capable after living in the world she'd been living in the past five years, allowing herself to get close to people again, to let real emotions in again. But it was the same as it had ever been.

She eased into the Lawson house, quickly and quietly. In theory, there should be no one to be quiet for, but it had always been her way. Soft and quiet as a tiny bird, disturbing as little as possible.

She wouldn't be able to clean up completely—the broken glass of the window would stay, but she couldn't leave a body for the poor Lawsons to find. Though as she crept though the house, something felt wrong. She knew it immediately.

And as she moved into the kitchen where all she found was a disturbing lack of a dead body, her heart sunk. She grabbed for the firearm at her side, even as she knew there was no point.

She could feel it as surely as she felt her heart speed in her chest.

The Crow was long gone.

Chapter Eight

Zach was at a loss.

He'd practically worn the finish off the patch of floor he'd been pacing for the past two hours, not knowing what to do, trying to convince himself there had to be a reasonable explanation for what he had seen.

Ava sneaking from her house—just an hour or so after she'd told him to his face that she was tired, implying she was headed to bed. And she should have been headed to bed considering she'd have to rise again at the crack of dawn, if not sooner, in order to start her baking for the festival guests.

But that was very much not what she had done.

Zach hadn't meant to be watching, but something in him was drawn to his windows that night, even after he'd turned his lights off and "gone to bed" too. He hadn't really gone to bed. All he'd done was tuck Chloe in, and then head to his room. Yes, he'd had intentions of turning in, but with all that had happened, there was no way in hell he was going to fall asleep anytime soon.

Still, he didn't want Chloe to worry, so he turned off his light and lay on his bed hoping by some miracle he'd actually drift off. But after lying there for a good fifteen minutes with thoughts rolling through his head, picking up speed as if they were on a runaway, downhill trajectory, he was even further from sleep than he had been when he lay down.

And then he heard the noise.

It wasn't a particularly loud noise, but it was very familiar.

For a moment he wondered if he was losing it. Had he fallen asleep and not realized it? Because what he heard was a sound he heard almost every day…but never until morning. Ava's garage door.

He checked the time on his phone.

Not quite midnight. Okay, so he wasn't losing it.

He got out of bed and moved the curtain a hair, just in time to see Ava's car backing out of her garage, down the driveway and out onto the street…all without turning on the headlights of the car.

Which was incredibly weird.

Because she wouldn't have anything to hide, right? And then, in a moment of extreme clarity, Zach realized she did have something to hide. She'd been acting weird ever since the kiss. And yeah, that kiss had changed everything, and maybe Ava was scared of what it meant—God, knew Zach was scared too—but Ava had never been one to hide from what worried her. She was more of a "get it all out in the open" kind of person—something that had given Zach more than his fair share of uncomfortable conversations.

Like the one he'd had the other night with her about Kimberly. The conversation he'd avoided like the plague for years. The one he knew would make him and Ava grow even closer because it was one of those "vulnerability moments," which he hated with the absolute breadth of his being, but apparently one that his subconscious was willing to have because maybe, just maybe, he was ready to move on. And damn it, if he was going to move on, he wanted to move on with Ava.

After Zach paced in his room for twenty minutes, a thousand scenarios running through his head with possible explanations for Ava sneaking out of her house in the middle of the night, he moved downstairs. Much more room to pace there.

But after another hour with no sign of Ava returning, he still hadn't come any closer to an explanation that made any sense.

Why would she feel like she had to sneak out? It wasn't like she answered to anyone, let alone Zach, who was likely the only person who might even notice her leave. He'd never ask that of her. But what was with the timing? All these years, he hadn't let himself go there, then lately, things had started to feel different. Like maybe he didn't have to be alone for the rest of his life. Like maybe, if he gave love another shot, it wouldn't have to end badly.

And then the kiss happened, and everything changed. Like the universe was confirming yes, finally, he could have something good without worrying it was all going to leave him. The kiss felt like a forever. Like everything in the world was clicking into place. Like he'd finally found a way to feel "right" when he'd always felt a little bit wrong somehow.

Zach could feel himself starting to spiral. The thoughts entering his mind barely even made sense anymore, but he was having about as much luck stopping them as he would stopping an avalanche with his bare hands.

He was also starting to feel a sense of panic, an urge to get out into the open air. The house was closing in on him. But there was Chloe to consider. She was usually a heavy sleeper and rarely woke up during the night, but if she did, he couldn't let her find the house empty.

He had an old baby monitor in her room, which he'd been

meaning to get rid of for years, but just for one night, he could sneak in and turn it on. But then he'd risk waking her.

He could leave a note, he supposed. He paced some more, trying to think of what might happen if Chloe woke up. She'd probably be headed for the bathroom and then straight back to bed, which wouldn't be an issue. But if she woke up and came looking for him, he'd feel like the world's worst dad if she couldn't find him and thought she'd been left alone. If that was the case, she'd go straight to his room, so he quickly wrote a note saying he'd be out in the front yard.

At least out there, he'd have room to pace. Room for his thoughts to—well, to what, he wasn't sure, but he supposed he hoped they'd leave or work themselves out or something.

He wrote two more quick notes—one for the kitchen in case Chloe went for water, and one he taped to the inside of the front door, in case she somehow missed the other two notes and made it all the way to the point she would head out the door. It was definitely overkill, but he wasn't going to take any chances stressing his kid out.

Outside, the air was cool, and it suddenly felt like he could breathe again.

But the thoughts still swirled, spreading like wildfire, becoming increasingly more intense by the second. One minute he was almost convinced Ava had just left to check on the stove or something at the coffee shop. The next he was in a full-blown panic imagining Ava being so disgusted by his kiss that she packed up and fled in the night, never to be seen again.

Unfortunately, he couldn't make any of the believable— or even a single one of the truly ridiculous—scenarios add up. It didn't make sense that she snuck out with no head- lights if it was something innocuous, like checking the coffee shop, and, well, the wild scenarios didn't fit Ava. She wasn't a runner.

A brief thought flitted through his head. The way she arrived in town had been sudden and unexpected, and for the first time he wondered what the circumstances had been. It hadn't been so out of the ordinary that he thought anything of it at the time, but...could there have been something off about her late in the day arrival? Or the fact he never saw anyone take a look at the house next door before the moment she moved in. Was that a thing? Did people buy houses off the internet without going to see them in person? Seemed like a rash, irresponsible thing to do—and Ava certainly wasn't that. But still, he supposed it was possible.

He rolled a dozen more scenarios over in his head. Reasons someone might buy a house sight unseen. Running from a domestic situation, financial instability—but then, how would one afford a house?—evading the police...

They were all terrible. Unless there had been some sort of bidding war over the house. But he was sure he would have heard about it if there had been. Not to mention the local Realtor, Sandy St. James, was not particularly known for keeping secrets under wraps. Half the town would have kept him in the loop on that one. Hell, probably 99.8 percent of the town, considering it affected him directly, being next door and everything.

He was so lost in his thoughts, still pacing between his house and hers that it took him much longer than it should have to hear the crunch of the gravel on the street, nearing Ava's driveway. There was no way to run back across to his place without being seen, but he didn't particularly love the idea of being caught out there pacing in the middle of the night either.

Ava had made it clear she wasn't interested in being anything more than friends, and pacing in front of her house was a look that was a hell of a lot more stalkerish than Zach preferred.

In a panic, he strode up the steps of Ava's front porch, clinging to the shadows.

And the moment he got up there, he realized he was trapped.

She was still driving with no headlights, and worse, she was already out of the car to lift her garage door manually, he assumed, so it would make less noise.

There was no question. She was absolutely hiding something. Most likely from him.

And, even though his curiosity had never been so piqued, he wished, more than anything, he could disappear into thin air, just for a couple of minutes.

Ava drove into her garage, and Zach wondered if he should make a break for it. Unfortunately, by the time the thought could fully form, she was already coming back out of her garage to close the door again.

He skulked farther into the shadows, wishing he was back to feeling as creepy as he had staring out the window earlier. Because his "I am such a creeper" factor had gone way up since then. It was shocking how easily he'd turned into an irrational being when all his life he'd been rational as hell.

Ava made her way across the short expanse of grass, then up the stairs, headed for her front door. Zach began to believe maybe, just maybe she would simply go inside and never know he'd been there at all, pleading to the heavens that if he were to escape this humiliation, he would never, ever do anything so stupid again in his life.

Her keys jingled as she reached toward the door, and

Zach's heart began to soar. It was happening! He was going to make it out of there unscathed!

And then, in a final second of absolute horror, mixed with a hearty dose of confusion, a light burst on out of nowhere, throwing them both into a dizzying flash of movement and terror. Zach terrified of getting caught, but realizing poor Ava was probably in fear of her life.

Although, as he stared down the barrel of the gun she'd pulled out from somewhere in her jeans' waistband, so fast he'd barely even seen her move, perhaps she hadn't been quite as caught off guard as he thought.

IN THE SPLIT second that passed, Ava fully expected to see Justin's steely blue eyes staring back at her, but those eyes were not the frigid blue she anticipated at all. They were warm and kind and…well, truth be told, looking fairly terrified.

"Jesus, Zach!" Ava yelled, quickly lowering the gun and shaking it a bit, like it was hot and she could only touch it gingerly. "What the hell are you doing? I could have killed you!"

She was out of breath, her heart beating fast after being jolted into action. It was only thanks to her training that she'd taken the nanosecond before she blindly reacted and pulled the trigger.

So close. Way too close.

The thought of losing Zach was too much, but imagining it could have been her own fault made her instantly sick. She moved closer to the porch railing to lean on it, feeling rather unsteady on her feet.

Zach stood speechless for a bit, hands in the air like someone in a damn movie "stickup" scene or something. Slowly, he lowered his hands.

"Um, sorry." He cleared his throat. "Didn't mean to startle you," he said weakly, lowering himself into a nearby chair, looking a little shaky and a little green around the edges.

Ava leaned hard into the railing she'd been clutching, her adrenaline waning fast, suddenly feeling exhausted and wondering what time it was. It had to be at least two in the morning if not later.

"Zach, what are you doing on my porch in the middle of the night? In the dark," she added, to make sure she pointed out how weird it really was. Maybe to make herself feel better for pulling a gun on her best friend.

Who, she realized, after what had gone on earlier, and then over the past couple of minutes, was maybe not actually her best friend anymore.

Zach had been staring at his quaking hands and finally looked up, a little dazed. "Um… I," he said, and looked around like he was trying to come up with some kind of plausible explanation, but then his shoulders dropped, and he let out a long sigh. "This is going to sound dumb, but I was out here getting some fresh air."

"Some fresh air," Ava said, the doubt heavy in her voice. "On my porch."

"No. Well yeah, but…" Zach trailed off again.

"Zach," Ava said, moving to sit across from him. She needed to be at eye level. "Talk to me. What's going on?"

He looked into her eyes then, and Ava wanted nothing more than to close the two-foot gap and latch on to those soft lips again, but there was no way they could go there. Not ever again.

"I just—" he let out another short breath, like he was giving up on trying to make it look like anything other than it was "—I was out here pacing, okay?" he said. "I saw you."

Ava's brows furrowed together, her brain scrambling to figure out what, exactly, he had seen. Her stomach instantly seized, thinking the worst. What if he had seen her shoot at the Lawson house?

"I saw you leave. In the dark. With no headlights on."

Oh.

To his credit, the words weren't accusing, just had a sense of…hurt or something behind them.

"Zach, I—"

He held up a hand. "It's none of my business. And I have no business being here right now either. I don't know what I was thinking." He moved to stand.

"Zach," Ava said, her heart hurting, stretching as if it were trying to reach for him. She should let him walk away—it would be better…safer for everyone—but she couldn't do it. Couldn't leave him like that. Couldn't let him think whatever the hell he might be thinking about her. And the kicker was, it shouldn't matter what he thought. But right then, it was the only thing that *did* matter. "Can you please sit? I… I don't know if we can figure all this out, but can we at least try?"

Zach settled back into the seat and nodded.

Ava looked around, suddenly realizing they were exposed out there. "Where's Chloe?" she asked, trying to keep her voice steady.

"Sleeping," Zach said.

"Let's go over to your place and talk," Ava suggested. "I wouldn't want her to wake up not knowing where you are."

"Yeah, okay," Zach said, and there was still something unsure in his voice, almost zoned out.

Ava let Zach lead the way down the porch steps as she

took a long look around, searching for any sign of movement—a flash of metal or glass in the moonlight, an out of place rustling of bushes—but she didn't sense anything.

She probably wouldn't even if there was danger. Justin was usually too good for that.

Which only sent her thoughts whirring again. Had he meant for her to see him back at the Lawson house? He had to have been wearing a vest to have gotten away. There hadn't even been any blood at the scene. Which meant what? Had he planned the whole thing and she'd completely fallen for it?

She felt like a damn fool. And the two of them absolutely, 100 percent, needed to get inside the house immediately and get the curtains shut.

Once inside, Zach seemed to get a little clearer, pulling some whisky out of the cupboard and pouring it into two small glasses while Ava shut the curtains.

"We should move to the living room," she said.

They'd be farther away from windows than at the kitchen table.

Zach didn't argue, just set the glasses down on the coffee table and put his head in his hands, pulling his fingers through his hair slowly before taking a sip from his glass and leaning back heavily into the couch.

After checking each window in the room, making sure everything was shut, locked and covered, Ava finally came to sit across from him.

"Ava, what's going on?" Zach asked. "Why do you have a gun?"

She knew it would be the question on his mind since the moment it had been pointed in his direction, and she couldn't blame him. Guns weren't especially common in the town of Ambrosia Falls, unless someone was using a toy one for a target practice game at the fair.

There was no way out of it, she decided. She was going to have to come clean.

Mostly.

She took a slow sip of the whisky, feeling every inch of the burn from her lips to her stomach, letting it take over and fill her with something, anything other than the dread of what she was about to say.

"When I came to Ambrosia Falls," she said, "it was because I was running from something. Well, someone, I guess."

Zach nodded, like he'd suspected her to say exactly that. He also looked like he was itching to jump in and ask a million questions, but he stayed quiet. Still.

So still it made Ava nervous, and she marveled at how often this man made her nervous. No one had ever done that to her before. No one had ever been so important.

"I was involved with a man," she began, hating how the damn story was already making her sound like a victim. She had never allowed that term to be something used to define her. But she sure as hell couldn't tell him the whole truth. She couldn't bear what he might think of her then. "He was great at first…you know how the story goes. And then he tried to hurt me, and he had powerful allies and so I was put into witness protection."

Zach's mouth opened slightly in surprise, but he remained quiet.

"And, as I'm sure you've guessed, after all these years, he's found me."

Finally, Zach spoke. "So, the fire. And the water tower? That was all…this guy?"

Ava nodded.

"Shit," he said. "He broke into your place."

Ava nodded. "Looks like it."

"And the police are on their way," he said. "Maybe."

"I wish we had never called them now," Ava said. "Knowing what we're up against, the police might be more in the way than they are of help. They'll think this is just some regular guy, not someone trained."

"Trained?"

Ava nodded. "Justin's…well, he's sort of an operative."

There was a pause that went on long enough to make Ava a touch queasy.

"Like CIA or something?"

"Kind of. He's more of an off-the-books kind of operative."

Zach let out a slow breath. "The kind that does the work the sanctioned operatives can't really get away with without certain people and agencies asking too many questions?"

"Exactly."

"So we have one of the world's most dangerous men after us? Here, in Ambrosia Falls?" His voice rose a bit at the end, and as much as Ava hated that she was freaking Zach out, it had to be one of the most adorable things she'd heard in a long time.

"He's not after us," Ava corrected. "He's after me. And I plan to fix that as soon as the sun comes up."

Zach looked a little panicked. "What does that mean?"

"Zach," she said, "I have to leave. It's the only way."

He shook his head, the panic morphing into a resolve that had Ava's heart melting faster than butter on a cooktop.

"No. You are not leaving. We've finally, I don't know,

started to figure out what this is," he said, gesturing between the two of them, "and I'm not about to let that go."

A sting formed behind Ava's eyes. The last thing she wanted was to never be able to see it through with Zach, but there was no other way."

"I've already tried to fix it, Zach."

"What do you mean you've already tried?"

"I tried to find him. To take him out." She hated that the way he thought of her was probably changing by the second.

"Like kill him?" he asked, saying the last words in a whisper.

She sighed. "Yeah."

He ran his fingers through his hair. "Why the hell would you do something so dangerous by yourself?" he asked, his eyes wild.

Ava contemplated coming clean. All the way clean. Contemplated filling him in on the fact that she was more lethal than Justin. That she'd had so many more years' experience behind her. Though that might not be true anymore, considering her experience had come to a standstill once she moved to Ambrosia Falls. She wondered what Justin had been up to since that fateful day five years ago.

"It's fine," she said. "I've learned to take care of myself."

"Well, you don't have to anymore."

"Of course I do, Zach. This is ridiculous. I'll go and everyone here will be safe. I wouldn't be able to live with myself if anything bad happened to the people here. Knowing it was my fault and I could have stopped it by leaving."

"You can't start over all over again," Zach said.

"I can," Ava replied. "I've done it before, and I can do it again."

"Well," he said, breathing hard. "Then I don't think I can start over all over again."

"Zach," Ava said, moving to turn away. She couldn't take the look in his eye. The one saying she meant everything to him. Of course, she only knew the look so well because the feeling was disastrously mutual.

Zach grabbed her arm and turned her gently to face him.

"Like it or not, it's not just you that you have to think about anymore. This town, all of us…we're your family now. And even if nothing more ever comes out of you and me, I'm your family now. You're my best friend, Ava. We're going to figure this out together."

Chapter Nine

Strangely, Zach was relieved. He'd obviously known something was up, and the fact it had nothing to do with the kiss made everything okay again.

Well, maybe not everything, considering Ava's life was being threatened by a professional damn spy or whatever, but he'd be lying if he said he wasn't relieved all of it meant that he and Ava might still have a chance to be together.

"Maybe he's already on the run," Zach said. "If you tried to take him out."

Ava shook her head. "I think he knew I was coming. He must have had it all planned out. He's messing with me."

"Jesus," Zach said. "This guy is sick."

"And," she said, "he's not playing by his usual playbook."

"So, what now?" Zach asked.

"The smartest thing is for me to get out of here—"

"Stop," Zach said. "You aren't going anywhere. We just need to find a way to get the cops out here faster."

Ava shook her head. "That will put them in danger too. They won't understand how Justin is. He's smart. He's more dangerous than anyone they've come across before."

She gave him a serious look, like they should give up too, but Zach hadn't waited five years with a massive crush to let it go the exact day he finally decided to do something about it.

"Okay, so where would Justin go?"

Zach hated the way this guy's name sounded in his mouth—he'd honestly love to get his hands on this guy who'd hurt the most important person in his world—but he pushed the feeling aside. For now.

Ava sighed. "In the old days, he would find someplace nice. Someplace that wouldn't be roughing it too much. Let's just say Justin likes his amenities. I found him in the Lawson house."

Zach raised his eyebrows. "He was in Gus and Millie's place?"

Ava nodded.

"So are we looking for another place like that?"

"I doubt it. He knew I was coming. Had taken precautions."

"So he knew you'd know his regular routine and was counting on you coming after him."

"I guess so," Ava said. "I thought he'd be just cocky enough to stick with his routine."

"I'm surprised he'd even think you'd come after him like that."

"Um, yeah," Ava said, shifting a little, like she was uncomfortable.

Zach figured he'd be a little uncomfortable too if something like this suddenly sprung up from his past. And even though Ava was a victim, she thought she was safe and had finally let people back into her circle again. Had finally begun to trust again, and now her whole world was imploding.

And if he knew Ava at all—which he liked to think he

did—she would even be a little embarrassed she hadn't been able to take care of it on her own. The woman was nothing if not fiercely independent. It was a quality he admired about her, a quality that, frankly, made him even more attracted to her, but at some point, she had to realize she didn't have to do everything on her own.

At least he hoped she would, since there was nothing he wanted more in the world than to take care of her in every way she'd let him.

He wasn't sure what the hell he was going to do once they found this guy, but he was anxious to make a plan and get it over with. More importantly, he was anxious to get on with his life with Ava. Assuming this whole thing with Justin was the reason she'd blown him off earlier.

Except…what if it wasn't?

Shit.

"Um, can we pause for a second and get something straight?" Zach asked.

"Um, sure?" Ava said, phrasing it like a question.

Zach stood and started to pace. Lord knew he'd done enough pacing for one night, but there was no way he could sit still and say what he was about to say. "Okay. So, the, um…" He cleared his throat and stopped pacing, turning to Ava. "The kiss."

Ava nodded once. "The kiss."

Zach's pacing resumed. "Yeah, so I'm just going to lay it all out there and say I don't actually think it was a mistake. And maybe you still do or whatever, or maybe you said it because of this Justin thing, but I thought we should, like, get on the same page about it."

He stilled. Turned. Looked at her, his heart filled with equal parts dread and hope.

Ava stared back. For what seemed like an impossible amount of time, though it might have only been a heartbeat. And then she smiled. A shy smile Zach had never seen on her—she was always the least shy person in the room—but somehow it made her look more like...herself.

Zach held his breath.

"I don't think it was a mistake either," she said.

Zach felt every speck of stress release from his body in a giant wave of relief, and for a moment, everything was right with the world. And then, knowing the seriousness of the situation they were in—a place where she could be taken from him at any moment—every muscle tightened up again almost as quickly as they had relaxed.

"Okay, good," he said, his voice serious. "Then we have to concentrate on getting this guy so we can, you know, do that some more."

Ava looked like she was working hard to hide a smile, and somehow almost even managed it. "Okay," she said. "Sounds reasonable."

"As reasonable as talking about taking out a guy can sound, I suppose," Zach said.

"Indeed," Ava agreed.

"Okay, so now that we have that out of the way," Zach continued, "I'm guessing this Justin asshole needs another place to hide out then."

"Probably," Ava said, deep in thought.

"Probably?" Zach asked.

"Yeah, but it doesn't matter where he is," Ava said, as she noticed the first traces of the rising sun break past the edges of the curtains in Zach's living room. "Because we're going to make him come to us."

AVA NEEDED SLEEP BADLY, but a quick glance at her watch told her it was time to get up. Except she hadn't actually gone to bed. It was a damn good thing she worked in a coffee shop, because she was going to have to be mainlining the stuff for the rest of the day.

"What do you mean, he's going to come to us?" Zach asked.

"It's the one thing he won't expect," Ava said. "He's going to assume I'm either going to run or try to go after him again. And since he's been a step ahead of me this whole time, he'll probably continue being a step ahead of me. So we have to do the one thing he doesn't think we'll do."

"Which is…nothing?"

"Exactly. At least for now until I can work out a real plan. If there's anything I know, it's that plans made under duress or exhaustion are never as good as plans that have had plenty of time to be thought through."

"So, what…we just go about our day as usual?" Zach asked, looking slightly horrified.

"It's me he wants, and I know how to be careful," Ava said.

"There is no way I'm going to let you out of my sight for a second," Zach countered.

Ava only rolled her eyes a little. "You're going to have to let me out of your sight for at least a second. Like, for example, when I go home in a few minutes to shower and change."

His lips twitched up into a half grin. "I mean, are you sure you don't need any supervision for those, um, difficult tasks?"

The thought of Zach watching her shower sent a thrill through Ava's body, but she managed to keep the crimson of her face tempered. "I'm pretty sure I can manage," she said, though she gave him a little smirk back that hopefully said once all this was over, she might be game for some sudsy supervision.

"Okay, I'll let you go get ready for the day, and I'll do the same over here, but you have to stay on the phone with me the entire time."

"Don't you think that's a little overkill?" Ava asked.

"Do I think it's overkill to take the absolute minimum amount of precaution when we know there is a trained killer after you? One which you've recently poked like a damn bear, except instead of just poking him you actually shot him?" He raised his eyebrows as if waiting in great antici-pation for her answer.

"Um, okay. You have a point," she reluctantly agreed. "Even though I still don't think he'll do anything."

"But that's what I don't get. Why don't you think he won't do anything?"

Ava shifted. "Because he's toying with me. The water tower, the fire, the pictures he left on my doorstep..." She decided not to let Zach in on the fact that the pictures had actually been left right there in the room while they were busy making out. "I'd bet my life he's not done yet. He has a plan, and if there's one thing I know about Justin, it's that he will not be satisfied unless his plan is acted out to per-fection. It's why we're taking today to regroup and do noth-ing. It's going to drive him to a tizzy wondering what the hell we're up to."

"I gotta say, it's probably not going to be a tizzy-free kind of day for me either," Zach admitted.

"I know. It's going to be tense. But we'll be on alert and make the best of it for now. If we get any time to ourselves at the coffee shop, we'll think about what our next steps will be—maybe even get a chance to talk them through."

Zach nodded. "I don't like it, but I'll agree to your plan."

"Good," Ava said, turning to head to the door.

"I just have one more question."

She turned back and he grinned.

"Would it be okay if I kiss you?"

Ava couldn't stop the smile from creeping across her face. "Um, sure," she said, cool as ever even though her mind was screaming *yes, yes, yes!*

He stepped toward her, then slowed, grabbing hold of her arms lightly, his hands shaking a little.

"I'm so nervous," he said, then let out a little chuckle.

She laughed a little too, her insides vibrating—the excited feeling that made a person shiver as if they're cold. "I'm still me," she said, though the idea made her feel guilty. She was still hiding so much from him.

"I know, that's why I'm so nervous," he said, his face inching closer until finally his lips met hers and she let out a tiny sighing moan, relief flooding over her.

Strange that relief was the sensation she felt, though she supposed she'd been building the moment up for so many years, and then there was the whole roller coaster of the day—yesterday now, she supposed—making every emotion hover so close to the surface that none of them would really be a surprise. Grieving the idea of losing Zach only moments after it felt like she really found him, and then the hope blooming again…it was all so much. And she knew she couldn't quite trust any of it.

Justin had to be dealt with first.

But Ava was determined to savor the kiss, trying like hell to burn it into her mind and make it last forever. But it's funny what the brain did when those moments were happening though. Almost the precise second a person decided they wanted to really remember something because it's so damn good, or delicious, or perfect, that betraying brain tended to check out like a traitor, making the moment fog up and become hazy, leaving only a vague whispery essence of the real thing. It was why Ava knew she would crave that kiss forever.

The kiss was soft, not as urgent as the one in the coffee shop, but still, it felt familiar. Not because it was their second kiss, but because it felt like Zach. This had been exactly the way she'd imagined being with him would be. Sure. Steady. Gentle, but strong at the same time. Where the first kiss had been a whirlwind, a frenzy, this one felt a whole lot like being safe.

Of course, brains didn't only betray with memory, but with recollection too. And again, with its precise timing, the moment even the idea of safe popped into her mind, she immediately remembered how very unsafe things were right then.

She pulled gently out of the kiss, reluctantly blinking back into the room.

"Well, that's a good start to the day," Zach said with a grin, his arms still around her.

She smiled and nodded. "It definitely is."

"Okay," Zach said, taking a step back, which only made Ava want to take a step forward to close the gap again. He pulled out his phone and started typing, and while Ava was still trying to figure out what he was doing, her own phone started vibrating.

She hit the button to answer. "Am I supposed to say hello?" she asked, smirking.

"No, you don't have to talk. Go get ready like you normally would. Just don't go out of reach of the phone."

"Got it," Ava said, nodding, then headed to the door and straight out, turning only to wave her phone in Zach's direction, letting him know she would keep it by her side.

Outside, Ava scanned the area for threats. If Justin was out there and had a scope on her, there was little she could do. But not seeing anything obvious, she made her way back to her place, thinking about what she'd said to Zach.

She didn't know if what she said was true—about how Justin wouldn't do anything rash because he was still toying with her. Hell, she'd shot him, riled the bear, and frankly had no idea what he'd do now—Justin had never been known for being the calmest agent out there, but she didn't have a plan and needed time.

And in the meantime, she would keep a closer watch on this town than anyone ever had before.

Chapter Ten

If Zach thought the bell over the door at The Other Apple Store had been bad before, it was absolutely driving him up the wall now. Never in his life had his senses been on such high alert, and he was suddenly suspicious of everyone, even people he'd known all his life. Which was ridiculous, but it wasn't like he could make the feelings go away.

And since it was the Apple Cider Festival, that damned bell kept chiming almost nonstop. A group of women would come in, and Zach would be suspicious of them, even though he knew Justin was a guy. A senior couple strolled in, and he'd be suspicious of them too. What if Justin had coconspirators of the geriatric variety? A family of four strolled in and Zach was especially suspicious…like seriously, why weren't those kids in school? Did we all just take our kids to random towns in the middle of the school year now? *Come on, people!*

The worst part was, he knew he was being ridiculous, but he couldn't help it. This thing with Ava was too important. He couldn't risk anything happening to it before it even got started. If they didn't see it through, he'd always wonder. And then his thoughts turned to the kiss that morning. It had been so different from the one yesterday. Maybe there hadn't been as many sparks flying as with the first one, but Zach kinda loved that. Because he knew sometimes their life could be full of passion, sometimes full of friendship, and sometimes simple appreciation and love. It was the perfect blend...much like the perfect cup of coffee, he thought, as Ava walked up and jolted him out of his daydream.

"Whatcha thinking about?" she asked.

"Um, nothing," Zach said, bringing the cup to his lips a little too quickly and sloshing coffee over the edge of the cup, thankfully missing his clothes by about a millimeter.

"Yeah." Ava nodded. "I've been thinking a lot about, um, nothing too," she said, and even shot him a wink before she moved on to the next table.

Cripes, Zach thought. Here he was daydreaming when he was supposed to be figuring out a plan to save the love of his life.

Wait. Love of his life? Was that what Ava was? No, it was way too early to know for sure. Of course, when does anyone ever know for sure, really?

Damn it! He was doing it again.

He shook all thoughts out of his head and concentrated only on finding a plan. A way to find this guy. A guy he didn't have even the slightest clue what he looked like, what he sounded like...nothing. Zach's shoulders slumped.

He'd never felt so helpless in his whole life.

The jingle of the bells above the door interrupted his thoughts for the thirty-eight millionth time. A man, all alone, which was suspicious for the festival. Most people came with their family, or a group of friends, usually the ladies, or with someone who had newly become special to them. The Apple Cider Festival was nothing if not "the perfect weekend date destination," as the regional papers loved to tout.

Zach watched him closely. The man could have ducked into the coffee shop while his wife and kids were off bobbing for apple-themed prizes or perusing the local apple butters and honeys. Lord knew it was exactly what Zach would be doing if he was forced to attend some weird town's festival against his will.

But the man wasn't looking like he was having a crappy time. In fact, he looked downright cheerful, which Zach would have loved to say was strange, but in this town, cheer was basically the religion. The damn guy looked like he fit in perfectly, which was just so annoying. But Zach was used to pushing little annoyances out of the way, so he decided to give the guy the benefit of the doubt. Who knew, maybe the poor guy was just happy not to be stuck in some work cubicle for the day.

The man gave his order of coffee and an apple fritter—a little basic, but a solid order nonetheless—to Maureen, who was manning the counter while Ava no doubt created some delectable concoction in the back.

Zach pretended to be engrossed in his computer screen as the man sat, choosing the table directly across from him so they were facing each other.

Zach could never understand this move. Why, of all the places in a restaurant or café, would someone choose to sit staring straight at another human? Talk about awkward. He supposed some people did it on purpose, since they loved to chat with strangers…another thing he couldn't figure out. Ava would love it, Zach thought, then suddenly realized that could be a real benefit to him once they were officially together, since she could be the one to field all the awkward "people encounters."

Zach pretended to work for a while, keeping a keen eye on

the stranger across from him, even though he'd pretty much decided the guy was harmless. Of course, it wouldn't hurt to know for sure, so he decided to take a sip of coffee, which he'd been avoiding since it would mean taking his eyes off his screen and potentially engaging with those around him, including the man in question. Which, if he was trying to glean any kind of information—like whether he was a cold-blooded, murderous spy—it would probably be the quickest and easiest way. Well, quickest, anyway. There was nothing easy about talking to strangers in Zach's book. He moved his cup to his lips and took a long sip, gazing all around until finally his eyes landed on the man.

"You look pretty deep in thought there," the man said the literal second Zach acknowledged his presence.

Zach had known it. The man had been waiting all along to talk to someone. Which Zach always thought of as kind of insulting, since it wasn't Zach this person was particularly in-terested in talking to—he could have been absolutely anyone in the world and this man would have been perfectly happy. Like, if you're perfectly fine talking with just anyone, it had to mean you really only wanted to hear yourself talk, right?

"Um, yeah, I guess so," Zach answered.

"Got a deadline?" the man continued. "I assume you must be a writer by trade if you're working that hard in the middle of a Wednesday," he said, grinning.

At least, Zach thought, it wasn't a goofy grin. The guy seemed like a normal guy.

"Uh, no deadline. Well, at least not yet," Zach answered. "Just kicking around a few ideas, seeing what they might turn into."

"Nice," the man said. "I used to write. Wasn't as good at it as I wanted to be, unfortunately."

Zach knew the feeling well. He was pretty sure every writer knew the feeling, really, and after the little nugget of common ground, he found he was the one who was suddenly asking questions. "What did you write?"

The man shrugged. "Nonfiction stuff mostly." He grinned. "The problem was the research. I hated the research. So much time spent feeling like you're not actually accomplishing anything even though you're laying the groundwork, or whatever."

Zach tilted his head back and forth in agreement. "Yeah, not my favorite either. Although there's still some research involved in fiction."

"Ah, fiction. Yes, that's true I suppose," the man said. "But it's not all research, all the time."

"So, were you a journalist then?" Zach asked, finding he was actually enjoying chatting with the guy.

"Educational books," he said. "And then creating online courses for schools after that."

"Interesting," Zach said. "Sounds like it would require a lot of—"

"Research," they both said at the same time, then shared a small chuckle.

"Nothing against the educational sector," the guy said, "but lately I've been craving something a bit more creative."

Zach nodded. "So what's next then?"

"Well, I don't know, to be honest. I've been toying with the idea of a novel."

"Also not easy work," Zach said, "but it is rewarding… mostly."

"I bet," the guy said, a bit of a gleam in his eye now.

"Tell you what," Zach said. "Why don't you we exchange numbers, and if you do decide to take that route, let me know.

I'm happy to lend a hand where I can." Writing was such a solitary practice, and could be discouraging, especially when starting out. If he hadn't had the help of a few key people early on in his career, he never would have gotten to where he was. He liked to pay it forward whenever he got the chance...as long as it wasn't someone who seemed like they were going to take advantage. Which, by now, he could usually spot a mile away. But this guy seemed genuine enough.

"That's very generous of you," the man said, pulling out his phone.

Zach did the same and they exchanged electronic business cards. "'Glen Abrams,'" Zach said, reading the info aloud.

Glen nodded. "The listing has my previous educational work info attached, but the number's still the same. This way, you'll have a better chance at remembering who I am down the road." He stood and moved closer to Zach's table, holding out his hand.

Zach stood and took it. "Perfect," he said.

"Well, I better get going," Glen said. "The wife's probably out there figuring a way to convince me we need to move out to the country," he said. "Not that I don't love the country, but I think I'm more of a city guy."

"Fair enough," Zach said, thinking he wished there were a few more guys as down to earth as he was in this world.

AVA'S STOMACH SEIZED, her lunch threatening to make an encore appearance as she stood in the shadows watching Zach shake hands with the man who wanted to kill her.

Had tried to kill her and was back to finish the job.

The moment their hands touched, a lightning bolt of clarity shot through her.

What the hell was she doing?

Every moment…every second she stayed in town was another moment she was putting the people she cared about at risk.

How could she have been so careless? She should have been packing the moment she discovered she hadn't taken Justin out back at the Lawson house.

She knew Justin would try something else to mess with her—that he wanted nothing more than to make her suffer the way he must believe he'd been suffering for the past five years—but she didn't think he'd go after the people around her. Not the ones closest to her. Sure, he put people in danger with the water tower and the fire, but those were simply potential innocent casualties—something Justin never cared enough about.

But she was the Sparrow, trained not to get close to people. Trained to easily walk away the moment it was time. Trained to never let her feelings get in the way.

Of course, if Justin had been watching her for any length of time, a thought making her intensely queasy all over again, he would know she'd dropped that notion a long time ago. Longer than she was even willing to admit to herself.

Worse, it was the reason she was still in town when she should have been long gone.

And she'd bet her life Justin had known exactly what he was doing. He knew the moment the people who were really in her life were threatened—something that happened simply by being in the same room with Justin—she would have no choice but to leave.

He was smoking her right out of her town. Right out of her new life.

She wanted to drop everything and go, just turn around, walk right out the door of that kitchen and never look back.

But that wasn't how the town of Ambrosia Falls worked. In about two minutes flat, someone would wonder where she'd gone. And about one minute later, someone would ask Zach if he'd seen her. And then he would come after her. She wouldn't even have a chance to pack the essentials—namely the supplies and weapons she had stashed in various corners of her house—before he'd be on her. Telling her she couldn't go. Telling her they were in this together. Telling her all the things that terrified her to her core.

Because they could not be in this together. Not really. Zach was a capable guy, but he wasn't trained like she was…or like Justin was. He wouldn't stand a chance out there. And she couldn't deal with him out there either. She'd be far more worried about protecting Zach than she'd ever be for herself. She didn't know what she'd do if something ever happened to Zach.

She could never live with herself.

A plan quickly formed in her head. She hated when plans came so easily. The easy plans were usually only easy because there was a lack of options. And this time, she only had one option—run—and Justin knew it as well as she did.

The afternoon went by quickly. Too quickly.

Ava was going back and forth in her mind about how to say goodbye to Zach. Imagining not saying goodbye to him was inconceivable but telling him she was leaving was not a choice either. He'd try to talk her out of it, or worse, try to follow her.

The only thing she could do was sneak away in the night, being far more careful this time to make sure he wouldn't see her leave. When she'd first arrived in town all those years ago, she'd made several contingency plans, and she still had a beat-up old Chevy truck in storage across town. She'd have to pack up the things she needed and make her way there on foot. It wouldn't be easy, since she wanted at least a few days' worth of supplies, but she'd been in worse situations.

If luck were on her side, maybe Justin wouldn't catch on about her other mode of transport right away. He'd know she was gone in the morning—right along with everyone else in town and probably within a twenty-five-mile radius too—but half a day's head start might be the best she could do. Especially if Justin didn't know what she was driving or which direction she'd gone.

Still, she couldn't leave without saying something to Zach. She couldn't be that cruel.

Around the time Zach packed up his stuff and was heading out to get Chloe from school, the idea of a letter came to her. And if she left it in his mailbox, he wouldn't see it until he checked for the mail in the morning, or hopefully longer. It would be perfect. She'd be long gone, and he wouldn't have too much of a chance to worry.

Then, of course, her thoughts started churning over what to write. It wasn't like she could just be all like, thanks for everything, byeee! Ugh.

But how could you tell someone how much they meant to you in one little letter? She hoped he already knew—at least somewhat—how large a role in her life he'd come to play, but she was sure he didn't fully understand how much he meant to her. He couldn't understand that he was everything, and everything was something she'd never even come close to before.

She had closed herself off her entire life, even with Justin, she realized. Coming to Ambrosia Falls she'd seen how the real world could be—simple, even if it wasn't easy, and filled with a comfort she had never known before.

It was like the town—and Zach—had woken her from a hazy dream world and, for the first time in her life, filled everything with color.

After the rush of folks buying their breads and desserts to take home for dinner, Ava locked up the store the same way she did every evening. She didn't take anything extra with her—everything she would need was back at her place. Her supplies were mostly ready to go. She just needed to gather them all from their hiding places around her house, then slip out into the night. Fingers crossed she'd be unseen, by Justin and, most especially, by Zach.

She drove home and parked her car in the garage like she always did, then went into the house and texted Zach first thing.

Hey, I'm home, but I'm beat. It was an easy excuse, considering neither of them had gotten any sleep the night before. I've double-checked all the doors and windows and have the security system on. Gotta get some sleep. Have a good night.

Short, sweet, and just familiar enough he wouldn't get suspicious. Even though everything had changed between them in the past couple days, they'd never texted each other anything more intimate than the sort of message she'd just written, so she hoped it would work.

A minute later, her phone dinged with a text.

Me too. Please be careful. See you in the morning.

You be careful too, she typed, feeling a twinge of guilt at the see you in the morning part.

She avoided the letter writing as long as she could, going around the house and collecting only the essentials—small weapons she could easily carry, food supplies meant for backwoods camping, a couple changes of clothes and a second pair of sturdy shoes in case the whole thing went south, and she had to make her way on foot. The final things she packed were various forms of ID—with several different aliases—and some thick rolls of cash she'd been slowly adding to each week over the years.

And then it was time. She set her bag by the back door and sat down at her kitchen table with a pen and paper. She'd gone back and forth all day about what to write, finally deciding she owed it to Zach to lay it all out there. Not the stuff about her history or why Justin was so focused on her, but about the way she felt.

Dear Zach,
By the time you see this letter, I'll be gone. Long gone, I hope. But I couldn't leave without saying goodbye. I know I'm robbing you of your chance to say it back, and I'll forever be sorry for that, but I couldn't figure out any other way.

I had to go. I love you and Chloe too much to keep putting you in danger.

You might notice I used the word *love*. And I want you to know I don't mean it in the way you love your parents or your friends. Yes, you are my best friend, but I also want you to know I've been madly, head over heels in love with you for years. Maybe since the moment I laid eyes on you. The problem was, I didn't really know what love was. I'd never let myself have that before, and I guess I kind of thought I'd go the rest of my life without it.

I haven't told you everything about my past, but what

you need to know is this: you were the reason I kept going. This interesting guy next door. The one who was so good with his kid, the one the whole town loved despite his efforts to push them all away, the one everyone knew they could count on. The one who made the days go by effortlessly, the one who gave me the inspiration for my recipes, the one who, without my even realizing it, was the reason I did everything I did.

Because that's who you are, Zach.

The one.

I thought love was something you *let* happen to you. I didn't know it could come along and hit you over the head, forever changing you whether you liked it or not. I was arrogant. I didn't think I could ever be touched by the big L word. But I was 100 percent wrong, and it's fine if you don't feel the same way back—in fact, I *hope* you don't, because leaving is going to be the hardest thing I've ever done and I do not want that for you.

I never want you to hurt. I never want Chloe to hurt.

Which is, of course, the very reason I have to go.

This whole town has stolen my heart, but the biggest chunk of it will always be set aside for you. Never change, Zach. Knowing your kind, incredible, grumpy self is still out there living, breathing, thriving, will be the only thing that continues to keep me going.

Kiss Chloe for me and please, do everything you can to live your best life.

With my love forever,

Ava

Ava didn't realize she was crying. She had to move. She had to keep the important people safe.

She decided to leave the letter in Zach's mailbox. With any luck he wouldn't think to check the box for a few days. The only tricky part would be getting it there without him noticing. Unfortunately, Zach liked to watch out his kitchen window. She knew this because she was also a watcher, and now that she thought about it, her watching was aimed way too often at Zach's house. She would sit several feet back from the window, so anyone glancing over wouldn't immediately see her, and watch him standing at that kitchen sink lost in thought.

But he wasn't there now.

It might be her only chance. Every part of her screamed to put it off, but she might not get another shot. She had to go now, before she lost her nerve.

She stuffed the letter in an envelope, scribbled his name on it, checked the window facing Zach's one more time and snuck quietly out her front door, stepping carefully to make as little noise on the gravel as possible. It had never bothered her that the mailboxes were all the way at the street before. It wasn't much of an inconvenience to walk the thirty or so steps to retrieve the mail, but in that moment, the distance seemed like miles.

She reminded herself to breathe as she moved. That was the thing about sneaking…your instinct was to hold your breath, which was, of course, the worse thing a person could do when trying to be quiet. Finally, she made it, pulling the mailbox open slowly. It squeaked a little, but she slipped the metal flap shut and turned back toward her house.

A few more steps and she'd be home free.

Which was precisely when the door to Zach's house burst open and he came flying down the stairs, a look of pure panic on his face.

"Zach?" she said, and as he ran toward her, the terrible empty feeling of having to leave morphed into something else. Something along the lines of nauseated terror. "What's wrong?"

"She's gone," he said, out of breath, jumpy and looking like he was on the verge of tears. "Chloe is gone."

Chapter Eleven

"Okay, let's not panic," Ava said, though it made it a hell of a lot harder for Zach not to panic when Ava looked like she was about to panic too.

His mind swirled. How could he have let this happen? He knew there was a dangerous person in town, and he hadn't even thought to make sure his daughter was by his side at all times? What was wrong with him? Sure, he'd grown up in this lazy small town his whole life and had literally never seen anything dangerous happen. There'd been some tragedies, of course. Accidents and weather-related catastrophes no one had seen coming. But the thought someone could do something to hurt the people of Ambrosia Falls on purpose… it didn't seem real.

Except he had known there was a threat. He should have been more vigilant.

Thought he had been, to be honest, though he supposed he didn't have it in him to think like a bad dude and had been so focused on keeping Ava safe he would never, in a million years, have thought Chloe was in danger.

"Let's get inside," Ava said, glancing around in a way Zach did not like.

He couldn't give two shits about his own well-being, but

at least had the presence of mind to know he couldn't help Chloe if he became incapacitated somehow, so he let Ava lead him up his front steps and into the house.

"Are you certain she's gone?" Ava asked, guiding Zach to a kitchen chair. "Like, does she have any hiding places or anything?"

Zach shook his head. "She's never really been a hiding kind of kid."

Ava started to pace. "What about friends? Would she sneak out to go see anyone, do you think? Was she mad about anything?"

"Mad?" Zach asked, putting his elbows on the table and leaning his head in his hands. He was having trouble catching any of the thoughts pummeling through his head.

"Like, did you guys get in a fight or anything?"

He looked up from his hands. "What? No. We weren't fighting. We had a normal dinner, the same as we do every day, and then she went upstairs to finish some homework. She was working on some big project for science class or something."

"So, she was up there for a while," Ava said.

Zach nodded. "At least I thought she was." He put his head back in his hands. "Oh God," he said, his voice strangled.

"Did you hear anything during the time she was up there?"

Zach shook his head. "Nothing. Which maybe should have clued me in? But I thought she was sitting at the desk in her room working. It's not like she would normally be roaming around or anything. And then I went to check on her and she was just…gone…" he said, his voice trailing off.

"Okay, so is it possible she could have simply come downstairs and headed out without you knowing?"

"She's never done anything like that before," Zach said.

"I mean, she walks to her friends' houses all the time, and to Mom's, but she's always told me where she was going."

"Maybe she forgot this time," Ava said, and Zach could tell the hope in her voice was false, even if it did inject a tiny spurt of it into him too.

"I guess. I mean, it would be the world's worst timed co-incidence, considering all the other stuff going on around town and what's going on with…you," he said, not sure how else to say what he was thinking.

That this was no coincidence at all.

"I agree," Ava said, "but we have to cover all our bases, right? It's the smart thing to do."

"I have to get out there. Start searching," Zach said, getting up from the table and starting to pace along with Ava.

"But," Ava said quietly, "search where?"

Zach stopped midstep. It hadn't occurred to him it might be pointless to rush out of the house and start randomly driving around. Where would he go? What would he do? And now that it was dark out, how would that even work? "Well, I have to do something," he said, trying to keep the anger out of his voice, though it wasn't working.

"I think we should at least call around to make sure she hasn't gone to a friend's house or your mom's or something before we jump to conclusions. I agree the timing is terrible, and we have to consider all the possibilities, but this is at least a place to start."

Zach swallowed hard, not liking any of it one bit. But he didn't have any other ideas. At least not any rational ones.

"So let's call around and see if anyone knows where she is. Just casually, you know, so more people don't get freaked out," Ava said. "Because if this is who we think it might be, we're going to want to keep this as simple as possible. We can't have all the people in town freaking out and getting in the way if we need to move to a plan B."

"Yeah, okay," Zach said.

At least it was something to do. There was absolutely no way he could do nothing. He just wasn't sure how he was supposed to keep the fear out of his voice as he called around.

An hour later Zach's panic was going into full-blown freak-out mode. No one had seen Chloe. Deep down, he'd known all along they wouldn't get anywhere with the calls, but they had to try.

"At least we managed not to freak anyone out, I guess," he said.

"I'm so sorry, Zach," Ava said, her eyes red as much from emotion as from exhaustion.

"It's not your fault," Zach said.

He wanted to be angry at Ava. To be mad she ever came to this town and put all of them in this position, though of course he couldn't be. She had been a victim in all this as much as anyone. More than anyone. She was the innocent bystander who did nothing besides being in the wrong place at the wrong time and getting involved with the wrong dude. And Zach knew a little something about getting involved with the wrong person. A person who turned out not to be who he thought they were at all, so he could hardly get mad at Ava for doing the same thing.

"This is definitely my fault," Ava said, a tear falling.

She looked like she was about to crumple, but Zach couldn't let that happen. He needed her to keep it together. Because if Ava fell apart, there was no way he wasn't going to follow.

"Nope," he said, putting his arms around her and pulling her close. "First of all, this isn't your fault. This is all shit you had no control over. You are not putting all this on yourself. And second, you simply can't go down that rabbit hole because I need you to keep me calm. If we both lose it, we have no chance. We have to keep it together for Chloe."

Ava pulled in a deep breath and nodded. "You're right. I'm just going to put all these feelings aside and deal with them later."

"Yup, we will deal with them later," he said. "Okay, so what's next?" he asked, as they broke apart from the hug.

"I'm not sure what we can do before the sun comes up," Ava said, making panic flash though Zach's eyes again. She put her hands up. "I'm not saying we're going to do nothing—I'm just saying things are going to be limited."

"I'm not going to sit here all night," Zach said.

"I know. I'm going to go upstairs and check Chloe's room, see if there are any clues there."

"Right, okay. I'll go check outside, under the window of her room—see if there's anything there," he said, heading for the door.

But before he got two steps out of the house, something stopped him cold.

An envelope—bright white contrasting against the dark porch floor.

"Ava," he called before she got too far away. "I think I found something."

THIS WAS 100 PERCENT her fault. It killed her to keep the real her a secret from Zach, especially with everything going on, but she couldn't come clean now. If she did, Zach would hate her, which she could live with, but she couldn't live with anything happening to Chloe. She needed Zach to trust her, to work with her, for their best chance at getting Chloe back.

She was halfway up the stairs when he called to her, his hands shaking as he turned toward her with an envelope in his hands.

Ava's stomach seized.

Zach came back into the house in a daze, shutting the door absently.

"Do you want me to open it?" Ava asked.

She wanted to be the one to handle whatever was going to be inside that envelope. She was trained to preserve evidence, to keep her cool no matter what the contents might be. But Chloe was Zach's daughter, and she had no right to be the first to see, even if this was about her in the end. Right now, all that mattered was Chloe. And Zach.

Ava cringed as Zach ripped into the envelope, thinking about all the things that could happen. There could be a dangerous substance, or worse, some kind of explosive even though the envelope appeared to be flat from where she stood.

Zach pulled a photo from the envelope, and Ava rushed over, praying it would be proof of life and not something much, much worse.

She let out a breath when Chloe's scared, but very much alive face looked back from yet another instant camera print.

"It's proof of life," Ava said quickly. "It means she's okay."

"Okay?" Zach said, his voice hitching. "She's tied up. There's a gag in her mouth."

"I know. And that's obviously bad, but it's not Chloe he wants."

"She looks so scared," Zach said, running his finger along Chloe's face in the picture.

"We're going to get to her," Ava said. "We just need to

find out where he's keeping her, and I'll surrender. He'll hand Chloe to you and this will all be over. Easy peasy," Ava said.

"That is not easy peasy," Zach said, an angry edge to his voice. "I'm not going to hand you over to this guy."

"It's the best option, Zach," Ava said, and she meant it.

She would do anything to save Chloe, and if that meant the end of herself, so be it.

"I don't care about easy," Zach said. "I care about getting Chloe back *and* keeping you safe."

Ava waved away his comment. "Whatever, either way we need to figure out where this is," she said, poking at the photo, "and get to her."

Zach flipped the picture over. *Don't even think about the cops, Sparrow.*

"Sparrow?"

"It's, uh, what he used to call me," she said, hoping he wouldn't ask too many questions.

"This guy is getting weirder and weirder," Zach said. "Although he clearly didn't do his research if he thinks cops are going to be a problem around here."

Ava took the picture from Zach to study it closer, starting to pace, hoping it would help her think.

"If he wants you to come and find her," he asked, "why doesn't he just tell us where she is? You'd think he'd have had plenty of time to set up traps for us or whatever."

Ava shrugged one shoulder. "That's not how Justin works. He only feels powerful when he's playing people. When he's messing with their minds."

"Is that what he's doing to Chloe?" Zach asked, with something wild behind his eyes.

Ava shook her head quickly. "I don't think he'll hurt her. Not if we do what he says. I mean, I don't think it's impossible, but Chloe isn't who he's after. He's doing this to hurt me."

"Okay, I get that, but how in the hell are we supposed to find her from this?" Zach asked, pulling the photo right out of Ava's hand, which, given the circumstances, Ava wasn't going to fight him on, no matter how much she needed to study it and hope for a clue.

"He must think we'll be able to figure it out somehow," she said.

Suddenly Zach stopped. "This was taken in the daylight."

Ava moved beside him, close enough so they could both see. "Right, I didn't even think of that. So if she was still here for dinner, that doesn't leave much of a time frame for it to still be light out. What time did you eat?"

"It was late. I cooked a roast, which always takes a while, but it's Chloe's favorite."

"So we're looking at a window of like, two hours, tops."

"Which means she can't be far, right?" Zach said, a tiny sliver of hope trickling into his voice.

"Yeah, if he got her to this…whatever this is," Ava said, motioning to the photo, "and then came back here again so quickly, it was only about an hour that we were making calls before we found the envelope."

"Jesus," Zach said, running his fingers hard through his hair. "I just realized this asshole was right here. We could have had him." Zach raced back to the front door and whipped it open.

Ava wasn't sure if he was expecting to find Justin right there on his doorstep, or what, but she knew he was long gone. Justin didn't take chances. He likely would have waited until he had a full view of the two of them to risk creeping up to the door. He was good at what he did. Damn good.

Ava just hoped she was still better.

Zach shut the door again and threw out a string of curses that would make a sailor blush.

"We should try to get some sleep," Ava said.

At a time like this, it was unlikely to happen, but she knew from experience sleep would make everything so much easier and the likelihood of success much greater.

"We can head out as soon as the sun starts coming up."

Zach flopped onto the couch and let out a half-hearted chuckle. "I can't see how there's any way I could sleep knowing Chloe is out there, scared and alone."

"I know," Ava said, "but we should try anyway. We'll be better for helping Chloe that way."

"We don't even know where we're going," Zach said.

"We'll figure it out."

"How though? We have no idea where to start." He held up the photo of Chloe. "This could be pretty much anywhere."

"We'll find her," Ava said, with as much confidence as she could muster.

"You don't know that. You can't know that," Zach said, a hint of anger breaking through the fear in his voice.

"I do know it," Ava said. "Because I know you, and I know me. And we aren't going to stop until we do."

Zach slumped his shoulders and nodded. Ava knew his mind would be reeling all night. She glanced at her watch. It was about five hours until the sun came up again.

And it would be the longest five hours of their lives.

Chapter Twelve

Zach knew he needed sleep but knowing that didn't get him any closer to actually getting any. Still, he tried to rest as much as possible as he studied the photo of Chloe. He could hardly stand to look at it, almost relieved she was gazing slightly away from the camera—he wasn't sure he'd be able to take seeing her fear head-on. Which made him feel like a coward, but his heart was already ripping in two catching even a glimpse of her.

He hoped Chloe would be able to sleep…at least she'd get a bit of a break if she did. She had to know he was coming for her, right? He hoped it would be enough to keep her spirits up, to stay strong and positive. A tiny smile played at the edge of his lips. He would bet his life Chloe was giving this Justin jackass a piece of her mind. Maybe that's why she had the cloth around her mouth. Chloe was a fierce, determined kid and would likely not be making it easy on the guy.

Of course, that realization terrified Zach, and he sent a silent plea out to the universe to keep her safe. He couldn't lose her.

He just couldn't.

Zach leaned his head back and closed his eyes, picturing Chloe's sweet face laughing at the dinner table. She'd been humoring him after he'd told a particularly bad joke about a snowman and "the Winternet," and she'd played right along even though she was way too old for the joke. She was so good at that. The bad dad jokes were kind of their thing. Sure, she—rightly—made fun of him over it, but she never told him to stop, even when her friends were around. And yeah, she might roll her eyes every now and then, but that was part of her charm. And part of what made it so fun to tell the stinkin' jokes in the first place.

He let out a heavy sigh as a tear escaped his eye, rolling down his cheek and toward his ear, but he couldn't be bothered to wipe it away. It didn't matter. Nothing mattered except finding Chloe.

Chloe, Chloe, Chloe. He had to find her…

Should they start with places close to town? She couldn't be more than two hours away, given the time frame they'd worked out earlier. Maybe they should start at the far end of that window—drive an hour out of town and work their way in? But which direction? And more importantly, how much ground could they cover before the sun went down again?

Zach's eyes snapped open.

"Hey," Ava said. Somehow, she was sitting in the chair across from him even though he hadn't heard her sit down. "You've been out for a few hours."

"I have?" Zach asked, then wiped a bit of drool from the corner of his mouth. "It didn't feel like I slept. The last thing I was thinking about was how much ground we can cover before sunset and then…"

A jolt went through Zach. "Where's the picture of Chloe?" he asked, a note of desperation in his voice.

Ava leaned over and grabbed it off the coffee table, holding it out to him.

He plucked it out of her hand and studied it. But this time he didn't look directly at Chloe. He looked past her, above her head to the window. It was how they'd known it was still daylight when the picture was taken. There it was.

"Look at this," Zach said, pointing to the direction the light shone in through the window. "The sun's coming in from this direction," he said, motioning to the area out past the left perimeter of the photo.

Ava let out a little gasp. "And we know the sun had to be close to setting when he took the picture."

"And the sun sets in the west...so this has to be west." He made the motioning gesture again.

"Which means this is north, east and south," Ava said, pointing to each edge of the photo as she said the directions.

"Which means this picture was taken somewhere south of town."

"Holy shit," Ava said.

Suddenly they were getting somewhere, Zach thought. "It's mostly woods out that way, which would make sense. I haven't gone hunting in years," he said. "Never liked the idea of shooting living things, you know? But I used to go with my dad when I was a kid. I think there are still a few hunting shacks out there."

"That's exactly what this looks like," Ava said, pointing at Chloe again. "It's small, likely one room, but has an area for a cot here and I'm assuming a bit of living quarters be-hind the photographer."

Zach knew Ava was avoiding saying kidnapper so he wouldn't get all worked up again, but avoiding it only served to bring it straight back to the forefront of his mind. "We need to get out there," he said, getting up.

"The sun will start coming up in about an hour. We can

gather supplies, and by the time we're ready to leave, it will be close to rising."

"Sounds good," Zach said, heading upstairs to get changed. Ava headed toward the front door. "Wait, where are you going?"

"Home. To change and get ready," she said, pointing toward the door.

"I don't think we should split up. I can change quickly, then we can head to your place where I can stand watch while you get ready."

Ava raised her eyebrows and opened her mouth as if she were about to argue but must have thought better of it. "Sure, sounds good," she said. "I'll go see what you have for food and water."

Zach nodded and continued up the stairs to put on a few layers. In his experience, the woods could be either way too hot or way too chilly depending on the time of day and the direction of the sun. He tried to think of every possible scenario and couldn't help but feel underprepared for all of them.

He headed back downstairs and fished in the closet for his hiking boots he used occasionally when he and Chloe decided it was time to get outside and see some nature.

Ava handed him a couple bottles of water and kept two for herself. "I'm pretty sure I don't have any of these at my place," she said, heading for the door.

Zach grabbed his keys and followed, letting her lead the way over to her place.

As they walked, Zach was on high alert. With the lights from their houses, they'd be sitting ducks if someone decided to shoot from out of the darkness. He strained to hear any noise that might be out of place but could barely think over the sound of the crickets. Had they always been that loud?

A friggin' elephant could charge past and barely be heard over the damn things.

But in a few steps, they'd made it to Ava's and Zach was safely closing the door behind them.

Ava went toward the back door to her house and retrieved a large backpack.

"Were you planning on going somewhere?" Zach asked.

Ava looked momentarily surprised, then gave him a little smile. "I learned a long time ago it's good to be prepared, that's all," she said with a shrug.

But Zach had been in her house dozens of times, and there had definitely not been an already packed bag leaning up against the back door. "Jesus," he said, rubbing his face. "You were going to leave."

Ava pulled in a long breath. "It's the only way, Zach. And this...what happened to Chloe only proves it. As soon as we find her, I'm either going to have to go with Justin, or if we get very lucky, I'll make it out too and can get a head start on him."

"You can't leave," Zach said.

Ava stood in front of him and looked him straight in the eye. "Except I have to."

Zach shook his head.

"We can't waste time arguing about it," Ava told him. "I have a second gun at the store. We should stop by and grab it before we head out."

"Why do you have even one gun?" Zach asked, but Ava just gave him a look.

Of course, he knew the answer. The guy who now had his daughter. It was going to take a while to rearrange the ideas he'd had of Ava's life before Ambrosia Falls into the truth he now knew. Trying to picture her under the influence of this guy, helpless and desperate, didn't compute with anything he knew about her. She'd always been so confident, so strong. He couldn't reconcile any other thoughts of her, no matter how hard he tried. And the way she was checking and double-checking her gear, which included doing a safety and ammo check on her handgun, did not make the visual of a helpless Ava any easier to grasp onto.

"How much gas do you have? Your truck will do better out on the rougher roads," Ava said, zipping her backpack with finality.

"Yeah, we should be good. Filled up a couple days ago."

"Great, let's go," Ava said, and Zach marveled at her businesslike tone.

Like she was a completely different person. Except, she wasn't a completely different person. This was just another side of her. A side that, even though it was jarring, made a hell of a lot more sense than some damsel in distress scenario.

A few minutes later they pulled up to the coffee shop, both jumping out of the vehicle. Zach was not about to leave Ava by herself for even a second. He didn't know what this Justin guy was capable of, but he was not going to make the mistake of underestimating him.

Zach thought he had been prepared for anything, but as he went to close the truck door, the silence-shattering siren and the red and blue lights bursting out of nowhere definitely caught him a teensy bit off guard.

And like a damn fool, he promptly stuck up his hands.

ZACH WAS NOT good at attempting to look innocent.

It was a good thing the guy was a writer, because he would certainly not make it as an actor, or you know, any profession requiring even the slightest hint of faking anything, anywhere, at any time.

"You okay there, man?" the officer said as he stepped out of his vehicle.

Ava shot Zach a look that she hoped conveyed he needed to lower his arms, and she hoped the officer wouldn't pick up on it in the early morning light.

"Oh, uh, yeah, sorry," Zach said sheepishly, lowering his arms. "You, uh, startled me a bit."

The officer nodded. "Yeah, sorry about that. I like to see how people react. Tells me a lot."

"Does it?" Zach asked politely, not doing a very good job at hiding the panic on his face.

"Is there anything we can do to help you out, Officer?" Ava quickly interjected, desperate to take the focus off Zach so he could hopefully regain some semblance of composure.

"Y'all are up a little early, aren't you?" the man asked.

Ava shrugged one shoulder. "I'm always up this early," she said. "Bakery owner." She motioned to the store.

"Ah," the officer said, raising an eyebrow. "Looks like a nice store. Was thinking I might have to come in for a coffee when you open."

"We'd love to have you," Ava said, turning on her small-town charm.

Which was strange. She'd settled into the small-town charm persona so fully over the last couple years it became who she was, except…she realized now she'd been in a different mode ever since she learned about Justin's reappearance.

Sparrow mode.

"And you?" the officer said, turning back to Zach.

"Oh, uh, just helping out a bit," he said. "You know, the Apple Cider Festival and all."

"You help with the baking," the officer said, a sarcastic lilt to his voice.

Zach's brows furrowed together, and Ava held her breath, terrified he was going to say something even more suspicious, but he simply said, "Of course," effectively conveying he couldn't understand why that would be strange at all and putting the sexism right back in its place.

"Got a lot of gear in there for a coffee shop," the officer said, flicking on a light and shining it into the second-row seat of the truck.

"Yeah," Zach said, "we were out hiking yesterday. I was a little tired afterward, and I guess I got lazy about putting our stuff away."

The guy nodded and took a step back. Ava got the feeling he decided they were harmless. "I hear there's been some trouble up this way," the officer said. "You guys know anything about that?"

"Sure," Ava said, jumping in. "Who doesn't? The water tower. The fire at the baking competition stage. Gotta say, I'm pretty bummed about that one." She leaned in close to the man. "I usually make a pretty good showing."

"I bet you do, what with being the town baker and all," the officer said, giving her a courtesy smile. "But you don't have any insight beyond the basics? No ideas as to how any of it happened?"

"Oh," Ava said, doing her best to look surprised, "unfortunately no. It's all just so...strange."

"And you?" he said, turning to Zach.

Zach shrugged, and it only looked a little forced. "No idea. Nothing like it has ever happened around here before."

"You lived here long?"

"All my life," Zach said.

The officer nodded, looking Zach up and down, making him squirm all over again.

"I'm sorry," Ava said. "I wish we could help, but if there's nothing else, I really do need to get started on my day."

"Right, no problem," the officer said, pulling a card out. "I'll be nosing around town a bit today, so if anything else out of the ordinary happens, I'd appreciate it if y'all could let me know."

"Sure thing—" Ava took the card and peered at the name "—Officer Banyan," she said, shooting him her best "no need to worry about me, I'm just an innocent baker" smile.

He tipped his hat and got in his car, backing away as Ava and Zach went into The Other Apple Store.

"Holy shit," Zach said, the moment they were safely inside. "What the hell do we do now?"

"We're going to have to make it look like we're doing exactly what we said we'd be doing. I figure there's another hour before the town starts coming to life and he'll have other things to be focused on. We can't risk moving your truck right away. I say we wait it out for a bit, then you calmly head out by yourself—it'll look like I'm staying here—make sure the coast is clear, then come around back and pick me up."

"I don't know if I can wait an hour," Zach said, starting to pace.

"If you're going to look all nervous and guilty, can you at least come back to the kitchen and do it?" Ava asked, pulling him toward the kitchen doors. "Officer Banyan is probably looking at us right now."

Zach let out a groan. "I am so bad at this," he said as they moved to the back.

"Not that bad," Ava said. "There were moments out there I almost believed you."

Zach rolled his eyes. "Almost? Great. I wonder what I looked like to a trained professional."

As a trained professional, Ava thought he'd done okay. Unfortunately, she couldn't exactly explain that to him.

"Jesus. Of all the times for the cops to show up," Zach said, able to pace freely now that they were out of view.

"I know, but I think we're fine. This might be better, anyway. Maureen will be here right around the time it should be safe for us to go. I'll tell her I have a migraine or something and ask if she can run the store for the day. I was planning on closing, but this will be better. It'll keep the town gossip down a bit."

Zach nodded. "Okay, yeah, you're probably right. But how in the hell are we going to kill this hour? I'm dying here. I have to do something."

"Easy," Ava said. "If the store is opening today, we have to get some baking done."

Zach looked as terrified as she'd ever seen him. Which, given the past several hours, was saying something.

"It's fine," she said. "I'll find you some easy stuff to do."

An hour later the place was full of baking smells and Zach still looked just as nervous. Ava couldn't fault the guy—he was hardly in an ideal mindset to be learning the ropes of a bakery, especially given that it had been a while since he'd had a proper sleep.

While he was watching over the mixer, adding dry ingredients a small amount at a time, Ava took a moment to retrieve the gun she had hidden in the back closet on the top shelf behind a box of old marketing materials. She wished she could go down into the crawlspace and really arm up, but that might be a little hard to explain to Zach.

When she got back to the kitchen, Maureen had arrived and was grilling Zach about why he was there.

He seemed to be doing about as good a job at improv with Maureen as he had with good ole Officer Banyan.

"I'm helping a bit. Ava's, um, not feeling well," he said, swallowing guiltily.

"Hey, Maureen, I'm so glad you're here," Ava said, trying to look exhausted.

Which, she had to admit, wasn't much of a stretch.

"I woke up with a migraine this morning," she continued. "As you can see, I roped Zach into helping. Is there any way you can run the store today?"

Maureen looked from Ava to Zach, then back to Ava again. "So you called Zach? That seems a little weird. Unless you already knew he was up or—" Her eyes grew wide.

At first Ava wasn't sure what Maureen had figured out, panicking that somehow she knew about Chloe. About Justin. About all of it.

And then Maureen smirked. One of those knowing smirks that said loud and clear she knew you were up to something, and she knew exactly what that something was, wink, wink. And then her expression changed to something akin to pure glee. "Sure. Yeah definitely. I can run the store today," she said, then added a quick, "It's about time," with a happy sigh.

Oh, jeez, Ava thought. *This'll be flying through town faster than wildfire once the store opens.*

It was taking a little longer for Zach to catch on to what was going on. "What's about time?" he asked.

"Nothing," Ava said, grabbing his arm and leading him toward the door. "Would you mind giving me a ride home? Maybe grab your truck and come around back to pick me up?" Ava said, lifting her eyebrows with a look that said, *Just go, I'll deal with this.*

"Yeah, sure," Zach said, still a little dazed as she pushed him out of the kitchen.

"Omigod, spill!" Maureen said the second Zach was out of earshot.

Ava groaned. "Maureen, it's nothing. It's not what you think."

"Mmm-hmm," she said, not believing it for a second.

Ava wished a secret affair was the only thing she'd be dealing with over the next few hours, but she supposed a little rumor was the least of her worries, even though it was…embarrassing somehow. Not that Zach would be embarrassing to be with—definitely not—but the fact the whole town was going to go nuts over the whole thing, all thinking like they knew better way before either of them did. And yeah, that might actually be true, but they didn't know the half of what had been holding them back from exploring the possibilities.

She sighed as she stepped out the back door of her shop. Zach was already waiting, looking tired, worried and so heartbreakingly handsome behind the wheel of his truck. If only there was a chance to properly explore those possibilities someday.

"She thinks there's something going on between us, doesn't she," Zach said, looking like he both wanted to kick himself for not figuring it out sooner, and like he wanted to crawl under the nearest rock and hide for a very long time.

"She does," Ava said, staring straight ahead.

"This is not good," Zach said. "The whole town is going to be talking."

Ava waved the comment away. "It'll be okay. In fact, it might be good. It will keep everybody distracted, at least for today. We'll have time to get to Chloe, I can get out of town, Justin will follow and forget Ambrosia Falls even exists and everything will be fine."

"How would any of that be fine?" he asked, his eyes wild.

"I'm sorry you'll have to deal with the fallout of all the gossip, but after I'm gone for a few days, everyone will forget all about it."

"That is not happening," Zach said.

"Zach, it's the only way. You know it's the only way."

"I absolutely do *not* know that it's the only way. And yeah, I'm good with focusing on Chloe for step one, but I'm not okay with you being bait for this guy to hurt yet another person I care about."

"You need to stop," Ava said.

"Stop what?"

"Caring about me. It's just not going to work."

"You and me won't work?" Zach said.

"Exactly."

He let out a hard breath. "Fine," he said, though he looked hurt. "That's not even what I'm worried about. And I'm not worried about any ridiculous gossip fallout either. This is about you being safe. Whether our friendship could ever become something else doesn't matter right now. What matters is the friendship itself, and frankly I'm pissed you're treating it like it's nothing."

"I know it's not nothing, Zach," Ava said, turning away, focusing on the passing landscape. "It's everything," she whispered.

Silence fell in the truck for the next several minutes.

Finally, Ava spoke. "Let's focus on Chloe. Nothing else matters if we don't get this next step right, okay?"

"I know, but…we're going to try to get this guy, right?"

Ava nodded. "In an ideal world, yes. But we can't assume we'll get close enough. And you said yourself you don't like the idea of hurting things. You won't even hunt, Zach."

"Innocent animals hunted for sport are very different from someone who is trying to kill the people I love."

Love.

Ava let that sit there, not knowing what to say in return. Especially since she wanted to scream at the top of her lungs that she loved him too.

"Just focus on Chloe," she eventually said instead.

Zach nodded. "Focus on Chloe."

And then I'm gone.

Chapter Thirteen

"I think we're a few miles out from the first shack," Zach said after they'd driven for more than an hour.

"We shouldn't get too close," Ava said. "He'll hear us coming from miles away if we pull up in a one-ton truck."

Zach pulled to the side of the road. "Do we try to hide the truck?"

Ava looked around. "If you can find a place, it might help."

"There was a trail about a half mile back," he said. "We could go a little way down there."

"Yeah, that would be better," Ava said, her eyes scanning as much of the terrain as she could see, which wasn't much considering they'd been on a forest road for the past fifteen minutes. "Will we be coming back to the truck after we check out the first shack? Or going on foot?"

"If I remember correctly, this road ends not too much farther from here. I think we're on foot from here on out."

Ava nodded. "Carrying packs is going to make it harder, but we'll have to suck it up. How many shacks are there?"

"Only three I know of, but that doesn't mean there aren't more. Like I said, this isn't really my world."

"Fair enough. With any luck, there will be trails leading to any shacks you don't know about."

They heaved their packs over their shoulders and headed out. Ava followed Zach since he knew the terrain better than she did.

After hiking in silence for about twenty minutes, Zach held up his fist military-style to alert Ava to stop. They moved much slower then, and as silently as possible, though Ava couldn't help but feel like Zach could use a little more training in being stealthy. Or you know, any at all.

Zach ducked behind a tree, and Ava followed his lead, easing behind another where she had a good view of both Zach and the tiny cabin in the distance.

"Okay, so how are we going to play this?" Zach asked.

He had imagined a scenario where he'd quietly charge forward, gun in hand and eyes darting, scanning for potential targets. And he had to admit, that's pretty much the way the whole thing went down, except he was still back behind the tree thinking it all through while Ava whisper-yelled, "Follow me," and then moved out exactly the way he'd envisioned himself doing it.

He had no choice but to follow, watching Ava aim her handgun steadily in one direction and then the other, stepping lightly but quickly, nearly silent on her feet, moving closer and closer to the shack.

One thought kept repeating in his mind. *How is she so good at this?*

She paused at one last tree, pointed in the direction she was about to go. She motioned for him to move in the opposite direction, which he did, the adrenaline pumping.

Even though Ava had the longer route, she somehow made her way around the shack first, seamlessly ducking under the single window in the back, then moving around to the front. While all this was going on, Zach felt like a lumbering bear as he made his way much more loudly around the closer side of the shack, thankfully not having any windows to avoid, and got around to the front in time to watch Ava take her last couple steps toward the door, lunge back, then kick her leg near the handle of the door. With wood splinters raining, the door burst open, and Ava stepped inside, pointing her gun first to the right, and then immediately to the left as Zach finally bumbled in after her like some kind of clueless old-timey deputy.

"Clear!" Ava yelled, as if she'd done it a hundred times before.

Jesus.

"Um, okay," Zach said, standing there blinking, his mind moving in all kinds of directions.

He was upset and pissed that Chloe wasn't there. He wanted all this to be over. He wanted to know the people he loved were safe.

And he also wondered how in the fiery depths of hell Ava was so calm under pressure, seemed to know how to expertly handle a weapon, not to mention maneuver like some kind of tactical genius.

"Um, what was that?"

Ava turned to him. "What do you mean?"

"That," he said, waving his arm in a circular gesture. "Like the whole...rushing in like you're some kind of navy SEAL or something."

It was Ava's turn to stare and blink for a moment. "Um, I guess I was copying people on the TV," she said, shrugging. "Did it look ridiculous? It probably looked ridiculous. I'm sorry, that's so embarrassing. I guess I...kind of got caught up in the moment or something."

Zach squinted at her. "No. No, it looked very believable," he said. "Like, weirdly believable."

"Huh," Ava said, nodding slowly. "Okay then, um, that's good I guess."

They stood for a moment, then Ava spoke again. "Well, this clearly isn't the shack in the picture—the view out the window isn't the same at all so, we should get going."

"Right," Zach said, hiking his pack a little higher on his shoulders. "There's one a little farther toward Aspen Hill."

"Great," Ava said, "lead the way."

Thirty minutes or so later they slowed again, hiding in the trees several dozen yards from the shack Zach led them to.

"I have a feeling this could be the one," he said.

Ava nodded, working her jaw. "Okay, let's take it slow… be extra cautious."

Zach was still nodding when Ava was on the move again. *Shit.* He hurried after her, trying to be as quiet as possible, but it seemed to be one of those situations where the harder you tried at something, the worse you were at it.

He pulled in a deep breath, letting it out slowly through his mouth, trying to calm his racing heart, but by the time they neared the shack, he was breathing like he'd just run up ten flights of stairs.

Like the last time, they paused to get their bearings.

And that's when Zach saw it. A small, red shoe. Exactly like a pair of Chloe's.

Saliva filled his mouth as his stomach performed an impressive reenactment of one of those spinning teacup rides.

Strange that the man would have the presence of mind to grab shoes for her as he somehow stole Chloe out of her second-story bedroom window. The planning and precision it would have taken was enormous. Sure, Chloe's bedroom window looked out onto the forested edge of town, so it wasn't likely he'd be seen, but he had to be quiet enough that Zach wasn't alerted, and with a kid like Chloe, that couldn't have been easy. To think of him gathering up shoes on top of it all was wild. Like the man had thought of everything, including precisely how to execute his plan.

It was not a thought that comforted Zach.

Ava was signaling to get his attention. She'd seen the shoe too. This was definitely the place. She put her finger over her lips to signal silence, then began to move. They followed the same procedure as at the last shack, though now that Zach knew what to expect, he was able to round the front of the building at the same time as Ava.

Still, she was the one who got to the door first and gave it a kick that might have been even more intense than the one at the last shack. She whipped her gun right, then left, then once again…and to Zach's horror, yelled "Clear!"

"What do you mean, clear?" Zach asked, rushing inside, his eyes frantically covering every inch of the room. "She was here. This has to be the place. Look at the window, it's the same as in the photo." He dug into the side pocket of his cargo pants to retrieve the photo even though he already knew he was right. "Her shoe is outside. She has to be here."

AVA'S HEART SANK, though she knew what she was feeling was nothing compared to what Zach must be feeling. Justin was an absolute bastard for putting them through all this. Not to mention what Chloe must be dealing with. She must be so scared. All alone with that jackass of a human who probably didn't know the first thing about kids. Ava could only hope he was feeding her decently and keeping her warm.

The silver lining was, she didn't think Justin would actually hurt Chloe…not yet, anyway. None of this was even about Chloe. It was about Ava, and Ava alone. Chloe was just another ploy. Another way to toy with her, to make her pay for finding him out and escaping all those years ago.

Zach started rummaging through some of the stuff in the cabin, lifting relatively recent food containers from the small counter, then throwing them back down again in disgust. He moved over to the bed and lifted the pillow, which was when Ava heard it.

A quiet, almost imperceptible high-pitched squeal. A squeal Ava had heard only once before…five years ago.

"Get out!" she yelled, yanking the back of Zach's shirt with more might than she knew she was capable of, and dove for the doorway, dragging Zach behind her.

He didn't question—didn't have time to question—following her lead as she turned and dove through the doorway as the first boom sounded, then a second…pieces of the shack exploding in every direction. Wood splinters shot through the air, then rained on them as Ava covered her head with her arms, hoping nothing more substantial was on its way down.

Since the shack didn't have much to it, the raining debris didn't take long to clear. Ava rolled onto her back to survey the damage. Her first thought was that the thing had been obliterated so fully that, if there hadn't been a black mark of ash where the shack once stood, no one would have known anything ever stood there at all. Her second thought was to wonder where the hell all the blood was coming from.

"Shit, Zach," she said, scrambling over to him.

He was breathing and conscious, but clearly in a lot of pain. The blood was pouring from his thigh at the base of a five-inch shard of metal still lodged in his leg.

"Don't move," Ava said, scrambling into her pack.

But Zach, of course, moved. And in the worst possible way too, realizing what was causing the blood...the pain. His hand flew to the shard and yanked, tearing the metal free from his leg.

The blood gushed faster.

Ava had never been one to get queasy at the sight of blood, but apparently when it's the man you've recently come to realize you loved, it wasn't so easy to keep your wits about you. Ava wanted to panic...had started to panic, but quickly realized she was all Zach had.

Come on, Ava, she said to herself. *Do not lose it. Keep your shit together and save the love of your life.*

AN UNEXPECTED KNOCK came at the front door.

The little girl's eyes grew wide...hopeful. Silly little bird, the Crow thought.

He picked the girl up off the sofa and carried her to a closet, tucking her gently inside.

He spoke quickly and quietly. "If you make a sound, it will be very bad for both you and your daddy." He looked straight into her eyes as he finished speaking. "And believe me, you do not want that."

Needless to say, the hope vanished from the girl's eyes, replaced by a fear that sent a satisfied calm through him. He was in control of the situation. All was going as planned.

He just needed to take care of whatever this little problem was knocking on his door.

He wasn't worried. He was trained for this and would handle whatever stood in his way. He would not fail this time.

"Hello there," he said, a pleasant smile pasted on his face. The Crow was surprised, but not rattled, to see a uniformed officer standing at the door. "How can I help you?"

"Officer Banyan," the uniform said. "I'm checking on some leads in the area." He peered over the Crow's shoulder, looking for clues, perhaps anything suspicious. Looking for mistakes.

But the Crow did not make mistakes. "Oh?" he said. "What do you mean by leads?"

"Well, there have been a few odd occurrences back in Ambrosia Falls, and I ran into a fellow from—" he flipped back a few pages in his notebook "—Pieville, down there at the apple festival thing, and he remembered something strange. He said the property in the woods should be empty right now. Said the owners headed down to Florida for a couple of weeks. But then he saw smoke from an outdoor fire the other day, and thought it was strange. And since I was asking him about anything strange he might have noticed, he filled me in," the officer said. "Thought I ought to come out here and take a look."

Damn snoopy small towns, the Crow thought, but he pulled out his best acting chops and feigned relief to the point of almost chuckling. "Well, I suppose that makes sense. I'm Jonathan, the Millers' son. And you're right, my parents did head down to Orlando for a bit. They asked me to come house-sit, though I didn't think I could until the last minute. I suppose that's why no one in town knew about me coming to stay." He finished off with a shrug he hoped said the whole thing was no big deal.

The officer nodded, buying his story hook, line, and sinker. *Sucker.* The Crow found people were quite trusting if you were nice to them. Even trained professionals.

Of course, no one ever expected anything bad to happen in a place like Ambrosia Falls, which made the whole thing about ten times easier. If it hadn't been for the real prize—

the Sparrow—he wouldn't even consider a job like this that was, frankly, a waste of his talents.

But this was the job he'd been thinking about for five years. On top of the years he'd put into the target before that. So much time invested. So much at stake.

The only one that really mattered.

"The Millners' son, you say?" the officer asked.

Typical. The man was testing him.

"Miller," the Crow replied, trying not to take offence at the juvenile treatment. Reminding himself the man was simply doing his job.

"Miller, right, right," Banyan said. "And you're the son?"

"Right. Jonathan, sir."

"And you're out here all by yourself?"

"Just me and my typewriter," he said. "Taking the opportunity to do a little work on the old memoirs."

The officer raised his eyebrows, then wrote the information in his notepad. It was unlikely he'd call around to check on the story of Jonathan Miller, but the Crow had done his research anyway. Art and Eliza Miller did indeed have a son named Jonathan, and the Millers only bought the place in Ambrosia Falls a few years ago. The folks in town likely wouldn't know what Jonathan looked like. Even if word got around the son was staying at the property, the Crow had no doubt he could deal with a few nosy neighbors. Maybe he'd tell them he was there for some peace and quiet and wasn't interested in getting to know the locals. The people in town wouldn't understand. Small-town people tended to live in small towns because they liked the socialization of knowing everyone around them, but they would let it go. They certainly wouldn't want to be accused of being something so heinous as "rude." They'd chalk it up to him being a "big city person," accompanying the phrase with knowing looks to their fellow gossips.

Even if a neighbor did show up, word would get around fast and that would be the end of it.

"So, uh, what did you mean about odd occurrences?" the Crow asked.

It was always better to keep a person talking, and not give them too much time to think. All the better for making people believe you're friendly and concerned, and if you were friendly and concerned, you were no longer a person worthy of suspicion.

Banyan waved a hand as if it were no big deal. "Some small petty crime stuff. Nothing major. Kids, I suspect."

The Crow made an agreeing, musing sound. "Probably bored in a place like this," he said, smiling at Banyan like he knew what he was talking about.

Banyan played right along as if the Crow had scripted the whole thing. "You got that right," he said with a chuckle. "Sorry to have bothered you. You have a good night now."

"Will do. Thanks, Officer," the Crow said, giving the man a wave as he turned to leave.

What a doofus, was all the Crow could think as the officer stepped off the porch and headed to his car.

Chapter Fourteen

Officer Banyan got into his car, careful not to look back at the house too much.

He had good instincts, and those instincts were telling him the man in that house was not telling the whole truth. In fact, he'd be surprised if he'd been told even a sliver of truth.

It wasn't so much that the guy was suspicious, it was that he was too smooth about the whole interaction. People tended to be nervous around the law, like that guy back at the bakery, but this guy was a little too sure of himself.

Banyan turned around in the wide yard and made his way back down the drive. He was out of sight of the house in a few seconds, the forest swallowing his car. He drove another minute before he got to the side road he'd seen earlier, and turned onto it, pulling his car to the edge to make a call.

"Hey, Vince," Jennifer, the dispatcher, said from the other end of the line. "How's it up there in Appleville, or whatever it's called?"

"Hey, Jen. It's…interesting."

"I bet," she said. "What can I do for you?"

"I need a lead checked out if you have a minute. There's a couple out here—Art and Eliza Miller. I've got a guy here who says he's their son staying on the property. Can you find out if there's anything I need to know about this Jonathan Miller? Something's got my spidey senses twigging about him."

"Well, you do have the best spidey senses around," she said. "I'll see what I can find out."

"Thanks, Jen," Banyan said, and hung up.

Research always took its sweet time, and Banyan had never been very good at waiting. Besides, with all the convenient forest surrounding the house, it would be a real shame to let it go to waste. There weren't many surveillance opportunities better than the one presenting itself to him on a silver platter.

He quickly collected his supplies and headed into the trees.

THE PAIN IN Zach's leg made every minute feel more like an hour, and every step he took—leaning much more heavily on Ava than he would have liked—was like a fire poker being slowly inserted into his muscle, then down into the bone.

Ava had been incredible under pressure. The picture of calm in a world suddenly filled with pain and chaos and confusion and hurt. His thoughts circled around Chloe and what she must be going through, then to the pain in his leg that would not be ignored for more than a moment at a time, and then back to Chloe again.

The first-aid kit in his pack was almost used up, and they had to get to better supplies sooner rather than later.

"You're doing great," Ava said as she helped him hobble along through the rugged terrain.

She had to be as exhausted as he was, but she was much better at hiding it.

The trip back to the truck took far longer than the trip

into the woods, and it was afternoon by the time they finally made it back.

"What are we going to do now?" Zach said, his voice choking.

Ava was helping him into the passenger side. "We're going to get you patched up, regroup, and decide what our next move is."

"We don't have time. We have to get to Chloe," he said, wincing as Ava started backing the truck out of the rugged terrain.

"I know," Ava said, "but we also have to stop the bleeding or you're going to pass out. And you're obviously no good to Chloe if you're unconscious."

No matter how much he wanted to argue, Zach knew she was right. He was weak and tired and needed to regain his strength.

It took several minutes to move through the not-quite-trail in reverse, but soon they were back on the road and rolling toward town. Somehow through the pain, Zach was able to find a few short bursts of something close to sleep—an intense sort of focused rest where he thought only of Chloe... of how they were going to get her back.

The trip felt long, but the clock confirmed they'd made good time. Ava must have driven way past the speed limit, and Zach was grateful for it.

Thankfully, their houses were at the end of their lane and backing the forest, so no one was around when they got back. Ava helped Zach out of the truck, his leg feeling like it had been lit on fire all over again.

"I have a good supply of first-aid stuff," Ava said, as she pointed him toward her house.

Zach didn't argue. Couldn't argue, really. Maybe it was the

pain or maybe it was the stress, but he could hardly focus, let alone come up with a plan.

The bandage around his leg was soaked through as Ava helped lift him up each step, and slowly, painfully, they made their way into her house. Ava sat Zach down at the kitchen table.

"I'll be right back. Don't move," she said, as she went in search of supplies.

Moving was both the last thing Zach wanted to do, and the only thing he wanted to do. He had to get to Chloe. He leaned his head back, resting it against the wall behind him, no longer able to stop the tears from flowing. He wasn't sobbing, just a stream coming from the corners of his eyes as if he'd turned on a faucet.

"I'm so sorry, Zach," Ava whispered as she knelt beside him to deal with his leg. "I'm so sorry I've done this to you and Chloe."

Zach raised his head, about to speak, and realized Ava had her own tears teetering on the edge of her lower lids. But she was keeping herself busy, cutting off his pant leg and pulling the used bandage away from his wound, which was enough to shock him straight out of the conversation. He tensed and ground his jaws together, trying not to scream out with the pain.

But oddly, it seemed to shock his brain back into working again. "What about a drone?" he said, gritting his teeth.

"For?" Ava asked, unscrewing the cap from a bottle of something Zach was pretty sure was not going to feel all that wonderful.

"It can cover a hell of a lot more ground than we can," Zach said, just before he shouted a curse as the antiseptic hit his leg.

"That could work," Ava said, moving quickly to dry the gash as best as she could.

She grabbed a large wound closure bandage, adhering it to one side of the gash and then the other, then pulling the wound closed, the whole thing holding it shut like a series of connected butterfly bandages.

"This should hold for a while," Ava said, as she covered everything with a large gauze pad, then neatly wrapped it.

His leg still hurt like hell—was going to hurt like hell for a while, Zach knew—but it was clean and closed and, with any luck, would hold until he could get proper stitches. At least the damn air was off it anyway, and he could maybe have a chance at saving his daughter.

"Okay," Ava said, putting her hands up as if to surrender. "So, drone, then. You have one, right? You any good at flying it?"

Zach gave her a side-glance. "I'm okay," he said. "And I'm all we've got, so I'll have to make damned sure I'm at my best."

Ava nodded once. "Great, let's do it before we lose the light. Can you walk?"

Zach leaned heavily on the table as he made his way to his feet. He was going to walk one way or the other. "Yup, I'm good," he said, only wobbling a little when the head rush hit him.

He paused for a second, steadying himself, then headed toward the door. "I'm going to need help with the drone."

Ava followed, and ten minutes later they were loading the drone case into the truck. It was about the size of a carry-on suitcase but was reinforced with metal and was heavier than it looked.

"Let's go," Zach said, heading toward the driver's side.

"Not so fast," Ava said. "First off, you are not driving with that leg, and second, we need to gear up."

Gear up? Zach thought. Wondering if maybe she wanted to gather more food, some more water, which would probably be smart.

The pain in his leg had morphed into something more like a heavy, pulsing ache that was much better than the gaping wound had been. He limped up the porch stairs and stopped in the doorway as Ava pulled a large painting—apparently on hinges—from the wall and began punching numbers into a large safe behind it.

"Okay," he said, looking behind him, then quickly closing the door.

"There are some duffel bags in the chest behind you," she said, opening the door to the safe.

But Zach was too stunned, watching Ava pull weapons out of the safe, a handgun and several knives. She followed up with a magazine of ammo and what looked like a...grenade?

"What the hell?" Zach asked.

"I'll explain in the car," Ava said. "But we need those bags."

Zach nodded, then turned to the chest, lifting the lid to see four large duffels.

"We'll need them all," Ava said, heading to the kitchen table with her haul.

Zach looked at the duffels, then at the items Ava was carrying, then back at the duffels. There was no way what she was carrying would come close to filling one of the bags, let alone four, but he grabbed them anyway, his mind spinning.

Ava set everything on the table and moved to the stove, bending to open the warming drawer on the bottom. It didn't look like there was anything inside, but she reached under the lip of the drawer, struggling a bit with her burned arm, and released something with a soft click. The floor of the drawer lifted to reveal a false bottom from which Ava proceeded to pull four shotguns.

"Um, okay then," was about all Zach could say.

She didn't stop there. Moving to the living room, Ava lifted the seat of an easy chair to reveal yet another secret compartment, this one filled with what looked like high-tech equipment.

"Night vision with heat signature capabilities," she said, as casually as if she were reading the day's specials at Margie's Diner downtown.

Zach added the goggle-like contraptions to one of the bags.

Next, she moved the coffee table and pulled up the area rug, revealing a cutout in the floor. She pulled the switch completely off a nearby lamp and inserted it into a hole that looked like a knot in the wood. The switch became a handle, which Ava quickly pulled, revealing two more guns and some body armor.

Of course.

"Put this on," Ava instructed, tossing what Zach could only assume was a Kevlar vest his way.

Around the house they went, Ava revealing compartment after compartment filled with rations, weapons and ammo until each of the duffels was full and Zach was feeling a bit like he'd been launched off the planet and had landed in a different world.

Zach and Ava stood staring at the bags, so full it was a miracle the damn table was even holding.

He glanced at Ava, then looked at the bags, then looked at Ava again. "Who are you, and what have you done with my happy-go-lucky, always positive, charming and harmless best friend?"

OFFICER BANYAN WAS perched in a prime spot inside the tree line overlooking the Miller property, which consisted of a few small outbuildings and a large barn, but he kept his eyes trained on the house. There hadn't been much movement, though he supposed there wouldn't be if the guy inside had been telling the truth and he was in there working on his memoirs.

He settled in to wait, binoculars in hand.

But it didn't take long to spot movement in the house.

The man, Jonathan, moved to one of the front windows and looked out. Then strangely, he moved on to another window on the side of the house that didn't even face the driveway and looked out that one too. He moved to the next window, went out of Banyan's sight for a few minutes—about the length of time he might need to look out a few more windows—then came back to the front of the house, looking in that direction one more time.

The man could have been admiring the scenery, Banyan supposed, but the way he was so methodical about it, almost tactical, something had to be up.

He lifted the binoculars and peered in, studying every detail in every corner of the house that was visible through the windows. He was about to pull back the binoculars and sit back for a bit when he spotted something rather disturbing.

A foot. And it most definitely did not belong to the man who answered the door. It was far too small, not to mention clad in a rainbow-striped sock. Banyan was the first to admit he didn't always catch every single detail, but he was sure he would have noticed bright, rainbow-striped socks if Jonathan—though he was beginning to doubt that was his real name—had been wearing them.

Unfortunately, the rest of the body the foot belonged to was out of sight.

He must have stared at the foot for ten minutes straight, until finally it twitched ever so slightly. Banyan let out a long breath, relieved the worst-case scenario, which had been strolling through his mind, was not reality.

Still, the man told him straight to his face he was there alone, and no matter which way you cracked that particular egg, the man had lied.

A few minutes later Banyan's phone vibrated.

"Hey, Vince," Jen said from the other end of the line.

"Hey, Jen," Banyan replied.

It was stunning how silent it was this far from civilization, and even though he was barely talking over a whisper, his voice cut through the quiet like a gunshot.

"I have your confirmation about that guy Jonathan," Jen said. "The Millers do, in fact, have a son by that name."

"So, he was telling the truth?" Banyan asked.

"Well, he didn't seem like a liar when I was talking to him."

"Wait, you talked directly to Jonathan Miller?"

"Just got off the phone with him," Jen confirmed.

Banyan's eyes shot back toward the forest house. "And did you happen to catch where he was at?"

"Sure did. Says he's packing for a trip to see his folks down in Florida. Leaves tomorrow," Jen said. "And Vince?"

"Yeah?"

"He says he's never been to his parents' place up in Ambrosia Falls. Been meaning to get there, but he usually just meets up with them in Florida once a year."

"I'll get back to you," Banyan said.

"Be careful out there, Vince," Jen said, hanging up.

Banyan's mind was whirling a mile a minute when he spotted movement in the house again. He quickly lifted his binoculars. The man—not Jonathan Miller, apparently—was bringing a plate of food over to the person who was just out of sight. The person did not reach for it, so the man eventually set the plate on the floor. Banyan peered through those binoculars so hard he forgot to blink, but the peering paid off. A few minutes later the person with the rainbow sock finally leaned forward to check out the plate of food.

Banyan wasn't sure what he'd expected, but an adorable preteen with an incredibly defiant look on her face had not been it.

Sure, a preteen could aim a defiant look at a parent, but there was something in the way they interacted. This girl was not that man's kid.

It took Banyan about zero point five seconds to decide he had to get to her.

The correct thing to do would be to call for backup, but he decided he couldn't wait. He shot off a quick text, hoping it would reach its destination—cell service was spotty—then began the descent toward the house.

Still inside the protection of the trees, Banyan double-checked his equipment—handcuffs, gun loaded, holster unsnapped. He didn't like the feel of any of it. The remote location, the eerie silence, the child in harm's way. It was a cop's nightmare scenario, the kind that tested the mettle and let you know if you had what it took. And Banyan knew there was no way in hell he was turning around and leaving that little girl behind.

He considered how to approach the situation. He could simply walk up and knock on the door…a better option if he had his squad car with him. But out here on foot, he still had the element of surprise working for him.

Best case scenario would be if he could get the girl and haul ass out of there before the man even knew she was gone. But hiking a scared kid through dense forest after she'd been abducted and through who knew what was probably not the best situation either.

Banyan took a deep breath. There was a very good chance he was going to have to take a shot at the guy. With any luck, he wouldn't have to take a fatal shot, but he needed to prepare himself in case it came to that.

Banyan pulled the gun from his holster and stepped out into the clearing. He moved quickly and quietly toward the structure, flattening himself against the house near one of the side windows, hoping he'd catch a glimpse of the girl. He needed to know exactly where she was before anything happened. He couldn't risk hurting her and didn't want to traumatize her more by witnessing a shooting if it could be helped.

He tried to figure how an abduction of a girl could relate to the other incidents in town but couldn't understand what the connection might be. What he did know was, it was too small a town and too small a time frame for all of it to be coincidence. Something worse than anything the residents of a town like Ambrosia Falls had likely seen was happening, and the man inside was the key to unlocking it all. If Banyan could, he'd like to take the man alive, but the girl was the priority…if she was in danger, he would do what he had to do to ensure her safety.

There was no movement visible inside. Banyan made his way toward the front door, ducking under windows, then climbed the steps silently. He reached for the knob, which turned easily in his hand. He supposed the man inside wasn't too worried about security way out there in the middle of nowhere.

Banyan eased himself inside, gun at the ready, heart beating a million miles a minute. It took a few moments for his eyes to adjust to the dim entrance, but soon he was moving into the living room where he'd first seen the girl.

She was no longer there.

He moved stealthily across one wall of the living room, making his way toward the kitchen area, gun leading as he rounded the corner. Quickly and methodically, he cleared the room, moving deeper into the house, entering a hallway.

He was about to pass the first bedroom on the right, peeking in and seeing it was empty, when something caught his eye. Something flickering inside a smaller space—a closet—on the other side of the room. He moved toward the lights, realizing the flickering was a security setup. He moved closer, entering the walk-in closet. If he could get a good look at the monitors, maybe he could find the girl.

Three screens sat on a small desk. The first showed four views of the inside of the house—the living room, the kitchen and a couple bedrooms. The second monitor showed various sections of land surrounding the property. This was when Banyan's tap-dancing nerves began to whirl their way into a frenzy. The third screen showed flashing words. *Perimeter Breach, Northeast Quadrant.*

That was the moment he knew. The moment he realized he had lost the very second he stepped out of the trees.

He turned to leave the closet. To give himself a chance to get out of there alive, but the small space was already going dark. The door was shut, then bolted behind him even though closet doors didn't typically have bolts on them.

The man had prepared the closet for this exact purpose. To lure anyone wanting to help straight there. And as a fog-like substance began filling the small space, the feeds on the first monitor changed, the girl popping up clearly on the screen. She was in a dark space, alone and looking pissed off...and scared. Banyan called out to her, yelled that he was there to help.

But he couldn't help. And the girl showed no signs of having heard him before his head became heavy and he slid down the wall.

His last thought before everything went black was, *I failed her.*

Chapter Fifteen

Ava and Zach were heading back to the forest. Unfortunately, they didn't have a specific target this time.

What they did have was about half an hour before they reached the last clear area appropriate for launching a drone before the forest got heavier.

Zach finally broke the silence. "So, I'm guessing there's a little more to your past than you've led me to believe."

Ava let out a long, slow sigh. This was the moment she'd been dreading for five years. The moment the people important to her found out she wasn't exactly who she said she was. She wasn't anything even close to the person she appeared to be.

"I'm so sorry, Zach. It was all part of the conditions of being in witness protection. Though it's not strictly witness protection in my case, more like asset protection."

"So you're an asset of the government."

"I used to be," Ava said. "But I haven't been active since I came to Ambrosia Falls. Everything about my life here has been legit since the day I arrived."

She hoped he understood that meant her feelings for him too—especially her feelings for him.

"So…judging from the arsenal you've got back there, were you some kind of assassin or something?"

Now that she had come this far, she couldn't lie to him anymore. Found she didn't want to keep anything from him anymore.

"Sometimes," Ava said, watching him out of the corner of her eye, but his face remained neutral. "And sometimes I was recon, and sometimes I was asked to be security, or backup, or sometimes I was needed for my expertise."

"Expertise in what? Were there a lot of national baking emergencies?" Zach asked, though his voice sounded more baffled than angry. More stunned than sarcastic.

"Baking has always just been a hobby," Ava said.

"Could've fooled me," Zach replied, and Ava smiled.

"I have an advanced degree in geology. I specialize in forensic geology, using trace evidence to track down suspects or persons of interest. I often got asked to assist in time-sensitive searches for victims or sometimes perpetrators. I have some sharpshooting too, so that was a big part of my job."

Zach swallowed hard.

"I'm still me though," she said.

"Still you. Right. You just have a little forensic geologist slash sharpshooter experience to pad your résumé with. No big deal, right?"

"I'm serious, Zach. This doesn't change who I've always been to you."

Zach shook his head, still clearly trying to wrap it around everything.

"And now that you know," Ava continued. "it means I don't have to hide any of this—" she waved her hand toward the bags in the back seat "—and we can go in there and get Chloe back using everything we've got available to us."

"That's the other thing I've been wondering about," Zach said. "Why the hell didn't you tell me all this when Chloe got taken? Why did we go up to that shack and make damn fools of ourselves falling right into his trap?"

"That's on me," Ava said. "I didn't think Justin would be so organized, so prepared. None of that was ever his strong suit. It's why he and I worked so many jobs together. I was the one who checked and rechecked each tiny detail of every job. He was the one who was good at storming in and causing chaos, which is a surprisingly rare quality to have, and if there was ever a master at it, it was Justin. This whole… careful, methodical, calculated side is something I've never seen from him before."

"So you underestimated him," Zach said, his voice accusatory.

"I'm not so sure it was underestimation so much as it was familiarity and knowledge of past behavior and skills. You want to know a target inside and out, which is why I thought I had an advantage here, but clearly Justin has changed as much as I have. Maybe more."

"Well, you did get one thing right, at least," Zach said. "This is all on you. And I may never see my daughter again. Sometimes, I wish I'd never met you."

The words stung. More than stung, they obliterated. And the worst part was, he was absolutely right.

ZACH HATED HIMSELF the moment the words left his mouth. He was hurt and angry and maybe a little embarrassed it had taken so long to catch on to the truth of who Ava really was. And worse, he was running on fear, terrified something unthinkable could have already happened to Chloe.

They drove in silence for a while, but when they neared

their destination, Zach couldn't take it anymore. "I'm sorry," was all he said.

Ava shrugged one shoulder. "You're not wrong. I did do this. I came into this town and into your lives out of nowhere. You didn't ask for any of it. I knew the risks, and I decided to get close to you and Chloe anyway. And as long as I live, it will be the biggest regret of my life."

Oof. Zach knew Ava was talking about putting them in harm's way, but it still stung to hear the woman he loved say she regretted ever knowing him. Of course, he had just told her the same thing only more harshly, so yeah. He could only hope she meant the words about as much as he did, which was not at all.

"And don't worry," she continued. "As soon as we get Chloe back, you'll never have to see me again—but I am trained for this sort of thing and probably your best chance at getting her back."

"Ava, that's not what—"

Ava put up a hand. "It's fine. It's…whatever. Right now, we need to focus on Chloe. She's all that matters."

Zach certainly couldn't argue with that, and they were nearing the edge of the trees anyway, so he let it drop. Ava pulled the truck into an approach off the road, stopping before they went too far down the rugged trail leading into a wheat field.

Ava opened the tailgate and pulled the drone case to the edge. Zach took over from there, opening the case and pulling the drone from the protective foam padding. He was about to walk it a few paces away, but Ava took it gently from his hands. Walking was not his strong suit at the moment.

Zach powered everything up, and within a few minutes, the drone was airborne, hovering high over the trees.

"This could take a while," Zach said. "There's a lot of area to cover in these trees."

Ava nodded. "It's what makes it perfect for hiding." She shook her head. "I should have anticipated this. The people who put me here should have anticipated this."

"I'm not sure there's a place in the world that doesn't have trees close by."

"Not this kind of dense forest though. A person could get lost in this indefinitely."

Zach focused on flying the drone and trying not to get discouraged. Not yet.

Ava shook out her body. "Okay, this isn't helping. I need to think. Think like Justin, only not exactly like Justin since he's been ahead of us this whole time."

"Okay, so what's his usual MO?"

"He's never been good at being uncomfortable," Ava said. "Or at being wrong. Which is probably why he's still after me after all these years."

"Why was he after you in the first place?" Zach asked.

It was the question he'd been wondering since he found out someone had been after her. He'd assumed she'd gotten swept up in the wrong crowd and witnessed something she shouldn't have, but that theory didn't really fly anymore.

"I can only assume he was an enemy operative. A sort of double agent, I guess, although we don't use that term in the real world. It's more of a TV thing."

Zach nodded, thinking over all the things that meant. "And you were with him for a while?"

"Years," Ava said, rubbing the bridge of her nose, like she was trying to stop a tingle. "I found his stash of surveillance on me. All the years we'd been together, and for a while before that even. He'd been gathering data, intel for who knows what purpose. He had a thousand opportunities to kill me... I don't know why he never did. I almost wish he would have," she said, trailing off.

There was a pause as Zach looked at her—beautiful, vulnerable, still the Ava he knew, just...with a few additional skills.

"I'm glad he didn't," Zach said.

Maybe it was the hope talking, but he couldn't bring himself to believe he would never see Chloe again. And knowing what he knew about Ava now actually made him feel better about the situation. Yes, he was still terrified beyond belief, but in a way, none of it seemed real. He still felt Chloe's presence, and he was going to cling to that feeling as hard as he damn well could.

Ava began to pace, thinking, mumbling a bit to herself, though Zach couldn't catch any of the words. He was busy trying not to let his drone crash. It had been a while since he'd been out flying, and the machine took more concentration than one might think.

"You wanna talk it out?" he asked.

Ava stopped and turned to him. "Maybe."

"Okay, so it was a surprise to you that he headed for the shack, I'm guessing."

"Very much so," Ava said, "but I figured he was trying to throw me off his trail. And I hate that it worked."

"It's smart, but we can be smarter. So, he had it pretty cushy at the first place he was at...the Lawson place."

Ava nodded. "It made sense because it was close. It was cushy enough for him...barely," she said, rolling her eyes, "and the family was going to be away for a while."

"But he likely guessed you'd know all that about him, so

he set it up so you would think you were getting the jump on him, when really, he was ten steps ahead."

"I hope not ten," Ava said, "but yeah, sounds about right."

"And then the shack."

"Which we can assume he only went to long enough to plant the explosives and take the photo of Chloe," Ava said.

"Right. And had we been thinking in terms of Justin, we might have realized it was a trap, but we were so focused on Chloe. I'd bet my last dollar he purposely got the window in the picture so he could throw us off the scent of where he was really staying."

"So where would he really be staying then?" Ava asked, more to herself than to Zach.

She started pacing again.

"Well, we know he likes a luxurious place if he can get it," Zach said, the wheels starting to turn a little faster up in the old hamster wheel of his.

"But we thought he'd stay close to town, which is why I headed to the subdivision on the lake first," Ava continued.

"But then he headed for the woods, which was smart. Easy to get lost. But if this was the place he'd planned on staying for the major part of his, what would you call it?" Zach asked.

"Operation," Ava said.

"Right. For the major part of this operation, I'd bet he'd still be looking for a nice, cushy place."

"If that even existed," Ava said, still pacing.

"Ah, but it does," Zach said, his heart rate climbing with a little zip of excitement. "The Miller place," he said, with a big smile.

"Who are the Millers?" Ava asked. "I thought I knew everyone in Ambrosia Falls."

"You do, but the Millers get their mail in Pieville."

Ava's eyes grew wide. "Can you find their place with the drone?"

"I think so," Zach said, quickly changing course.

Several minutes later Zach was maneuvering the drone over a patch of forest about twelve miles away. "I don't know exactly where it is, I've never been out there, but Arnie Jackson was out helping build it about ten years ago. Said the place was huge. They built it on an old ranch site, apparently."

"Sounds like it would be the perfect place for Justin," Ava said, looking like she didn't particularly like the taste of his name on her tongue.

"But wouldn't he realize we'd figure it out eventually?" Zach asked, his eyes glued to the monitor, praying for a break in the trees.

"That's exactly what he's counting on," Ava said. "He wants me to come to him."

Zach swallowed. He very much did not like the sound of that.

Just then, off to the far side of the monitor, Zach spotted something. The edge of a clearing. He quickly maneuvered the drone toward the clearing, hoping the machine was too high for the whir to be heard from the ground.

"I've got something," Zach said.

Ava came to stand beside him, leaning toward the small screen.

"That's got to be it," she said.

"Has to be. There's a vehicle in the drive."

"Could be the Millers'," Ava said.

"Could be," Zach agreed. "I wish I knew more about them."

"Wait, what's that?" Ava asked, pointing to something shiny in the trees.

Zach changed the path of the drone again, centering over the object in question. "Is that a car?"

"I think so," Ava said. "Weird place for a car. And what's that dark strip on the top?"

"Holy shit. I think it's a police vehicle," Zach said, panic sneaking into his voice. "The asshole said no cops. Why the hell are there cops?" He turned to Ava, his eyes wide. "Maybe they have Chloe already. We have to get out there."

Ava remained silent.

Chapter Sixteen

At least we have a new target, Ava thought as she steered the truck toward their destination. But she was worried. The police car presented a whole host of new problems, and she did not like adding variables to the mix. And a cop was a huge variable.

Sure, there was a chance the officer had somehow caught on to Justin, taken him down and rescued Chloe, but that was very unlikely. Still, the police vehicle was well hidden from both the road and the place where Justin was squatting, so maybe he or she was just watching. Waiting for backup. Of course, that meant another set of eyes on their rescue, which could go either way. A cop could think they were the bad guys and keep them from doing what they needed to do. Or they could decide to help.

The fact that Justin specifically said no cops did not put her at ease. He would have to know she had nothing to do with this officer showing up—they'd been trained to work outside the confines of organized law enforcement, at least the kind the public knew about, anyway. The "no cops" thing had been for Zach's sake. People who'd lived their whole lives following the law would automatically think to phone the police, but Ava was far beyond any of that. If there was anything she couldn't take care of herself, she had resources beyond typical law enforcement.

Maybe the whole police vehicle thing was another ploy by Justin to throw her off her game. She just couldn't figure out what the reasoning behind it might be.

It took time to get out to the remote location. More time than it did getting to the place they could park before they went on foot to the shacks, but this time they wouldn't have to trek so far through the forest.

"I think we should stay away from the police car," Ava said. "On the off chance it's a plant by Justin to mess with us, we won't want to get too close."

"A plant?"

Ava shrugged. "I can't figure out any good reason to do something like that, but if there's one thing I've learned over the past few days, it's that I do not have as much insight into Justin's thinking as I thought I did. It could simply be something he's using to distract us, so we'll miss something else. We need to stay alert...be ready for anything."

"I don't know how to be ready for anything," Zach said.

"Just try not to be too surprised, no matter what happens."

Zach raised an eyebrow. "Considering our current situation, and the things I've discovered about the person I'm closest to, I'd say you could pretty much send a steamroller right over me and I'd say it was par for the course."

"Good," Ava said, trying to ignore the sarcasm laced in his words.

It would be good if he was angry. Even better that he was angry with her. It would mean Chloe was his only priority. Maybe, with any luck, he wouldn't worry too much about what she was doing.

Because she was going after Justin. And she wouldn't let a

little thing like her personal safety get in the way. She would end this one way or the other. If Justin was gone, there'd be no more threat to Chloe and Zach. And the same applied if she was the one who was gone instead. Either way, she was going to make sure Chloe and Zach were safe.

"We're getting close," Zach said, watching the pin he'd dropped on his phone map based on the drone footage. He hoped he wouldn't lose the signal, since cell service was pretty spotty in the area.

"The police car is in there, I think," Ava said, pointing to the recently car-trampled grass leading into the ditch.

A short distance later they approached the gravel drive leading into the acreage and up to the farmyard. From the drone, it had looked like the house was about a half mile in. The place must be a nightmare in the winter. A person could be stranded there for days if they didn't have a snow-plow of some sort.

"I'm going to go past. See if there's somewhere we can ease into the trees like the police car did."

Zach nodded, his neck craning to see as far as he could up the drive, which, given the sharp curve near the entrance, was not far at all.

About a quarter mile past the turnoff, Ava eased the truck off the road and into the ditch, continuing through a small break in the trees. She weaved a little way farther until she was sure the vehicle couldn't be seen from the road. The grass would be trampled, just like with the police car, but there wasn't much she could do about that.

"We need to go up the hill and try to get a read on the place," Ava said. "Figure out what our next move is going to be."

"I don't like this," Zach said. "Chloe is in there all alone.

He's one guy. With all this firepower, we should be charging in there and taking him down."

Ava shook her head. "That's way too risky for Chloe. What if she got caught in the line of fire? Justin may know he needs Chloe for leverage to get me out here, but once I'm in his line of sight, he won't think twice about using her for a shield."

Zach cursed under his breath. "I hate this."

"I hate it too," Ava said. "We can't carry all this up the hill. Take what you're comfortable with and follow me," she told him, tucking a handgun into the back of her pants and a knife at her ankle. She hung the infrared goggles around her neck.

"We'll come back for what we need once we know what we're up against."

Zach rummaged through the bags while Ava doublechecked her ammo. "Do you need help with any of that?"

"I think I'm okay. I haven't used one of these in years," he said, checking a gun of his own, "but I do know a bit. Like I said, I used to hunt."

Ava nodded once. "Sounds good," she said, hoping Zach would not have to use his weapon. If the guy was against hunting animals, who knew what it might do to him to aim at a person.

THEY MOVED UP the hill quickly, slowing as they neared the top. Staying low, Zach followed Ava as she crept to the point where she could see the farmyard. All was still and quiet.

Ava put the goggles on, then began to whisper as Zach crept up beside her. She lowered to her stomach and Zach followed suit.

"So, these don't work like they do in the movies," Ava

said. "We're not going to be able to see the outline of a person unless they're outside. Through walls we have to use our best guesses. Walls are insulated and aren't the best way to get a good read, but we might get lucky and catch someone walking past a window or something."

Zach was disappointed, but realized there wasn't much he could do about it. He nodded and put his goggles on anyway.

"I can't stand sitting here waiting for something to happen," Zach said. "I need to get to Chloe. She must be so scared."

"I know," Ava whispered, "but this is the way it has to be. If we go in there unprepared, the person we're putting most at risk is Chloe, and that is the last thing we want to do."

"I get that in my head, but this is killing me. I need to know if she's down there."

"Give it a few minutes," Ava said, studying every inch of the yard, searching for anything out of the ordinary. "Looks like there's a heat spot inside the barn."

"Just one?" Zach asked, turning his attention to the barn.

"I think so. Like I said, it's hard to tell through walls."

"So, let's go in there and get him," Zach said.

"Except we don't know it's him. It could be Chloe, or even an animal."

"If it's Chloe, that's even better, we can grab her and get the hell out of here."

"Assuming it's not a trap," Ava said.

Zach let out a long sigh. He just wanted to know his kid was okay and get her to safety.

"Look, I know this is hard. It's killing me too," Ava said. "But we have to play this smart. If it's Chloe, great, but there's no telling what kind of trap he may have set. And if it's Justin in there, things could get ugly fast, and if he goes down—" she let out a long sigh "—we need to know where she is before anything can happen to Justin."

Zach understood what Ava was getting at then. "In case he has her stashed somewhere it'll be hard to find her."

Ava nodded, not looking at all happy he'd arrived on the same page.

They lay in silence for a few minutes, watching…waiting. Zach's thoughts jumped from being certain something catastrophic could have happened to being so sure Chloe was alright. Because she had to be. Any other outcome was unthinkable. Any future without her was impossible. And then his thoughts moved to scolding. Cursing himself for even thinking about any of that when all his attention should be 100 percent on getting to her. Rescuing her. Making sure she was okay and spoiling her for the rest of her life. And yeah, in his head he knew spoiling her wasn't good for her in the long run, but that didn't stop him from making pleas with the universe that if she ended up okay, he would do anything and everything in his power to make this up to her.

But being stuck inside his own head was not helping anyone, least of all Chloe.

"What are you thinking?" Zach asked.

"It's so quiet. Too quiet," Ava said. "Too still."

"Do you think he's not even here?" Zach asked, his disappointment already rising.

"No, I think he's here somewhere," Ava said. "It's like I can feel him, but something isn't right. If he had a plan, there would be something obvious, or at least a hint at something. I can't figure out what his strategy is."

"I bet that's exactly what he's hoping for," he said. "Get you off your game. Get you lost inside your head, guessing what his next move is going to be."

Ava nodded. "Yeah, and I've been thinking about that. Trying to decide whether he'd do something exactly opposite of what I would expect, or if that's too predictable now too."

"If it were me, I'd do both," Zach said.

"Me too," Ava agreed. "Which means we have nothing. No strategy."

"We have instinct," Zach said, "and mine is telling me to get back to the vehicle, load up with as much shit as we can possibly carry, get Chloe out of there and end this bastard."

Ava nodded. "I guess waiting isn't getting us anywhere at this point. You sure you're up for this? Going up against Justin is no joke."

"I couldn't give a flying rat's butt who we're going up against. It's not about him."

"I'm not sure there are flying rats—at least I hope to hell there aren't—but I get what you're saying," Ava said, easing her way down the low hill a bit, then slowly standing.

Zach followed, but he had only taken a few steps before the ground beneath them shook. The world in front of them lit up in a series of flashes, one after the other. The noise was booming, shattering the serenity of the forest.

"Holy shit," Zach said.

Ava stood motionless, mouth hanging open.

"Ava?" Zach asked. He'd never seen her in shock like this, and if she—the trained spy-type professional person, or whatever, exactly, she was—was in shock, things must be very bad indeed.

"I think we can assume Justin knows we're here," Ava said, her eyes still wide with a sort of faraway look in them. "I'm pretty sure that was your truck."

"Along with all of our ammo and guns?" Zach asked, his voice squeaking a little.

Ava nodded.

"We have to get to Chloe now!" Zach said. "Please tell me we can go find her now. We have to get her away from this guy."

Ava looked from Zach to the area where the truck had exploded, then back to Zach again, her face finally morphing from shock to something closer to determination. "Yeah, we gotta go now," she said, turning toward the house.

Zach was on her heels. "What's the plan?"

"I have absolutely no idea."

Chapter Seventeen

Since Justin clearly had the advantage of location and planning, Ava had hoped to even the playing field with the element of surprise and sheer firepower, both of which had just blown up right in front of her face.

He'd known exactly what her plan had been. It was a thought that sent stone-cold fear through every inch of her body. She always thought she'd be able to outsmart Justin when the time came, but she realized he'd had five years to plan what to do when he found her. Five years she'd spent rebuilding her life instead of thinking about Justin.

They'd been the best five years of her life, and she wanted to end this asshole for making her go back to her old life. How could she have fallen for his BS in the first place? She'd always been the better operative—more careful, more intuitive, more prepared. But now she wondered if all that had been true, or if he'd played it that way all along and she was simply the world's biggest sucker.

The worst part was that now—when her skills and confidence mattered the most—was not the time to start doubting her abilities, to start feeling inadequate.

She had to save a beautiful, smart, hilarious little girl, and save her dad while she was at it. If she could just do that, she'd gladly lay down her life and give Justin what he wanted. What happened to her after Zach and Chloe were safe mattered exactly zero percent.

"Are we going for the barn?" Zach asked.

"Probably," Ava said, slowing down as they neared the edge of the trees.

She motioned for Zach to stop, as she eased behind a large tree. Zach did the same a few feet away.

"I want to check the heat signature one more time," she said. "Might look different now that we're closer."

She pulled the googles up from around her neck. Zach did the same with his.

"Shit," Ava said, closing her eyes to the blinding light.

Zach made a surprised sound as the same glare burned into his eyes. "Jesus, what the hell is that?"

"He must have lit a bunch of fires in there," Ava said, trying to blink the bright spots from her vision.

"How is it not burning down then?"

"Not sure," Ava said. "They must be contained somehow. Maybe in metal containers or something."

"I am really starting to hate this guy," Zach said, throwing out the greatest understatement Ava had ever heard.

"Yeah, welcome to the club," she said, with a half-hearted smirk.

"He clearly wants us to go into that barn," Zach said. "Which means I am highly disinclined to do so."

Ava thought for a moment. Zach was right. Justin obviously wanted them in the barn…using the fires as a sort of calling card slash bait situation. So that was exactly where Ava was going to go. But she sure as hell wasn't letting Zach get anywhere near it.

"Let's go for the house," Ava said. "Stay low. You go

around the front, and I'll take the back. With any luck we can catch him by surprise from one angle or the other."

She pulled the gun from her waistband and nodded for Zach to do the same.

"Promise me one thing," she said. "If you find Chloe first, get her out. Don't worry about where I am. Your only job is to get her out—I'll be right behind you."

The moment Zach gave his nod, Ava sprinted from the trees and headed toward the back of the house, clearing the corner of it in seconds. A quick glance back assured her Zach was headed toward the front of the house. She waited a few more beats, hoping to hell it would either take Zach a bit to get inside, or there wouldn't be a good view toward the barn from in there. She didn't need a lot of time, but if he spotted her, everything would be lost. There was a still a chance she could handle Justin if left to her own devices, but she definitely wouldn't be able to handle him if she had to make sure Zach was safe too.

If she knew Justin at all—though after the past couple of hours, she wasn't sure she ever did—he would be focused on one thing and one thing only.

Her.

And maybe it was instinct, or maybe it was the fact that she felt like she did still know the Crow, at least in the most fundamental sense, but Ava somehow knew Chloe was not in that barn. He would be keeping her somewhere that wouldn't be easy to find. He wanted to keep Zach busy...keep him away.

And to have her, his Sparrow, all to himself for one last fight.

ZACH TRIED LIKE hell to get his hands to stop shaking but was having no luck. It had to be the nerves or adrenaline or something, but either way, he took a moment—just a second—to breathe and try to center himself. The life of his daughter depended on what he did in the next few minutes.

Thank the Lord Ava was right there with him. He wasn't alone. Chloe wasn't alone.

Two breaths in, two breaths out, then he tried the door. Locked.

He wondered if the real owners of the house ever locked their doors. They were so deep into the middle of nowhere it seemed impossible some random criminal would stumble upon the place, but he supposed no one was ever completely immune to the outside world encroaching into their existence. The current situation was proof enough of that.

There was little reason to worry about noise—Justin clearly knew they were there—but Zach's instincts told him to be as quiet as possible. Still, the only way in seemed to be to break one of the small windowpanes on the door and reach in to unlock the door like they always did on TV. He was about to do it too, when he noticed an open window halfway down the side of the house. He figured it would be a whole lot quieter to cut through a window screen than it would be to smash a damn pane of glass.

He just needed to find something to step onto to get up to the window. Anything would do, like…one of the chairs sitting around the firepit a few yards away. He rushed over and grabbed one, hoping Ava wasn't already inside and wondering where in the hell he was.

He made quick work of the screen with his pocketknife and eased one leg over the windowsill, pushing off with his other leg to sort of jump up there. And damn if it didn't hurt quite a bit more than he expected with the gaping wound that had only been closed a short while earlier.

He bit his lip through the pain as he struggled through the window.

It was not a graceful endeavor.

He glanced around, taking in the room, half expecting Ava to already be far enough into the house to catch a glimpse of her, but she was nowhere to be found. Maybe she was halfway to clearing the whole place by now, Zach thought, and figured he'd better get a move on if he was to be of any use at all.

He began on the main floor, moving through the living room, eyes darting, ears perked, skin prickling with adrenaline and anticipation. Easing his way toward what he thought might be the kitchen, he peeked around the corner. It was, in fact, a kitchen, and it was very empty and very quiet.

Zach let out a long, slow breath, trying to find his composure, his bravery, his wits. And while he was pretty sure he didn't actually find any of those things, desperation and fear propelled him forward anyway.

Where the hell was Ava? He did not think he would be doing this alone.

But he was so close to Chloe now. He could feel it.

Moving back through the living room, he started down a short hallway. Peeking into the first room on the right, he found a bedroom. Nothing seemed out of the ordinary. Without going in, he moved on to the next bedroom down the hall. Same thing. The third bedroom was as empty as the others. His frustration grew as he moved to the bathroom at the end of the hall, even flinging the shower curtain open and half-expecting someone to jump out at him.

He had "cleared" all the rooms and come up with nothing. But of course, he hadn't really cleared them completely, had he? He'd determined there was no one obvious lurking in any of them, but he had to look closer. Closest to the third bedroom, he moved into that room first, gun at the ready. He whipped the door back and pointed his gun in that direction, heart beating hard and feeling like an absolute imposter. Who was he trying to kid? He had no idea what he was doing. Still, what other choice did he have?

Zach ducked and lifted the bedspread, readying for the jump scare of his life, but again, nothing happened. He moved on to the closet, taking a deep breath before thrusting the door open then aiming the gun into every corner.

Empty.

He really hoped no one was watching him, because this whole daring rescue thing was making him feel like the biggest amateur on the planet.

He moved into the next bedroom across the hall, going through all the same motions with the same result.

Zach headed down the hall, backtracking his way to the first bedroom. He did the behind the door thing, the under the bed thing, then moved on to the closet. But this time, when he moved to the closet, he wasn't met with nothing.

There was a latch on the door.

On the outside. His heart began to race. There would never be a latch on the outside of a closet door unless someone on the outside was keeping someone on the inside against their will.

Zach slowly opened the latch, visions of Chloe jumping into his arms already rolling through his mind as he whipped the door open.

The first thing he registered was that Chloe was not there. His heart fell straight to his feet and through the floor.

The second thing he registered was even though Chloe wasn't there, the closet was not empty. A man lay on the floor, and Zach couldn't tell whether he was dead or passed out. A strange shot of excitement moved through him...if this was Justin, then maybe everything was already okay. Maybe Ava had somehow gotten in there and secured him in the small space, perhaps already on her way to Chloe. Unfortunately, the third thing he registered was that the man was wearing a police uniform, and also, that he looked familiar.

Shit.

The cop from that morning in town. Banyan?

He had no idea how the officer had gotten to Justin ahead of them, but it actually made Zach feel more secure, his shoulders easing a bit. The police knew what they were doing. Except, he realized in the next heartbeat, even if Banyan had found Justin, he hadn't fared too well going up against him, and the low vibration of dread in his stomach started all over again.

Guess they knew the origin of the police cruiser in the woods now.

And then, as these things rushed through his mind, Zach registered a fourth thing. There was a strange smell in the room...a little bit earthy, and a lot chemical. He looked at the officer on the floor. Had the man been gassed?

Without thinking, Zach just moved. And yeah, probably not the best idea to go rushing into a small space that might still be filled with gas, but that apparently didn't matter to his brain. He shoved the gun into the back of his pants, then grabbed the man under the armpits, gathering all his strength to pull him out of there.

The thought had occurred to him that maybe it was already too late, and perhaps he shouldn't be moving a body—especially if this place was about to become a crime scene—but even as he was thinking those things, Zach knew he couldn't leave a defenseless man in a situation like that, even if it might already be too late.

After a few strong heaves, Zach maneuvered the officer out of the closet and into the bedroom. He thought about putting him on the bed, but all of a sudden, he was feeling a little…dizzy?

His breathing was heavy from the excursion. Which meant he'd taken in some of the gas. He hoped to hell it wasn't lethal, and hoped to even deeper depths of hell this asshole hadn't done anything like this to Chloe.

Zach had never been so scared, so full of adrenaline, so motivated to…he wasn't sure what. Find Chloe, for sure, but then he wanted to do something else. To find this man who had his daughter and make sure he never did anything like this to anyone ever again.

He did not like the feeling. It wasn't him.

The air in the bedroom was probably already compromised, but in Zach's mind, it only made sense to shut the closet door and keep as much of it contained to that small space as possible. But when he moved toward the closet, he saw the screens. Four of them, clearly receiving pictures from surveillance cameras around the property.

He was torn. This could be the answer to exactly where Chloe was, not to mention where Ava had gotten to, but getting close enough to see, and maybe even figure out the basics of the system, would mean going all the way inside the closet and risking getting caught in there himself…maybe permanently.

The room seemed to tilt around him.

But the other choice was to continue wandering around the house aimlessly, and then move on to the grounds if he had no luck. But all of this was already taking too long.

Every second Chloe was out there, scared and alone, was one second too many.

He almost decided it wasn't worth the risk. He was of no use to Chloe or anyone else if he was unconscious…or worse, and he moved to close the door, ready to seal it shut and latch it back up, but then a flash. Movement across one of the screens and he was pulled in, as if he had no control over his feet. He yanked his shirt up over his nose, realizing it wasn't going to help much, but it was all the protection he had and peered into the screen.

But the screen was so dark, like maybe he hadn't actually seen anything at all.

He blinked, then blinked again, convincing himself it had been a trick of the eye. He'd wanted so badly to see something that he dreamed it all up.

He started backing out of the closet when the flash came again. Someone running across the top left screen. The feed was dim, but the place looked like…the barn. And someone had just moved from behind one large beam to the next.

Ava.

What the shit was Ava doing in the barn?

But Zach knew the answer with a certainty that sent a chill straight to his bones. She was going after Justin, and she was doing it alone. Except screw that, Zach thought, already halfway there in his mind. He didn't think about what he would do when he got there; he only knew he had to help.

And then the screens all flashed, changing to new feeds, and he saw the one thing he'd been hoping to see, so scared he might never see again.

The face of his beautiful daughter.

Chapter Eighteen

The barn door slid open with a wail. So much for taking the sneaky route, Ava thought as she eased inside. Even though the sun was just beginning to set, the inside of the barn was incredibly dim, and her eyes needed time to adjust. Time she didn't have.

Ava's first instinct was to slide the door shut again, though it did cross her mind she might need a quick escape. But the thought of Justin being able to get out without her realizing it and going after Zach or Chloe won out, and she squeak-slid the door shut again.

Her eyes still a bit compromised, Ava felt like a fish in a fishbowl—vulnerable…exposed. She needed to find cover.

She began to make out shapes in the shadows. The place was a veritable smorgasbord of farm implements ranging from large tractors and machinery all the way down to pitchforks and rakes, and a million other potentially deadly instruments in between.

The infrared goggles were useless. Justin had set at least a dozen fires in the main open space of the barn, contained in old wheel wells on top of concrete blocks. It was a maze in there, with stalls running in one direction, then turning and continuing in another. Which would have been fine if Justin hadn't already had time to memorize the place.

First rule of operatives—know the territory. Which went hand in hand with the second rule—confuse your opponent whenever possible.

It was a built-in element of surprise situation on repeat.

"Hello, Sparrow," a creepily disembodied voice echoed through the barn.

What the hell had he done? Install a damned speaker system?

"I've been waiting for this moment for a long time."

It's funny the things a person forgot when given ample amounts of time. Ava was surprised to learn she'd forgotten his voice. Or not forgotten it, really, but it had been such a long time since she'd thought about his voice, the sound of it took her by surprise. Made so many memories come rushing back.

Funny thing was, very few of them were happy. Though she supposed that had a lot to do with the fact she rarely allowed herself to be happy back then. Given how she'd been living the past five years and how different her life was, the thought broke her heart a little. She'd never noticed it back then, but after experiencing a joyful life, she wasn't sure she could go back to a life like her old one.

"I haven't," she said under her breath, glancing around for any hint as to where he might be.

Her eyes landed on a speaker built into the wall. So, the intercom system was in place before Justin got there. Maybe it was a way to communicate between the house and the barn, or maybe they'd had ranch hands at one point and this was the easier way to get messages to their staff. With any luck, it would be an older system, which would mean there was likely a dedicated room where a person would have to make the announcements from. New technology was definitely handy sometimes but could be a real pain in the ass to trace with all the Bluetooth and wireless and everything.

She eased down the wall, glad she had dark clothes on.

Her eyes were finally starting to adjust, and she spotted a wire running up a post in front of her. Tracing the wire with her eyes, she moved farther down the length of the barn, following it to a small room built into the back of the structure.

Silently she moved into position outside the door of the room, kicking it open, so ready to shoot. So ready for all this to be done.

But the room was empty.

"Aw, Sparrow, you didn't think it would be that easy, did you?" came the disembodied voice.

No, Ava thought, but she'd be lying that she hadn't hoped he'd be that careless and underestimating of her.

And now she knew he was watching her too. Hard to track someone when they had eyes on you, but you had absolutely no idea where they were. But it was dim inside the barn, the windows shuttered, the only light coming from the fires.

Ava moved quickly, ducking behind the nearest fire. If he was using infrared to track her, she would use his own fire trick against him. She moved again to the next nearest fire, then the next. It wouldn't be impossible to track her, but she was damn well going to make it as hard as she could.

The real problem was, she had no idea where the hell Justin even was. And he probably had her exact location pinpointed.

She closed her eyes...had to think. If she were Justin, where would she go?

And then, with the intuitive clarity that used to fuel her every move, honed over years in her former life, she knew.

Up.

Justin would be somewhere above, in the loft. Advantage was at the high ground where you can see your enemy coming. Usually. She had to figure a way to go up without waltzing right into some trap he'd no doubt set for her. She desperately needed an advantage of her own. *She* needed the higher ground.

A quick glance around told her there were several ladders leading to the hayloft, and she'd bet her life each one of them was booby-trapped somehow. And if she knew Justin, those traps would do harm, yes, but it would not be enough to kill her—only to weaken her so he could toy with her some more.

Coward.

But Ava didn't need to get to the loft. She needed to get higher. She needed to get to the roof.

Of course, getting onto the roof of a barn was not an easy task considering a two-story barn was usually thirty feet up, and this one was no exception. She also needed to get there without Justin knowing what she was up to.

She needed a distraction.

And as the final rays of sun shone through the edges of the shuttered windows, the dust dancing around as it passed through the sun streaks, an idea started to form. Dust. So much dust. Highly flammable dust if given the proper variables.

And she'd passed a bunch of yard and lawn tools on her way into the barn that would come in very handy, indeed. Bags of grain lay stacked against the nearest stall. The feed looked like it had been there for a long time, as if the animals the grain had been intended for had been gone awhile and no one ever got around to getting rid of it. If Ava were very lucky, maybe the grain had even begun to form the dusty black mold that was very bad for a person to breathe in, but that would be perfect for her plan.

Ava crept back to the pile of yard tools and pulled out what she needed. The gas-powered leaf blower wasn't going to be quiet, but if her plan worked it wouldn't matter if Justin knew where she was.

Because she would not be there for long.

Making her way back to the sacks of grain, Ava pulled out the small knife from its sheath near her boot and made a long, quick slice down the front of each stack. Grain began to leak out. She put her knife away and pushed the primer button a few times before yanking the cord. It made a hideous sound, no doubt instantly alerting Justin to her location.

She pulled the cord again, and again—hideous sound, no start.

Scrambling came from above, and she knew she'd only get one more chance.

She yanked that damn cord with every ounce of strength she had and the thing finally, blessedly, roared to life.

In one swift move, Ava kicked over the stacks of grain, causing a huge plume of dust to billow into the air as she pointed the leaf blower toward its destination—the nearest fire, and on the other side of it, a nice, convenient stack of hay, dry and brittle, and best of all, gloriously flammable.

It hadn't been Justin's best move to light those fires, Ava thought as she ran in the opposite direction toward one of the shuttered windows.

Even though they were behind her, Ava knew the flames were huge. The heat was heavy at her back, and as she scrambled the few feet to the window and pushed the shutter open, she risked a glance back and smiled as the flames licked their way around the edges of the haystack.

It wouldn't keep Justin busy forever, but if he had some master plan to deal with her in the loft, he'd have to put out the fire first. Footsteps pounded on wood somewhere deep inside the barn and Ava knew she was right.

She flung one leg over the windowsill, then eased to the ground on the other side, gently closing the shutter behind her.

Problem one down. Now there was just the little matter of how to get onto the roof of the exceedingly tall, and extremely daunting—now that she was getting a good look at it—building. She ran a full circle around the barn, pleased to see a bit of smoke billowing from the east side—Justin was no doubt losing his shit, which made her extremely happy—but there was no obvious way up the structure.

Scratch that.

There was one very obvious way, but Ava really did not want to take it. Unfortunately, there were no trees, or any structures around that might be hiding a handy-dandy ladder that might happen to reach all the way to the roof either, so it made her decision easy.

The decision was easy, but the execution definitely wouldn't be. Back when she was in the field, she might not give too much thought to it, but now that she'd let herself... soften for five years, she was not sure how this was going to go.

Off the front of the barn, there was a pulley system that must have once been used to transport feed, or hay, or who knew what up to the second floor of the barn. The heavy metal contraption was bolted above the second-floor door, close to the roof.

Ava took a deep breath and let it out in a big, determined whoosh. It was now or never, she knew, and jumped up onto the long rope dangling near the ground. Inch by inch she eased up the rope, moving hands above her head, then pushing with her legs, trying her damnedest not to look down. But the moment she had that pesky thought that she should not look down, the task, of course, became impossible.

Halfway up, Ava began to think the whole thing had been a very bad idea. Her arms, not used to the kind of stress, began to shake, but she tried to kind of zone out, to keep moving and not think too much. Eventually she made it to the heavy metal wheel part of the pulley and above it, the strong wooden post, about six inches square. She hadn't thought this next part all the way through. She was only taking it one step at a time, and with her arms as weak and spent as they were, she wasn't sure she could hoist herself up to the post. Although, given the situation she was in, so high from the ground, she wasn't entirely sure she could make it back down either, so again, easy decision…and a difficult execution.

She tried to visualize her plan. Maybe she could kick her feet up and go legs first, but the thought of dangling upside down made her shove that idea away pretty quickly. She honestly still didn't know if it was going to work when she decided to simply go for it, moving her legs up close under her, gripping the rope with her feet and pushing herself partway above the post, steadying herself by grasping the post and heaving her way the final few inches.

As she straddled the post, her heart raced, and everything else shook, and then, even worse, she accidentally looked down. A little zip of wooziness forced her to scramble up over the edge of the roof to its relative safety faster than she could say giddyap.

Which was definitely also faster than she could process that she just climbed to the roof of a barn that was, you know, on fire.

But a girl couldn't have everything. One step at a time was about all a person could handle in a situation where their ex-boyfriend slash stalker slash attempted murderer is after them and everyone they love.

Legs still shaking, Ava made her way to the first of two little vent stacks with the cute tiny roofs on the top of the barn. She supposed they had a name but had absolutely no idea what it might be. And absolutely no desire to care, what with the whole burning building beneath her and everything. Which was when she decided to risk a peek, leaning a bit toward the east side of the barn. There was smoke, but it didn't seem any worse than before, and since it wasn't streaming out of the vent she was currently leaning on, she figured Justin must have it under control. It would have been pretty careless to light a bunch of fires inside an old dusty barn filled with hay and not have a few extinguishers lying around.

The slats in the vent stack allowed Ava a bit of a view back into the barn. It was almost as dark in there as it was becoming outside, the last whispers of light melting into darkness as she rested, knowing that what had gotten her this far had been the easy part.

And then a shadow crossed as she watched, a darkness breaking the muted orange of the glowing fires. The path of the shadow was determined, confident, not evading or using maneuvers to try to stay hidden. Either Justin was very sure of his plan, or he had no idea about her perch above.

He moved fast, and almost instantly past where she could see, heading for the back of the barn. Ava got up and hung on to the vent stack as she eased around it. The roof was steeply pitched, but she was surprised at how steady she felt up there. Though she supposed anything would feel steady after the monstrous climb of doom she'd just performed.

Careful of making noise, Ava made her way down the roof, stepping carefully in the dark, testing each step before putting her full weight on it. It was an old barn, but it was sturdy, and she made it to the second vent stack in a minute or so.

Jackpot.

Justin wasn't directly below the vent, but he was in her line of vision. Surrounded by monitors and electronic equipment, the guy had a whole intelligence center going on right inside that rustic old barn. She should have known. Justin wasn't one to trust his instincts, always preferring the backup of technology to show him the easiest way.

And then on one of the screens, she saw something. A man, wandering through the house, and she couldn't help herself—her body moving of its own accord—when she leaned in a bit further to get a better look.

And that's when she heard the big crack.

But she didn't have time to figure out where it was coming from before the world in front of her gave way, the vent falling in on itself.

Which was precisely when she began to plummet.

ZACH KNEW ONLY two things. He had to get to Chloe, then he had to get to Ava. He had absolutely no idea how he was going to do either of those things, but he was going to damn well do them anyway.

The screens flashed again, and Chloe's face appeared. She was somewhere dark. The grainy gray feed of Chloe's face looked like night vision, but the sun was still peeking out over the horizon, the setting sun coating everything in a sickly pink glow.

Which meant there weren't any windows wherever she was.

His guts started to churn. What if she wasn't in the house at all? Or anywhere on the property? The bastard had moved her at least once, even if it was stopping only long enough to take a picture at the old hunting shack.

But Zach knew he had no choice. He had to search every inch of the property because, well, frankly he had no other option. So he began to search, knowing full well it was an exercise in frustration and he was going to descend further and further into panic the entire time.

The screens flashed once more and Zach trained his eyes on Chloe, studying every inch of the screen for some kind of clue to let him know where she might be. And then he saw it. A small circle a bit brighter than the rest of the feed, as if a tiny bit of sun was trying to break through. A knot in a piece of wood, maybe? Or even a crack? But before the screen switched again, Zach knew one small thing more than he did before. He'd had frenzied visions of underground spaces, bunkers, panic rooms impossible to get into, but now he knew she was in a space where there must be at least one window—a covered window, but a window nonetheless.

Zach took a big breath and screamed, "Chloe!"

He'd forgotten where he was and a wave of dizziness washed over him, making him thrust an arm out to grab the wall, nearly falling. He moved back out of the closet, stepping over the police officer and wondering how deadly the gas was. But the thought pushed to the back of his mind as he stumbled toward the door of the bedroom.

"Chloe!" he yelled again, the effort forcing him to pause and lean on the doorframe.

His vision swirled for a moment, then righted itself, like the worst head rush of his life. As long as the effects weren't permanently affecting him, he was damn well going to use every moment he had to get to his daughter.

He moved back toward the living room. There was a chance Chloe could be in the basement, and he wasn't about to leave the place without exhausting every possible chance he had at finding her.

As another wave of dizziness rolled through, his head feeling heavier, his body moving slower, his thoughts getting thicker, he made his way to the large windows. If the gas was this potent, and if there was any chance Chloe was anywhere nearby, he needed to air the place out. He thought about going back and closing the bedroom door the gas was coming from, but if there was any chance Banyan was still alive, he couldn't do that. The officer had clearly already been through a hell of a lot. Judging from the headache already threatening to strangle Zach's efforts at finding Chloe and Ava, if the officer did wake up, he was going to be suffering, and Zach couldn't bear to make that even worse.

He struggled with the old windows that clearly hadn't been opened for a while, but finally got the crank to move the tiniest bit. After another lurch or two, the window gave way, a whoosh of fresh air pouring in, aided by the window he'd climbed through on the other side of the room. He repeated the effort with one more window, then moved toward the basement stairs, which he'd seen near the entrance.

The stairwell was dim, but even as he was descending, Zach could already sense this wasn't going to be where he found Chloe. The light from the stairway would have illuminated the feed from the camera more, he was sure of it, but he supposed, in his hazy stupor, it was possible there could be a room built down there that was darker.

The sensation as he made his way down the stairs was similar to being drunk, with brief moments of clarity alternating with bouts of fogginess through which he concentrated hard, trying to find lucidity again. And then, without fully knowing how he'd gotten there, he was standing in the middle of an empty room, light streaming in through windows on all sides.

Chloe was nowhere to be found.

Still, Zach fumbled to open every door in that basement. He wasn't sure in the end how many there were, it felt like a hundred, but even he knew that didn't make sense.

He blinked a few times and shook his head, which seemed to help a little, then made his way back up the stairs to the main floor. The task took far more exertion than it should have, but he got the sense the toxin was already weaker than before, and maybe he was on the other side of it. His head still felt like it was in a vise and his eyelids were heavier than ever, but the fresh air as he crested the top of the stairs helped even more.

"Chloe!" he yelled one more time before reaching for the doorknob to leave.

He had no idea what his plan was, but he'd exhausted every possible hiding place in the house.

But as he turned the knob, a clunk sounded. A clunk from somewhere inside the house.

"Chloe?" he yelled again, this time more questioning, his heart starting to beat a little faster.

The clunk sounded again, and this time Zach was ready for it, listening intently for where it was coming from.

The ceiling?

It took Zach far longer than it should have to figure it out. How could he have been so dense?

The attic.

Zach figured it must be the gas, or at least that was the story he was going with as he stumble-ran through the house searching for an access panel. Living room, nothing. Kitchen nothing…he went through the bedrooms, even stepping over the police officer to peek into the closet of horrors, but still nothing until he reached the back bedroom on the left, tucked away inside the closet, where he finally found what he was looking for.

"Chloe, I'm coming!" he yelled, then ran back to the kitchen for a chair, positioning it under the panel and sliding it open.

But even with the chair he was still too far below the opening to see inside. With the still-foggy brain, Zach didn't know where he summoned the strength—it must have been pure adrenaline—but somehow, he jumped and pulled himself partway through the small hole, and still half hanging out, he scanned the dark space.

A scurrying noise came from somewhere in the shadows, and Zach braced himself once more.

But it wasn't an enemy to fight that he saw. It was his amazing Chloe—hands tied and a cloth around her mouth— but otherwise looking healthy and uninjured.

Relief flooded him, and he didn't even care how much he shook with the effort of hanging there as his daughter looped her arms around his neck and began to cry.

Chapter Nineteen

Everything hurt.

Ava started to move slowly, trying—unsuccessfully—not to groan, unsure as to what might be injured or broken…or what might be coming at her next. Eventually she rolled onto her back, and nothing seemed to be broken, but her muscles screamed. This was going to hurt tomorrow.

If she made it to tomorrow.

A slow clap started from somewhere in the rafters. "You always did know how to make an entrance," Justin said.

Ava couldn't see where he was, exactly, but from the direction of his voice, she got the general idea of his whereabouts being ahead of her and to her right. She had seen him just before her fall though, so he couldn't have gotten far.

"Asshole," she said under her breath, realizing—as she picked a few splinters of wood from her shirt—that he had to have doctored the vent stack, set it to crumble.

The first one she leaned against had been as strong as the day it was built, but the second folded in on itself like the origami game she used to play as a kid to determine her future. She was still waiting on her "large fortune" and "many cats."

"I have to say, you've played into my plan exactly as you were supposed to," his voice said, faraway and tinny.

A speaker.

He'd known exactly what she was going to do before she did it. Of course, he'd had the advantage of time—scoping out the property and putting measures in place to ensure she did what he expected. She wondered if he'd even bothered to booby-trap the ladders or if he knew she'd assume they'd been tampered with.

Ava began to realize one thing. In the time she'd been slowly getting to her feet, Justin could have taken her out six times. But that wasn't what he wanted. He wanted to toy with her. To make her suffer—both physically and mentally. He wanted to control her.

And she hated that she'd played right into his game. Her face burned…with rage, embarrassment, she wasn't sure. Probably a combination of both. She used to be better than this.

She needed to be better than this.

"Where's Chloe?" she spat, wiping at the bit of blood on her lip.

"She's safe," Justin said. "Might take a while for that… gentleman of yours to find her though."

Of course. Justin would do everything in his power to keep Zach busy. To keep him away while he played out his sick game. To have Ava all to himself. To do what he failed at the first time.

But Ava wasn't going to make it easy. If it was a choice between saving herself or saving Zach and Chloe, it wasn't a choice. She'd gladly sacrifice for them, and she was prepared. But if there was a chance, a way to keep the life she'd built…well, she was going to bloody well try for it. And lucky for her, she didn't care about teaching anyone any lessons, or whatever the hell it was Justin was trying to do or prove. The first chance she got she would take him out. No questioning, no overthinking, no excuses. She reached behind her back for her gun.

Shit.

It must have dislodged in the fall. Ava glanced back to the pile of rubble wondering if it was worth trying to find, when a shadow jumped out at her. Except, of course, it wasn't just a shadow. It was the man she hoped she'd never see again. She was caught off guard, knocked to the floor, tumbling, tangling with him. She never wanted to be this close to him again. Had fiery, burning nightmares about it after the bunker explosion.

But as they rolled once more, Ava realized something. All those years spent worrying about Justin finding her, terrified about what might happen, were for nothing. In fact, now that he'd found her, she realized it was the best thing that could ever happen.

Because truly, this was the only way to end it.

She wrapped one leg around Justin's waist and used the momentum of the roll to heave herself to the top position. Justin anticipated the move and countered, but it was enough to untangle them and send her scrambling a few feet away.

Justin got to his feet quickly, but so did Ava, finally coming face-to-face with the man who'd very nearly killed her five years ago.

"Good to see you, Sparrow," he said, the words not so much being spoken as they were oozing out of him.

"Afraid I can't say the same," Ava said, "though it is a little alarming to see you this way."

"Scared?" he asked.

Ava scoffed. "I meant your appearance is alarming, not the situation," she said.

Justin had always been vain, and Ava knew how to hit him where it hurt. He was an attractive person, most spies were—it helped their marks trust them—and he would still be considered handsome. But he had definitely aged, and Ava wasn't above using any tactic she could to get inside his head.

His eye twitched and she knew she was on the right track, but then he smiled.

They were giving each other a wide berth, circling the loft of the barn. Ava's hands were out at the ready, as were Justin's, though he clearly had the advantage, considering the knife in his hand.

"It has been a long five years," he said, as if shrugging the comment off, but Ava knew better.

"Really?" she said, as if she didn't have a care in the world. "Because they've been the absolute best five years of my life."

She wasn't lying either…she'd give anything to go back to her warm little Ambrosia Falls house and be quite content for the rest of time. She'd kind of fallen into being an operative in the first place. It was cliché, a recruiter singling her out in college, citing her advanced marks and athletic abilities, but even then, Ava knew her desirability as an agent had more to do with the fact that she didn't have any close family left, or many other connections for that matter.

Ugh, and she hated to admit it, but all that was probably how Justin had been able to get close to her too. Once someone became an operative, they couldn't live a normal life anymore. It was inevitable that operatives tended to attract each other like magnets…it was really the only way to have a relationship at all.

Of course, there was a whole lot of risk in getting involved with an agent, which Ava knew as well as anybody, she just never thought she'd be gullible enough to fall for it. Which was, of course, her real mistake. Believing she was smarter than Justin…less gullible. Except she'd been the one who got played. She supposed it was inevitable, this instinct to continue assuming she was smarter than him—everyone believed they were smarter than everyone else in the room most of the time. But she wasn't about to underestimate him again.

She would, however, do her damnedest to make sure he thought she'd become a whole lot weaker than she had. Her limp, as she moved slowly, never taking her eyes off Justin, was real, but she might have been exaggerating it…just a little. Maybe more than a little. She swiped at her lip again, reminding Justin of the cut he put there with his clever, clever ways.

"Looks like it hurts," Justin said, a gleam in his eye that Ava decidedly did not like.

It was a little too wild, a little too unhinged.

"It's fine," she said, though she didn't try to sell the point too much.

As she said it, Justin lunged, knife hand out. He was trying to catch her off guard again, trying to make her duck to the left, which would have sent her tumbling over the edge of the loft, but she was too well-trained. Ava didn't even have to try to memorize the details of her surroundings anymore, it happened automatically, and instinct thrust her in the opposite direction.

They continued to circle, Ava watching Justin's eyes, his hands…every twitch of every muscle, her mind working, trying to come up with a plan. She was moving toward the rubble of the vent stack, her gun at the forefront of her mind. She had no doubt Justin had a gun on him somewhere too, but it would likely be hard to get it, and he wouldn't pull it out unless she had one too. He wanted a fair fight. He'd been beaten by Ava before, and his tiny ego wouldn't allow for him to win at a disadvantage. He'd have to win fair and square.

Her feet slid across the floor, the dirt and hay and splintered bits of woods dampening the sound of their footfalls.

She was beginning to form a tiny inkling of a plan. It was a terrible plan, but it was all she had. It was too much to hope she'd happen upon her gun, but if she could get to one of the sharp splinters of wood, one large enough to do a little damage if embedded in the right appendage at the right angle, she could have a chance. Of course, that was a lot of ifs. If she saw an appropriate piece...if she was able to get a hold of it...if she was able to get close enough to Justin to do some damage. But it was what she had. He wasn't going to wait around all day before he made another move.

Justin lunged for her, a flame from one of his fires glinting off the blade, and Ava put her plan into motion. She ducked, rolling along her right shoulder, grabbing as much debris from the floor as her hand would hold as she went. She jumped back to her feet and spun to face him, checking her treasures. There was a single splinter that might do, and as she discarded the rest, she made her own lunge toward Justin, driving the splinter home with all her might, but at the last second, he saw it coming and turned, just enough for the wood to dig into his shoulder instead of closer to his chest where she'd been aiming.

Justin let out an animalistic wail, clearly injured, but also clearly even more pissed off now as his eyes went wild and he came straight for her.

Ava had no time to react as he hit her full-on with his entire weight, sending them both toward the railing of the loft area. The wood railing only crackled for a second before it gave way, sending them into free fall, a sensation Ava had hoped she wouldn't experience again, let alone so soon. Though maybe because she'd already been through this once in the past few minutes, she was less caught off guard than Justin seemed to be. His wild eyes filled with fear. She swung a leg around his body and used the momentum to spin them both, hoping like hell he would be the one to hit the floor first.

ZACH LIFTED HIS precious cargo down from the attic and set her on the floor. He was as gentle as he could be as he bent down and removed the cloth from around her mouth and cut the rope free from her hands.

Even though she hadn't done it in years, Chloe scurried up and clung onto his neck, not letting go even when he stood, ignoring the slice of pain shooting though his leg. Pain was nothing, not when he finally had his daughter back.

He moved back down the hall carrying his only child, and tears filled his eyes when Chloe whispered, "I knew you'd come."

He held her close as he continued to stumble toward the door, realizing for the first time he hadn't thought about what he might do when he found Chloe. They had no truck to retreat to, no safe space to go to figure out their next move.

Suddenly, Chloe stiffened. "What's wrong, Dad?"

She pulled back and looked at him, alarm filling her eyes.

"Nothing's wrong anymore, sweetheart," he said, taking another step toward the door.

"Dad," Chloe scolded. "What's wrong with your leg? You shouldn't be carrying me."

"I don't want to let you go," he said, continuing to stumble along.

"Dad!" she said, louder this time. "Stop. Put me down. Please."

Zach didn't want to admit it, but his leg *was* making it a whole lot more difficult to rescue Chloe. He didn't want to be hurt, he didn't want to admit it was hampering the whole "brave, strong dude" thing he had going on, but he wasn't some sort of superhero. He was just a guy who would do anything for his kid.

"It's okay, Chloe," Zach said.

"Dad," Chloe said, her tone more serious than a veteran teacher dealing with the school bully for the fourth time that semester. "Put. Me. Down."

Zach eased Chloe out of his arms as gingerly as he could, trying not to wince. "I want to make sure you're okay."

"Yeah, same," she said, putting her hands on her hips.

A little pang of something—sadness that she was growing up so fast, maybe—shot through him, but he knew this was the real Chloe. The very capable, caring and concerned kid he wasn't quite sure how he raised to be so amazing, and so completely herself.

"I'll be fine," he said, trying not to let his limp betray his words.

Chloe side-eyed him like she knew he was full of it, which he absolutely was. The truth was, his leg hurt like hellfire pokers were twisting around in there, but his job wasn't done yet, so he wasn't about to stop and try to do something about it.

"Come on," he said, leading her toward the door. "We need to figure out what to do next."

"We have to get Ava and get out of here," Chloe said matter-of-factly, as if the whole thing was obvious.

"How did you know Ava was here?"

"*He* kept talking about her," Chloe said, the word coming out like she had a bad taste in her mouth. "It was so annoying. And then he started calling her some dumb bird name." She thought for a moment. "Sparrow, I think. It was so weird. He is *so* weird."

Zach marveled at how even a kidnapping could do little to keep Chloe's feistiness at bay. "That's one word for it, I guess," he said.

Chloe smiled conspiratorially like she knew a few other choice words her dad might prefer to call the guy.

"Okay, you're right. Ava is out here, and I have to find her, but first I need to find someplace safe for you."

"I can come with you—" Chloe started to say, but Zach put up a hand to cut her off.

"There is no way that is happening," he said in the tone of voice he hated to use, but under the circumstances, it was warranted.

Chloe sighed. "Fine." The word came out with a little pout, but Zach knew she wasn't going to argue.

He hoped to hell that tone was never going to stop working on the poor kid, no matter how much it hurt him to have to use it, since he had no idea what he would do if he didn't have it in his arsenal.

Zach unlocked, then opened the door slowly, peeking out first to make sure the coast was clear. He had an idea in the back of his mind, one that made a lot of sense, but something didn't feel quite right about it. Still, he and Chloe crept out of the house, and after looking in every direction, moved quickly toward the edge of the trees. His instincts screamed at him to run, but something held him back.

They made it to the tree line, and after about eight more feet, Zach stopped.

"What are we doing?" Chloe whispered.

"I don't know," Zach whispered back.

He glanced around again, then headed in the same direction. A few yards more and he stopped. He looked at Chloe.

"What?" she asked, knowing something was up.

He leaned back on a fallen log to give his leg a bit of a rest. As he looked at Chloe, whose eyes were wide with concern and questioning, he decided to be honest.

"I don't know what to do," he said.

"Okay," Chloe replied, as if she had expected as much.

"It's just… I know where there's a place that should be safe, and you'd be sheltered and out of harm's way."

"Okaaaay," Chloe said again, this time dragging the word out as if to say, *spit it out, Dad*.

Zach sighed. "But something doesn't feel right about it."

Chloe shrugged. "So, we don't go there. You always have to trust your instincts, Dad."

The kid was right. Thinking about taking Chloe to the cop car should have been a no-brainer, but visions of his own truck blowing up sent shivers down his spine. If anyone had been even close to the truck when it went…well, he didn't even want to think about that.

He nodded once. "You're right," he said.

He had, after all, always taught Chloe exactly that—trust your gut.

"I don't know where you'll be safe. And I need to know you're safe."

Chloe looked around. "What about right there?" she said, motioning with her hand to exactly where he was sitting.

"With me?" Zach asked, wishing for nothing more than to be able to do exactly that and keep her with him for eternity, but he couldn't leave Ava.

"No," Chloe said, delivering another magnificent eye roll, "under the log you're sitting on."

Zach shifted, looking over his shoulder. The ground was covered in tall fernlike vegetation that would provide almost total cover.

"I can hide in the space under there."

It was pretty brilliant. Still, Zach was hesitant. "What if there are bugs under there?" he asked.

She looked up at him through her lashes, very much *not* impressed. "I am not the one who is afraid of bugs," she said, shaking her head the tiniest bit.

Right. Right, it was absolutely him that did not love the creepy-crawlies.

Like, at all.

"What about rain?" he asked.

Chloe squinted up at sky—what little of it she could see through the trees—and stitched a "seriously?" kind of look onto her face. "There aren't even any clouds. And besides, I'll be under a log, the rain isn't going to get me."

"It could seep down under there," Zach said, raising an eyebrow as if daring her to challenge his logic.

"Um, so I guess my butt will get a little wet then," she said, shooting him an "are we done this ridiculous argument yet" look, already starting to crawl under the log.

Zach stood and tested the fallen tree trunk to make sure it was sturdy and wasn't about to fall on her head or anything, but the thing felt like it was stuck there with concrete.

"Fine," he said. "But you need to stay right here."

Chloe nodded.

"I am so serious, Chloe. After everything, can you imagine what would happen if I come back here and you're gone?"

Chloe peeked out from the log. "I'm guessing your head would pop right off."

And the way she said it—so grim—Zach couldn't help but bark out a laugh. "That is exactly correct. My head would pop off and that would be the end of me."

Chloe's face softened but was still serious. "I'm not going anywhere, Dad. I promise."

"Okay," he said, knowing she was telling the truth. "Just stay here, stay quiet. I don't know, try to sleep or something, and I'll be back as soon as I can."

"Don't worry about me, Dad," she said, as Zach leaned over to plant a kiss on the top of her head. "I'm getting pretty used to entertaining myself."

Zach smiled, but as he stood, a pang of sorrow whooshed through him. The poor kid had been kidnapped and left to essentially fend for herself. Nothing to keep her mind busy, and here she was pretty much taking care of him.

And there he was, leaving her all alone again.

"I will be back soon," he said, turning before she could see the glistening in his eyes.

After everything she'd been through, the last thing Chloe needed was to be worried about him.

Chapter Twenty

The good news was, the landing had forced the jagged stake all the way through the fleshy part of Justin's shoulder so it poked through to the other side. The not so good news was—as Ava blinked, another round of pain shooting through her body—she noticed her eye was about half an inch from being impaled on said piece of wood.

Unfortunately, Justin noticed too.

He twisted his body, trying to move the stake farther toward Ava's head as her eyes snapped shut and she felt the heavy graze of the wood across her eyelid.

Justin rolled as he twisted, trying to get the upper hand, but with his injured shoulder he was sluggish, and as he moved above her, Ava took advantage of the momentum to maneuver her foot into his torso and kick him away. She scrambled to her feet quickly, at the same time Justin also righted himself.

As they faced off yet again, Ava spoke.

"It doesn't have to be this way, Justin. I'm not in the business anymore. Whoever you were working for—the people who wanted me gone—don't matter anymore. I'm no threat to anybody out here."

Justin plastered on a wild smile. "Sounds exactly like

someone who was trying to pretend they had a nice, quiet life in the boonies would say."

They continued to move slowly, circling again, though they were both moving slower, and with decidedly more effort than before.

Ava sighed. "I'm not working anymore, Justin. If I was, you would have heard about it by now."

"There are plenty of jobs that have been unclaimed or unaccounted for over the past five years. A surprising amount, really. And this place," he said, motioning around him, though Ava knew he meant the entire area of Ambrosia Falls, "is a perfect cover. Remote. No one questioning your comings and goings."

"I live in a small town, Justin," Ava said. "Everyone knows my comings and goings. Believe me, Ambrosia Falls is not a place one can easily keep their business to themselves."

Justin shrugged. "Maybe…maybe not. Either way, my employers are not willing to take that chance." He paused for a moment, as if mulling over whether he should say the next part. Apparently, he decided to go for it. "Besides, I've been waiting way too long for this moment to walk away now."

Ava wasn't surprised. She knew this had long been personal for Justin, even if her emotions over him, other than anger, had ended ages ago.

"I'm sorry to hear that," Ava said in the most impersonal tone she could muster. Nothing frustrated Justin more than not being taken as seriously as he wanted. Sure, the situation was certainly serious, but Ava was going to try damn hard to make Justin think he meant nothing to her. Which, if he hadn't been literally in her face, would be true. "It's going to be tedious having to deal with you."

Justin squinted at her, and Ava knew he was trying to formulate a comeback. She used the moment to lunge for him, aiming toward his bad shoulder. If that piece of wood hurt going in, it was going to burn like the rage of a teen with a bad attitude being pushed back out. She balled her fist and impacted him with the fleshy, outside part of her hand. The wood sliced into her a little, but it was nothing compared to the way it sliced back through Justin, his wail confirming it was not an overly pleasant experience.

Ava desperately needed her gun, but she couldn't be sure Justin hadn't set traps on the ladders, and knowing Justin, if an incendiary of some sort had been set, it wouldn't just be a simple flash-bang to scare someone off. It would do some damage.

She couldn't risk it.

But Justin was already gathering himself, and she needed time to think. She turned and fled down a corridor in the barn, a wall on one side and a row of animal stalls on the other. She considered ducking into one of the stalls, but once inside, she'd be trapped, so she kept running.

"Sparrooow," Justin called, dragging the word out, and it was just like him to be all creepy, as if he were the evil star of his very own horror movie.

What an egotistical ass.

Ava rounded the corner of the passage, making her way back into the main area of the barn, the fires still burning around the room, the heat stifling, an eerie red glow making the whole place seem like it was simmering in a bath of embers.

Ducking and using each firepit as cover, Ava made her way back toward the pile of yard tools she'd found the leaf blower in, and tried to quietly grab something she could use as a weapon. While she successfully managed to get her hands on a simple garden rake, she'd made a god-awful clatter—loud enough to raise the devil himself, which was actually pretty fitting, given her surroundings.

She wheeled around, sure Justin would be right behind her, but he was still a bit of a distance away, just coming around the corner of the passage he followed her through.

Justin smirked in a kind of "aw, isn't that cute" kind of way, looking sadly at her rake.

What a cocky jackass, she thought, and since the rake was all Ava had, she moved toward Justin, wanting nothing more than to end this. But as she made her way across the room, Justin slowly and deliberately reached out his good arm, grabbing hold of a tool of his own that had been conveniently leaning against the wall, hidden behind a few bales of hay. Which, she realized, he'd probably planted there earlier.

A gleaming, and rather sharp-looking pitchfork.

Ava glanced around the massive space, wondering what other items might be conveniently hidden around the place. Not that she had much time to think about it, since she hadn't stopped moving even when Justin pulled out the damn giant fork.

She just needed to be better than him, that was all there was to it. And yeah, maybe she'd let her training lapse a little in the past few years, and yeah, Justin had probably done the opposite, biding his time by honing his skills, but she was still confident. She'd always been better than him. At least that's what she was telling herself, even if a tiny voice somewhere deep in her head was whispering to her consciousness with inklings of doubt.

And maybe it was the doubt that got her. Threw her off her game, because as she neared Justin, something about the glint of the pitchfork distracted her. Or maybe it was the look on Justin's face, like he had so much hatred for her and honestly, Ava didn't know why. Didn't know what she'd ever done to him besides bring him close and make a life with him.

Ava raised her rake. It felt far too flimsy in her hands, far too old and maybe even ready to break, but it was all she had, and she brought it down hard, aiming for Justin's head, sure it wouldn't knock him unconscious, but maybe, if she was lucky, it might do some kind of brief damage. She imagined her follow-through might skim past the nasty gash on his shoulder, but as it turned out, there was no follow-through.

Only two tines of a pitchfork settling neatly and deeply into her forearm as her hands were raised above her head.

The pain was inconceivable. Ava had been hurt before— it had been an inevitability in her past life—but this was breath-stealing, instant agony, the sharp metal piercing straight through her already burned arm. She yanked back in reaction, the tines coming free, but then the blood began to race from her body as if it were being chased from within, pouring to the floor.

Ava tried to run, tried to put pressure on the wounds to staunch the blood and buy some time—it needed to be stopped or, well, Ava didn't want to think about that—but Justin was ready, yanking her back by her hair and throwing her to the ground, straddling himself on top of her.

And then his hands were around her throat. She didn't know how he still possessed so much strength—his injured shoulder should have made it impossible to even move his arm, but he must have been running on pure adrenaline as he squeezed with both hands, the right one doing most of the work.

Ava tried to move beneath him, struggled to bring a leg up and shift him off her, but he was too strong.

Her thoughts became cloudy, and then suddenly the only thing she could focus on was Justin. She didn't want to give him the satisfaction—it was exactly what he wanted—but it was his eyes. Eyes that held so much in them, a wild, possessive rage. A fury fueled by years of failure and obsession and need to destroy...by the embarrassment of having lost once, and a vow it would never happen again.

Then, as the world started to pull in from the edges of her vision, a darkness taking its place, the look changed to something else.

Joy. Pleasure in the fact that he had won.

Ava closed her eyes. She couldn't watch the sick satisfaction washing over his features.

And then, a magnificent, unholy clunk reverberated through the air, and the weight on top of her shifted as her world faded to black.

THE SHOVEL FELT heavy in his hands. He'd never once wanted to hurt someone like that, but seeing Justin choking Ava, Zach didn't think, he just reacted.

As he shoved the unconscious Justin to the floor, Zach was shocked at how pale Ava looked. Almost lifeless.

He moved quickly to her side, leaning his head close, listening for her breathing.

At first, he heard nothing, but then, the faintest flutter of air moved through her lips, and it was like his whole body exhaled. And that's when he felt it. Something wet soaking into his jeans, and even though the fires were going, the barn was still pretty dim, and he could only see whatever it was, was dark, almost black. He swiped at the stuff and his hands came away red, his stomach clenching.

Instantly, Zach noticed Ava's arm was covered in it too, and he knew he had to move fast—there was so much blood. He pulled his outer shirt off and wrapped it as tightly as he could around Ava's forearm, hoping with everything he had in him that it would be enough. After everything they'd been through, he couldn't lose her now.

He picked her up, the burning in his leg a constant reminder this was not an okay situation, and with one last glance at the lifeless-looking Justin, he hurried out of the barn and into the cool night air, only then realizing he didn't know how he was going to get her out of there. His truck was long gone, and he couldn't trust the police car.

But… Justin must have gotten out into the woods somehow, Zach realized, rushing toward the house, and its attached garage. The main door on the garage was locked, so he headed to the front door of the house. The garage was connected through the front entrance and Zach made his way there quickly, elated to see a small SUV parked neatly in the center. He flung open the passenger seat and set Ava in as gently as he could, though a small moan wisped past her lips, which was both relieving and a little scary at the same time.

But nothing was more of a relief than a quick glance at the ignition where the keys were dangling. Perhaps Justin was preparing for a quick getaway. He buckled her seat belt and shut Ava's door, running to the driver's side and pushing the button to open the garage door as he slid behind the wheel.

He hit the gas and backed out of the garage fast, simultaneously rolling down the window.

"Chloe!" he yelled, still moving backward, turning the

wheel until the headlights hit the edge of the forest. "Chloe, we gotta go!"

Zach was nearly to the edge of the trees, readying to throw the vehicle into park and race back into the woods, but, bless her heart, Chloe was already running out, as if she'd been waiting for this moment all along.

She flung open the back door, scrambled inside, and had the door shut faster than Zach would have thought possible. Her seat belt was on in seconds.

As Zach hit the gas and headed out the winding driveway, he glanced at Chloe in the rearview mirror. "Have you been practicing that or something?"

Chloe shrugged a shoulder. "Maybe a little in my head while I was waiting for you to come back."

Zach shook his head in amazement.

"What? I had a lot of time to think and worry," Chloe said, sounding a little defensive.

It was around that time Chloe noticed Ava was not looking too hot in the passenger seat.

"Dad!" she said, alarmed. "Is she okay?"

Zach glanced back at Chloe again and hated the look he saw on her face—terror mixed with confusion. He wished he still had the innocent confusion of a kid, wondering how something so terrible could happen to a good person.

"I hope so," Zach said.

He wanted so badly to tell Chloe Ava would be fine, but the truth was, he had no idea. He had no medical training, and truthfully, he'd only done what he'd seen people do on TV to wrap her wound. He knew it had to be tight, but beyond that, he had no clue.

"I'm going to be fine," Ava croaked, surprising them both.

She hitched up a little in the seat and turned to face Chloe. "Your dad saved me."

Chloe smiled then. "Me too."

And Zach's whole being burst with an uncomfortable prickle of a thousand emotions coursing through him. Embarrassment. Pride. A sense of not being worthy. Of not feeling like he'd done anything special, and in fact, like he'd done everything all wrong.

But most of all he felt grateful to be sitting there with the two most important people in his world.

"I don't need a hospital," Ava said. "I can deal with all this."

"Of course you need a hospital," Zach said. "You've lost a lot of blood."

Ava shook her head. "I can manage at home," she said, and then she looked at him, the expression on her face serious, like she was trying to tell him something without telling him something.

Something she didn't want to say in front of Chloe.

And then, with his heart breaking in two, and wondering how many times a heart could break in one day, Zach understood. They couldn't go to the hospital. She couldn't be stuck in a hospital with Justin still out there. She'd be a sitting duck.

He cleared his throat. "Yeah, okay," he said. "We'll just head home."

He didn't dare glance back to see what he knew would be an even more confused look on the face of his daughter as the vehicle fell silent for the rest of the drive home.

"I'd like to help you with that," Zach said, pulling into his driveway.

He wondered if it was okay to park the strange SUV right

there in plain sight, but it wasn't like Justin didn't know where they both lived anyway, so he wasn't sure what the point would be. Unless, of course, the police came looking... though something told him the car was clear of any connection with Justin or any suspicion of any kind, really.

"Yeah," Ava said, gingerly moving to release her seat belt.

Chloe—the one Zach had been worrying about the longest over the past...how long was it? A day? God, it felt so much longer than that—had already bounded out of the vehicle, as if completely unscathed by the whole ordeal. He didn't have any illusions that she wouldn't have some mental scars, but he was going to do everything in his power to make sure she had help, both professional and his own, in dealing with it all.

His first order of business was to be by Chloe's side as she crawled into bed, exhausted.

"Are you sure you don't want to talk about anything?" he asked, but Chloe shook her head. "I'm fine, Dad," she said, a "just leave it alone" tone to her voice. Clearly, she was not in the mood for some exhaustive rehash of everything right then.

Chloe gently pushed him out of her room so she could change—she was all about the privacy these days—and Ava met him in the hallway.

"You think she'll be okay?" he asked her.

He was the parent. He should have been the one to feel certain about what his daughter was feeling one way or the other, but he honestly had no clue. Why did all the other parents always seem like they knew exactly what they were doing? Were they all faking it too?

"Give yourself a break," Ava said, like she was reading

his mind. "She'll be fine, and if she's not, the two of you are going to figure it out together."

Zach nodded, though he was far from convinced.

Chloe opened her door again and they both stepped inside as she crawled into bed.

"Think you'll be able to sleep?" Zach asked.

Chloe nodded. "I can barely keep my eyes open."

"Okay good," Zach said, then did something he hadn't done in years.

Turned on the old baby monitor he used when Chloe was little and hadn't gotten around to putting away yet. Although, truth be told, he'd still used it over the years without Chloe knowing about it. It was a habit he'd only stopped about a year ago, though he wished he hadn't. Maybe he could have prevented this whole thing before it even started.

"Are you serious, Dad?" Chloe said, giving him a look that said she was not at all impressed.

"Just for tonight, okay?" Zach said. "I just need reassurance for right now."

Chloe sighed. "Fine, but we are not going to make a habit of this, right?" she asked, sounding more like she was the parent.

Zach smiled and stepped back while Ava sat on the bed. "Good night, sweet girl," she said, bending to kiss Chloe on the forehead.

"I'm glad you're okay," Chloe said.

Ava's eyes filled with tears then, and a thrum struck Zach's heart. Ava cared so much for Chloe, and Zach realized he would give anything to have this every night. Minus the abduction/explosions/revenge situation, obviously.

"I'm glad you're okay," Ava managed to whisper, booping Chloe on the nose.

She quickly got up and passed Zach as she left the room. He got the feeling she was trying to hide the extent of her emotions from them, but he wasn't fooled. Ava cared so much more than she would ever let on.

The only thing was, Zach couldn't figure out why she needed to hide anymore.

Ava was almost done rebandaging her arm by the time Zach limped back downstairs, the receiving end of the kid monitor in hand.

She was looking better after some water and clean bandages.

"You did a good job of this," she said, motioning to her arm and the discarded pile of cloth. "Sorry about your shirt."

"I was worried it might be too tight," he said.

Ava shook her head. "It can never be too tight in a situation like this. More importantly, how's your leg?"

"I have no idea," Zach said, suddenly looking exhausted as he flopped into a chair. "I'm sure I'll live."

"After everything that leg has been through, we should check on the wound closure bandage."

Zach nodded and pulled his pants off, a sheepish look crossing his face. "I kind of hoped it would be different circumstances the first time I took my pants off in front of you," he said.

Ava let the corner of her mouth curl up in a half smile. "Me too."

But she went to work, not wanting to drag out a moment of Zach's pain longer than she had to.

"You should go into town for proper stitches tomorrow," she said, "but for now, this bandage is actually holding."

"Yeah okay," he said.

"And get some sleep," she told him, as she got up from her chair.

"Oh, um…right. Sleep. That's a thing," Zach said, his thoughts jumping all over the place.

He thought…hoped she might stay. It didn't seem right that they would, what? Just go their separate ways after everything? And yeah, maybe things had gotten intense between the two of them, but maybe he was reading too much into everything. Zach suddenly felt like a fool. He realized he'd built up everything in his head to be bigger than it was. They'd really only shared two kisses, after all, and had barely discussed what they even meant.

But she was his best friend, and two passionate kisses had to mean something.

Still, he supposed they could figure it all out tomorrow. He was pretty damn exhausted too.

She headed to the door, and on the porch, she turned back to Zach. "I'll see you tomorrow," she said, kissed him on the cheek and headed toward her house.

Chapter Twenty-One

Ava was not going to see Zach tomorrow. She wouldn't see him tomorrow, or on any other day in the near future.

Justin was still out there somewhere, and the only thing she could do now was run. He wouldn't have a way to inform her if he tried to go after Zach or Chloe again, no way to use them as leverage if she could get far enough, fast enough. He would leave them alone and come after her.

But it was going to be the hardest thing she'd ever done. Leaving them.

A tear rolled down her cheek as she climbed the steps to her front door and slipped inside, needing to gather a few things before she left Ambrosia Falls forever.

In less than half an hour, Ava was ready to go.

She took one last look around her house. It had been such a good house, everything she needed in a time where her whole world was imploding, and it had built her back up. Gave her back her life. No, gave her a brand-new life so much better than the one before, and damn it, she was going to miss the place. Which was a new feeling for her. She couldn't remember ever being attached to a place, not even as a kid. But this house, and Ambrosia Falls in general, were special places.

She could only hope the next people to live here would

appreciate it as much as she did. She hoped they'd be nice. Zach and Chloe deserved to have great neighbors.

Ava flipped her living room light off for the last time, then turned to head out the door, jolting as she saw the dark figure in the open doorway. At first, it didn't compute. How had someone gotten the door open so quietly? But then she realized she'd left it unlocked. Even with all that was going on, she was slipping. So used to not having to lock her doors in the quiet little town, she'd done the same thing again, purely out of habit.

Cursing herself in her head, she readied to bolt in the other direction, when the figure spoke.

"You're leaving?"

They were just two little words, but they were filled with more emotion than Ava had ever heard in such a short phrase. Anger, confusion, disbelief, but most of all hurt. If a broken heart could stand up and talk, those two words were exactly what it might sound like.

"Zach," Ava whispered, unsure how to answer.

He stepped farther into the house, a stream of moonlight falling onto his face. In one hand he held the little walkie-talkie-like receiver from the baby monitor, which almost made Ava smile, and in the other hand he held...a letter?

Oh no.

"I was about to head to bed when I remembered. I'd been so caught up with Chloe missing and everything, I didn't have a chance to stop and wonder what the heck you were doing at my mailbox."

Ava swallowed, knowing she'd been exposed. That letter was supposed to be for later. For when she was gone.

"But then I was in the shower, and I remembered. You know, the way you always remember things when your mind finally has a chance to slow down and not think for a second, and then everything you missed during the day comes tumbling back at you?"

Ava nodded slowly. Her mind was whirling, panicked, dumbfounded. This wasn't the way things were supposed to go.

"I remembered a little flutter of a thought that something was weird about you standing out by my mailbox. There's nothing out there to see. Nothing to do. Just a mailbox." He held up the letter. "This is you leaving, isn't it?" he said, the crack in his voice giving away more than his face even, in the near darkness.

"I'm sorry," was all Ava could say, the words coming out in a whisper, and tears filled her eyes.

"You don't have to leave, Ava. You can't leave, not after this," he said, the letter shaking a little.

"I have to," Ava said, trying to pull her shoulders back, trying to show she was serious. The only problem was all her body wanted to do was break down into a heap on the floor and sob.

"You don't have to, Ava," Zach said. "You could stay here. We could figure this out together."

She shook her head. "We can't, Zach. It's too dangerous."

And that's when Zach held the letter in both his hands and held it closer to his face to read through the dim light. "'I've been madly, head over heels in love with you for years. Maybe since the moment I first laid eyes on you.'" He looked into her eyes then. "It's like you took the words right out of my head. This is all exactly how I feel. And now, after everything, I don't know how I could bear to lose my best friend. But I don't know how I could bear to lose the love of my life too."

"I know," Ava managed to say. "But this is the only way. Maybe someday but..."

She picked up the bag she'd packed and tried to push past him, but Zach put his hand out to stop her.

"Let me go, Zach. It's the only way to save the two of you," she said, pulling out of his gentle grip and spinning around toward the door.

And was immediately blocked by a very large, very solid body.

An arm attached to said body reached up, and Ava readied herself for another fight, not knowing how much she had left in her to do so. But the arm kept reaching, not in her direction, but toward...the wall?

The lights flicked on, and Ava was momentarily blinded, blinking, wholly discombobulated. And then her vision adapted, and a familiar face came into view.

ZACH DIDN'T KNOW who the hell this guy was, but he swore he would take him out if he laid one finger on Ava. He hadn't known he had it in him, but all the violence of the night seemed to be simmering right on the surface, and Zach was ready to punch the bushy, gray handlebar mustache right off the guy if he had to.

"George?" Ava said, confusion heavy in her eyes.

"Hey guys, am I interrupting something?" the older man said, with an expression on his face that was not at all subtle about the amusement he was getting out of the situation.

"George? What the hell are you doing here?" Ava asked, looking like she was readying to punch him in the shoulder for scaring her like that.

The man—George—sauntered in without a care in the

world and quietly shut the door before he sat on the couch, taking up more space than seemed possible on the large sofa.

"Well," George said, "I wanted to let you know we got him."

"What are you talking about?"

"We got the Crow."

What the hell was that supposed to mean, Zach wondered, but to be frank, George was kind of an intimidating man, and Zach didn't particularly think interrupting him was the best idea.

"What?" Ava asked, as if it were impossible to believe what George was saying. She moved to a chair near George and sat. "How are you even here?" She shook her head a little, as if trying to clear it.

"Well, it's a bit of a long story, and it kind of looks like you were getting ready to leave, so maybe I should leave it for another time."

The guy was starting to remind Zach of his annoying uncle Arthur, who loved the sound of his own voice and dragged his stories out just to get another few seconds of attention.

"George!" Ava said.

And that was all it took. George chuckled a little, but finally started explaining. "I have an old army buddy who's helped me out quite a bit over the years. In fact, he helped me set you up here in this charming little town."

Ava's eyebrows knit together in the most adorable way, as Zach moved to sit. He tried to be discreet about it, but hobbling around mostly on one leg tended to draw attention.

When everyone was settled, George went on. "I think you all may have had a run in or two with him."

Ava's eyes alighted with understanding. "The cop."

George nodded admiringly. "Officer Banyan, to be exact. He and I have kept in touch with one another all these years. In fact, he's been keeping an eye on you." He turned to Ava, his eyes twinkling.

"Is he okay?" Zach interrupted. "The last time I saw him, he looked kind of...dead."

"Luckily, not quite," George said. "When I didn't hear from him when I was supposed to, I got the hell out here and tracked his phone. Lost the signal a little way away from the acreage, but I eventually got to him. He was pretty loopy, but I called the ambulance out to that nice acreage in the forest and they're getting him right as rain. He's at the hospital now."

"Holy shit," Ava said. "And Justin?"

"Told ya," George said. "We got him."

Wait. The Crow is Justin? Realization flooded over Zach. "And you're Sparrow," he said, remembering what Chloe had repeated from her captor.

"Yes," Ava said absently, apparently still trying to wrap her head around everything. "So, it's over?"

"It's over," George said, putting his hand on her knee like a father might. "It's really over this time. They've got Justin in custody. I still don't know who he's working for, and we don't want to risk revealing your real identity, or the fact that Zach here," George continued, turning to acknowledge Zach, "and Chloe are involved, so the state authorities have agreed to work with us to keep all that quiet. But the charges of break and enter out at the acreage, as well as the attempted murder of Officer Banyan, should keep him behind bars for a very long time."

Ava opened her mouth to say something, but nothing

came out. She shook her head again as if she still couldn't believe it.

Hope was building inside of Zach, but he was scared to say anything, afraid he might jinx…well, everything.

"Well," George said, clapping his hands together, almost as if washing them clean of the whole ordeal, "I'd better get over to the station. Make sure everything goes smoothly."

George bent down and kissed Ava on the top of the head. "See ya around, kid," he said, then turned to Zach and held his hand out.

Zach stood—after a bit of a struggle—and shook it. "Nice to meet you, sir," he said.

"Likewise," George said, with a nod of his head.

And with that, George sauntered away like he hadn't just delivered the kind of news that changed lives forever.

"What the hell was that?" Zach asked.

Ava blinked. "I think," she began, the words tentative. "I think it was George giving me my life back. Again."

"What do you mean 'again'?"

"He was the one who saved me from Justin the first time. Five years ago. I'd sent him a text, and he got to me, some-how found the strength to pull me out of a burning inferno."

"Jesus," Zach said, shaking his head at the idea Ava might have been through worse than any of them had gone through that day. "I'm sorry."

Ava shrugged. "But in the end, it brought me here."

Zach couldn't hold back any longer from asking the question his mind had been quite distractedly screaming at him for the past ten minutes. "So does this mean you can stay?"

Ava seemed to be thinking about it as he held his breath. He didn't know if he could take another letdown tonight. Or for the next half century or so.

"I think," she said, pausing once more to give it a final mulling. "I think I can," she told him, her eyes widening in delight like a kid at a carnival.

Zach finally saw the thing he now knew he'd been wishing for, for years. An understanding surging between them that the time for questioning was past, and in its place, a realization that they belonged to each other. He went to her, his leg not quite letting him forget he was hurt, but since his entire life had been stolen away and then given back to him in a matter of hours, he was not about to waste even a single second more.

Chapter Twenty-Two

Zach knelt on his good leg in front of Ava's chair and leaned up for a kiss, and what else could Ava do but meet him halfway, her heart thrumming, her skin humming, and everything inside her tingling.

The kiss was slow, and maybe even a little questioning still, each of them asking, *are you sure?* Of course, neither of them had ever been so sure of anything in their lives.

Ava slipped her hands under the edge of his T-shirt and lifted it over his head, holding his gaze, trying not to wince at the pain zipping through her arm. Concern filled Zach's eyes and Ava hated that she was stopping the moment of intimacy, but his focus only turned to her injured arm, holding it so gently, so lovingly, then softly wisping the lightest of kisses along it.

The carefulness, the tenderness should have brought forth thoughts of sweetness. But knowing that this man, this beautiful, good, courageous man cared for her so wholly—cherished her—made it, oddly, the most seductive moment she'd ever known. Each almost imperceptible brush of his lips triggered sensations that hadn't been roused in years.

Maybe it was relief knowing the moment that had been building for years, maybe even from the first time she saw him that night on her front porch, beer in hand, and each moment after, had finally led them to meaning everything to each other. First as best friends and now to this...to their very own forever. Forever was not a concept Ava had allowed herself to think about, and even now it scared her, but as Zach made his way up her arm with his kisses, over her shoulder and to her neck, thoughts started to retract, becoming far away and unimportant.

Zach found her lips again just as he found the hem of her shirt, pulling it up and pausing for breath as he maneuvered her good arm out of it, then over her head, so careful when he slid it over the bandage on her other arm. He flung the shirt gently to the couch and turned back to her, just looking at her for a moment.

"Hey," he said, his voice husky and ragged.

"Hey," she said back, smiling and wholly content.

Over the years they'd built this thing where they checked in with each other, brought each other back to the moment when things started to get a little too stressful, a little too overwhelming, a little too...well, grumpy on Zach's end. Ava knew this was what they were doing now. Checking in. Coming back to the moment. Connecting.

All this time she'd been so afraid to lose Zach, but she realized it wasn't just Zach the man, it was their relationship. It was the reason they had never gone down this path before, the fear that things would change.

The moment lasted only a second before their lips met again, but it shoved away all the uncertainty and solidified that they were still going to be them—best friends. And now, obviously more, but still them. Ava felt something heavy lift from her.

Suddenly, she was so alive, so hungry for this man she

loved more than she'd loved anything in her life, her hands exploring, moving across his skin. His lips drowning her in a desperate kiss before moving downward, kissing his way along as his hand fumbled behind to release her bra, his lips finding her breast, ravenously taking it into his mouth. Every nerve came alive, pulsing, thirsting for more. She couldn't get enough as he moved to the other side, his strong hands tight around her as he grazed, licked, and, in Ava's admittedly biased opinion, unabashedly thrilled his audience of one, her breath coming in gasps.

She fumbled for his button, his zipper, excruciatingly difficult with only one good hand and a need so urgent she thought she might die if she didn't get to him.

"Let me help," Zach said, grinning and regrettably moving away from her, leaning heavy on the arm of the chair as he mostly used only his good leg to stand.

What a pair they were, Ava thought, though she had to admit, she was absolutely going to enjoy this show while it lasted. Once balanced on one leg, Zach gingerly peeled his jeans partway down, the bandage stark white against his skin, though that was decidedly not where her attention landed given the rather impressive arousal situation going on.

He stopped halfway through the removing of his pants and Ava turned her attention back to his face, which was looking a bit more sheepish than you'd expect someone to be in that situation.

"What?" Ava asked, concern rising.

"I, uh, kinda need to sit down for this part," he said, kind of shrugging and hobbling over to the couch, flopping heavily and struggling to free himself of the particularly difficult and maddening jeans.

Ava tilted her head, a smile spreading across her face. "Works for me," she said, standing.

As she stood, she imagined she'd strip in an erotic, seductive way, but with her injured arm, she struggled with her own jeans, the button difficult but not impossible with the use of one good hand, then the actual removal of them being a kind of wriggling, hopping affair.

Sexy it was not, but at least they were both finally free of all obstacles.

"Quite a pair we make," Zach said, with a little chuckle.

Ava moved slowly toward him, gloriously exposed and feeling pretty damn sultry again all of a sudden. She moved close, pausing to allow him a good, long look, his eyes alight with appreciation, before she spoke. "The best pair, in my opinion," she said.

Zach smiled. "One might even say a perfect pair," he said, as he reached up for her, pulling her toward him.

Ava straddled her legs around his, careful of his injury, their lips meeting—urgently now, desperate to achieve their full pairing. As he lifted her and she slid onto him, she cried out in the relief of someone who'd waited and wanted for way too long.

Zach leaned his head back and closed his eyes, releasing a slow breath ending in a low groan like he'd been waiting just as long for this kind of relief. But there was so much more relief to be had as Ava began to move, slowly at first, then quickening as he rose to meet her in a rhythm so natural it was like they were made for each other. Zach found her breast with his mouth again and it was like a string that ran straight through her was pulled taut, the pressure building to unsustainable levels, and then he began to suck, ever so gently. Ava nearly whimpered with need, and as he thrust to meet that need, he sucked harder, the string stretching to the point of no return, and then finally, gloriously breaking as she erupted with a cry that sent Zach reeling over the edge too, surging to his own climax with a sexy, primal roar of a sound as he held her tight—protective, loving, like he was never letting her go.

And she hoped to hell he never would.

Epilogue

They decided a car accident was the best way to explain Zach's limp, Ava's messed-up arm, and the fact that Zach was missing a truck. Officer Banyan had been true to his word, only reporting what was necessary to put Justin in prison and keep him there for a very long while.

Ava and Zach made their debut as a couple two days later by taking a slow walk, hand in hand up Main Street, right through all the people from town who were packing up their booths and tents, the air filled with scents of a crisp fall breeze, some remnants of apple-scented goodies and a touch of sadness that it was all over for another year.

Everyone turned to stare, but not one gaze in the crowd had even the slightest hint of surprise. In fact, as the pair approached, there was more than one murmur of the word *finally* and quite a few knowing glances and approving nods.

When they reached The Other Apple Store, Maureen was waiting for them on the stoop.

"Thank you so much for keeping the place going," Ava said, as she hugged her friend.

"Of course," Maureen said. "We were so worried when you didn't show the other morning, but I figured the least I could do was man the store for a day. When we heard about the accident, I nearly fainted. I'm so sorry I didn't come looking for you or send help or something."

Even though they were bombarded with questions, Ava and Zach kept their answers to the onslaught of questions as vague as possible. Decided to go for a hike. Truck ran off the road. Took them a while to get help and make it back.

Keep it simple and boring, so fewer questions would be asked.

"What you did was exactly what I needed," Ava said, hugging her one more time.

"Well, would you look at that," Barney said, stopping his packing to raise a hand over his eyes to block the sun.

Someone let out a low whistle from a few stalls down and Miss Clara gasped. "Captain Applebottom!" she yelled, as she started running toward her prized chicken. "You've come back to me!"

Sure enough, as Ava gazed up the street, Captain Applebottom was strolling back on into town as if he didn't have a care in the world—safe, sound and pecking at the ground every few steps.

"Guess the little guy wasn't too keen on being the town's damn mascot," Zach said, eyes twinkling with newfound respect. "Now that is one smart bird."

And as Miss Clara scooped Captain Applebottom into her arms, the town resumed its packing.

So many people she'd come to know and love over the years—Barney, who was already on Miss Clara's case for letting Captain Applebottom get loose in the first place, Donna Mae from the antique store, Jackson packing up his hardware sale, Annie, who was helping some of the others since her knitting had been washed out in the water tower incident, and so many others. People she tried not to let into her heart but who had wriggled their way in anyway.

She felt a warm hand take hers. Zach. The only best friend she'd ever had, and from across the street, Chloe running toward them, clearly with a plan on her mind.

"Can we get one last apple-cinnamon ice cream?" she asked Zach.

"Who? You and me?" Zach asked.

Chloe rolled her eyes. "Obviously not," she said. "Me and Emma. We want something for the walk to the park."

Zach chuckled and dug into his pocket for some money as Ava took a good, long look at her town.

At all the people milling around doing their thing, at Zach, who looked as content as she'd ever seen him, at Chloe rushing back toward Emma, and she realized, for the first time since she'd arrived in Ambrosia Falls, there was absolutely nothing hanging over her head. Nothing stopping her from letting the whole town fill her up. Nothing in the way of enjoying each single mundane, everyday moment. Nothing that could ever force her to leave.

Zach pulled her hand back into his like that was its new home now. "Well, thank goodness that's over," he said, in his signature grumpy way.

For all the quirks of the town and the people in it, Ava realized with a grin, there was not a single thing she would change.

"Yup," she said, a smile spreading across her face. "And I absolutely can't wait till next year."

* * * * *

COMING SOON!

We really hope you enjoyed reading this book.
If you're looking for more romance
be sure to head to the shops when
new books are available on

Thursday 24th October

MILLS & BOON

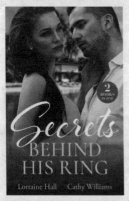

LET'S TALK

Romance

For exclusive extracts, competitions and special offers, find us online:

f MillsandBoon

X @MillsandBoon

⌾ @MillsandBoonUK

♪ @MillsandBoonUK

Get in touch on 01413 063 232

afterglow BOOKS

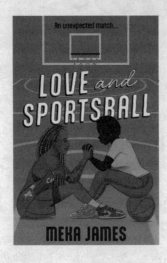

 Sports romance

 Sports romance

 Workplace romance

 Workplace romance

 One night

 Spicy

OUT NOW

Two stories published every month. Discover more at:
Afterglowbooks.co.uk